Chas. F. Heebner

Manual of pharmacy and pharmaceutical chemistry

Designed especially for the use of the pharmaceutical student and for pharmacists

in general

Chas. F. Heebner

Manual of pharmacy and pharmaceutical chemistry
Designed especially for the use of the pharmaceutical student and for pharmacists in general

ISBN/EAN: 9783742833082

Manufactured in Europe, USA, Canada, Australia, Japa

Cover: Foto ©Andreas Hilbeck / pixelio.de

Manufactured and distributed by brebook publishing software
(www.brebook.com)

Chas. F. Heebner

Manual of pharmacy and pharmaceutical chemistry

MANUAL

OF

PHARMACY

AND

PHARMACEUTICAL CHEMISTRY.

DESIGNED ESPECIALLY FOR
THE USE OF THE PHARMACEUTICAL STUDENT AND
FOR PHARMACISTS IN GENERAL.

BY

CHAS. F. HEEBNER, Ph. G.,

GRADUATE IN PHARMACY OF THE COLLEGE OF PHARMACY OF THE CITY OF NEW
YORK, CLASS OF '81; INSTRUCTOR IN THEORY AND PRACTICE OF PHAR-
MACY, AT THE COLLEGE OF PHARMACY OF THE CITY OF NEW YORK

NEW YORK:

PUBLISHED BY THE AUTHOR.

1887.

PREFACE.

THE special aim of this work is to afford a short but instructive course in the Department of Pharmacy.

It is the outgrowth of a want long felt by students at the various Colleges of Pharmacy, for a book especially adapted to their use as a *class-book*, or *note-book*. All the unnecessary matter of many text-books has been here eliminated.

The amount of material presented, as well as the arrangement of the various topics and the manner of their treatment, has been simplified as far as can consistently be done; thereby producing a work of such a nature, that the student will find it most advantageous as a book *for study* in reviewing the subjects for the class, and preliminary to examinations.

For a similar reason, it commends itself as a book of reference to Pharmacists ; also to Pharmaceutical students or drug clerks, especially in preparing for the examinations of the various Boards of Pharmacy. It cannot take the place of lectures in Pharmacy, nor replace many of the exhaustive works on this subject, some of which should be read in connection with this work.

Many of the facts within the following pages represent compilations from authorized sources, with many original explanations and practical hints.

It was the author's intention to have placed this treatise in the hands of the Pharmaceutical public, two years since, but illness retarded the completion of the necessary work.

It is hoped that the MANUAL OF PHARMACY AND PHARMACEUTICAL CHEMISTRY may prove of material service to those for whom it has been prepared.

CHAS. F. HEEBNER.

Oct. 26, 1887.

TABLE OF CONTENTS.

INTRODUCTION.

PHARMACY. PHARMACOPŒIAS. DISPENSATORIES.............................. 13

PART I.

METROLOGY. GRAVITATION. Weight. Weighing. The Balance. Systems of
 Weights. Troy. Avoirdupois. Apothecaries. Liquid Measures. Metric
 System. Specific Gravity, and Methods for Determination. Specific
 Volume. Rules for Proportionate Mixing.............................14-33
COLLECTION, PREPARATION, AND PRESERVATION OF BOTANICAL DRUGS. Des-
 sication. Garbling...34-35
MECHANICAL SUBDIVISION. Comminution. Contusion. Trituration. De-
 gree of Subdivision. Levigation. Elutriation.....................36-37
HEAT. Its Determination. Sensible Heat. Latent Heat. The Thermom-
 eter. Comparison of Different Thermometric Scales. Bunsen Burner.
 Blowpipe. Crucible...37-39
PROCESSES REQUIRING HEAT. Sublimation. Ignition. Incineration. Calci-
 nation. Fusion. Torrefaction. Reduction. Deflagration. Oxidation.
 Carbonization. Methods for controlling Heat. Boiling Point.........39-41
SOLUTION. Simple. Chemical. Saturated and Super-saturated Solutions.
 Circulatory Displacement. Solvents. Complex Solution. Dialysis....41-43
MACERATION. DIGESTION. INFUSION. DECOCTION.........................43-44
PERCOLATION. Methods. Relation to Fluid Extracts. Requisites for their
 reliable preparation. Determination of Menstruum. Quantity of Per-
 colate. Test for Exhaustion. Theory of Percolation and Exhaustion.
 Re-percolation (Illustration).....................................45-51
PROCESSES. Lixiviation. Expression. Filtration. Colation. Clarifica-
 tion. (Various methods). Decolorization and Deodorization. Sedi
 ment. Decantation. Syphon..52-53

VAPORIZATION. Evaporation—Spontaneous and In Vacuo. Distillation. Simple. Apparatus Required. Fractional and Destructive Distillation. Sublimation.... 54–55

SEPARATION OF SOLIDS FROM SOLUTION. Crystallization. Methods. Amorphous. Dimorphous. Isomorphous. Mother Liquor. Water of Crystallization. Efflorescence. Deliquescence. Size of Crystals. Granulation. Crystallography. Precipitation. Washing the Precipitate. Character of Precipitate. Examples.............................55–58

GENERATION, ABSORPTION, AND COLLECTION OF GASES. 58–59

CLASSIFICATION OF PHARMACOPŒIAL PREPARATIONS.

LIQUIDS. Aceta. Aquæ. Collodia. Decocta. Elixiria. Extracta. Fluida. Glycerita. Infusa. Linimenta. Liquores. Mellita. Misturæ. Mucilagines. Oleata. Oleo-resinæ. Spiritus. Syrupi. Tincturæ. Vina..................... 59–61

SOLIDS. Abstracts. Cerata. Chartæ. Confectiones. Emplastra. Extracta. Massæ. Pilulæ. Pulveres. Resinæ. Suppositoria. Triturationes. Trochisci. Unguenta...61–63

PART II.

INORGANIC PHARMACY.—PREPARATIONS.

Aqua. Aqua Destillata....... 64

ACIDS. Definition. Basylous Radical. Acidulous Radical. Salts. Acidum Sulphuricum. Acidum Sulphuricum Aromaticum. Acidum Sulphuricum Dilutum. Acidum Sulphurosum. Acidum Hydrochloricum. Acidum Hydrochloricum Dilutum. Acidum Nitro-Hydrochloricum. Acidum Nitro-Hydrochloricum Dilutum. Acidum Nitricum. Acidum Aceticum. Acidum Aceticum Dilutum. Acidum Aceticum Glacial........64–70

ALKALIES AND THEIR COMPOUNDS.

POTASSIUM SALTS. Source. Reactions. General Impurities. Potassii Carbonas. Potassii Bicarbonas. Potassii Nitras. Potassii Bitartras. Potassii Tartras. Potassii et Sodii Tartras. Potassii Acetas. Potassa. Potassa cum Calce. Liquor Potassæ. Potassa Sulphurata. Potassii Chloras. Potassii Citras. Potassii Sulphas. Potassii Sulphis: (Other salts of Potassium found elsewhere)............................. 70–77

CONTENTS.

SODIUM SALTS. Source. Reaction. General Impurities. Tests. Sodii Chloridum. Sodii Carbonas. Sodii Carbonas Exsiccatus. Sodii Bicarbonas. Soda. Liquor Sodæ. Sodii Acetas. Sodii Benzoas. Sodii Boras. Acidum Boricum. Sodii Chloras. Sodii Nitras. Sodii Salicylas. Sodii Sulphas. Sodii Sulphis. Sodii Sulpho-Carbolas. Liquor Sodii Silicatis. (Other Sodium Salts found elsewhere).................77–85

AMMONIUM SALTS. Sources. Ammonia. Reactions. General Impurities. Tests. Ammonii Chloridum. Ammonii Sulphas. Ammonii Carbonas. Liquor Ammonii Acetatis. Ammonii Nitras. Aqua Ammoniæ. Linimentum Ammoniæ. Spiritus Ammoniæ Aromaticus. Aqua Ammoniæ Fortior. Spiritus Ammoniæ. Ammonii Benzoas. Ammonii Bromidum. Ammonii Iodidum. Ammonii Phosphas. Ammonium Oxalate. Ammonium Citrate. Ammonium Tartrate 85–90

ALKALINE EARTHS AND THEIR COMPOUNDS.

CALCIUM SALTS. Sources. Tests. Calx. Liquor Calcis. Syrupus Calcis. Calcii Bromidum. Calcii Carbonas Præcipitatis. Creta Præparata. Pulvis Cretæ Compositus. Mistura Cretæ. Trochisi Cretæ. Calcii Phosphas Præcipitatis. Calx Sulphurata..................... 91–94

MAGNESIUM SALTS. Sources. Tests. General Impurities. Magnesii Sulphas. Magnesii Carbonas. Magnesia. Magnesia Ponderosa. Trochisci Magnesiæ. Magnesii Citratis Granulatus. Liquor Magnesii Citratis....94–97

BARIUM SALTS. (None officinal). Tests. Barium Sulphate Barium Chloride. Barium Carbonate. Barium Peroxide. Barium Hydroxide....... 97

STRONTIUM SALTS. (None officinal). Tests. Strontium Nitrate 98

LITHIUM SALTS. Source. Tests. General Impurities. Lithii Carbonas. Lithii Benzoas. Lithii Bromidum. Lithii Citras. Lithii Salicylas.... 98–99

CERIUM SALTS. Cerii Oxalas. Cerium Nitrate........................... 99

ALUMINIUM SALTS. Source. Tests. General Impurities. Alums.—Composition. Alumen. Alumen Exsiccatum. Aluminii Hydras. Aluminii Sulphas....................... 100–101

THE HALOGENS AND THEIR SALTS.

CHLORINE. Properties. Tests. Aqua Chlori. Calx Chloratæ. Liquor Sodii Chloratæ. Javelle Water. IODUM. Source. Preparation. Purification. Tests. Syrupus Acidi Hydriodici. Potassii Iodidum. Sodii Iodidum. Iodoformum. BROMUM. Source. Preparation. Tests. Potassii Bromidum. Sodii Bromidum. Acidum Hydrobromicum Dilutum. CYANOGEN SALTS. Cyanogen. Potassii Ferrocyanidum. Potassium Ferricyanide. Ferrocyanide of Iron. Potassii Cyanidum. Acidum Hydrocyanicum Dilutum. Ammonium Sulphocyanide................101–111

PREPARATIONS OF THE METALLIC AND NON-METALLIC ELEMENTS.

SULPHUR. Occurrence. Sulphur Sublimatum. Sulphur Lotum. Sulphur Præcipitatum. Sulphuris Iodidum. Lac Sulphuris. Hydrosulphuric Acid. Carbonei Bisulphidum.... 111-113
PHOSPHORUS. Preparation. Oxides. Amorphous Phosphorus. Acidum Phosphoricum. Acidum Phosphoricum Dilutum. Oleum Phosphoratum. Pilulæ Phosphori. Sodii Phosphas. Sodii Pyrophosphas. Calcii Hypophosphis. Sodii Hypophosphis. Potassii Hypophosphis. Hypophosphorous Acid. 114-118
FERRUM. Tests. Ferri Chloridum. Liquor Ferri Chloridi. Tinctura Ferri Chloridi. Ferri Iodidum Saccharatum. Syrupus Ferri Iodidi. Syrupus Ferri Bromidi. Ferri Lactas. Ferri Sulphas. Ferri Sulphas Exsiccatus. Pilulæ Aloes et Ferri. Ferri Sulphas Præcipitatus. Mistura Ferri Composita. Ferri Carbonas Saccharatus. Massa Ferri Carbonatis. Pilulæ Ferri Compositæ. Ferri Oxalas. Liquor Ferri Subsulphatis. Liquor Ferri Tersulphatis. Ferri Oxidum Hydratum. Trochisci Ferri. Emplastrum Ferri. Ferrum Reductum. Pilulæ Ferri Iodidi. Ferri Oxidum Hydratum cum Magnesia. Ferri et Ammonii Sulphas. Ferri Hypophosphis. Liquor Ferri Acetatis. Tinctura Ferri Acetatis. Ferri Valerianas. Liquor Ferri Citratis. THE SCALE SALTS. Characteristics, etc. Ferri et Ammonii Tartras. Ferri et Potassi Tartras. Ferri et Ammonii Citras. (Vinum Ferri Citratis.) (Liquor Ferri et Quininæ Citratis.) Ferri et Strychninæ Citras. (Vinum Ferri Amarum.) Ferri Citras. Ferri et Quininæ Citras. Citrate of Iron, Quinine, and Strychnine. Ferri Phosphas. Ferri Pyrophosphas. (Dialysed Iron.)..118-130
MANGANUM. Occurrence. Tests. Mangani Oxidum Rubrum. Mangani Sulphas. Potassii Permanganas. 130-132
ARGENTUM. Occurrence. Tests. Argenti Nitras. Argenti Nitras Dilutus. Argenti Nitras Fusus. Argenti Oxidum. Argenti Cyanidum 132-133
CUPRUM. Occurrence. Tests. Cupri Acetas. Cupri Sulphas. Ammoniated Copper.............................. 134
PLUMBUM. Occurrence. Tests. Plumbi Oxidum. Liquor Plumbi Subacetatis. Emplastrum Plumbi. Plumbi Acetas. Plumbi Carbonas. Plumbi Iodidum. Plumbi Nitras..135-137
CHROMIUM. Occurrence. Tests. Potassii Bichromas. Acidum Chromicum...137-138
CADMIUM. Occurrence. (No Officinal Preparations.) Cadmium Iodide. Cadmium Sulphate..138-139
ZINCUM. Occurrence. Tests. General Impurities. Liquor Zinci Chloridi. Zinci Chloridum. Zinci Oxidum. Zinci Sulphas. Zinci Corbonas Præcipitatus. Zinci Bromidum. Zinci Iodidum. Zinci Valerianas.....139-142
ARSENIUM. Occurrence. Tests. Antidotes. Acidum Arseniosum. Liquor Acidi Arseniosi. Liquor Potassii Arsenitis. Arsenii Iodidum. Liquor Arsenii et Hydrargyri Iodidi. Sodii Arsenias. Liquor Sodii Arseniatis. Scheele's Green. Paris Green........... 142-145
STIBIUM. Occurrence. Tests. Antimonii Sulphidum. Antimonii Sulphi-

dum Purificatum. Antimonii Sulphuratum. Pil. Antimonii Comp. Antimonii Oxidum. Pulvis Antimonialis. Antimonii et Potassii Tartras. Syr. Scillæ Comp. Vinum Antimonii. Mist. Glycyrrhizæ Comp.....145–147

BISMUTHUM. Occurrence. Tests. Bismuthi Subcarbonas. Bismuthi Subnitras. Bismuthi Citras. Bismuthi et Ammonii Citras..............147–149

HYDRARGYRUM. Occurrence. Preparation. Tests, etc. Emplastrum Ammoniaci cum Hydrargyro. Emplastrum Hydrargyri. Massa Hydrargyri. Unguentum Hydrargyri. Hydrargyri Chloridum Corrosivum. Hydrargyri Chloridum Mite. Pil. Catharticæ Comp. Hydrargyri Iodidum Rubrum. Liq. Arsenii et Hydrargyri Iodidi. Hydrargyri Oxidum Rubrum. Hydrargyri Oxidum Flavum. Oleatum Hydrargyri. Hydrargyri Cyanidum. Hydrargyri Subsulphas Flavus. Hydrargyrum Ammoniatum. Liq. Hydrargyri Nitratis. Ung. Hydrargyri Nitratis. Hydrargyri Sulphidum Rubrum....................................149–154

PART III.

ORGANIC PHARMACY.

Relations of Pharmacy to Organic Chemistry. Composition of Plants. Cassification of Proximate Principles 155

THE CELLULIN GROUP.

CELLULOSE. Gossypium. Cotton and Linen Fibre. Tests. Pyroxylinum. Collodium. Collodium Flexile. Collodium Stypticum. Collodium cum Cantharide. Paper. Preparation. Chartæ. Parchment Paper. Oxalic Acid..156–158

DESTRUCTIVE DISTILLATION OF CELLULIN. Acidum Aceticum. Methylic Alcohol. Pix Liquida. Syrupus Picis Liquidæ. Oleum Picis Liquidæ. Pitch. Carbo Animalis. Carbo Animalis Purificatus. Creasotum. Aqua Creasoti. Acidum Carbolicum Crudum. Acidum Carbolicum. Acidum Salicylicum. Oleum Succini. Coal. Coal Tar.............159–162

AMYLACEOUS BODIES AND THEIR DERIVATIVES.

AMYLUM. Amylum Iodatum. Glyceritum Amyli. Dextrin. Glucose. Fehling's Test. Saccharum. Syrupus. Saccharum Lactis. Caramel. Mel. Mel Despumatum. Confectio Rosæ. Mel Rosæ....................162–165

WAX. Cera Flava. Cera Alba. Ceratum......... 165–166

EXUDATIONS OF PLANTS.

GUMS. Definition. Classification. Acacia. Mucilago Acaciæ. Syrupus Acaciæ. Tragacantha. Mucilago Tragacantha. Mucilagines.... 167–168

GUM RESINS. Definition. Ammoniacum. Asafœtida. Cambogia. Myrrha. Misturæ..... 168–169

RESINS. Definition. NATURAL RESINS. Mastiche. Pix Burgundica. Pix Canadensis. Guaiaci Resina. Gutta Percha. Scammonium. ARTIFICIAL RESINS. Resina. Resina Jalapæ. Resina Podophylli. Resina Scammonii. Extractum Colocynthidis Comp.................... 170–172

OLEO-RESINS. Definition. NATURAL OLEO-RESINS. Terebinthina. Oleum Terebinthinæ. Terebinthina Canadensis. Copaiba. Massa Copaibæ. DERIVED OLEO-RESINS. Preparation. Oleoresinæ....................172–174

BALSAMS. Definition. Balsamum Peruvianum. Balsamum Tolutanum. Styrax. Benzoinum. Adeps Benzoinatus. Acidum Benzoicum 174–175

MALTUM. Extractum Malti...175–176

FERMENTATION. Various Kinds. Products. Whiskey. Brandy. Gin. Rum. Alcohol. Dilute Alcohol. Fusel Oil. Vinum Album. Vinum Album Fortior. Vinum Rubrum. Acidum Tartaricum. (Acidum Citricum.) Spiritus Vini Gallici. Spiritus Frumenti..............................176–180

ALCOHOL DECOMPOSITION PRODUCTS. Æther. Spiritus Ætheris. Æther Fortior. Spiritus Ætheris Comp. Oleum Æthereum. Æther Aceticus. Spiritus Ætheris Nitrosi. Amyl Nitris. Chloral. Butyl Chloral Hydrate. Chloroformum Venale. Linimentum Chloroformi. Chloroformum Purificatium. Mistura Chloroformi.................... 180–185

VOLATILE OILS. Definition. Description. Source. Reactions. Composition. Methods of Preparation. En-fleurage. Preservation. Restoration. Adulterations. Tests. Oils derived by the Action of Ferment. Table of Officinal Volatile Oils.......................................185–189

STEAROPTENS FROM VOLATILE OILS. Camphora. (Camphor Monobromata.) Menthol. Thymol. Test....................................189–190

FIXED OILS AND FATS. Definition. Description. Chemical Composition. Stearin. Palmitin. Olein. Purification. Decomposition. Protection. Restoration. Preparation. Adulterations. Tests. Table of Officinal Fixed Oils and Fats....................................191–193

EMULSION. Definition. Theory. Emulsifying Agents. Emulsion of Cod Liver Oil. 192

SAPONIFICATION DERIVATIVES. Soaps. Preparation. Soluble Soaps. Insoluble Soaps. Description. Chemical Composition. Sapo. Sapo Viridis. Tinctura Sapo Viridis. Linimentum Calcis. Emplastrum Plumbi. Glycerinum. Nitroglycerin. Acidum Oleicum. Oleates. Precipitated Oleates..192–196

ALKALOIDS. Occurrence. Composition. Solvents. Nomenclature. Formation of Salts. General Methods of Extraction. Theory of Isolation. Opium. Opium Denarcotissatum. Assay. Extraction of Morphine. Cinchona. Assay. General tests for Alkaloids. Table of Officinal Alkaloids..................................... 107–204

CONTENTS.

GLUCOSIDES. Definition. Characteristics. Chrysarobinum. Elaterium. Picrotoxinum. Salicinum. Santoninum. Sodii Santoninas. Unofficinal Glucosides 205–206

ORGANIC ACIDS. Acidum Gallicum. Acidum Tannicum. Valerianic Acid. 207 DRUGS CONTRIBUTED BY THE ANIMAL KINGDOM. Acidum Lacticum. Acidum Oleicum. Adeps. Oleum Adipis. Cautharis. Carbo Animalis. Cera Flava. Cera Alba. Cetaceum. Coccus. Fel Bovis. Ichthyocolla. Moschus. Oleum Morrhuæ. Pepsinum Saccharatum. Tests. Saccharum Lactis. Sevum. Vitellus. UNOFFICINALS. Castoreum. Gelatin. Colla. Koumiss. Pancreatin, etc... 207–211

TOXICOLOGY. Poisons. Definition. Antidote. Definition. General Remedies. General Antidote. Classification of Poisons. Symptoms. Special Antidotes..... 211–213

MANUAL OF PHARMACY

AND

PHARMACEUTICAL CHEMISTRY.

INTRODUCTION.

PHARMACY. The art or science of preparing, preserving, and compounding substances for the purposes of medicine; the profession of a pharmacist. The name is also applicable to the place where medicines are compounded and dispensed.

PHARMACOPŒIA. An authorized treatise on the several kinds of medicine, and formulas for preparing them. There are in use at the present day about twenty-three different Pharmacopœias, authorized by as many nations. The U. S. Pharmacopœia was published in 1820, and the several decennial revisions in 1830, 1842, 1851, 1863, 1873, and 1882 respectively. These revisions are conducted by a convention of men appointed for that purpose, by certain pharmaceutical and medical bodies; other Pharmacopœias are produced through the respective governments.

DISPENSATORY. A commentary on one or more Pharmacopœias, giving the history, properties, doses, etc., of officinal and unofficinal drugs. There are three Dispensatories published in the United States, viz.: The National Dispensatory, U. S. Dispensatory, and King's Dispensatory (Eclectic).

PART I.

METROLOGY.

Metrology is the determination of the bulk or extension of substances (*measure*); their excess of gravitating force (*weight*); and the relation of these to each other (*specific gravity* and *specific volume*).

GRAVITATION. The attraction existing between all *masses*.

WEIGHT, in any terrestrial substance, is the *excess of attraction* which the earth and the substance have for each other, over and above the attraction of each in opposite directions, by the various heavenly bodies.

By the law of gravitation, an attraction is exerted by the sun, moon, and other planets for a body near the earth, as well as for the earth itself, and *vice versa*,—but on account of the rapid diminution of the force, by the increase of distance (inversely as the square of the distance), the earth's attraction overcomes that of the heavenly bodies, and draws the body toward itself.

WEIGHING, is the determination of the excessive attraction by the earth by comparison with a substance of known gravitating force. Accomplished by means of various instruments known as steelyards, scales, etc., all dependent upon the principle of the balance. The instruments employed by most pharmacists for weighing are called Balances.

THE BALANCE.

The *Knife-edges* of a balance are the sharp points (made either of steel or agate) which act as bearings for the beam. They are three in number, two of which are known as *Points of Suspension*,—the points at each end of the beam, from which the pans are suspended; and one, the *Point of Support*,—the point at the middle of the beam which supports it upon the upright.

The *Centre of Gravity* is in a perpendicular line extending through the point of balance.

Conditions upon which the stability, sensibility, and accuracy of the balance depends.

1. The Centre of Gravity must be situated *below* the Point of Support (the central knife-edge).

2. The Centre of Gravity should be as *near to* the Point of Support as possible.

3. The three knife-edges should be in the same plane, and their edges parallel to each other.

4. The construction of the beam should be as light as possible; light but strong and inflexible.

5. Within limits, sensibility increases with the length of the arms.

6. Also affected by the friction between the knife-edges and planes (which in fine balances should be made of agate).

7. The Points of Suspension should be equi-distant from the Point of Support.

SYSTEMS OF WEIGHTS USED IN PHARMACY.

There are four, viz.: Troy, Apothecaries', Avoirdupois, and Metric.

TROY WEIGHT, used by jewellers. The grain and ounce were adopted by the U. S. Pharmacopœia, 1870.

3⅛ grains	= 1 carat.		
24 grains	= 1 pennyweight.		
20 pennyweights	= 1 oz.	=	480 grs.
12 ounces	= 1 lb.	=	5760 grs.

APOTHECARIES' WEIGHT, used in the compounding of medicines.

20 grains	= 1 scruple—Ʒ.		
3 scruples	= 1 drachm—Ʒ	=	60 grs.
8 drachms	= 1 ounce—℥	=	480 grs.
12 ounces	= 1 pound	=	5760 grs.

(Of the above denominations, all are employed in pharmacy excepting the pound.)

AVOIRDUPOIS WEIGHT, used in the purchase of drugs, and for general commercial transactions; also recognized by the Br. P.

27½ grains	= 1 drachm.	
16 drachms	= 1 ounce—oz.	= 437.5 grs.
16 ounces	= 1 pound—lb.	= 7000 grs.

etc. (The oz. and lb. are the denominations usually employed.)

The only denomination common to the above three systems is the *grain*.

Derivation of the Grain. According to a law enacted in 1266, in England, "An English penny weighed thirty-two wheat corns, taken from the midst of the ear and well-dried; twenty such pence make an ounce, and twelve ounces one pound." Another law, enacted in 1304, reads "that every pound of money or of medicines is of twenty shillings' weight, but the pound of all other things is twenty-five shillings' weight. The ounce of medicine consists of twenty pence, and the pound contains twelve ounces," etc.

LIQUID MEASURE.

Medicines are measured by means of graduated conical or cylinder glass vessels, known as *graduates*. Systems of measures used in pharmacy. There are three, viz.,—*Liquid* or *Wine*, *Imperial* or *British*, and *Metric*.

Liquid or Wine Measure; used in the U. S.

60 minims—$\mathfrak{m}$ = 1 fluidrachm—$f\mathfrak{Z}$.
8 fluidrachms = 1 fluidounce—$f\mathfrak{Z}$ = 480 $\mathfrak{m}$.
16 fluidounces = 1 pint　　— O = 7680 $\mathfrak{m}$.
8 pints　　　 = 1 gallon —*Cong.* = 61240 $\mathfrak{m}$.

Imperial or British Measure; recognized by the British Pharmacopœia.

60 minims—$\mathfrak{m}$ = 1 fluidrachm—$f\mathfrak{Z}$.
8 fluidrachms = 1 fluidounce—$f\mathfrak{Z}$ = 480 $\mathfrak{m}$.
20 fluidounces = 1 pint　　—O = 9600 $\mathfrak{m}$.
8 pints　　　 = 1 gallon　—*Cong.* = 76800 $\mathfrak{m}$.

COMPARISONS OF WEIGHTS AND MEASURES.

Sixteen troy ozs. = 7680 grs.; sixteen Av. ozs. = 7000 grs. (680 grs. less) : 16 troy ozs.= about $1\frac{1}{16}$ Av. lbs.

Distilled water at 60° F. (30 inches barometer). One cubic inch weighs 252.45 grs.

Liquid or *Wine Measure.* One fluidounce weighs 455.7 grs.; one pint, 7291.2 grs.; one minim, .95 gr.; one gallon, about $8\frac{1}{4}$ av. lbs.; one gallon contains 231 cu. in.

Imperial Measure. One fluidounce water (under above conditions) weighs 437.5 grs.; one pint, 8750 grs.; one gallon, ten Av. lbs.: one minim, .91 gr.

Terms used in referring to Domestic Measures, and their equivalents; viz. :

Teaspoonful = one fluidrachm ; dessertspoonful = two fl. drs. ; tablespoonful = four fl. drs. ; wineglassful = two fl. ozs. ; teacupful = five fl. ozs. ; tumblerful = 12 fl. ozs.

The U. S. Pharmacopœia recognizes no general system of weights or measures. In most cases the term *parts* is used, referring to weight, and applicable to any system. In a few instances (formulas for Fluid Extracts) *cubic centimeters* are employed to denote the amount of finished product. The *gram* and *grain* are also used in certain formulas (pills and troches).

Problems.—1. If one pint elix. potass. bromid. contains 1⅛ troy ozs. of the chemical, how much in each fluidrachm ?

2. One pint elixir bromide of sodium contains 1280 grs.; how much in one fluidrachm?

3. How much powd. coca leaves must I employ to make one pint of elixir, each fluidrachm to contain 20 grs. ?

4. One gallon of the elixir represents 11.7028 Av. ozs.; how much calisaya bark to each fluidrachm?

TESTING OF GRADUATES. With the graduate standing on a level surface, pour into it 455.7 grs. distilled water at 15.6° C. (60°F.): the liquid should measure one fluidounce. Or pour into the graduate 30 cm^3 of water, which is the equivalent to a fluidounce.

METRIC SYSTEM.

The Metric System of Weights and Measures is based upon the *decimal* system, the various denominations increasing and decreasing by tenths.

Its use is *legalized* in America and England, and made obligatory by all other governments of the civilized world.

The *unit* or *standard* is the **Meter** (μέτρον, a measure), which is the unit of linear measure, and represents $\frac{1}{10000000}$ of a quadrant of the earth's polar circumference, equivalent to 39.37 English inches. The **Gram** is the unit of weight; the **Liter** of capacity (although the *cubic centimeter* is oftener and more desirably used) ; the **Are**, of surface measure. The denominations representing the subdivisions of any unit are expressed by prefixing the Latin numerals *deci, centi,* and *milli* to the unit, meaning respectively one tenth, one hundredth, and one thousandth; the multiples are expressed by prefixing the Greek numerals, *deka, hecto, kilo*, and *myria*, meaning ten, hundred, thousand, and ten thousand.

Comparison of the Value of the Several Denominations.

```
10,000.000—Myra—(M.)
 1000.000—Kilo—(K.)
  100.000—Hecto—(H.)
   10.000—Deka—(D.)
    1.000—Unit (Meter, Gram, Liter, Arc).
     .1—Deci—(d.)
     .01—Centi—(c.)
     .001—Milli—(m.)
```

Derivation of the Are. The square of ten meters (one Deka-meter), representing one square Hecto-meter $= 100 \text{ m}^2$.

Derviation of the Gram. The meter is divided into one hundred equal parts, called *centi-meters ;* upon one centi-metre as a base, a cube is erected having for its three dimensions, one c. m. each; the contents of this cube will be one cubic-centimeter (cm^3), measuring one milli-liter. This quantity of distilled water at its maximum density ($4° \text{ C.} = 39.2° \text{ F.}$) and 30 inches barometric pressure, weighs *one gram* $= 15.432$ grains.

Derivation of the Liter. The meter is divided into tenths, called deci-meters. If a cube is erected, having a deci-meter for each of its three dimensions, its contents will be ($1 \times 1 \times 1 = 1 \text{ dm}^3$) one cubic deci-meter ($dm^3$) ; the capacity of which is one *Liter.*

One Liter $= 1000 \text{ cm}^3 = 33.81 f\text{℥} = 2.113$ pints.

One liter of distilled water at $4° \text{ C.}$ (30 in. barometer) weighs 1000 grams $= 1$ kilo-gram $= 15432$ grains $= 2.2$ lbs av.

Abbreviations. The term *Kilo.* refers to kilogram; while cm^3, or c.c. are used to express cubic centimeters.

To convert metric *weights* into other systems: Reduce to grains by multiplying the number of grams by 15.432 and divide by the number of grains in the denomination of the system required.

To convert metric *measures* into other systems : Find the number of cm^3, multiply by 15.432, and divide by the number of grains of water in the denomination of the system required.

To convert *weights* of other systems into metric weights : Reduce to grains and divide by 15.432 ; the quotient will represent the number of grams.

To convert *measures* of other systems into metric measures : Reduce to grains (as though water were referred to), and divide by 15.432 ; the quotient will represent the number of cm³.

In writing the various metric denominations, it is advised to substitute the decimal point by a perpendicular line, and thereby avoid possible errors in placing the point. For example.

R

Pulv. Aloes............	9	74
Pulv. Myrrhæ.........	6	50
Pulv. Rhei............	13	00
Ol. Menthæ pip........	0	65
Misce fiant pilulæ No. 100.	

R

Chloralis..............	8	00
Potass. Bromidi........	12	00
Syr. Zingiberis........	32	00
Syrupi...............	96	00
Misce fiat mistura, etc.	

In the above there can be no mistaking of the quantities desired, as *all solids are weighed*, and *all liquids measured;* gram being the unit of weight, and the cubic-centimeter of measure.

Examples to test the knowledge of the student, on writing and convert-ing the metric system into other systems:

How many c. m. in 1 D. m. ?   D. m. in 1 K. m. ?   c. g.in 1 d. g.? c. g. in 1 H. g. ?   D. g. in 1 Kilo?   m. l. in 1 D. l. ?   H. l. in 1 M.l.? g. in 1 H. g. ?   c. g. in 1 D. g. ?   etc.

1. What is the cost of 18425 grams tartaric acid at $1.00 per Kilo. ? *Ans.* $18.425.

2. Cost of 425 grams zinc sulphate at 33⅓ cents per Kilo. ?   *Ans.* $0.14+.

3. Cost of 7500 grams potassium chlorate at 50 cents per Kilo. ?

4. Cost of 6218 grams potassium bromide at $1.40 per Kilo. ?

5. Cost of 2¼ lbs. alum at 22 cents per Kilo. ?

6. Cost of 150 Kilos. iodine at $2.75 per lb ?   *Ans.* $907.50.

7. Cost of 60 Kilos. citric acid at 3½ cents per oz. ?

8. Cost of 25 grams quinine at $1.10 per oz. ?

9. How many grams in 42 troy ozs. ?

10. How many inches in 25 meters?

11. How many f ℥ in 1 liter?

12. How many grams in 1 Av. oz. ?

13. How many Av. lbs. in 2000 grams?

14. Cost of 1 liter at $1.25 per d. l. ?   *Ans.* $12.50.

15. Two casks hold respectively 136 and 125 liters of water ; what is the weight of water that both will hold?   *Ans.* 261 Kilos.

16. From 735 c. m. subtract 3 m. 86 c. m. ?   *Ans.* 3 m. 49 c. m.

17. From 9 m. 8 m. m. subtract 57 m. m. ?   *Ans.* 8 m. 51 c. m.

18. *a.* Wishing to find the capacity of a bottle, I weigh it (having no measure); its weight is 520 grams; filled with water it weighs 1 K. 810 grams; what is its capacity? *Ans.* 1 K. 290 grams.
b. How many fl. ozs.? *Ans.* 43 f ℥ 312.18 grs.—or 43 f ℥. 5.28 f ℈.

19. Add 43 H. g., 25 K. g., 27 c. g., 3204 m. g., 68 D. g., 27½ g., and 52¼ D. g. *Ans.* 30538.474.

Work.

43 Hecto-grams,	4300	
25 Kilos.,	25000	
27 Centi-grams,		27
3204 Milli-grams,	3	204
68 Deka-grams,	680	
27½ Grams,	27	5
52¼ Deka-grams,	527	5
	30538	474

Ans. 30 Kilos 538 grams 474 milligrams, or 30,538 grams 474 milligrams.

NOTE.—In *reading* of denominations of weight, always give the number of *grams;* then follow with the fraction, reading it as so many of the *lowest denomination;* or mention the number of *Kilos.*, then the remaining *grams*, and the number of the lowest denomination.

20. Add 225 c. g., 83 d. g., 10002 m. g., 250 grams, 2½ D. g., 183 K. g., 19 H. g., 205 m. g. *Ans.* 185195.757.

21. Add 27½ grams, 438 c. g., 2786 D. g., 3487½ c. g., 42½ K. g., 235 d. g., 32½ M. g., 8¾ K. g., 16 m. g., 84 d. g., 23½ H. g., and give answer in av. lbs., ozs., and grs., using three decimal places throughout (1 gram = 15.4 grs.). *Ans.* 894 lbs., 5 ozs., 374 grs. ·

22. Add 425 D. g., 8¼ K. g., 3¾ M. g., 825 d. g., 460 m. g., 18 grams. *Ans.* 50350.960.

23. Add 54 d. g., 10 D. g., 4 c. g., 14 K. g., 7 M. g., 2638 d. g., 5 m. g., 18¾ grams, 42½ D. g., 10 M. g., 26 m. g. *Ans.* 184813.021.

24. Add 5 K. g., ½ H. g., 5 M. g., 500 grams, 50 d. g., ¼ c. g., 5 m. g., 5 c. g. *Ans.*

25. Add ¼ M. g., 50 H. g., 5 K. g., 500 D. g., 5000 grams, 50 c. g., ¼ d. g., 5 m. g. *Ans.* 25000.555.

26. Add 210 d. g., 42 D. g., 6 m. g., 456 c. g., 4368 m. g., 22 H. g., 3½ M. g., 6¼ grams, 248 d. g., 86 m. g., 43 grams, and reduce to Troy ozs. and grs.

27. I have ten vessels filled with water, which hold respectively 265 d. g., 44 m. g., 235 c. g., 45 D. g., 266 K. g., 18¾ grams, 525 d. g.,

3002 grams, 46 d. g., 25638 m. g.; how many pints are represented by the whole? *Ans.* 570.57 pts.

SPECIFIC GRAVITY.

Specific Gravity is the relation of weight to volume; or, the weight of a substance, as compared to the weight of an equal volume of another substance, taken as a unit.

Unit. The unit for the specific gravity of all solids and liquids is distilled water at 60° F. and 30 inches barometric pressure; for *gases*, either hydrogen or air is taken as the unit.

The specific gravity of U. S. P. officinals is taken at 59° F. (with a few exceptions) in order to avoid fractions in the *Centigrade* equivalent; 59° F. = 15° C., while 60° F. = 15.6° C.

The principle for determining specific gravity was discovered by Archimedes, the philosopher. King Hiero, of Syracuse, having ordered a golden crown made, suspected its purity when completed, and demanded that Archimedes should test it. The latter, after many unsuccessful attempts, was about to give up in despair, when one day, while taking his bath, he observed that, the deeper his body became immersed, the greater the quantity of water that overflowed the sides of the tub, showing that he displaced an equal volume of water. He rushed through the streets, naked, shouting "Eureka! Eureka!" and procuring a piece of pure gold of the same weight as the crown, compared the specific gravities of the two, when the latter was found deficient.

Laws on which Specific Gravity is Based. 1. Fluids buoy up all solids with a force equal to the weight of liquid displaced.

2. Floating bodies displace their weight of liquid; immersed bodies their bulk.

Methods for the Determination of Specific Gravity. 1. Hydrostatic Balance (for *solids* only). 2. Specific Gravity Bottle (*solids* and *liquids*). 3. Loaded Cylinder (for *liquids* only). 4. Hydrometer (for *liquids* only).

HYDROSTATIC BALANCE.

The Hydrostatic Balance is merely an accurate prescription balance, so arranged that one of the pans is suspended by shorter cords, and has a hook attached from the bottom, from which a substance may be attached by means of horse-hair or a piece of thread, for the purpose of weighing the substance in water.

Methods of use. I. *For solids insoluble in, and heavier than, water.* Determine the weight of the substance in air; immerse it in water and again note its weight; the difference between these two weights (i.e., its loss of weight in water) represents the weight of liquid displaced, or the weight of an equal volume of water. Having the weight of the substance, and the weight of an equal volume of water, a comparison represents the sp. gr.—; water being the unit, we divide the weight in air by the weight of an equal bulk of water, the quotient representing the sp. gr.

II. *For solids soluble in, and heavier than, water.* Weigh the substance in air, and again in some liquid of known sp. gr., in which it is insoluble; the difference represents the weight of an equal volume of the liquid used. On dividing this into the weight in air, the quotient multiplied by the specific gravity of the liquid used gives the sp. gr. of the substance.

Example 28. A piece of lead weighs in air 228 grs., in water 208 grs.; what is its sp. gr.? $228 - 208 = 20$; $228 \div 20 = 11.4$, *Ans.*

The above loses in weight in water $228 - 208 = 20$ grs.; hence, 20 grs. is the weight of an equal bulk of water; 228 grs. representing the weight of the lead—then $228 \div 20 =$ the sp. gr. or 11.4. (*Note:* The Rule of Three facilitates calculations in Specific Gravity, but is recommended by the author only to be used for rapid calculating, *after the student has become thoroughly conversant* with the principles of sp. gr. In all cases the weight of liquid displaced is the *first term*, the weight in air the *second term*, and the specific gravity of the liquid used the *third term;* thus $20 : 228 :: 1.000 : x = 11.4$.

Ex. 29. A nail weighs in air 50 grs., in water 43 grs.; what is its sp. gr.? *Ans.* 7.14.

30. A piece of gold weighs 700 grs., in water 66.4 grs.; what is its sp. gr.? *Ans.* 19.4.

31. A piece of copper weighs 360 grs. in air, in water 320 grs.; what is its sp. gr.? *Ans.* 9.

32. A silver chain weighs 848 grs., in water it weighs 768 grs.; what is its sp. gr.? *Ans.* 10.6.

33. A platinum crucible weighs 749 grs., in water it weighs 714 grs.; what is its sp. gr.? *Ans.* 21.4.

34. A piece of phosphorus weighs 45¾ grs., in air, in water 25¾ grs.; what is its sp. gr.? *Ans.* 1.83.

35. A solid, soluble in water, weighs in air 680 grs., in ether (s. g. .750) .540 grs.; what is its sp. gr.? $680 - 540 = 140$; $680 \div 140 =$

4.85 × .750 = 3.63, *Ans.* (The loss of weight in ether is 680 — 540 = 140 grs., which represents the weight of an equal bulk of ether. 680÷140 = 4.85 = sp. gr. as compared to ether for a unit, but as ether is only .750 as heavy as water, we will have to multiply by .750 in order to make the answer compare to water as the unit. 4.85 × .750 = 3.63, *Ans.*

36. Weight of a solid in air is 845 grs., in benzine (s. g. 0.835) 795 grs.; what is sp. gr.? *Ans.* 14.11.

37. Weight of a piece of alum 124 grs., in oil of turpentine (sp. gr. 0.872) 62 grs.; what is sp. gr.? *Ans.* 1.74.

38. Weight in air 1250 grs., in ether fortior (sp. gr. .725) 1200. grs.; what is sp. gr.? $1250 - 1200 = 50$; $50 : 1250 :: 0.725 : x = 18.125$, *Ans.*

39. A lump of sugar weighing 100 grs. was found to weigh when immersed in oil of turpentine (sp. gr. 0.87) 45.62 grs. What is its sp. gr.?

40. A piece of sodium chloride weighs 450 grs.; in alcohol (sp. gr. 0.820) 375 grs. What is its sp. gr.? *Ans.* 4.92.

III. *For solids lighter than, and insoluble in water.* As a floating body displaces its own weight of water, it is necessary to attach a heavy body to immerse it, before we can arrive at the *weight of an equal volume* of water. Consequently it becomes necessary to attach a heavy body sufficiently large to sink the lighter, to one arm of the balance, and counterpoise it; to the cord from which it is suspended, the light body is attached, which, on account of the buoyant power of the water, raises the heavy weight; now the weight required to restore the equilibrium of the balance must be added to the weight in air, the sum representing the weight of an equal bulk of water; on dividing the weight in air by this weight, the sp. gr. is attained.

Ex. 41. A piece of wax weighs in air 240 grs. For a sinker I use a nail weighing in water 86 grs.; the wax and nail weigh in water 76 grs.; what is the sp. gr. of the wax? $86 - 76 = 10$; $240 + 10 = 250$; $240 ÷ 250 = 0.96$. If the wax had been placed in water without the nail attached, it would have displaced 240 grs. of water; but by attaching to the nail it is wholly immersed, and displaces 86 — 76 = 10 grs. more water; then $240 + 10 = 250$ grs., is the weight of an equal volume of water; or, $250 : 240 :: 1.000 ÷ x = 0.96$.

42. A piece of cork weighs 154 grs.; I use a sinker weighing 921 grs. in water; the cork and sinker weigh together in water 425 grs. What is the sp. gr.? $921 - 425 = 496 + 154 = 650$ grs., weight of an equal volume of water; $154 ÷ 650 = 0.236$, sp. gr.

43. Weight of wax in air 2334 grs. A sinker is counterpoised in water and the wax attached, when it requires an addition of 75 grs. to overcome the buoyant power of the wax. What is its sp. gr.? *Ans.* 0.969.

44. A light substance weighs 120 grs. in air; being attached to a piece of lead and weighed in water, the united weight is 40 grs., while the lead alone in water shows 50 grs. What is its sp. gr.?

45. A sample of wax weighs 300 grs.; on attaching to a piece of copper counterpoised in water, the two combined lose 7 grs. in weight. What is the sp. gr. of wax?

46. One cubic inch of cork weighs 60.6 grs. What is its sp. gr.?

IV. *For solids lighter than, and soluble in water.* Proceed as in the previous method, using a liquid that is not a solvent for the substance, and multiply the result by the sp. gr. of the liquid.

Ex. 47. A piece of potassium weighs in air 200 grs.; a lead sinker weighs in petroleum (sp. gr. 0.75), 350 grs. ; with the potassium attached their combined weight in water is 347.6 grs. What is the sp. gr. of the potassium? $350 - 347.6 = 2.4 + 200 = 202.4$; $200 \div 202.4 = .988 \times .75 = .741$, *Ans.*; or $202.4 : 200 :: .75 : x = .741$.

SPECIFIC GRAVITY BOTTLE.

I. *For Liquids.* Perhaps the simplest and best method of taking the sp, gr. of liquids is the Specific Gravity Bottle. It generally consists of a flat bottom globular flask with slender neck, on which a mark is placed to indicate the level of a liquid; in some cases the neck is accurately fitted with a perforated glass stopper. A counterpoise of the exact weight of the flask accompanies it. The flask may hold exactly 100 or 1000 grs. of distilled water at 15.6° C.

Determination of the Specific Gravity of a Liquid. Fill the flask to the mark on its neck with the liquid, and weigh the contents, using the counterpoise to represent the tare of the bottle. This weight divided by 100 or 1000 will give the sp. gr. of the liquid, since the same volume of water weighs 100 or 1000 grs. according to the flask used : i.e., divide the weight of the contents by the weight of an equal bulk of water. *Ex.* A 1000-gr. flask will hold 1420 grs. of nitric acid, which at once shows the specific gravity, viz.: $1420 \div 1000 = 1.420$.

Care of Specific Gravity Bottles. Should be wiped dry to remove adhering moisture ; and handled as little as possible while containing the liquid under operation, to prevent change of temperature.

An ordinary prescription bottle may be used for the same purpose as a specific gravity flask, by first weighing and making a counterpoise; it is then filled with distilled· water at 15.6°C. (60° F.), the level of the liquid marked, and the weight of its contents noted. The sp. gr. of any liquid may be readily determined by filling the bottle with it, and weighing. This latter weight divided by the weight of water will show the sp. gr. *Ex.* A bottle holds 525 grs. water; the same bottle holds 609 grs. of hydrochloric acid; then $609 \div 525 =$ the sp. gr. 1.160.

Ex. 48. A bottle holds 1250 grs. of water; the same bottle holds 1332.85 grs. dilute sulphuric acid. What is its sp. gr.? $1332.85 \div 1250 = 1.067$, *Ans.*; or $1250 : 1332.85 :: 1.000 : x = 1.067$.

49. A bottle holding one fl. oz., holds 569.6 grains of glycerin or 373.67 grs. alcohol; or 330.38 grs. stronger ether; or 838.49 grs. sulphuric acid; or 1353.43 grs. bromine. What is sp. gr. of each?

50. A bottle holding one cubic inch, when filled with aqua ammonia contains 448.13 grs. What is its sp. gr.?

51. A bottle that will hold 500 grs. of water, when filled with mercury weighs 6750 grs. What is its sp. gr.?

52. A one-liter flask holds 1840 grams of sulphuric acid; what is the sp. gr.?

II. *For Solids* (in the form of a powder). Weigh the powder, and place in a counterpoised flask of known capacity; add a small quantity of distilled water, and shake to remove air-bubbles; then fill the flask with water to the established mark on the neck, and weigh again. From the combined weight of water and substance, subtract the amount due to the substance; the difference represents the weight of water in the flask. Subtract this weight from the weight of water the bottle originally held, and the difference represents the weight of water that the bulk of the powder now occupies, or the weight of an equal bulk of water. Having the weight in air, and the weight of an equal bulk of water, dividing the former by the latter gives the sp. gr.

If the powder is soluble in water, use a liquid of known sp. gr. in which it is not soluble, and proceed as above, and multiply the result by the sp. gr. of the liquid.

Ex. 53. A powder weighing 360 grs. is placed in a flask (which holds 1000 grs. of water), and the latter is filled with water; the combined weight of powder and water is 1260 grs. What is the sp. gr. of the powder? 1260 grs. (weight of powder and water) less 360 grs. (weight of powder) = 900 grs. (weight of water in flask) ; 1000 grs. (quantity of water the flask will hold) less 900 grs. = 100 grs. (weight of an equal bulk of water) ; 360 ÷ 100 = 3.6, *Ans.*; or 100 : 360 :: 1000 : x = 3.6

54. 200 grs. of calomel is placed in a flask (1050 grs. water capacity) and the latter filled with water; the combined weight is 1123 grs. What is the sp. gr.? 1123 − 200 = 923 grs. (water in flask); 1050 − 923 = 27 grs.; 200 ÷ 27 = 7.4, *Ans.*

55. Powd. silver weighs 105 grs.; bottle holds 300 grs. water ; silver and water, when bottle is filled, weigh 395 grs. What is sp. gr.?

56. A powder weighs 300 grs.; placed in a 5000 gr. flask, and filled with water, the combined weight of powder and water is 5250 grs. What is the sp. gr.?

57. One troy oz. powder, placed in a 1250 gr. flask and filled with water; the combined weight of powder and water is 1575 grs. What is the sp. gr.?

58. Calomel 100 grams is placed in a one-liter flask, and the latter filled with water; contents of flask weighs 1086 grams. What is the sp. gr.?

THE LOADED CYLINDER.

The Loaded Cylinder is used for determining the specific gravity of dense viscid liquids—such as balsams, oils, etc.—that are not easily removed from hydrometers or sp. gr. bottles, which are constructed of thin glass, and easily fractured.

Construction. Merely a rod of glass, or some metal that will sink in the liquid. It displaces its own bulk of the liquid.

Use. 1. Weigh the cylinder in air, then in water, and note the loss, which is the weight of an equal volume of water. 2. Weigh in the liquid under consideration and again note the loss, which represents the weight of an equal volume of the liquid. 3. Having the weights of equal volumes of water and the liquid under consideration, divide the latter weight by the former.

Ex. 59. A glass rod weighs in air 57 grs.; in water 35.5 grs.; in oil 39 grs. Sp. gr. of latter? 57 less 35.5 =21.5 (weight of equal volume of water); 57 less 39 = 18 (weight of equal volume of oil); 18 ÷ 21.5= 0.837, *Ans.*; or, 21.5 : 18 :: 1.000 : x = 0.837.

60. Cylinder weighs 80 grs.; in water 61 grs.; in solution chloride calcium 52 grs. Sp. gr. of solution ?

61. Glass rod weighs 100 grs.; in water 91 grs.; in sulphuric acid 84.44 grs. Sp. gr. of acid?

62. Glass rod weighs 200 grs.; in water 180 grs.; in glycerin 175 grs. Sp. gr. of glycerin?

63. Glass stopper loses by immersion in water 171 grs.; in another liquid 143 grs. Sp. gr. of latter?

64. Loaded cylinder weighs 200 grs.; in water 140 grs.; in solution chlor. zinc 106.7 grs. Sp. gr.of latter?

HYDROMETER (*for liquids only*).

Construction. A glass tube with a graduated stem, having a bulb at the lower end, loaded with mercury or small shot, to keep the instrument in an upright position.

Principle. *Floating bodies displace their own weight of a liquid;* therefore, the volume of liquid displaced weighs as much as the whole instrument; consequently, the lower the sp. gr. of the liquid, the deeper will the hydrometer sink.

Graduation. The point to which the instrument sinks in water at 60° F. is called 1.000 or 1000. It is then placed in a heavy or light liquid of known sp. gr., the corresponding point of immersion marked on the stem, and the interspace equally subdivided. The point to which the instrument sinks in the liquid indicates the sp. gr.

It is seldom that a hydrometer is graduated for liquids both *lighter* and *heavier* than water, as the instrument would be on the one hand either long and cumbersome, or on the other hand the graduations would be close and indistinct. For this reason, we have in general two kinds of instruments:

1. For liquids lighter than water, with the water-mark low down on the stem.

2. For liquids heavier than water, with the water-mark near the top of the stem.

For special uses, hydrometers are made, having only a portion of the graduated scale on either of the above; or having arbitrary scales of graduations,—such as the Alcohometer, Lactometer, Urinometer, Saccharometer, Acidometer, Barkometer, *and* Elacometer., etc.

Arbitrary Graduations. Baumé's, Trallé's, Cartier's, Twadell's, all of which should be avoided, and are being rapidly replaced by the Specific Gravity scale.

Baumé's hydrometers, which were the first of these peculiarly graduated instruments, may answer as a type.

1. *Pèsé-Esprit, for liquids lighter than water.* The point to which the instrument was immersed in a 10% salt solution was marked 0°,

and the point at which it rested in water was called 10°, and the intervening space equally subdivided.

2. *Pèsé Sirop* or *Pèsé Acide, for liquids heavier than water.* The points at which the instrument rested in water and a 15% salt solution, were respectively marked 0° and 15°—and uniformly graduated between these points.

Rules for converting Beaumé Degrees to Sp. Gr. Scale, and vice versa.

1. *For heavy liquids.*

$$B° \text{ to } S. G. = \frac{145}{145 - B°}; \quad S. G. \text{ to } B° = 145 - \frac{145}{S. G.}.$$

2. *For light liquids.*

$$B° \text{ to } S. G. = \frac{150}{B° + 140}; \quad S. G. \text{ to } B° = \frac{140}{S. G.} - 130.$$

Reading of Hydrometers. These instruments are constructed to be read from above the surface (i.e., the top of the meniscus), because they are often used with colored and opaque liquids which prevent reading from below. [Meniscus: the tendency of all liquids (excepting mercury) to adhere to the sides of a vessel, due to capillary attraction, produces a semi-circular surface in narrow vessels, called a *meniscus.*]

Ex. 65. A hydrometer weighing 300 grs. sinks to a certain point in water; how much must it weigh to sink to the same point in glycerin (sp. gr. 1.250)? $300 \times 1.250 = 375$ grs.; or, $1.000 : 1.250 :: 300 : x = 375.$

Explanation: Since the hydrometer displaces its own weight of any liquid, the above instrument displaces 300 grs. of water; in order to displace the same volume, or 375 grs., of glycerin (this liquid being $\frac{1250}{1000}$ as heavy as water, and $\frac{1250}{1000} \times 300 = 375$) it must weigh 375 grs.

From the above facts we deduce the following principle: *The weights of equal volumes are to each other as the sp. gr. of the liquids.*

Rule. *Multiply the weight of the hydrometer by the sp. gr. of the liquids.*

66. How much should a hydrometer (weighing 100 grs.) weigh, to sink to same point in sulphuric acid (1.840) as it does in water?

67. A hydrometer weighs 500 grs. It sinks in water to a certain point, how much should it weigh to sink to the same point in stronger water of ammonia (0.900)?

68. Hydrometer weighs 250 grs. It rests at a certain point in

water; how much weight must be added to cause it to rest at the same point in nitric acid (1.420)?

69. A hydrometer displaces 375 grs. of water; how much stronger ether (0.725) will it displace? and how much sulphuric acid?

Determination of Specific Gravity, Weight or Volume, when two of the factors are given.

I. Weight and Measure given, to find Specific Gravity. *Divide the weight given, expressed in grains, by the weight of an equal bulk of water*; or S. G. $= \dfrac{W}{V}$.

Ex. 70. 44 troy ozs. of a liquid measure 32 fl. ozs.; what is its sp. gr.? *Ans.* 1.448.

44 troy ozs. = 21120 grs.; 32 fl. ozs. water weighs (32 × 455.7) 14582.4 grs. If the same quantity of the liquid weighs 21120 grs. then its sp. gr. is (21120 ÷ 14582.4) 1.448.

71. 16 troy ozs. measure 14 fl. ozs.; what is the sp. gr.?

72. One Imperial fluid oz. of a liquid weighs 366½ grs.; what is its sp. gr.?

73. 1 liter sulphuric acid weighs 2839.488 grs.; what is its sp. gr.?

74. Equal volumes of benzol (sp. gr. 0.850) and glycerin weigh 34 and 49 parts respectively; what is the sp. gr. of glycerin? *Ans.* 1.225.

II. Measure and Specific Gravity given, to find Weight. *Multiply the weight of an equal volume of water by the sp. gr. and the result represents the number of grains;* or, $W = V \times S.G.$

Ex. 75. How many Av. ozs. will one pint glycerin (1.250) weigh? 1 pint of water weighs 7291.2 grs. × 1.250 = 9114 grs.; 9114 ÷ 437.5 = 20.83 ozs., *Ans.*

76. What will 2 pints ether (0.750) weigh, in troy ozs.?

77. What will 20 fl. ozs. of a liq. (0.835) weigh in grams?

78. How many Av. lbs. and ozs. will 1 gal. Monsel's solution (1.555) weigh?

79. What will 500 cm³ of nitric acid (1.420) weigh? 710 grams.

80. What will 10 L. ether (0.725) weigh in Kilos.?

81. How many grains will 250 cm³ of nitric acid weigh?

III. Weight and Specific Gravity given, to find Measure: *Divide the weight (in grains) by the sp. gr.; the quotient represents the weight in grains of an equal volume of water,* or $V = \dfrac{W}{S.G.}$

Ex. 82. Measure of 20 troy ozs. of sulphuric acid (1.840) in fl. ozs.? *Ans.* 11.448 fl. ozs.

20 troy ozs. = 9600 grs. ÷ 1.840 =: 5217. 3 grs. = weight of an equal volume of water.   5217.3 ÷ 455.7 = 11.448 fl. ozs.

83. Measure (fl. ozs.) of 18 Av. ozs. glycerin (1.250)?

84. Measure (fl. drachms) 20 troy ozs. nitric acid (1.420)?

85. Measure (cm³ and liters) 12 Kilos of a liquid (1.200)?

86. Measure (fl. ozs. and grs.) of 7291.2 grs. of hydrochloric acid?

SPECIFIC VOLUME.

Specific Volume, or Comparative Volume, is the relation of volume to weight; that is, the volume of a liquid as compared with another liquid of equal weight used as standard.

Unit or Standard.   Distilled water at 15.6° C. (60° F.), 30 inches barometer.

Theorem.   The volumes of equal weights of two liquids are to each other inversely as the specific gravity of the liquids.

Explanation.   To arrive at this explanation, we will return to a theorem in specific gravity for our introduction.   Suppose we have before us two vessels, of one quart capacity each, and place a pint of water in the one, and the same quantity of glycerin in the other; we have now *equal volumes* of the two liquids; and if we represent the weight of the water as 1, the relative weight of the glycerin is 1¼ the sp. gr., showing the latter to be 1.250 times as heavy as water, —hence *the weights of equal volumes are to each other as the sp. gr. of the liquids.*   But now, to reverse the above, let us again return to the two vessels containing one pint each of water and glycerin.   Their volumes, being equal, are represented by the ratio 1 : 1, or 1000 : 1000; but we have unequal weights, as glycerin is 1.250 or 1¼ times as heavy as water, and in order to have *equal* weights of both liquids, we must add ¼ pint of water to the pint already in the vessel, making the bulk of water 1¼ times that of the glycerin; now if we represent the volume of glycerin as 1000; the comparative volume of water will be represented by 1250, or their ratio as 1000 : 1250; therefore the volume of glycerin will be $\frac{1000}{1250}$ as great as that of the water, and hence the axiom: *The volumes of equal weights are to each other inversely as the sp. gr. of the liquids.*

Ex. 87. What is the specific volume of ether (.750)?   *Ans.* 1.33
0.750 : 1.000 :: 1 : x = 1.33, or $\frac{1000}{750}$ = 1.33

88. A hydrometer displaces a definite quantity of water; what will be the comparative volume displaced by sulphuric acid (1.840)?
Ans. .54   1840 : 1000 :: 1 : x, or $\frac{1000}{1840}$ = .54

89. The portion of a glass tube immersed in water is represented by one half its length; what portion of its length will be immersed in nitric acid (1.420)? $\frac{1.000}{1.420}$ of .5 = .35 or 1.420 : 1.000 :: .5 : x = .35

· 90. Three fourths of a tube is immersed in alcohol (.820); what portion will be immersed in glycerin (1.250)?

91. A hydrometer weighing 650 grs. has six tenths of its length immersed in chloroform (1.490); what portion will be immersed in hydrochloric acid? What is the weight of hydrochloric acid displaced?

FORMULA FOR DETERMINING THE QUANTITIES TO BE EMPLOYED, IN MIXING DRUGS OF UNLIKE PERCENTAGE STRENGTH, OR DIFFERENT SPECIFIC GRAVITIES, WHEN A MIXTURE OF DEFINITE STRENGTH OR SPECIFIC GRAVITY IS DESIRED.

Example. A pharmacist having on hand water of ammonia of 4% and 24% strength, wishes to mix them, to make a mixture that shall contain 16% of ammonia; what proportions of each shall he employ? *Ans.* 8 parts of 4%, and 12 parts of 24%.

METHOD. $16 \begin{array}{c|c} 4] & 8 \\ 24] & 12 \end{array}$ PROOF.

8 lbs. at 4% = 32 lbs. at 1%
12 " " 24% = 288 " " 1%
20 lbs. mixture 320 lbs. at 1% =

16)320
20 lbs. at 16%.

Explanation. The gain and loss of the percentage strength of the two solutions, as compared with the mean percentage, must balance. Hence we compare a percentage less than the mean, with one greater—4% with 24%. On every part of 4% water of ammonia employed to make the 16% mixture, there is a gain of 12%; and on every part of 24% used in the 16% mixture, there is a loss of 8% of ammonia. Therefore, as the gain and loss on equal parts of each are to each other as 12 to 8, we must take parts that are to each other as 8 to 12.

Rule. 1. Write the values in a column, and the mean value on the left. Link the ingredients in pairs, one less than the mean with one greater; and take the difference between the mean and the numbers representing the percentage strength of each ingredient, and write it opposite the value with which it is linked. These differences are the relative quantities of the ingredients taken in the order in which their values stand.

2. If the quantity of one ingredient is given; to find the corresponding quantities of the others, multiply their differences by the ratio of the given quantity to the difference of the ingredient it represents.

3. If the quantity of the mixture is given; to find the quantity of the ingredients, multiply their differences by the ratio of the given quantity to the sum of the differences.

Example. In what proportions must powd. opium, of 8, 10, 15, and 16% morphine strength be taken, to make a mixture of 14% strength? *Ans.* 2, 1, 4, and 6 parts respectively; or 1, 2, 6, 4.

(No. 1.)	(No. 2.)	*Proof No.* 1.	*Proof No.* 2.

$14\begin{cases} 8 \\ 10 \\ 15 \\ 16 \end{cases} \begin{matrix} 2 \\ 1 \\ 4 \\ 6 \end{matrix}$	$14\begin{cases} 8 \\ 10 \\ 15 \\ 16 \end{cases} \begin{matrix} 1 \\ 2 \\ 6 \\ 4 \end{matrix}$	$2 \times 8 = 16$
		$1 \times 10 = 10$
		$4 \times 15 = 60$
		$6 \times 16 = 96$
		___
		13 13)182
		    14
			$1 \times 8 = 8$
			$2 \times 10 = 20$
			$6 \times 15 = 90$
			$4 \times 16 = 64$
			___
			13 13)182
			    14

Example. Having powd. opium containing 7, 8, 9, 12, 16, and 20% morphine; how shall I mix them to produce a 14% product?

$$14\begin{vmatrix} 7 \\ 8 \\ 9 \\ 12 \\ 16 \\ 20 \end{vmatrix} \begin{matrix} 6 \\ 2 \\ 2 \\ 2 \\ 6 \\ 7 \end{matrix} + 5 + 2 = 13$$

$$6 \times 7 = 42$$
$$2 \times 8 = 16$$
$$2 \times 9 = 18$$
$$2 \times 12 = 24$$
$$13 \times 16 = 208$$
$$7 \times 20 = 140$$
$$\overline{32}\quad 32)448$$
$$14$$

Example. A pharmacist desires some powd. opium containing 12% morphine; how much shall he use each of 6, 8, 10, 13, 14, and 18% powder? *Ans.* 6, 2, 2, 2, 13, and 7 respectively.

Example. It is desired to dilute stronger water of ammonia (28%) to make a 10% water of ammonia; what proportions shall I use? *Ans.* 10 parts of 28% sol.; 18 parts of water.

$$10\begin{vmatrix} 28 \\ 0 \end{vmatrix} \begin{matrix} 10 \\ 18 \end{matrix}$$ Water is represented by 0.

Example. How shall I mix powd. opium (14% morphine) with milk sugar, to make a uniform mixture containing 12% morphine? *Ans.* 12 parts of powd. opium, and 2 parts milk sugar.

Example. A drug-broker wishes to mix 500 lbs. of powd. jalap containing 14% resin, with lots containing 9% and 11% to make a mixture containing 12.5%. How many pounds must he use of each lot?

$$1.25 \begin{vmatrix} 14 \\ 9 \\ 11 \end{vmatrix} \begin{matrix} 1.5 \\ 1.5 \\ 1.5 \end{matrix} \quad \begin{matrix} 1.5 + 3.5 = 5 \\ \\ 500 \div 5 = 100 \end{matrix} \quad \begin{matrix} 500 \\ 1.5 \times 100 = 150 \\ 1.5 \times 100 = 150 \end{matrix}$$

Example. How many ounces of resins of scammony containing respectively 85, 90, and 92% of resin, must be mixed with 54 ozs. assaying 75% resin, to form a mixture that will test 80%? *Ans.* 10 ozs. of each.

Example. How many grams each of powdered opium, assaying respectively 9, 10, 12, 16, and 18% morphine, must be used to make a mixture of 100 grams that will contain 14% morphine? *Ans.* 21.052 grams, 9%; 10.526 grams, 10%; 10.526 grams, 12%; 31.578 grams, 16%; and 26.315 grams, 18%.

$$14 \begin{vmatrix} 9 \\ 10 \\ 12 \\ 16 \\ 18 \end{vmatrix} \begin{matrix} 4 \\ 2 \\ 2 \\ 4 + 2 = \\ 5 \end{matrix} \quad \begin{matrix} 4 \times 5.263 = 21.052 \text{ grams.} \\ 2 \times \text{ ``} = 10.526 \text{ ``} \\ 2 \times \text{ ``} = 10.526 \text{ ``} \\ 6 \times \text{ ``} = 31.578 \text{ ``} \\ 5 \times \text{ ``} = 26.315 \text{ ``} \end{matrix}$$

$$\dfrac{19)100}{5.263} \qquad \overline{99.997 \text{ grams.}}$$

Example. I desire to produce 240 gallons of bay-rum containing 60% alcohol, by mixing several lots containing respectively 70, 62, 58, and 50% alcohol; how much of each shall I use? *Ans.* 100 gals. of 70%, 20 gals. of 62%, 20 gals. of 58%, and 100 gals. of 50%.

Example. 100 ozs. of a lot of tincture nux vomica assays 2½% of extract, how much alcohol shall I mix with it to produce the officinal tincture (2% extract)? *Ans.* 25 ozs.

Example. Wishing to make 5 lbs. solution of soda sp. gr. 1.120, and having on hand a solution, sp. gr. 1.400—how much water must I use to produce the quantity of the sp. gr. desired? *Ans.* 1 lb.

$$1.120 \begin{vmatrix} 1.400 \\ 0 \end{vmatrix} \begin{matrix} 1.12 \div .28 \\ \text{or the ratio of} \\ 0.28 \div .28 \end{matrix} \quad \begin{matrix} = 4 \times 1 = 4 \\ \\ = 1 \times 1 = 1 \end{matrix}$$

$$\dfrac{5)5}{1} \qquad \overline{5}$$

Example. How much glycerin shall I mix with water to make 25 lbs. of a solution, sp. gr. 1.160? *Ans.* 2.32 lbs.

COLLECTION, PREPARATION AND PRESERVATION OF BOTANICAL DRUGS.

Division of the plant into parts for the use of the pharmacist. Root, stem, pith, bark, buds, leaves, flowers, fruit and seed. Each part requires the observance of special rules, regarding its collection, dessication and preservation for medicinal uses.

Time for General Collection. At that period of the plant's growth, when the peculiar juices are most abundant in the portion desired.

Collection of Special Parts.

Roots. *Of annual plants*, should be collected just before the flower forms. *Of biennials*, late in the autumn of the first year or very early in the spring of the second year. *Of perennials*, immediately after the first appearance of the plant above ground.

Stem. *Of herbaceous plants*, should be collected after foliation, but before floration.

Bark. *Of trees*, should be collected in the *spring*; *of shrubs*, in the *autumn*, at which seasons they can be most readily detached from the wood, on account of the ascent and descent of the sap. The outer portion or epidermis should always be discarded.

Leaves. Gather when fully developed and before they begin to wither and fall. *Of biennials*, during the second season. (*Ex.*, Hyoscyamus, Digitalis, etc.)

After the appearance of the flowers, the leaves begin to lose their activity, the juices going to develop the fruit. The slowly developed leaves of a dry season are considered to be most active.

Herb or Flowering Tops. By this term we refer to the *whole plant* (though often the root is rejected), which should be collected while the plant is in flower.

Flowers. May be gathered just before they are perfectly developed; the scent is less lively, and the color paler in fully expanded flowers in consequence of the ovary growing at the expense of the accessory organs. The French or *red rose* is always gathered in bud, the astringent principle and red color being then most developed. Flowers should be collected at about midday, or as soon as the sun has dried off the dew.

Fruit. *Berries.* Collect when *perfectly ripe*, but not *dead ripe;* the vegetable acids have not then been so completely converted into sugar, and the aroma is fresher and stronger.

Seeds. When perfectly ripe.

DESSICATION.

The process of removing water from a solid substance at a low temperature.

Botanical drugs are generally bulky, and are liable to become mouldy, hence dessication is resorted to with a view to reducing their bulk, aiding their preservation, and facilitating subdivision.

In order to facilitate dessication by the exposure of a large surface to the air, substances of vegetable origin (with a few exceptions, the roots of burdock, belladonna, etc.) should be cut in thin slices transversely to the direction of the vascular and fibrous tissue, thereby opening the cells and ducts of the part used. The knife used should be sharp, to prevent tearing of the cellular structure and loss of juice. (*Ex.*, fleshy or succulent roots, etc.—squill bulb, jalap tuber, colchicum corm, columbo root, etc.).

Seeds require very little drying, if any.

Flowers are dessicated in the shade without artificial heat to avoid the loss of essential oils.

Roots, herbs, barks, and *leaves* that contain no volatile principles may be dessicated at a temperature not exceeding 150° F.; it is well to employ this temperature in order to destroy the eggs deposited by insects. Worm-eaten jalap (if the resin is sought) is most profitable, as the parasite eats only the starchy matter.

The natural moisture in botanical drugs varies from 30–80% of their weight. (Elecampane root, 88%; Stramonium leaves, 90%.)

Garbling. This process, to which the drug should be subjected after dessication, consists in the separation of impurities and adulterations, as well as decayed or deteriorated portions.

Gums, gum-resins, and resins often contain pieces of bark, stone, gravel, etc., which should be removed.

Tests. The tests for botanical drugs, except those containing important alkaloids (for which there are prescribed methods of assay), are few; the most readily applied being *taste, odor, fracture, color of powder, medicinal activity,* and a microscopical examination.

Preservation. Botanical drugs, whether in powder form or not, are best preserved from deterioration by keeping in a dry place enclosed in vessels which will admit air but exclude light. Unless they contain volatile oils, they will keep well in paper boxes. A vial of ether or chloroform placed in the container, prevents the destruction of the drug by insects.

Odorous and inodorous drugs should always be kept separated.

Mechanical Subdivision of Drugs.

Comminution. The process of reducing a vegetable substance to finer particles. Drugs must be subdivided before use in the various manipulations of pharmacy, for the purpose of increasing their surface, thereby allowing a freer action of solvents, and facilitating the extraction of the medicinal principles.

The various forms of subdivision are obtained by—slicing (*Ex.*, *squills*), chopping, cutting (*Ex.*, *columbo*), crushing, filing, rasping (*Ex.*, *guaiac*), sawing (*Ex.*, *rhubarb, camphor*), bruising, grinding, grating (*Ex.*, *nutmeg*), sifting, levigating (*Ex.*, *prepared chalk*), elutriating (*Ex.*, *purif. sulphide antimony*), triturating, granulating (*Ex.*, *acacia*), subliming (*Ex.*, *sulphur, camphor*), and precipitating (*Ex.*, *calcium phosphate*).

Processes usually conducted by the use of the mortar:

Contusion or **Bruising, and Trituration.** For *contusion* or *bruising*, the mortar should be made of metal (iron or brass), deep, and with flaring edges; the pestle should be heavy, and the convexity of its base should coincide with the concave surface of the mortar; the motion is a succession of blows. The process is hastened by working small portions of drug at a time, and sifting frequently. For *trituration*, shallow mortars of Wedgewood ware or porcelain, without flaring edges, are best adapted. The motion is a circular one, with downward pressure.

Grinding, or Pulverization. Usually accomplished on a large scale by means of drug mills of various construction, and sieves; or on a smaller scale by the use of mortar and sieve.

Sifting. The process of separating the coarser from the finer particles of pulverized substances; and is generally performed by pressing them through the meshes of fine wire, horsehair, or muslin sieves.

Fineness of Powders.—Graded by terms expressing the number of meshes to the linear inch of the sieve, through which the powder will pass. Not more than a small portion should be able to pass through a sieve having ten meshes *more* to the linear inch.

Gradation of Powder.

Coarse,	or No. 20 ———	20 mesh sieve.	
Moderately coarse,	" 40 ———	40 "	"
" fine,	" 50 ———	50 "	"
Fine,	" 60 ———	60 "	"
Very fine,	" 80 or more	80 "	" or more.

Dusted Powders. Powders carried to a certain height by draughts of air caused by the revolution of mill-stones, and deposited on shelves within the inclosure.

Granular Powder. A powder obtained in the form of small granules made uniform by rejecting that which passes through a No. 30 mesh, and that which fails to pass through a No. 20 mesh.

Levigation. The process of reducing to fine particles by rubbing with a small quantity of water. (*Ex.*, powd. salep, nux vomica, ignatia). Performed on a slab with a muller, or in a mortar with a pestle.

Elutriation. The process of removing the coarser from the finer, or heavier from lighter particles by mixing them with water, so that the finer, light, powdery portion may be poured off after the coarser particles have subsided. (*Ex.*, prepared chalk.)

DETERMINATION AND APPLICATION OF HEAT.

Heat or temperature is measured by the thermometer, which indicates the *degree* of heat, but not the *amount*.

Sensible Heat is that which can be shown by the thermometer.

Latent Heat. The heat that a body gives out or takes up, in passing from one state to another.

The latent heat of water is 142.56° F.; that is, ice at 32° F., in changing to water at 32° F., absorbs 142.56° of heat.

Illustration. Take 1 lb. water at 174.56° F. and mix with it 1 lb. water at 32°. When the temperature has become uniform, we have 2 lbs. water at 103.28° F., the mean proportional between the two temperatures. Again, take 1 lb. water at 174.56° F., and mix with 1 lb. chopped ice at 32° F.; on taking the temperature of the mixture, when the ice has become entirely converted into the liquid state, we have 2 lbs. water at 32° F., while 142.56° of temperature have been lost or absorbed by the ice.

THE THERMOMETER.

An instrument consisting of a glass tube of small bore terminating in a bulb, and containing mercury or alcohol, which, by its expansion or contraction, according to the temperature to which it is exposed, indicates the degree of heat by the position of the top of the liquid column on a graduated scale.

Method of Construction. A glass tube with bore of uniform diameter, and a bulb blown at one end, is heated over a lamp, causing the air in it to expand, forming a partial vacuum. The heated tube is inverted, and the open end plunged into a vessel of mercury.

On cooling, the air in the tube contracts, thereby drawing the mercury into the bulb. The latter is then heated till the mercury overflows at the top, when the tube is quickly sealed by a blowpipe.

Method of Graduating. The fixed points are the boiling and freezing points of water; these are determined by placing the instrument into melting ice for a time, and the point to which the mercury rises, represents the *freezing-point;* on immersing it in steam from boiling water for a time, the height of the mercurial column is noted, which represents the *boiling-point.*

SCALES IN USE.

Fahrenheit, Centigrade or Celsius, and Reámur.

Comparison.

	F.	C.	R.
Boiling Point..	212°	100°	80°
Freezing Point.	32	0	0

The intervening spaces are equally subdivided (making 180 degrees on F. scale, 100 in C., and 80 in R.) as well as the extension above the boiling-point and below the freezing-point.

WATER is not adapted for use in the thermometer, on account of the fact that it does not expand and contract regularly; it becomes a solid at 32° F. (0° C.) and a gas at 212° F. (100° C.). At 39.2° F. (4° C.) it is at its *greatest density*, and expands by either an increasing or diminishing temperature from that point.

ALCOHOL is often used in thermometers to indicate *low* temperatures because of its low freezing-point (its boiling-point is 170° F., (76.6° C.), but on account of its lightness and great expansive power, a long column of the liquid must be employed, making an unwieldy instrument.

MERCURY is best adapted for use in thermometers. On account of its weight, only a short column is required; it does not adhere to the sides of the tube; has a low freezing-point, $-40°$ F. ($-40°$ C.) and high boiling point 669° F. (357° C.); expands and contracts regularly.

Relation of Fahrenheit and Centigrade Scales.

180° F. = 100° C.; 9° F. = 5° C.; or, 1° F. = $\frac{5}{9}$° C. and *vice versa.* 1° C. = $\frac{9}{5}$° F.

Conversion from One System to the Other.

1. Above 32° Fahrenheit to Centigrade.—*Rule.* Subtract 32°; × 5, and ÷ 9 = C°.

2. Between 0° and 30° F. to C.—*Rule.* 32° − F.°; × 5 + 9 = C.°.

3. Below 0° F. to C.—*Rule. Minus* F.° + 32; × 5 ÷ 9 = C.°.

Centigrade Degrees to Fahrenheit.

4. Above 0° C. to F.—*Rule.* C.° × 9 + 5; add 32° = F.°.

5. Between 0° and −17.7° C. to F.—*Rule.* C° × 9 + 5 = x; 32° − x = F.°.

6. Below −17.7°.—*Rule. Minus* C° × 9 + 5 − 32° = F.°.

In each of the above instances the calculations with 32° are necessary in order to learn the number of degrees the given temperature represents, above or below the freezing-point.

GENERAL RULES. The two following rules will answer for all cases, providing the algebraic signs are properly observed:

To reduce F.° to C.°.—*Rule. Add* − 32° × 5 + 9 = C.°.

To reduce C.° to F.°.—*Rule.* Multiply by 9 + 5, add + 32° = F.°·

Example. Reduce 10° C. to F. *Ans.* 50° F.

Reduce 65.5° C. to F. *Ans.* 150° F.

21.1° C. = 70° F.; 93.3° C. = 200° F.; − 20° C. = − 4° F. − 40° C. = − 40° F.; − 9° F. = − 22.7° C.; 20° F. = − 6.6° C.; 190° F. = 87.7° C.; 100° F. = 37.7° C.; 60° F. = 15.6° C.

DIRECT APPLICATION OF HEAT.

Sources of Heat. The combustion of coal, illuminating gases, alcohol, kerosene, charcoal, sperm oil, etc.

Media of Application. Stoves, furnaces, lamps, Bunsen burners, blowpipes, etc.

Apparatus for Applying a High Heat. Bunsen burner, blowpipe, crucible, sand bath, etc.

Bunsen Burner. The combustion of gas in the presence of a good supply of oxygen from the air, drawn from the bottom of and through the centre of the burner. Burns with a light-blue flame.

Blowpipe and its Use. A metallic or glass instrument by which a current or blast of air is forced from the mouth through a flame, for the purpose of reducing or oxidizing chemical subtances.

Crucible and its Use. A cup-shaped vessel or melting-pot, so tempered and baked as to endure extreme heat without melting. Made of the following materials, viz.—platinum, plumbago, clay, Wedgewood ware, iron, silver, porcelain, etc.

Processes Requiring a High Heat.

SUBLIMATION. The process by which a solid is changed into vapor, by the application of heat, and recovered in a solid form by passing into a cooled receiver. *Examples*—Benzoic acid from benzoin. Corrosive sublimate. Calomel. Chloride ammonium. Sulphur. Camphor. Iodine, etc.

Powder sublimates are obtained when there is a great difference in temperature between the condenser and retort, and *cake sublimates* when the temperature of the condenser is but little below that at which the volatile body sublimes.

IGNITION. A process of strongly heating either an organic or inorganic substance, with access of air, the residue left being sought. *Examples.* Quantitative tests for various salts, including manganese sulphate, sol. chloride iron, chloride of gold and sodium, etc.

INCINERATION. A process similar to ignition, except that it is applied to *organic substances*, with a view to burning up the carbonaceous principles, converting them into CO_2, which usually remains in the ash, combined with an alkali present.

CALCINATION, OR DEHYDRATION. A process of strongly heating inorganic crystalline substances, with a view to the removal of water, CO_2, or other volatile constituent. *Examples.* Dried alum, sodium pyrophosphate, magnesia, lime, etc.

FUSION. A process of heating an organic or inorganic substance until it liquefies or melts. *Examples.* Melting of wax, spermaceti, the preparation of fused nitrate of silver, arsenic iodide, zinc chloride, diluted nitrate of silver, etc. By fusion, chemicals are made to dissolve in their own water of crystallization.

TORREFACTION OR ROASTING. A process of heating organic substances to change their qualities, by the modification of certain constituents, without altering others or charring. *Examples. Torrefied rhubarb;* representing a loss of the cathartic power of rhubarb without imparing its astringency. *Coffee;* some empyreumatic principles are generated, without the destruction of its important alkaloidal principle, caffeine.

REDUCTION. A process of reducing inorganic substances to obtain a lower degree of combination, or the element itself, by the aid of some reducing agent. *Example.* Reduced iron from the oxide, As. from As_2O_3.

DEFLAGRATION. A process of heating one inorganic substance with another capable of yielding oxygen (permanganates, chlorates, nitrates, etc.), producing sudden combustion, without explosion. *Example.* Sodium arseniate.

OXIDATION. 1. A process of heating with access of air, inorganic substances having a strong affinity for oxygen, which element they absorb from the air. 2. Also accomplished by the action of nitrates, chromates, manganates, sulphates, chlorine, etc., with the application of heat. (*Ex.*—1. ZnO, PbO, $As_2 O_3$, etc. 2. Phosphoric acid, valerianic acid, solutions of ferric salts, etc.)

CARBONIZATION. A process of heating organic substances without access of air, until the volatile products are driven off, and a charred residue remains, having a black color like charcoal. *Examples.* Charcoal, kelp, etc.

Methods for Equalizing and Controlling Heat; and the Temperatures attainable.

Water bath; below 212° F.

Saline baths; saturated solutions chloride sodium, 227° F.; chloride calcium, over 300° F.

Steam bath ; above 212° F.

Super-heated steam bath ; *i.e.*, steam under pressure. Pressure 5 lbs. = 226° F.; 10 lbs. = 240° F., etc.

Oil bath ; below 500° F.

Glycerine bath ; below 482° F.

Paraffin bath ; below 680° F.

Hot air bath; Sand-bath; and Card-teeth bath; for extreme temperatures.

Boiling Point. The *boiling point* of a substance is modified by the pressure of the air, or the vapor formed, and by the nature of the containing vessel. A liquid boils, when the tension of its vapor equals or exceeds the pressure of the superincumbent atmosphere. On the summits of some high mountains, water boils at a temperature as low as 185° F. (85° C.)

SOLUTION.

The process of placing a substance in contact with a liquid, thereby causing it to take the fluid state and become intimately mixed with the liquid. The liquid used to produce this change is called the *solvent* or *menstruum*, and the product a *solution*.

SIMPLE SOLUTION. When the dissolved body may be recovered without having undergone any chemical change, on the evaporation of the solvent, or its removal in some other way. *Examples.* Chlorine in water, carbonic-acid gas in water, glycerine in alcohol, chloride of sodium in water, etc.

Phenomenon exhibited during the Process. Reduction of temperature ; but with dehydrated salts, increased temperature.

CHEMICAL SOLUTION. A solution in which the dissolved body undergoes some chemical alteration, either in composition or decomposition. *Examples.* Copper in sulphuric acid, zinc in hydrochloric acid, syrup iodide of iron, solution chloride of iron, etc.

Phenomena accompanying Chemical Solution. Generation of heat; effervescence; light (sometimes); changes of color, odor and taste; and *always* a new product.

Methods for Facilitating Solution. Mechanical subdivision ; heat (except with gases, and some calcium salts,—*viz.,* tartrate and citrate); agitation.

Saturated Solution. A solution that contains as much of the dissolved body as it can take up at the normal temperature.

The degree of concentration of a saturated solution depends on the temperature of the atmosphere, and in order to establish a standard for comparison, the U. S. P. indicates the solubility of officinals at 15° C. (59° F.) in water, and in alcohol—thus, potassium iodide is soluble in water 0.8 parts, in alcohol 18 parts ; potassium bromide is soluble in water 1.6, in alcohol 200 parts. A solution that is saturated with one solid may also dissolve another, and on this principle many salts are purified.

Super - saturated Solution. A solution made by heating the solvent, and dissolving to saturation at the temperature employed.

Usually carried on at the boiling - point of the solvent. The U. S. P. states the solubility of chemicals in boiling water, and in boiling alcohol—thus, quinine is soluble in boiling water 700 parts, boiling alcohol 2 parts; silver nitrate in boiling water 0.1, in boiling alcohol 5 parts.

By a reduction of the temperature of an over-saturated solution, the excessive of dissolved body is thrown out of solution, in the form of crystalline or amorphous masses; consequently a means of purification.

CIRCULATORY DISPLACEMENT. The process of effecting the solution of a solid, by placing it on a perforated diaphragm (or in a bag) that is immersed just below the surface of the liquid. That portion of the liquid having the greatest solvent power is always in contact with the solid, thereby keeping up a continual circulation in the fluid ; hence the term *circulatory displacement.*

Solvents. The simple solvents used in pharmacy are as follows, arranged in order of importance : Water, Alcohol, Ether, Glycerin,

Benzine, Chloroform, Carbon Bisulphide, and Oils. Acids, Amylic Alcohol, Wine, and Vinegar are less frequently employed.

Principles dissolved by:

Water. Gums, albumen, sugars, pectin, etc.

Alcohol. Volatile oils, resins, alkaloids, etc.

Ether. Fats, oils, resins, oleo-resins, alkaloids, etc.

Glycerin. General solvent and preservative agent.

Chloroform. Oils, resins, alkaloids, gutta-percha, etc.

Benzine. Oils, resins, alkaloids, etc.

Oils. Solvents for both fixed and volatile oils, resins, coloring matter, etc.

COMPLEX SOLUTION. The liquid obtained by treating bodies (such as barks, roots, herbs, etc.) composed of both soluble and insoluble principles, with a solvent suited to the principle desired, leaving behind the insoluble portions.

Apparatus employed for making Complex Solutions. Mortar and pestle, percolators, infusion and decoction mugs, macerating jars, still and condenser.

Processes for effecting Complex Solution. Maceration, Digestion, Infusion, Decoction, Dialysis, Distillation, and Percolation.

DIALYSIS.

The separation of crystalloids from colloids, by diffusing through a septum or diaphragm.

Crystalloids. Substances capable of assuming a crystalline form. (*Examples,* salt, sugar, chemical salts, etc.)

Colloids. Amorphous bodies; usually forming gelatinous masses with water, as glue, gelatin, starch, gums, dextrin, etc.

The Septum or **Diaphragm** may be most advantageously made of parchment paper, which is now used to replace bladder, parchment, skins, etc.

Construction of Dialyser. A short cylinder of glass (having one aperture covered with a septum), into which the substances are placed in liquid form. This vessel is floated in distilled water, and by the force of *osmosis*, the crystalloids pass through the septum into the water, while the colloids remain in the dialyser. There are two kinds of *osmosis* exhibited during the above process, viz.: *Endosmosis*, the passage of the denser liquid into the lighter; and *Exosmosis*, the passage from the lighter to the heavier

The application of the process of Dialysis has been resorted to, in the preparation of **Dialysed Tinctures** * (which were originated, and their preparation practically demonstrated, by the author), in which the active crystalline principles have been separated from gummy, resinous, extractive, and coloring matter.

Preparations made by Dialysis. Dialysed Iron; many of the costly chemical salts are purified by dialysis.

MACERATION.

The process of treating a complex substance to the action of a fluid, at a temperature between 60°-90° F., until the soluble portion has all been dissolved. This process is very little used at present, as it leaves a finished tincture in the residue.

Apparatus for Conducting Maceration. Wide-mouthed bottles or jars, into which the drug is placed, and the proper menstruum poured on it; it is then set aside, and agitated occasionally, for 2–16 days, when the liquid is poured off, and the residue expressed to recover the remainder of the liquid.

DIGESTION.

The process of subjecting a complex substance to the action of a fluid, above the normal temperature, yet below the boiling point of the liquid.

Infusion.

The process of treating a coarsely comminuted complex substance to the action of either hot or cold water for a specified time, and straining. The solution obtained is called an *Infusion.*

Two officinal infusions are made by percolation, the remainder by the general process as above.

Strength. An ordinary infusion, the strength of which is not directed by the physician nor specified by the U. S. P., should represent 10% of the drug.

Decoction.

The process of treating a coarsely comminuted complex substance with water, and boiling for a greater or less period of time, finally cooling and straining. Strength; when not designated by the physician nor directed by the U. S. P., should be 10%.

---

* See thesis by the author, on *Dialysed Tinctures*, N. Y. College of Pharmacy, 1881; *New Remedies*, May, 1881, p. 132; *Pharmaceutical Journal and Transactions*, III. Series, No. 570. Proceedings. A. P. A., 1881, p. 101.

PERCOLATION.

Percolation (*per, colo,* to strain, or trickle through), also known as Displacement. A process, whereby a solution of vegetable principles is obtained, by passing a liquid solvent through a powdered drug.

Apparatus. The apparatus used to hold the powder is a **Percolator**; it is a cylindrical or conical vessel of glass or stoneware, with a funnel-shaped termination at the smaller end, the aperture of which is fitted with a cork bearing a glass tube, provided with a closely fitting rubber tube, at least one fourth longer than the percolator itself, and ending in another glass tube, whereby the rubber tube may be so suspended that its orifice shall be above the surface of the liquid in the percolator.

Forms of Percolators. 1. *Conical* (funnel-shaped); 2. *Cylindrical* (length four or five times its diameter); 3. Well-tube (Dr. Squibb's) percolator. The 1st., is used for tinctures mostly; the 2d., for fluid extracts; 3d., for general use.

The *Well-Tube Percolator* is probably the most complete form for use with either small or large quantities of drug. A glass welltube is placed in the centre of a slightly tapering jar or pot, and held in place by the drug packed about it. The menstruum, after percolating through the drug, accumulates in the well-tube, from which it is removed by a syphon, so arranged that the rate of removal may be regulated.

Menstruum; the solvent employed.

Percolate; the liquid passing from the percolator, containing the soluble constituents in solution.

Residue or **Marc**; the inert, insoluble portion remaining after the completion of the process.

Classes of Preparations requiring Percolation in their Process of Manufacture. Eleven, viz.: *Aceta, Aquæ* (several by percolation through cotton, impregnated with a volatile oil), *Elixiria, Extracta, Extracta Fluida, Infusa* (two), *Mellita* (one), *Oleo-resinæ, Tincturæ, Syrupi,* and *Vina Medicata.*

The **Fluid Extracts** depend entirely for their strength and re-liability on the skill with which percolation is conducted; consequently, the application of this process to their manufacture is selected as a means to outline the several steps of percolation.

Requisites for the Preparation of a Reliable Fluid Extract.
1. Reliable Drug. 2. Uniform Powder. 3. Proper Menstruum.
4. Uniform Moistening. 5. Uniform Packing. 6. Proper Application of Menstruum. 7. Maceration. 8. Percolating at a Proper and Uniform Rate. 9. Quantity of Percolate obtained.

1. Reliable Drugs. Obtained by careful garbling, and subjecting to microscopical and other examinations.

2. Uniform Powder. Obtained by the use of two sieves, one having ten meshes more to the linear inch than the size of mesh desired; reject the portion passing through the finer, and reserve all passing through the coarser. The *degree* of comminution depends upon the structure of the drug, the solubility of its active principles, and the rapidity with which it absorbs the menstruum. Drugs possessing a loose texture can be used in a coarse condition (*Examples*, Dandelion, Rhubarb, Sarsaparilla), while those having a tough, horny structure must be in a fine powder. (*Examples*, Nux Vomica, Ignatia Bean, etc.)

3. Proper Menstruum. The menstruum can be determined only by experiment. It is necessary to use such an one as is best adapted as a solvent for the active principles desired, and leaving undissolved in the residue the inert and objectionable principles; it should also be chosen with a view to the permanence of the finished fluid extract under the influence of changes in temperature, etc. If the active constituents exist in a saccharine, albuminous, or other water soluble principle, the character of the menstruum would be chiefly water, while on the other hand if an oil, resin, or certain alkaloidal principles are desired, alcohol should predominate. A drug containing one or more of each of these two classes of constituents would be percolated with dilute alcohol.

The menstrua for officinal Fluid Extracts comprise the following solvents,—either singly or combined. Alcohol, water, boiling water, glycerin, ether, aqua ammonia, hydrochloric and acetic acids. When one or more of the solvents are to be used in combination, they should invariably be mixed before applying to the drug.

4. Uniform Moistening. Most vegetable drugs, in their natural condition, are in a moist state, but after dessication and comminution the cellular tissue becomes dry, hard and tough, and like a dry sponge will not readily absorb moisture, but when dampened absorption follows immediately. If the powdered drug were packed in its dry state, the subsequent application of the menstruum would produce a swelling of the particles to such an extent as to prevent the passage of the liquid through the drug. Previous moistening is then necessary, in order to produce a quick absorption of menstruum, and to facilitate its uniform descent through the packed drug.

Method. The drug is placed in a suitable vessel, and the necessary quantity of menstruum poured on, and it is thoroughly stirred with a spatula, or suitable instrument (when operating with a large amount of drug, the hand is used) until it appears uniform. The moist powder is then passed through a coarser sieve, in order to break up any lumps, that although externally moist (owing to the adhesive nature of certain drugs), may be dry internally,—as is true with licorice, cascara sagrada, buckthorn berries, etc.

Quantity of Menstruum for Moistening: Dependent on the nature of the drug, and character of the menstruum. In all cases the moistened particles should cohere to form a mass when pressed in the hand, but should readily fall apart when subjected to a slight rolling pressure by the fingers and thumb. When moistened to *excess*, the drug invariably packs itself too hard.

5. **Uniform Packing.** When working with the amount of drug specified in the Pharmacopœia, the entire quantity may be poured into the percolator at once (having previously arranged the porous diaphragm of felt or cotton over the orifice), but a larger amount must be packed in fractions. The first portion is simply shaken down, the next subjected to a slight uniform pressure with the closed hand, and each subsequent layer packed with an increased pressure, using however, *a uniform degree of pressure throughout each separate layer.* Ligneous drugs should be very firmly packed, while drugs of a more loose cellular structure are subjected to a moderate pressure. Again, the alcoholic strength of the menstruum regulates the pressure to be applied. It must be correspondingly firmer, as the menstruum is stronger in alcohol. Nux vomica, aconite, ginger, orris, etc., requiring a strong alcoholic menstruum, may be packed *"firmly,"* while gentian, wild cherry, dandelion, rhubarb, etc., having menstrua of diluted alcohol, are packed *"moderately."* Unless properly packed, the menstruum does not descend uniformly and slowly.

6. **Application of the Menstruum.** When well packed, a disk of paper or muslin is spread upon the surface, and held down

by a layer of pebbles or some suitable weight, to prevent the pouring on of the menstruum from disturbing the packing of the surface of the drug.

The menstruum may now be added in portions, until it ceases to be absorbed, care being taken that the drug is kept continually covered with a stratum of the liquid, to prevent the formation of fissures through the mass, through which the menstruum would rapidly pass. The percolator is then covered to prevent evaporation.

7. **Maceration.** Since the soluble and active principles of vegetable matter are in a dry condition, and contained in cells which are more or less broken up by the process of comminution, the powder is submitted to maceration for a specified period of time, before percolation proper begins, thus securing contact with the solvent for a longer time, while the cells are completely softened and expanded, without the unnecessary use of a large quantity of menstruum.

The **period of maceration** specified is two days, but a corre· spondingly longer time is adopted when working large quantities, from 4–10 days.

8. **Percolating at a Proper and Uniform Rate.** Unless the quantity of material in operation is largely in excess of the Pharmacopœial quantities, the rate of percolation should not exceed the limit of 10 to 30 drops per minute. The rate is about 60 drops per minute with large manufacturers. To begin percolation, the rubber tube is lowered and its glass end introduced into the neck of a bottle previously marked for the quantity of liquid required for the product.

The rapidity may be increased or lessened by raising or lowering the receptacle, or in the Well-tube Percolator by raising or lowering the glass syphon.

When the process is properly conducted, the first percolate will be nearly saturated with the soluble constituents of the drug; the successive portions having a paler color, until finally devoid of taste, color and odor, except those due to the menstruum itself.

9. **Quantity of Percolate Obtained.** 100 cm³ for each 100 grams of drug by the following process: Percolate 70–90% of the required amount and *reserve;* continue percolation till the drug is exhausted; evaporate this second percolate to a soft extractive consistence, and dissolve in the reserved percolate; filter, and add through the filter sufficient menstruum to complete the required measure.

1000 cm³ (15432 grs. of water) represent 1000 grams (15432 grs.) of powder; 15432 grs. water = 16128 minims. If 16128 minims (2.1 pts.) represent 15432 grs. (2.2 lbs. Av.) then *one minim represents 95-100 grains of drug.*

Exhaustion of the Drug. Can only be determined by a previous knowledge as to the constituents that the menstruum will extract. Usually, freedom from color, odor, and taste is the test—but there are exceptions; with some drugs the *absence of color* in the percolate would be the test, as is the case with red saunders, cochineal, saffron, etc., where the color alone is desired. The *absence of a precipitate,* or *a cloudiness when mixed with water* (due to an oily or resinous body), is the test for exhaustion in some drugs, such as guaiac, lupulin, cannabis indica, etc. The *absence of bitterness* in others, due to bitter alkaloids—colchicum, cinchona, opium, nux vomica, etc. The *absence of astringency* in drugs having tannin as their valuable principle,—as catechu, white oak bark, galls, kino, etc.

Recovery of Alcohol or Ether from the Residue: By distillation and subsequent rectification, or by percolation with water, after having previously mixed with sawdust, excelsior, sand, or some other inert substance. Expression is also often employed.

Theory of the Principles of Percolation and Exhaustion. Having carefully followed all the details for conducting percolation perfectly, all of the drug particles are necessarily under the same pressure of surrounding menstruum, as in maceration ; and on account of the gravitation of the liquid in the mass, it passes *through* the porous particles rather than *around* them.

A small proportion of the menstruum is at first gradually absorbed into each particle (by endosmosis) till filled. Other portions of the menstruum which is continually added, are deflected by the upper surface of the drug particles, and directed into a circuitous course towards the orifice of the percolator; but every particle of menstruum has had a strong tendency to pass in a straight line, from the surface of the drug to the outlet, consequently, it penetrates the porous surface of each drug particle in the direction of this straight line, to a distance controlled by its falling force, and the resistance and solubility of the surface. This force is then divided, one portion being retained by the deflected particle in its retarded course, and the remainder distributed to the interior of each drug particle.

This force from without, destroys the counterbalance between cohesion and gravitation, by giving the balance of power to gravita-

tiou, and a downward current is established within the drug particles. This current is, by density of the moving matter, by friction,
and by the length and area of channels, rendered indefinitely slow,
and can only be hurried within the extremely limited compass in-
volved in the keeping of a line of particles behind. Any further
supply of menstruum is in excess, and after the surface of the drug
particles are washed free from soluble matter, and are saturated
with particles of menstruum in slow motion; this excess serves only
to dilute the solution and wash it away as it is slowly pushed through.

Thus a copious supply of menstruum would, in time, wash the drug
particles free from soluble matter, and the latter would be in a very
dilute solution. If, however, the soluble constituents are required
in concentrated solution, the excess of menstruum which simply
flows between the drug particles must be avoided.

The outlet of the percolator must be closed, and only enough
menstruum added to keep the upper surface constantly covered.
The soluble matter will then all be in dense solution, the menstruum
between the drug-particles sharing with the particles themselves, the
portion of soluble matter which was on or near the surface, and if
the outlet of the percolator be opened, so as to allow the liquid to
flow out only at the rate of one drop each minute for example, the
laws of hydrostatics require that this rate shall be supplied from
every atom of the total contents of the percolator.

Hence the current established in all parts of the percolator
must be very slow, and by this diminished velocity, must be
proportionately relieved from friction and increased in power;
or in other words, the currents *between*, are retarded approxi-
mately to the same rate as the currents *within* the drug particles, and hence, the superincumbent vertical lines of particles of
liquid are not deflected from the surfaces of the drug particles,
but pass through them in the straight lines required by gravitation, becoming more and more highly charged with the soluble
matter until they escape below comparatively undiluted..*

Objections to the U. S. P. Method for Fl. Exts.

The temperature required for evaporation of the second percolate,
is njurious to the activities of some constituents, while any volatile
oils or volatile alkaloids are almost entirely lost, and often an extract
is obtained that is practically insoluble in the first percolate. By

---

* The above represents essentially the theory advanced by Dr. E. R. Squibb.

the process of *Re-percolation*, or *Fractional Percolation*, the application of heat is avoided

RE-PERCOLATION.

This process consists in dividing the powdered drug into portions, and percolating each portion separately, in such a manner, that a mixture of the more concentrated portions of each percolation, produces a liquid of fluid extract strength.

Illustration. Take 44 Av. ozs. of powdered drug, and percolate to obtain 42 fl. ozs. of fluid extract. Divide the drug into three portions, the *first* representing 22 ozs., the *second*, 14 ozs., and the *third*, 8 ozs. Moisten the 22 ozs. with the menstruum, pack, macerate, and percolate till 8 fl. ozs. have passed, which *reserve*. Continue percolation to exhaustion, and use this second percolate to moisten the *second* portion, which prepare for percolation as before. Reserve 14 fl. ozs. of percolate, and exhaust the drug. Use this second percolate to prepare the *third* portion for percolation; percolate till 20 fl. ozs. pass—and mix with the previously reserved portions, making 42 fl. oz. in all.

Should the percolate have a color or taste after 20 fl. ozs. have been taken from the third portion, then continue percolation to exhaustion, reserving the percolate to be used as menstruum in subsequent operations.

Another method (Dr. Squibb's). Divide 32 parts of powdered drug into four portions of 8 parts each. No. 1 is moistened, packed, macerated and percolated until exhausted. Reserve the first 6 parts, and use the remainder to macerate No. 2, which percolate, and reserve 8 parts; repeat the process with No. 3, and No. 4, reserving 8 parts of percolate from each. Mix the reserved portions, thereby making 30 parts total. The weaker percolate of the fourth portion is reserved for subsequent operations, when from each 8 parts of drug, 8 parts of percolate are obtained.

It has been proven, that the first 12 ozs. of percolate contains from 70–78% of the total extract obtainable from 16 troy ozs. of drug.

Preservation of Fluid Extracts. The bottles containing them should be tightly corked, and not exposed to direct sunlight, or to any great or sudden changes in temperature. Thereby, loss of alcohol by evaporation is prevented, and the deposition of sediments retarded.

LIXIVIATION.

A process similar to percolation, by which soluble substances are separated from insoluble porous matter. *Ex.* The exhaustion of wood ashes with water to obtain pearlash, and nut-galls to obtain gallic acid.

EXPRESSION.

The forcible separation of liquids from solids, effected by various kinds of Presses, viz., hydraulic press, screw press, filter press, roller press, spiral twist press, and lever press.

FILTRATION.

The process of separating an undissolved substance from a liquid, by passing through the pores of a medium, the latter being impervious to the undissolved substance. The medium is called the *Filter*, the undissolved substance retained on the filter, the *Precipitate*, and the liquid obtained, the *Filtrate*.

Filtering Media; Paper, paper pulp, asbestos (for strong acids), ground glass (for strong alkalies), sand, charcoal, precipitated calcium phosphate, etc.

Paper Pulp. The best method for obtaining good paper pulp, is to beat up filter paper with liquor potassa, wash with water and dry.

Rapid filtration may be effected by various means, —viz., heat, pressure, aspirators, filter pumps, etc.

The support for the filter is called a *funnel*.

COLATION, OR STRAINING. A process of filtration, the medium for separation being a cloth or porous substance, such as muslin, flannel, gauze, felt, bolting cloth, etc. The support for a strainer is called a *tenaculum*.

CLARIFICATION.

The process of separating from a liquid, undissolved matter which impairs its transparency and which cannot be removed by filtration.

Methods. 1. *By the Application of Heat;* thereby increasing the fluidity of the liquid, and enabling the heavy particles to either rise or fall, depending on their density. On rising to the surface they may be skimmed off.

2. *By the use of Gelatin.* Used when the liquid contains tannin (to which its cloudiness is due), forming with it an insoluble compound, which subsides.

3. *By the use of Albumen.* On the application of heat, the albumen coagulates and envelopes the suspended matter which caused opacity, and carries it to the surface. The white of an egg is usually sufficient to clarify one gallon of the liquid.

4. *By the use of Milk.* This method is adopted with liquids containing free acids; the latter coagulates the casein of the milk, which carries the particles producing cloudiness with it to the bottom. Used to clarify sour wines and vinegars.

5. *By the use of Paper Pulp.* This affords a mechanical separation, the paper acting as a filter, filling the pores of the strainer.

6. *By Fermentation.* Dependent on the principle that the albumen present in most vegetable juices becomes insoluble in the alcohol generated by fermentation, and deposits.

DECOLORIZATION AND DEODORIZATION.

Processes by which substances are deprived of color and odor. Usually accompanies the process of clarification, and is accomplished by the use of animal or vegetable charcoal.

Sediment. Insoluble matter separated by gravity, from the liquid in which it has been suspended, and hence differs from a precipitate (see page 57).

DECANTATION.

The process of removing a liquid from another liquid or insoluble solid, by pouring it off, or by the use of a syphon, or pipette.

In decanting, care must be taken not to disturb the deposit, nor to allow the liquid to run down the sides of the vessel. Avoided by greasing the lip of the vessel, and by using a glass rod as a guiding rod.

Syphon and its Use. A bent tube having one arm shorter than the other. When once filled with water, and the short arm immersed below the surface of the liquid, the atmospheric pressure forces the liquid up the shorter arm, while the excess of weight of the liquid in the longer arm causes a continuous flow.

The flow takes place only when the discharging orifice is lower than the surface of the liquid, and no part of the tube is higher above it than the point to which the same liquid will rise by atmospheric pressure, that is, thirty-three feet for water, thirty inches for mercury, etc.

VAPORIZATION.

The act of vaporizing; or the process of changing a solid or liquid into the form of vapor.

EVAPORATION.

The liberation of a liquid below its boiling-point in the form of vapor, directly from the surface exposed to the air, with a view to the involatile portion.

Employed in the preparation of Extractum Ergotæ, Fel Bovis Inspissatum, the scale salts, the concentration of syrups, fluid extracts, etc.

Process conducted by the use of the various baths, etc., described on page 41.

Spontaneous Evaporation. Evaporation at the normal temperature of the atmosphere, without the employment of artificial heat.

Evaporation in Vacuo. Evaporation conducted in a closed vessel, having appliances attached for removing the atmospheric pressure. The liquid boils at a low temperature, evaporation proceeding actively at 120° F. In the manufacture of cane sugar, the syrup is concentrated in a vacuum pan before crystallization, in order to prevent discoloration by high temperatures.

DISTILLATION, SIMPLE.

The process of converting a liquid into vapor by the aid of heat, and passing the vapor into a cooled chamber called a **Condenser**, where its latent heat is abstracted, and it is deposited as a liquid called the **Distillate**. The involatile, or less volatile portion remaining, is termed the **Residue**. This process is resorted to with a view to the volatile body, or both the volatile and involatile.

U. S. P. preparations employing distillation: Abstracts, extracts, fluid extracts, oleo-resins, distilled water, etc.

Apparatus used for conducting this process: Alembic, Retort, Still, Condenser, Receiver, Worm, etc.

The Retort is a long-necked flask of glass or other material, having the neck bent to form an acute angle with the body of the flask. The *tubulated* and *stoppered* retorts are arranged with an opening at the top, that they may be readily refilled, and at the same time a continuous flow of the liquid kept up.

Receiver. A flask having a heavy glass rim around the top of the neck,—the latter tapering so as to fit the exit-tube of the retort. When the receiver has an orifice at the top, it is called *tubulated;* if an opening at the bottom tapered and drawn out to a point, for the purpose of drawing off and measuring the distillate, it is called *quilled.* These have been superseded by the Liebig's condenser.

Liebig's Condenser. A glass tube fitted by means of corks into a glass, copper or tinned iron tube ; into the lower end of this second tube a stream of cold water is passed, which on becoming heated by the condensing vapors passing through the glass tube, is discharged at the upper end. The glass tube is connected at one end with the retort, at the other with the receiver.

Safety Tube. A modified funnel tube, bent in the form of an S, for the purpose of regulating sudden disengagement of vapors, thereby avoiding explosions.

Stills. The modified forms of the alembic and retort, now extensively used. When the neck of the still is connected with a spiral coil of pipe immersed in water to condense the vapors, this form of condenser is termed a **Worm.**

FRACTIONAL DISTILLATION.

A process by which constituents of different volatilities are separated, by collecting and removing the distillates obtained at different temperatures. *Examples.* Various gases, benzine, benzol, naphtha, gasoline, kerosene, etc., obtained by the fractional distillation of Petroleum.

DESTRUCTIVE OR DRY DISTILLATION.

A process by which organic bodies are subjected to a gradually increased heat out of contact with air, whereby their original complex conditions are broken up into simpler forms. *Example.* Production of pyroligneous acid, tar, creosote, etc., from wood, or illuminating gas, carbolic acid, ammonia, etc., from coal.

The following four products are always obtained during destructive distillation :

	From Wood.	From Coal.
1. *Gas.*		
2. *Liquid.*	{ Acid reaction. (Pyroligneous Acid.)	{ Alkaline reaction. (Ammonia, *representing animal matter.*)
3. *Tar.*	Creosote.	Carbolic Acid.
4. *Charcoal.*	Charcoal.	Coke.

Sublimation. See page 39.

CRYSTALLIZATION.

The process which chemical substances undergo in passing from a liquid or gaseous state into a solid, to assume definite and regular geometrically formed bodies. These mathematical forms are termed **Crystalline,** and the bodies possessing them called **Crystals.**

Amorphous (from Greek α μορφέ—without form), not susceptible to crystallization ; *Dimorphous,* crystallizing in *two* forms; *Polymorphous,* in several forms; *Isomorphous,* a term applied to substances having the same form of crystal, but having unlike properties.

Methods for effecting Crystallization. 1. By deposition during the evaporation of a solution. 2. By deposition from a supersaturated solution on cooling, or partial cooling. 3. By fusion. (*Examples.* Sulphur, bismuth, antimony, etc.) 4. By sublimation. (*Examples.* Benzoic acid, iodine, corrosive sublimate, etc.) 5. By precipitation. (*Examples.* Mercuric iodide, oxalate of iron, etc.)

Mother Liquor. The solution remaining after the first crop of crystals has been separated ; it is a saturated solution of the salt, and may contain another salt, as well as coloring matter and other impurities, hence crystallization is a means of purification. By concentrating the mother liquor and cooling, another crop of crystals can be obtained; this process may be repeated until the liquid is freed from crystalline matter.

Water of Crystallization. The water appropriated by most substances and entering into combination when passing into the crystalline state. Under *ordinary circumstances* the amount of water in the same crystal is uniform.

Efflorescence. The property that certain crystals possess, of parting with some of their water of crystallization at the ordinary temperature, forming a dry powder. (*Ex.,* Carb. soda, zinc sulphate.)

Deliquescence. The act of absorbing moisture from the air. Such crystals are called *Hygroscopic.* (*Ex.,* Calcium and magnesium chlorides, sodium phosphate, etc.) Water of crystallization in certain salts ; viz , the sulphates of iron (ferrous), zinc, and magnesium have each seven molecules of water ; quinine sulphate has seven ; the alums have twenty-four, etc.

The Size of Crystals is dependent upon the rapidity of evaporation, and the degree of concentration of the solution. *Large* crystals are obtained from cold saturated solutions, by slow evaporation ; *small* crystals by *rapid* cooling of supersaturated solutions.

Crystallization is facilitated by suspending some foreign substance in the solution, such as threads, wire, pieces of wood or lead, around which the crystals quickly form. (Milk sugar is crystallized on pieces of wood, rock candy on threads, etc.) The presence of a perfect crystal induces the formation of perf .et crystals throughout the solution.

GRANULATION.

The process of obtaining broken crystals by rapidly stirring an evaporating saturated solution or a supersaturated solution while cooling. Many chemical salts are purified by this process, by avoiding the impurities of the water of crystallization taken up by larger crystals. (*Ex.*, potass. chlorate, ammon. chloride, etc.)

Creeping of crystals. Certain crystals possess great powers of absorption, thereby carrying mother liquor through themselves, and causing new crystals to form on their upper surface. This process is repeated by the crystals until finally a coating has formed over the top and outside of the vessel. In the preparation of expensive salts and alkaloids this proves a considerable loss, and may be remedied by making a line of melted paraffin around the inner surface of the vessel.

CRYSTALLOGRAPHY.

The science of the geometrical forms of crystals.

All crystalline substances have forms belonging to one of the seven systems of crystallography, viz.:—

I. *Regular cubic* or *monometric.* II. *Quadratic* or *dimetric.* III. *Hexagonal* or *rhombohedra.* IV. *Rhombic* or *trimetric.* V. *Oblique prismatic* or *monoclinic.* VI. *Diclinic.* VII. *Doubly-oblique prismatic* or *triclinic.*

PRECIPITATION.

The process of forming an insoluble substance from a solution, by the means of light, heat, or chemical action. The insoluble body formed is the **Precipitate ;** the substance producing the precipitate is called the **Precipitant ;** the liquid remaining above the precipitate is the **Supernatant Liquid.**

Objects of Precipitation. Purification, subdivision, and the formation of new compounds.

Example. If a solution of mercuric chloride is mixed with a solution of potassium iodide, double decomposition results, forming mercuric iodide and potassium chloride, the former depositing while the latter remains in solution in the supernatant liquid. *Reaction.* $HgCl_2 + 2KI = HgI_2 + 2KCl$.

Washing. In order to recover the mercuric iodide free from potass. chloride, the supernatant liquid must be removed (by decantation or syphoning), and the precipitate well washed by introducing it upon a filter and pouring water over it, until the filtrate shows no trace of the dissolved body.

When washing precipitates *entirely* insoluble in water, use *hot* water; or *cold* water when *slightly* soluble.

Character of Precipitates. Their physical characteristics are expressed by the terms: *crystalline, amorphous, granular, flocculent, dense, bulky, heavy, light, curdy, gelatinous,* etc. A thick, tenacious or gelatinous precipitate left on decanting the supernatant liquid is called a *Magma. Heavy precipitates* are produced by concentrated hot solutions (*Ex.,* heavy carbonate of magnesia), while dilute solutions produce *light precipitates.* Precipitating Jars, are vessels of glass or stoneware, slightly tapering from the bottom upwards.

Examples of U. S. P. preparations made by this process: Lead iodide, mercuric oxide, white precipitate, aluminium hydroxide, alkaloids, etc.

Generation, Collection and Absorption of Gases.

Various gases are frequently required in the production of certain pharmaceutical preparations, and as tests.

(*Examples.* Chlorine Water, Syr. Hydriodic Acid, Aqua Ammonia, etc.)

The most important gases are CO_2, H_2S, Cl, NH_3, and HCl.

Solution. Effected by conducting the gas a short distance below the surface of the liquid used as a solvent, when, as it bubbles up through the liquid, absorption takes place to a greater or less degree dependent upon whether the gas combines with the water to form a compound or not. (*Ex.,* NH_3 and HCl form compounds with water, and are readily absorbed, but Cl, CO_2, and H_2S not as readily.) Solubility is increased by forcing the gas into the liquid under pressure.

Washing. They should invariably be passed through water in a wash bottle for purification, before solution.

Changes of Temperature. Gases are more rapidly absorbed by *cold* than by hot liquids, consequently, the receivers should be kept cool.

By the action of sunlight, chlorine water decomposes and becomes hydrochloric acid.

Having described all of the processes resorted to in producing galenical preparations, a classification of these products follows.

CLASSIFICATION OF PHARMACOPŒIA PREPARATIONS.

I. Liquids.

ACETA—VINEGARS (MEDICATED). *Number* 4.

Solutions of medicinal organic constituents obtained by percolating the drug, using dilute acetic acid as a menstruum. The menstruum produces soluble salts with the alkaloidal principles, besides having antiseptic properties.

AQUÆ—WATERS (MEDICATED). *Number* 14.

Waters which have been impregnated with volatile substances. Made by, 1, *Simple Solution*, 2, by *Absorption*, 3, by *Percolation*, through cotton impregnated with the substance ; and 4, by *Distillation*.

COLLODIA—COLLODIONS. *Number* 4.

Solutions of pyroxylin or gun-cotton in a mixture of stronger ether and alcohol, impregnated with a medicinal agent. Used externally, by application with a brush ; on evaporation of the solvent, a film remains, which acts as a protection or brings the medicament in direct contact with the skin. Made by, 1, *Solution*, and 2, *Percolation*.

DECOCTA—DECOCTIONS. *Number* 2.

Solutions of the active principles of vegetable drugs obtained by boiling with water.

ELIXIRIA—ELIXIRS. *Number* 1.

Sweetened and aromatized alcoholic preparations or cordials, containing minute quantities of medicinally active ingredients in solution.

EXTRACTA FLUIDA—FLUID EXTRACTS. *Number* 79.

Permanent, concentrated solutions of the active constituents of vegetable drugs, of such a strength that 1 cm³ contains the medicinal principles and represents the virtues of 1 Gm. of the drug. Made by, 1, *Percolation*, 2, *Re-percolation*.

GLYCERITA—GLYCERITES. *Number* 2.

Solutions of medicinal substances in glycerin. Made by *Trituration*, either with or without heat.

INFUSA—INFUSIONS. *Number* 5.

Aqueous solutions of the soluble principles of vegetable drugs, obtained by *Maceration* or *Digestion* in hot or cold water.

LINIMENTA—LINIMENTS. *Number* 10.

Liquid or semi-liquid preparations having for a base cotton seed oil, alcohol or turpentine, intended for external use, and are applied to the skin with friction. Made by *Solution*, and *Digestion*.

LIQUORES—SOLUTIONS. *Number* 26.

Aqueous solutions without sugar, in which the substances acted upon are wholly soluble in water excepting solutions of volatile substances. Gutta-percha solution alone has a menstruum *other than water*. Made by, 1, *Simple Solution*, 2, *Chemical Solution*.

MELLITA—HONEYS. *Number* 3.

Mixtures of honey with certain medicinal substances.

MISTURÆ—MIXTURES. *Number* 11.

Aqueous liquid preparations which contain insoluble substances in suspension. Made by *Trituration*.

MUCILAGINES—MUCILAGES. *Number* 5.

Aqueous solutions of gums or mucilaginous principles of vegetable drugs. Made by *Maceration*, either with or without heat.

OLEATA—OLEATES. *Number* 2.

Solutions of metallic oleates or alkaloids in oleic acid. Made by *Trituration*.

OLEORESINÆ—OLEORESINS. *Number* 6.

Liquid preparations consisting of an oil, either fixed or volatile, holding resin and other constituents in solution. Made by percolating the drug with stronger ether till exhausted, and distilling off the ether from the percolate.

SPIRITUS—SPIRITS. *Number* 22.

Alcoholic solutions of volatile substances, either solid, liquid, or gaseous. Made by, 1, *Simple solution*, 2, *Chemical solution*, 3, *Chemical reaction*, 4, *Maceration*, 5, *Absorption*.

SYRUPI—SYRUPS. *Number* 34.

Concentrated solutions of sugar in watery fluids, with or without medication. Made by, 1, *Solution* with heat, 2, *Agitation* without heat, 3, *Digestion* or *Maceration*, 4, *Percolation*, 5, *Simple admixture*.

TINCTURÆ—TINCTURES. *Number* 73.

Alcoholic solutions of non-volatile, medicinal substances, prepared by *Percolation*, *Maceration*, or *Solution*. Solutions in aromatic spirits of ammonia and ether are included under the same name, although specially distinguished by the titles of Ammoniated and Ethereal Tinctures.

VINA (MEDICATA)—MEDICATED WINES. *Number* 11.

Solutions of medicinal substances, organic or inorganic, in stronger white wine, made by *Percolation*, *Maceration* and *Simple Solution*.

II. Solids.

ABSTRACTA—ABSTRACTS. *Number* 11.

Solid powdered preparations representing the soluble constituents of vegetable drugs combined with sugar of milk, so that one part represents two parts of the drug. Made by exhausting the drug by percolation with alcohol, evaporating, diluting with milk sugar to the required weight, and powdering when dry.

CERATA—CERATES. *Number* 8.

Unctuous preparations which in consistence are midway between plasters and ointments, sufficiently soft to be spread at the ordinary temperature, and yet firm enough to adhere to the skin without melting.

Cerates, as the name indicates, contain cera (wax), an ingredient. Oil, lard, or petrolatum is used as a basis. Made, 1, by *Fusion*, 2, *Incorporation*.

CHARTÆ—PAPERS. *Number* 3.

Preparations intended for external use, resembling plasters spread upon non-absorbent paper, the process necessarily varying with the nature of the substance.

CONFECTIONES—CONFECTIONS. *Number* 2.

Soft solids formerly known as *conserves* and *electuaries*, in which one or more medicinal substances are incorporated with a saccharine body, for the purpose of preservation and convenient administration.

EMPLASTRA—PLASTERS. *Number* 17.

Solid tenacious preparations, intended for external use, harder than cerates, yet pliable and adhesive at the temperature of the body, and requiring heat to spread them. They have for a basis, 1, Lead plaster, 2, Resin Plaster, 3, Gum Resins, 4, Burgundy Pitch.

EXTRACTA—EXTRACTS. *Number* 32.

Preparations obtained by removing the medicinal principles from crude drugs by solution, and evaporating to a solid or semi-solid consistence. Made by percolation and subsequent evaporation, with introduction of glycerin if necessary.

MASSÆ—PILL MASSES. *Number* 3.

Solid masses kept in bulk, to be used in making pills.

PILULÆ—PILLS. *Number* 15.

Medicaments in the form of small globular, ovoid, or lenticular solids, intended to be swallowed without being previously masticated.   Pill masses are composed of two parts, viz.—*active ingredients,* and *excipient.* The latter is the substance used to give the mass its proper consistence. Excipients to be used with *soft* or *liquid substances,* are inert powders, as licorice root, bread crumb, soap, acacia, starch, etc.

With *powders* syrup, honey, glucose, mucilage, confections, glycerin, glycerite of starch, etc., are used.

Coatings for pills. Sugar, gelatin, tolu, gold or silver foil.

PULVERES—POWDERS. *Number* 9.

Compound powders.

RESINÆ—RESINS. *Number* 4.

Solid preparations consisting principally of the resinous principles of vegetable drugs insoluble in water. Made by *Precipitation, Distillation,* or *Percolation distillation* and *precipitation.*

SUPPOSITORIÆ—SUPPOSITORIES.

Solid preparations intended to be introduced into the rectum, urethra or vagina, to produce medical action, and of such a consistence that they will melt at the temperature of the body. Their form is usually conical with rounded apex, made by pressure, moulding or rolling.

Base. Cacao butter, on account of its low fusing point, and its property of becoming solid at a temperature just below that point.

Method of preparation. Mix the medicinal portion (previously brought to a proper consistence, if necessary) with a small quantity of cacao butter by rubbing together, and add the mixture to the remainder of the cacao butter previously melted and cooled at 95° F. Then mix thoroughly and pour into suitable moulds, which are cooled by being placed on ice, or immerced in iced water. In the absence of suitable moulds, the above mixture may be cooled, divided into parts of definite weight and made into a conical or other form by the fingers.

Unless otherwise specified, Suppositories should be made to weigh about 15 *grains* or 1 *gram*.

TRITURATIONES—TRITURATIONS. *Number* 1.

Powders prepared by triturating a medicinal substance with a definite quantity of milk sugar. Strength—10% of the medicinal substance.

TROCHISCI—TROCHES. *Number* 16.

Mixtures of medicinal substances with sugar or extract of licorice, formed by the aid of mucilage into stiff pasty masses, and divided into flat circular, oblong, rectangular, or stellate pieces usually weighing about 10 or 20 grains. Prepared by incorporating the ingredients into a plastic and adhesive mass, rolling into a thin sheet, and cutting into proper shape with a lozenge cutter.

UNGUENTA.—OINTMENTS. *Number* 26

Fatty preparations of such a consistence that they may be easily rubbed on the skin, and becoming gradually liquefied while in contact.

Bases. Lard or benzoinated lard, combined in some cases with a very small quantity of wax. Made by, 1, *Fusion*, 2, *Incorporation*, and 3, *Chemical Reaction*.

PART II.

PREPARATIONS.

Inorganic Pharmacy.

(H$_2$O—18) Aqua.—Water.

Natural water in the purest attainable state.

Description. A colorless, limpid liquid, odorless and tasteless at ordinary temperatures, and remaining odorless while being heated to boiling; neutral reaction; containing no more than 0.01% of fixed impurities.

(H$_2$O—18) Aqua Destillata.—Distilled Water.

Prepared by distillation, refusing the first 5%, and the last 15% of the distillate.

Description. A colorless, limpid liquid; odorless; tasteless; neutral reaction. Should contain no metals, sulphates, chlorides, calcium, ammonia and ammonium salts, or organic matters: and no fixed residue on evaporating one liter.

ACIDS.

An **Acid** is a compound of an electro-negative radical or a halogen with hydrogen, which hydrogen it can part with in exchange for a metal or basylous radical.

Basylous Radical. A metal or unsaturated group of elements possessing electro-positive properties, and capable of displacing the replaceable hydrogen of an acid to produce a salt. In inorganic chemistry, bases or basylous radicals are generally metals, their oxides or hydroxides.

Acidulous Radical. An element or unsaturated group of elements possessing electro-negative properties, and capable of combining with hydrogen to form an acid, or with a basylous radical to form a salt.

Salt. A body formed by the union or attraction of bases with acids, or basylous on acidulous radicals.

(H$_2$SO$_4$—98) ACIDUM SULPHURICUM.—SULPHURIC ACID.
(Oil of vitriol.)

Preparation. Sulphur or iron pyrites (FeS$_2$), is burned in a furnace so arranged that the sulphurous acid gas is mixed with air; in the same furnace by the heat of the burning sulphur, nitric acid is generated from a mixture of nitrate of sodium and sulphuric acid, the fumes of nitric acid being carried with the mixed sulphurous oxide and air into a leaden chamber, where the current of these gases comes in contact with a jet of steam.

Reaction. 3SO$_2$ + 2HNO$_3$ + 2H$_2$O = $\widehat{N_2O_2}$ + 3H$_2$SO$_4$.

$\begin{pmatrix}\text{Sulphurous}\\\text{Oxide.}\end{pmatrix}$ $\begin{pmatrix}\text{Nitric}\\\text{Acid.}\end{pmatrix}$ (Steam.) $\begin{pmatrix}\text{Nitrogen}\\\text{Dioxide.}\end{pmatrix}$ $\begin{pmatrix}\text{Sulphuric}\\\text{Acid.}\end{pmatrix}$

The N$_2$O$_2$ takes up O from the air and becomes N$_2$O$_4$ (nitrogen tetroxide) which immediately decomposes into N$_2$O$_2$ and O$_2$—the latter being utilized to oxidize more SO$_2$. This process is continually repeated, the N$_2$O$_2$ acting as the O carrier to the SO$_2$. The following may serve to illustrate the entire changes that take place.

S + O$_2$ = SO$_2$ ┐ SO$_3$ + H$_2$O = H$_2$SO$_4$
S + O$_2$ = SO$_2$ ┼ SO$_3$ + H$_2$O = H$_2$SO$_4$
S + O$_2$ = SO$_2$ ┼┼ SO$_3$ + H$_2$O = H$_2$SO$_4$
HNO$_3$
HNO$_3$

H$_2$O
N$_2$O$_2$ ┼ N$_2$O$_2$ + O$_2$ = N$_2$O$_4$
O$_3$ ┘ N$_2$O$_4$ = N$_2$O$_2$ $<$ O + SO$_2$ = SO$_3$ + H$_2$O = H$_2$SO$_4$
O + SO$_2$ = SO$_3$ + H$_2$O = H$_2$SO$_4$

The dilute acid taken from the leaden chamber, called "chamber acid" (50° B. sp. gr. 1.52–1.58), is evaporated in shallow leaden pans until its density is 60° B. sp. gr. 1.70–1.75 called "pan acid," and finally concentrated by distilling in glass or platinum stills to 66° B. sp. gr. 1.840.

Description. Colorless liquid, of an oily appearance, inodorous, strongly caustic taste, strong acid reaction. Sp. gr. 1.840—contains 96% absolute sulphuric acid. Miscible in all proportions with alcohol and water, with evolution of heat. Chars organic matter.

Test for Identity. White precipitate with soluble barium or lead salts, insoluble in hydrochloric acid.

Impurities and tests. *Lead:* Acid (1) + alc. (4) = white ppt. *Nitric Acid— With diluted acids:* + Sulphate of iron = brown or reddish zone. *Hydrochloric Acid:* + Sol. sulphate of silver = ppt.

Iron: + Water ammonia (excess) = brown ppt. *Copper:* + Water ammonia = brown ppt. *Arsenic:* + H_2S = yellow ppt. *Arsenious* or *Sulphurous Acid:* Diluted acid + test zinc; the gas evolved blackens paper wet with solution nitrate of silver.

Officinal Preparations. 1. Acidum Sulphuricum Aromaticum. 2. Acid. Sulphuricum Dilutum.

ACIDUM SULPHURICUM AROMATICUM.—AROMATIC SULPHURIC ACID. (Elixir of Vitriol). Add sulphuric acid (200) to alcohol (700) and allow to cool. Add tinct. ginger (45), oil of cinnamon (1), and alcohol to make 1000. Contains about 20% of officinal sulphuric acid, partly in the form of ethyl-sulphuric acid ($C_2H_5HSO_4$), Sp. gr. 0.955.

ACIDUM SULPHURICUM DILUTUM.—DILUTED SULPHURIC ACID. Acid (1) + water (9). Pour the acid *into* the water under constant stirring, to avoid sudden evolution of heat. Sp. gr. 1.067—contains 10% of officinal sulphuric acid.

(H_2SO_3—82) ACIDUM SULPHUROSUM.—SULPHUROUS ACID.

Made by heating sulphuric acid and charcoal together; the gas evolved is passed into ice-cold distilled water.

Reaction. $4H_2SO_4$ + C_2 = $2CO_2$ + $4SO_2$ + $4H_2O$.
(Sulphuric Acid.) (Charcoal.) (Carbon Dioxide.) (Sulphur Dioxide.) (Water.)

Tests for Identity. 1. White precipitate with barium chloride, soluble in hydrochloric acid.

2. Add to diluted H_2SO_4 and test zinc; H_2S is evolved, which blackens paper moistened with solution of silver nitrate.

3. Decolorizes and deoxidizes an acid solution of potassium permanganate.

Description. A colorless liquid; sulphurous odor and taste; strong acid reaction. Sp. gr. 1.022–1.023, contains about 3.5% of SO_2, and 96.5% of water.

Impurities and tests. H_2SO_4 (*limit*); + HCl + $BaCl_2$ = white ppt.

(HCl—36.4) ACIDUM HYDROCHLORICUM.—HYDROCHLORIC ACID.
(Muriatic acid.)

Preparation. The action of sulphuric acid on sodium chloride; distilled in glass or iron retorts.

Reaction. $2NaCl$ + H_2SO_4 = Na_2SO_4 + $2HCl$.
(Sodium Chloride.) (Sulphuric Acid.) (Sodium Sulphate.) (Hydrochloric Acid.)

The gaseous HCl is passed into distilled water, until the liquid has attained the proper degree of concentration.

Description. A colorless, fuming liquid, of a pungent suffocating odor, and an intensely acid taste, and strong acid reaction. Completely volatilized by heat. Sp. gr. 1.160—contains 31.9% absolute hydrochloric acid, and 68.1% water.

Impurities and tests. *Iron:* Dilute acid (1–10) + NH_4OH, or $(NH_4)_2S$ = Ppt. *Copper:* Dilute acid (1–10) + NH_4OH = Blue color. *Lead:* Dilute acid + NH_4HS = Black color. *Chlorine:* Dilute acid (1–5) + sol. KI = Liberation of iodine. *Sulphuric Acid:* Dilute acid + Ba $(NO_3)_2$ = White ppt. *Sulphurous* and *Arsenious Acid:* Dil. acid + test zinc; gas evolved blackens paper wet with nitrate of silver solution.

Officinal Preparations. Diluted Hydrochloric Acid. Nitro-Hydrochloric Acid. Diluted Nitro-Hydrochloric Acid.

ACIDUM HYDROCHLORICUM DILUTUM. (Diluted Hydrochloric Acid). Acid (6) + water (13)—mix. Sp. gr. 1.049—contains about 10% absolute hydrochloric acid.

ACIDUM NITROHYDROCHLORICUM. (Aqua Regia. Nitro-Muriatic Acid). HNO_3 (4) + HCl (15). Mix in large glass vessel. When effervescence ceases, pour into g. s. botts. Keep in cool place in bottles not more than half full.

Reaction. HNO_3 + $3HCl$ = Cl_2 + $NOCl$ + $2H_2O$.
$\begin{pmatrix}\text{Nitric}\\\text{Acid.}\end{pmatrix}$ $\begin{pmatrix}\text{Hydrochloric}\\\text{Acid.}\end{pmatrix}$ (Chlorine.) $\begin{pmatrix}\text{Chloro-}\\\text{nitrous Acid.}\end{pmatrix}$ (Water.)

Description. Golden-yellow, fuming liquid: very corrosive, having strong odor of chlorine. Dissolves gold, platinum, and the higher metals (hence called *aqua regia*), forming chlorides.

ACIDUM NITROHYDROCHLORICUM DILUTUM (Diluted Nitro-Hydrochloric Acid): HNO_3 (4) + HCl (15). Mix, and when effervescence ceases, add distilled water (76).

(HNO_3—63). ACIDUM NITRICUM.—NITRIC ACID. (Aqua Fortis).

Preparation. Made by the decomposition of $NaNO_3$ (Chili nitre), or KNO_3 (Calcutta nitre) by H_2SO_4, in iron or glass retorts.

Reaction. $NaNO_3$ + H_2SO_4 = $NaHSO_4$ + HNO_3
$\begin{pmatrix}\text{Sodium}\\\text{Nitrate.}\end{pmatrix}$ $\begin{pmatrix}\text{Sulphuric}\\\text{Acid.}\end{pmatrix}$ $\begin{pmatrix}\text{Sodium}\\\text{Bisulphate.}\end{pmatrix}$ $\begin{pmatrix}\text{Nitric}\\\text{Acid.}\end{pmatrix}$
or by using more nitrate, the following reaction :
$$2NaNO_3 + H_2SO_4 = Na_2SO_4 + 2HNO_3.$$

The sodium sulphate does not froth so readily, and is easily removed from the retort. The gas is passed into water, until it acquires the proper density; concentrated by distillation from conc. H_2SO_4, which abstracts water.

Description. A colorless, fuming, very caustic and corrosive liquid; strong acid taste and reaction; suffocating odor. Sp. gr. 1.420—contains 69.4% absolute nitric acid, and 30.6% water.

Impurities and tests. *Iron :* $+$ Aq. ammon. (excess) = brown ppt. *Copper :* $+$ Aq. ammon. (excess) = blue color. *Lead :* $+$ Aq. ammon. $+$ NH_4HS = blk. ppt. H_2SO_4 : $+$ Barium nitrate = white ppt. HCl : $+$ Silver nitrate = white ppt. *Iodine :* Dil. acid (1–10) $+$ gelatinized starch = blue color. *Iodic Acid :* After above test, add H_2S cautiously = blue zone. *Arsenic Acid :* Fleitmann's test (see Arsenic).

Officinal Preparations. Diluted Nitric Acid. Nitrohydrochloric Acid. Diluted Nitrohydrochloric Acid.

ACIDUM NITRICUM DILUTUM (Diluted Nitric Acid). HNO_3 (1) $+$ water (6)—mix. Sp. gr. 1.059—contains 10% absolute HNO_3.

(HC$_2$ H$_3$O$_2$—60) ACIDUM ACETICUM. ACETIC ACID.

Preparation. Obtained during the destructive distillation of wood, at a temperature much less than that necessary to produce charcoal. The process is conducted in sheet-iron cylinders: the condensable vapors are condensed in tubes immersed in cold water, while the uncondensable gases are carried into the furnace to be burned as fuel. The condensed portion contains methylic alcohol, acetones, furfurol, acetic and various other acids, and empyreumatic products, in a watery liquid; and an oily layer of tar, empyreumatic oils, resins, cresylic and phenylic compounds, and other hydrocarbons. The watery liquid constitutes *Crude Pyroligneous Acid* or *Wood Vinegar*, from which methylic alcohol may be obtained. To recover the acetic acid, the pyroligneous acid is treated with milk of lime in excess, for the purpose of forming calcium acetate, as well as to remove various tarry products as insoluble calcium compounds. The calcium acetate solution freed from precipitate is evaporated to dryness, and heated till it chars, then redissolved in water, the solution treated with H_2SO_4 and distilled. Owing to the difficulty in regulating the heat to prevent the decomposition of calcium acetate, the solution of this salt is usually decomposed by sodic sulphate.

Reaction. $Ca(C_2H_3O_2)_2 + Na_2SO_4 = 2NaC_2H_3O_2 + CaSO_4.$
$$\left(\begin{smallmatrix}\text{Calcic}\\\text{Acetate.}\end{smallmatrix}\right) \quad \left(\begin{smallmatrix}\text{Sodic}\\\text{Sulphate.}\end{smallmatrix}\right) \quad \left(\begin{smallmatrix}\text{Sodic}\\\text{Acetate.}\end{smallmatrix}\right) \quad \left(\begin{smallmatrix}\text{Calcic}\\\text{Sulphate.}\end{smallmatrix}\right)$$

The calcic sulphate (gypsum) is filtered out, and the filtrate evaporated to dryness; the dry mass is heated to above 260° C (500° F.) to destroy the empyreumatic compounds, and finally purified by dissolving in water, decanting from the sediment, adding sulphuric acid, separating the liquid from crystals of sodic sulphate and distilling.

Reaction. $NaC_2H_3O_2 + H_2SO_4 = NaHSO_4 + HC_2H_3O_2.$

Acetic acid is also made by pouring a mixture of alcohol and water upon beech shavings, the alcohol becoming oxidized by the action of the air.

Description. A clear, colorless, volatile liquid of distinct vinegar-like odor, purely acid taste and reaction. Miscible in all proportions with water and alcohol. Sp. gr. 1.048—contains 36% absolute acid, and 64% of water.

Acetic Acid "No. 8," of commerce (so-called because it was used in the proportion of one part in eight to make diluted acetic acid or distilled vinegar) has the sp. gr. 1.040—and contains 28.8% absolute acid.

The **Specific Gravity** of acetic acid is not a reliable criterion of its strength, since the acid of maximum strength increases in its relative weight on being mixed with water, until the percentage is reduced to 79%, when the maximum density is reached. An acid of 43% has the same sp. gr. as one of 100%; and between 72—85% the density shows very little variation. Hence, a better test than sp. gr. is its neutralizing power of volumetric sol. soda.

Identification Test. Neutralize with NH_4OH, add Fe_2Cl_6 = deep-red color, $+ H_2SO_4$ becomes colorless. On heating with H_2SO_4 the characteristic odor of vinegar is given off.

Impurities and tests.

Lead, Copper, Tin: $+ H_2S$ = ppt. *Iron:* $+ NH_4OH$ = brown ppt. *Calcium:* $+$ Ammon. oxalate $(NH_4)_2C_2O_4$ = white ppt. *Copper:* $+ NH_4OH$ = blue tint. *Empyreumatic substances:* Supersaturate with KOH = smoky odor or taste. Diluted acid (1–5) $+$ test sol. potass. permanganate = colorless solution. *Organic substances:* $H_2SO_4 +$ boil = dark color. *Nitric Acid:* $+ FeSO_4 + H_2SO_4$ = red brown zone around the crystal. *Sulphuric Acid:* $+ BaCl_2$ = white ppt. *Hydrochloric Acid:* $+ AgNO_3 =$ white ppt. *Sulphurous Acid:* $+ AgNO_3$ and warming = dark color.

Officinal Preparations. Diluted Acetic Acid.

ACIDUM ACETICUM DILUTUM (Diluted Acetic Acid). Acetic Acid (17) + distilled water (83)—Sp. gr. 1.0083—contains 6% absolute acid.

ACIDUM ACETICUM GLACIALE.—GLACIAL ACETIC ACID.

Preparation. Made by heating pure crystallized sodium acetate until the water of crystallization is expelled, and the salt is fused. The residue is powdered, mixed with conc. H_2SO_4 and distilled.

Reaction. $NaC_2H_3O_2 + H_2SO_4 = NaHSO_4 + HC_2H_3O_2.$

Description. At or below 15° C. (59° F.) a crystalline solid ; at higher temperatures a colorless liquid. Sp. gr. 1.056–1.058; nearly or quite absolute acid. Ten parts should dissolve one part oil of lemon.

[*Note.* Other acids are treated of elsewhere under the important elements entering into their composition.]

ALKALIES AND THEIR COMPOUNDS.

POTASSIUM, SODIUM, AMMONIUM, AND LITHIUM.

Ammonium (NH_4) is a *compound* and *volatile* alkali, while the others are *simple* and *fixed*. The **elements** of the simple alkalies are obtained, by exposing their carbonates mixed with charcoal to a high heat, when the metals vaporize and may be condensed.

Reaction. $K_2CO_3 + 2C + Heat = K_2 + 3CO.$
     (Potassium   (Carbon.)   (Potassium.)   (Carbon
     Carbonate.)   Monoxide.)

Preservation. On account of being readily oxidized in contact with air, these alkali metals must be kept under petroleum naphtha.

POTASSIUM SALTS.

SOURCE. 1. **Ashes of land plants;** Plants take their inorganic constituents from the soil, and when incinerated leave them behind as ashes. The ash of most plants contains potassium, sodium, calcium and silica among other elements. 2. **"Suint"** (from the water used in washing sheep); 3. **Argols** (the deposits in wine casks) ; 4. **Calcutta Nitre** (KNO_3—occurring as an efflorescence on the soil); 5. The principal source at present is **Kainite** or **Karnellite,** an impure chloride obtained from the Stassfurt mines, Germany.

Properties and tests. Potassa is a very strong alkali and completely neutralizes the strongest acids. The salts are colorless, unless the acid itself has a marked color, and have a neutral reaction, except those made from the weak acids, which are alkaline.

Readily soluble in water, and in conc. solutions are precipitated white by ammonium perchlorate, tartaric acid, and sodium bitartrate; and yellow by sodium picrate and platinic chloride. The flame when viewed through blue glass is of a purplish tinge.

General impurities to be tested for: *Alkaline earths* (a limit): + Test sol. Na_2CO_3 = cloudiness. *Chloride* (a limit): + HNO_3 + $AgNO_3$ = white ppt. *Sulphate* (a limit): + HNO_3 + $Ba(NO_3)_2$ = white ppt. *Carbonate:* + dilute acid = effervescence.

$((K_2CO_3)_2, 3H_2O.$—330) Potassii Carbonas.—Carbonate of Potassium.

(Salt of Tartar, so-called because formerly made from crude cream of tartar, or argols.)

Made by leaching or lixiviating wood - ashes with water, and evaporating the concentrated solution to obtain a dry mass when cool; this constitutes *crude potash* of a brownish color, consisting principally of carbonate with metallic and organic impurities; on calcining, a white, anhydrous salt is obtained, called *pearlash.* By treating the latter with cold water, decanting and filtering the quite clear solution and granulating, the *pure* carbonate is obtained.

May also be obtained by heating the bicarbonate in a crucible to redness, dissolving and granulating.

Reaction. $2KHCO_3$ + Heat = K_2CO_3 + $\overset{\frown}{CO_2}$ + H_2O.
$\begin{pmatrix}\text{Potass.}\\\text{Bicarb.}\end{pmatrix}$ $\begin{pmatrix}\text{Potass.}\\\text{Carb.}\end{pmatrix}$ $\begin{pmatrix}\text{Carbon}\\\text{Dioxide.}\end{pmatrix}$ (Water.)

Also the potassium salts from the Stassfurt mines are converted into a sulphate, and then into carbonate by a process similar to that of Leblanc for soda, by heating with lime and charcoal, forming K_2CO_3 and an insoluble oxysulphide of calcium.

Description. White, crystalline or granular powder, *very deliquescent;* odorless; strong alkaline taste, and reaction.

Solvents. Water (1)—insol. alcohol.

Impurities and tests:

Silica: Add HNO_3—evap. solution, and treat residue with water = a residue remains. *Alkaline Earths* (a limit): Test sol. Na_2CO_3

= only a cloudiness. *Chlorides* (a limit): + HNO_3 + $AgNO_3$ = only slight turbidity. *Sulphates* (a limit): + HNO_3 + $Ba(NO_3)_2$ = only slight turbidity.

Officinal Preparation. Unguentum Sulphuris Alkalinum (Alkaline Sulphur Ointment).

Sulphur (20), K_2CO_3 (10), H_2O (5), Benzoinated Lard (65).

($KHCO_3$) POTASSII BICARBONAS. BICARBONATE OF POTASSIUM.

Made by passing carbon dioxide (generated from marble, $CaCO_3$, by aid of H_2SO_4) into a concentrated solution of potass. carb.— evaporating and crystallizing; the unchanged carbonate remaining in the mother-liquor. *Salaëratus* is an impure powdered bicarbonate of potassium.

Reaction. K_2CO_3 + H_2O + CO_2 = $2KHCO_3$.
(Potassium Carbonate.)   (Water.)   (Carbon Dioxide.)   (Potassium Bicarbonate.)

Description. Colorless, transparent crystals, permanent in dry air; odorless; saline and slightly alkaline taste; feebly alkaline reaction. Sol. water (3.2), alm. insol. alcohol. At a red heat loses 31% of its weight.

Impurities and tests. General impurities and *Carbonates* (limit): Vol. sol. $BaCl_2$ = ppt. or opalescence.

(KNO_3—101) POTASSII NITRAS.—NITRATE OF POTASSIUM.
(Nitre. Saltpetre.)

Found native as an efflorescence on the soil near dwellings in India. Now obtained from the impure KCl of the Stassfurt mines by decomposition with native nitrate of sodium (Chili saltpetre). Equivalent quantities of the two salts are boiled together with water until sodium chloride separates; then, by concentration, all of the latter salt separates, and the solution is allowed to cool, when potassium nitrate crystallizes out.

Purified by recrystallization and granulation.

Reaction. $NaNO_3$ + KCl = KNO_3 + $NaCl$.
(Sodium Nitrate.)   (Potassium Chloride.)   (Potassium Nitrate.)   (Sodium Chloride.)

In granulating, the impurities of the mother-liquor locked up in the crystals are removed.

Description. Colorless, transparent crystals, or a crystalline powder, permanent in the air; odorless; cooling, saline, and pungent taste; neutral reaction. Sol. water (4), alm. ins. in alcohol.

Impurities and tests. General impurities, and *Metals :* $+$ H$_2$S, or $+$ (NH$_4$)$_2$S = ppt.

Officinal Preparations. 1. Argenti Nitras Dilutus (See Silver). 2. Charta Potassii Nitratis.

(KHC$_4$H$_4$O$_6$—188) POTASSII BITARTRAS.—BITARTRATE OF POTASSIUM. (Cream of Tartar.)

The *crude tartar* or *argols*, which is deposited in wine-casks during fermentation, is composed of potassium bitartrate and calcium tartrate, coloring and extractive matter. On boiling with water, adding clay, and subsequently filtering through animal charcoal (to remove coloring matter), and repeatedly re-crystallizing, a quite pure salt is obtained.

Description. Colorless, or slightly opaque crystals, or a white, gritty powder ; odorless, pleasant acidulous taste, and acid reaction. Sol. water (210)—very slowly sol. in alcohol.

Impurities and tests. General impurities and *Calcium Tartrate* (*more than 6%*) : Vol. sol. ammonium oxalate.

Officinal Preparations. PULVIS JALAPÆ COMPOSITUS. (Compound Powder of Jalap. Cathartic Powder.) Powd. Jalap (35), Powd. Cream of Tartar (65). Hydragogue cathartic. Dose, 10–30 grs.

((K$_2$C$_4$H$_4$O$_6$) H$_2$O—470) POTASSII TARTRAS.—TARTRATE OF POTASSIUM. (Soluble Tartar.)

Made by neutralizing potassium bitartrate with potassium bicarbonate in the presence of water, filtering out the calcium tartrate (impurity in cream of tartar) which subsides, and crystallizing.

Reaction. $KHC_4H_4O_6 + KHCO_3 = K_2C_4H_4O_6 + H_2O + CO_2.$
(Potassium) (Potassium) (Potassium) (Water.) (Carbon)
(Bitartrate.) (Bicarbonate.) (Tartrate.) (Dioxide.)

Description. Small, transparent, or white crystals or a white deliquescent powder. Odorless; saline, slightly bitter taste; neutral reaction. Sol. water (0.7)—alm. ins. alcohol.

Impurities and tests. General impurities, and *Calcium :* $+$ (NH$_4$)$_2$C$_2$O$_4$ = white ppt.

(KNaC$_4$H$_4$O$_6$, 4H$_2$O—282) POTASSII ET SODII TARTRAS.—TARTRATE OF POTASSIUM AND SODIUM. (Rochelle Salt.)

Made by adding potassium bitartrate to a solution of sodium carbonate, filtering out the precipitated calcium tartrate; evaporating and crystallizing.

$$2KHC_4H_4O_6 + Na_2CO_3 = 2KNaC_4H_4O_6 + H_2O + CO_2.$$

(Potassium) (Sodium) (Potassium and) (Water.) (Carbon)
(Bitartrate.) (Carbonate.) (Sodium Tartrate.) (Dioxide.)

Description. Colorless, transparent crystals, slightly efflorescent, or a white powder; odorless; cooling, saline and bitter taste; neutral reaction. Sol. water (2.5)—alm. ins. alcohol.

Impurities and tests. General impurities, and *Ammonium salts :* Heat with KOH = ammonia vapors.

Officinal Preparations. PULVIS EFFERVESCENS COMPOSITUS. (Compound Effervescing Powder. Seidlitz Powders.) NaHCO₃, 40 grs., and KNaC₄H₄O₆ 120 grs. in blue paper; H₂C₄H₄O₆, 35 grs. in white paper. Each to be dissolved in water separately, and the solutions mixed, and drank at once.

(KC₂H₃O₂—98) POTASSII ACETAS.—ACETATE OF POTASSIUM.

Made by neutralizing acetic acid with potassium bicarbonate, evaporating, fusing and granulating.

Reaction. $HC_2H_3O_2 + KHCO_3 = KC_2H_3O_2 + H_2O + CO_2.$

(Acetic) (Potassium) (Potassium) (Water.) (Carbon)
(Acid.) (Bicarbonate.) (Acetate.) (Dioxide.)

May also be prepared by the mutual decomposition between lead acetate and potassium carbonate.

Reaction. $Pb(C_2H_3O_2)_2 + K_2CO_3 = PbCO_3 + 2KC_2H_3O_2.$

(Lead) (Potassium) (Lead) (Potassium)
(Acetate.) (Carbonate.) (Carbonate.) (Acetate.)

Description. White, satiny crystalline masses, or a white, granular powder; very deliquescent; odorless; pungent and saline taste; neutral or faintly alkaline reaction. Sol. water (0.4), alcohol (2.5).

Impurities and tests. General impurities, and *Organic Impurities:* + H₂SO₄ = discoloration of acid.

(KOH—56) POTASSA.—CAUSTIC POTASH. (Potassium Hydrate.)

Made by the action of slaked lime on K₂CO₃ in solution. The solution is decanted from the precipitate and evaporated, fused and cast into moulds.

Reaction. $K_2CO_3 + Ca(OH)_2 = 2KOH + CaCO_3.$

(Potassium) (Calcium) (Potassium) (Calcium)
(Carbonate.) (Hydroxide.) (Hydroxide.) (Carbonate.)

Purification. By treatment with barium hydroxide, to separate sulphate as barium sulphate, and alcohol which dissolves only the caustic potassa.

Description. White, hard, dry solid, generally in the form of pencils; very deliquescent; odorless, or having a faint lye odor; acrid caustic taste, and alkaline reaction.

Contains 90% absolute KOH. Sol. water (0.5), alcohol (2).

Impurities and tests. General impurities, and *Silica :* Sol. + alcohol = ppt. *Organic Matter :* Solution has color. *Carbonate :* + acid = effervescence.

Officinal Preparations. 1. Potassa cum Calce. 2. Liq. Potassæ.

POTASSA CUM CALCE. POTASSA WITH LIME. (Vienna Caustic.) Made by rubbing together equal weights of potassa and lime, till a uniform powder is obtained. A milder caustic than potassa.

LIQUOR POTASSÆ.—SOLUTION OF POTASSA OR POTASH.

Preparation. Made by double decomposition between $KHCO_3$ in solution and milk of lime, $Ca(OH)_2$. The solution of the bicarbonate is heated to drive off the excess of carbonic acid, while potassium carbonate remains in solution.

$$2KHCO_3 + Ca(OH)_2 = 2KOH + CaCO_3 + CO_2 + H_2O.$$
$$\left(\begin{smallmatrix}\text{Acid Potassium}\\\text{Carbonate.}\end{smallmatrix}\right) \left(\begin{smallmatrix}\text{Calcium}\\\text{Hydroxide.}\end{smallmatrix}\right) \left(\begin{smallmatrix}\text{Potassium}\\\text{Hydroxide.}\end{smallmatrix}\right) \left(\begin{smallmatrix}\text{Calcium}\\\text{Carbonate.}\end{smallmatrix}\right) \left(\begin{smallmatrix}\text{Carbon}\\\text{Dioxide.}\end{smallmatrix}\right) \text{(Water.)}$$

Extemporaneous formula. Dissolve KOH (56) in water (944).

Description. A clear, colorless liquid, odorless; very acrid and caustic taste, strong alkaline reaction; miscible with water and alcohol. Sp. gr. 1.036—contains 5% KOH.

Impurities and tests. General impurities, and *Foreign Impurities:* Evap. neutralized solution to dryness; residue + water = some insoluble matter. Test to distinguish from Liq. Sodæ: KOH + conc. sol. tartaric acid = white ppt. soluble in excess of KOH.

POTASSA SULPHURATA.—SULPHURATED POTASSA.

(Liver of Sulphur.)

Made by melting together in a crucible, sublimed sulphur (1) and K_2CO_3 (2), pouring on a marble slab while hot, and allowing to cool. This preparation is not a definite chemical compound.

$$3K_2CO_3 + 4S_2 = 3K_2S_3 + K_2S_2O_3 + 3CO_2.$$
$$\left(\begin{smallmatrix}\text{Potassium}\\\text{Carbonate.}\end{smallmatrix}\right) \text{(Sulphur.)} \left(\begin{smallmatrix}\text{Potass.Tri-}\\\text{Sulphide.}\end{smallmatrix}\right) \left(\begin{smallmatrix}\text{Potass.Thio-}\\\text{Sulphite.}\end{smallmatrix}\right) \left(\begin{smallmatrix}\text{Carbon}\\\text{Dioxide.}\end{smallmatrix}\right)$$

Description. Irregular pieces of a liver-brown color when fresh, but gradually turning yellow; faint, disagreeable odor; bitter, alkaline taste and reaction.

($KClO_3$—122.4) POTASSII CHLORAS.—CHLORATE OF POTASSIUM.

Preparation. A solution of caustic potassa is obtained by the decomposition of K_2CO_3 with $Ca(OH)_2$, and Cl generated from manganese dioxide and HCl is passed into the mixture until absorption ceases, with the following result:

Reaction. $6KOH + 6Cl = 3KCl + 3KClO + 3H_2O.$
(Potassium Hydroxide.) (Chlorine.) (Potassium Chloride.) (Potassium Hypochlorite.) (Wate .)

On boiling the solution it decomposes, forming a chloride and chlorate.

$3KClO + 3KCl + Boil = KClO_3 + 5KCl.$
(Potassium Hypochlorite.) (Potassium Chloride.) (Potassium Chlorate.) (Potassium Chloride.)

The solution is filtered, evaporated and crystallized; purified by re-crystallization, most of the chloride remaining in the mother liquor.

On account of the cheapness of KCl obtained from the Stassfurt mines, the chlorate is now most advantageously made from that salt, by the aid of calcium hypochlorite; on boiling a solution of the latter salt, calcium chloride and chlorate are formed.

Reaction. $3Ca(ClO)_2 = 2CaCl_2 + Ca(ClO_3)_2.$
(Potassium Hypochlorite.) (Calcium Chloride.) (Calcium Chlorate.)

When solution of calcium chlorate is heated with potassium chloride, the following mutual decomposition results:

Reaction. $Ca(ClO_3)_2 + 2KCl = 2KClO_3 + CaCl_2.$
(Calcium Chlorate.) (Potassium Chloride.) (Potassium Chlorate.) (Calcium Chloride.)

Description. Colorless crystals or plates; pearly lustre; permanent in air; odorless; cooling saline taste; neutral reaction.

When strongly heated it gives off all of its oxygen, while potassium chloride remains. Sol. water (16.5)—slowly sol. in alc.

General Impurities: A trace of *chloride* is allowed.

Potassium chlorate should never be triturated with tannin, sulphur, sugar, or any oxidizable or combustible substance, except in the presence of water; or, if used in dry mixtures, the ingredients should be powdered separately, and mixed by means of a sieve and without friction, in order to avoid violent explosions.

Officinal Preparation. Trochisci Potassii Chloratis—5 grs. in each.

($K_3C_6H_5O_7,H_2O$—324) POTASSII CITRAS.—CITRATE OF POTASSIUM.

Made by saturating citric acid with potassium bicarbonate, filtering, evaporating and crystallizing.

Reaction. $H_3C_6H_5O_7 + 3KHCO_3 = K_3C_6H_5O_7 + 3CO_2 + 3H_2O.$
(Citric Acid.) (Potass. Bi- carbonate.) (Potassium Citrate.) (Carbon Dioxide.) (Water.)

Description. White, granular deliquescent powder; odorless; cooling, faintly alkaline taste; neutral or alkaline reaction. Soluble in water (0.6)—very slowly soluble in alcohol.

Impurities and tests. General impurities, and *tartrate:* Conc. sol. $+ HC_2H_3O_2 =$ white crystalline ppt.

(K_2SO_4—174) POTASSII SULPHAS.—SULPHATE OF POTASSIUM.

Obtained as a by-product in the manufacture of iodine, nitric and hydrochloric acids, etc. Also made from Kainite, a mixture of sulphates and chlorides of potassium and magnesium.

Description. Colorless crystals; odorless; sharp, saline, bitter taste; neutral reaction. Sol. in water (9), insol. alc.

Impurities and tests. General impurities, and *metals:* $+ (NH_4)_2S$ or $H_2S =$ ppt.

(K_2SO_3—194) POTASSII SULPHIS.—SULPHITE OF POTASSIUM.

Prepared by passing SO_2 into a solution of K_2CO_3 until the CO_2 has been expelled, and then adding more carbonate to form a neutral salt.

Reaction. $K_2CO_3 + SO_2 = K_2SO_3 + CO_2.$
(Potassium Carbonate.) (Sulphur Dioxide.) (Potassium Sulphite.) (Carbon Dioxide.)

Description. White, opaque crystals, somewhat deliquescent. Sol. water. Impurities and tests: *Sulphate:* $+ HCl + BaCl_2 =$ white ppt.

NOTE.—The following salts of potassium are treated of elsewhere: Potassium bichromate (*under Chromium*); bromide (*under Bromine*); cyanide, and ferrocyanide (*under Cyanogen*); hypophosphite (*under Phosphorus*); iodide (*under Iodine*); permanganate (*under Manganese*).

SODIUM SALTS.

SOURCES. 1. **Sea water** ($NaCl$); 2. **Mineral and brine springs;** 3. **"Barilla" or "Salicor"** (ash of plants growing near the sea); 4. **Chili Nitre** ($NaNO_3$); 5. **Borax springs and lakes;** 6. **Cryolite** ($6NaF. + Al_2F_6$).

Properties and Tests. The Salts of Sodium are more frequently used than those of Potassium, on account of their comparative cheapness, and greater solubility; they are colorless, unless the acid has a distinctive color, and have a neutral reaction, except those with weak acids. The flame has an intense yellow color, not visible through blue glass. Readily soluble in water, and yield a white crystalline ppt. when neutral or alkaline, with metantimoniate of potassium,—but as other metallic salts have a similar reaction, it is not a reliable and practical test.

General Impurities. *Sulphate* (limit): $+ HCl + BaCl_2 =$ white ppt. *Chloride* (limit): $+ HNO_3 + AgNO_3 =$ white ppt. *Carbonate* : $+$ Acid $=$ effervescence. *Metals:* $+ H_2S$, or $(NH_4)_2S =$ ppt. *Alkaline earths:* $+ Na_2CO_3 =$ cloudiness.

(NaCl—58.4) SODII CHLORIDUM.—CHLORIDE OF SODIUM.
(Common Salt.)

Found native in salt mines as impure *rock salt*, which may be purified by solution and re-crystallization. Also obtained from the *brine* of salt springs, which is evaporated by solar heat and allowed to crystallize, producing rock salt, or when evaporated at a boiling temperature, producing a finer grade, or *table salt.* Extracted from sea-water by evaporation or freezing. When frozen, sea-water yields pure ice and a concentrated saline solution.

Description. White, shining, hard, cubical crystals, or a crystalline powder, permanent in air (the deliquescence often observed being due to the presence of magnesium or calcium chloride as impurities); odorless; purely saline taste; neutral reaction: sol. water (2.8) —alm. insol. in alcohol.

Impurities and tests. General impurities and *Iodide* or *Bromide* : Evap. alc. sol. to dryness; dissolve residue in water, add gelatinized starch and chlorine water $=$ colored tint.

(Na₂CO₃.10H₂O—286) SODII CARBONAS.—CARBONATE OF SODIUM.
(Purified Sal Soda.)

Made extensively from sodium chloride and from cryolite, involving three important processes :

1. Leblanc's Process. Common salt is first converted into sodium sulphate by heating with H_2SO_4—the resulting product being called the *salt-cake.*

Reaction. $\quad 2NaCl + H_2SO_4 = Na_2SO_4 + 2HCl.$
$\begin{pmatrix}\text{Sodium}\\\text{Chloride.}\end{pmatrix} \begin{pmatrix}\text{Sulphuric}\\\text{Acid.}\end{pmatrix} \begin{pmatrix}\text{Sodium}\\\text{Sulphate.}\end{pmatrix} \begin{pmatrix}\text{Hydrochloric}\\\text{Acid.}\end{pmatrix}$

The dried sulphate is powdered and mixed with chalk and coal, and heated to fusion, with the following reaction :

$$Na_2SO_4 + 4C + 2CaCO_3 = Na_2CO_3 + CaS.CaO + 4CO + CO_2.$$
$\begin{pmatrix}\text{Sodium}\\\text{sulphate.}\end{pmatrix} (\text{Coal.}) \begin{pmatrix}\text{Calcium}\\\text{Carbonate.}\end{pmatrix} \begin{pmatrix}\text{Sodium}\\\text{Carbonate.}\end{pmatrix} \begin{pmatrix}\text{Calcium}\\\text{Oxysulphide.}\end{pmatrix} \begin{pmatrix}\text{Carbon}\\\text{Monoxide.}\end{pmatrix} \begin{pmatrix}\text{Carbon}\\\text{Dioxide.}\end{pmatrix}$

The resultant black product (termed *black ash* or *ball soda*), is lixiviated with cold water, which dissolves out the sodium carbonate (and some hydroxide which is also formed) from the insoluble impurities. The solution is evaporated to dryness, and the residue calcined with charcoal, converting it fully to a carbonate. Solution and evaporation yield *soda-ash*, containing about 50% of sodium carbonate. Repeated re-crystallization produces the pure salt.

2. **Cryolite Process.** Cryolite ($6NaF, Al_2F_6$) a mineral found in Greenland, consists of fluoride of sodium and aluminium, and represents the chief source of the sodium salts in the United States. When a mixture of cryolite and chalk is heated to redness, the following reaction results :

$$(6NaF + Al_2F_6) + 6CaCO_3 = 3Na_2O, Al_2O_3 + 6CaF_2 + 6CO_2.$$

(Cryolite.) $\begin{pmatrix}\text{Calcium}\\\text{Carbonate.}\end{pmatrix}$ $\begin{pmatrix}\text{Sodium}\\\text{Aluminate.}\end{pmatrix}$ $\begin{pmatrix}\text{Calcium}\\\text{Fluoride.}\end{pmatrix}$ $\begin{pmatrix}\text{Carbon}\\\text{Monoxide.}\end{pmatrix}$

The sodium salt, which is soluble, is extracted by lixiviation, and decomposed by passing CO_2 under pressure through the solution, aluminium hydroxide precipitating, with sodium carbonate in solution.

$$(3Na_2O + Al_2O_3) + 3CO_2 + 3H_2O = 3Na_2CO_3 + Al_2(OH)_6.$$

(Sodium Aluminate.) $\begin{pmatrix}\text{Carbon}\\\text{Dioxide.}\end{pmatrix}$ (Water.) $\begin{pmatrix}\text{Sodium}\\\text{Carbonate.}\end{pmatrix}$ $\begin{pmatrix}\text{Aluminium}\\\text{Hydroxide.}\end{pmatrix}$

3. **Solvay's Process.** Also known as the *ammonia-soda* process. Consists in conducting under pressure, into a cold solution of common salt, first ammonia gas, and afterwards CO_2, with the following result :

$$NaCl + NH_3 + CO_2 + H_2O = NaHCO_3 + NH_4Cl.$$

$\begin{pmatrix}\text{Sodium}\\\text{Chloride.}\end{pmatrix}$ (Ammonia.) $\begin{pmatrix}\text{Carbon}\\\text{Dioxide.}\end{pmatrix}$ (Water.) $\begin{pmatrix}\text{Sodium}\\\text{Bicarbonate.}\end{pmatrix}$ $\begin{pmatrix}\text{Ammonium}\\\text{Chloride.}\end{pmatrix}$

The sodium salt is deposited, while the ammonium chloride remains in solution. By heating the bicarbonate to redness, dissolving and crystallizing, the carbonate is obtained.

Reaction. $2NaHCO_3 + Heat = Na_2CO_3 + H_2O + CO_2.$

$\begin{pmatrix}\text{Sodium}\\\text{Bicarbonate.}\end{pmatrix}$ $\begin{pmatrix}\text{Sodium}\\\text{Carbonate.}\end{pmatrix}$ (Water.) $\begin{pmatrix}\text{Carbon}\\\text{Dioxide.}\end{pmatrix}$

Description. Large, colorless crystals, very efflorescent; odorless; sharp alkaline taste and reaction. Sol. water (1.6), insol. alc. Should contain at least 98% of pure, crystallized Na_2CO_3.

Impurities and tests. General impurities, and *Alumina* (if made from cryolite); $+ HCl + $ excess $NH_4OH + $ boil $= $ gelatinous ppt.

($Na_2CO_3 2H_2O$—142) Sodii Carbonas Exsiccatus. Dried Carbonate of Sodium. Na_2CO_3 (200) is exposed to warm air till effloresced, then heated till it becomes a fine powder weighing 100 parts.

SODII BICARBONAS VENALIS.—COMMERCIAL BICARBONATE OF SODIUM.

Preparation. Sodium carbonate is placed in a chamber, so arranged that water may be drained off; CO_2 is then admitted, and sodium bicarbonate is formed, while the water of crystallization is liberated and carried off to prevent its solvent action.

Reaction. $Na_2CO_3,10H_2O + CO_2 = 2NaHCO_3 + 9H_2O.$
$$\left(\begin{smallmatrix}\text{Sodium}\\\text{Carbonate.}\end{smallmatrix}\right) \left(\begin{smallmatrix}\text{Carbon}\\\text{Dioxide.}\end{smallmatrix}\right) \left(\begin{smallmatrix}\text{Sodium}\\\text{Bicarbonate.}\end{smallmatrix}\right) \text{(Water.)}$$

Also prepared by Solvay's process (see Sodium Carbonate).

($NaHCO_3$—84) SODII BICARBONAS.—BICARBONATE OF SODIUM.

Made by purifying the commercial bicarbonate, by placing it in a glass percolator and washing with cold water, until the washings cease to give a ppt. with magnesium sulphate, thereby removing carbonate, traces of sulphate and chloride, and ammonium salts.

Description. A white, opaque, odorless powder; cooling, mildly saline taste; alkaline reaction. Sol. water (12), ins. alcohol. Should contain at least 99% pure $NaHCO_3$; and the commercial, at least 95%.

Impurities and tests. General impurities, and *Ammonia* (if made by Solvay's process): $+ NaOH +$ heat $=$ ammoniacal odor. *Carbonate* (more than 3%): $+ HgCl_2 =$ red ppt.—only white cloud if *less* than 3%.

Officinal Preparations. 1. Mistura Rhei et Sodæ (Mixture of Rhubarb and Soda) $NaHCO_3$ (30), Fl. Ext. Rhubarb (30), Spts. Peppermint (30), and water ft. 100. 2. Trochisci Sodii Bicarbonatis (three grs. in each).

($NaOH$—40) SODA.—CAUSTIC SODA. (Sodium Hydroxide.)

Made by the double decomposition between sodium carbonate in solution, and milk of lime, heated to boiling.

Reaction. $Na_2CO_3 + Ca(OH)_2 = 2NaOH + CaCO_3.$
$$\left(\begin{smallmatrix}\text{Sodium}\\\text{Carbonate.}\end{smallmatrix}\right)\left(\begin{smallmatrix}\text{Calcium}\\\text{Hydroxide.}\end{smallmatrix}\right)\left(\begin{smallmatrix}\text{Sodium}\\\text{Hydroxide.}\end{smallmatrix}\right)\left(\begin{smallmatrix}\text{Calcium}\\\text{Carbonate.}\end{smallmatrix}\right)$$

The solution is decanted from the precipitated calcium carbonate, and evaporated to a solid mass.

Description. White, hard, opaque, solid, fibrous pieces, or white cylindrical pencils; deliquescent in moist air, but efflorescent in dry air; odorless; acrid and caustic taste; alkaline reaction.

Sol. water (1.7)—very sol. alc.

Impurities and tests. General impurities, and *Organic Matter :* Aqueous solution is colorless. *Silica :* Aq. sol. (1 in 2) + alc. = ppt.

Officinal Preparation.—LIQUOR SODÆ (Solution of Caustic Soda). Made by double decomposition (see Soda), or by dissolving soda (56) in water (944).

Description. A clear, colorless liquid. Sp. gr. 1.059—containing 5% of NaOH.

($NaC_2H_3O_2.3H_2O$—136) SODII ACETAS.—ACETATE OF SODIUM.

Made by saturating acetic acid with Na_2CO_3, evaporating, and crystallizing.

Reaction. $Na_2CO_3 + 2HC_2H_3O_2 = 2NaC_2H_3O_2 + CO_2 + H_2O.$
$\begin{pmatrix}\text{Sodium}\\\text{Carbonate.}\end{pmatrix}$ $\begin{pmatrix}\text{Acetic}\\\text{Acid.}\end{pmatrix}$ $\begin{pmatrix}\text{Sodium}\\\text{Acetate.}\end{pmatrix}$ $\begin{pmatrix}\text{Carbon}\\\text{Dioxide.}\end{pmatrix}$ (Water.)

Description. Colorless, transparent crystals; efflorescent in dry air; odorless; saline, bitter taste; neutral or alkaline reaction.

Sol. water (3), alc. (30).

Impurities and tests. General impurities, and *Organic Matter :* Salt + conc. H_2SO_4 = color to acid. *Silica :* Sol. + HNO_3 + evap. = residue not all soluble in water.

($NaC_7H_5O_2.H_2O.$) SODII BENZOAS.—BENZOATE OF SODIUM.

Made by saturating benzoic acid in solution with $NaHCO_3$, evaporating and crystallizing.

Reaction. $HC_7H_5O_2 + NaHCO_3 = NaC_7H_5O_2 + CO_2 + H_2O.$
$\begin{pmatrix}\text{Benzoic}\\\text{Acid.}\end{pmatrix}$ $\begin{pmatrix}\text{Sodium}\\\text{Bicarbonate.}\end{pmatrix}$ $\begin{pmatrix}\text{Sodium}\\\text{Benzoate.}\end{pmatrix}$ $\begin{pmatrix}\text{Carbon}\\\text{Dioxide.}\end{pmatrix}$ (Water.)

Description. White amorph. powder; efflorescent; odorless, or having faint odor of benzoin; sweet astringent taste; neutral reaction. Sol. water (1.8), alcohol (45).

($NaHSO_3$—104) SODII BISULPHIS.—BISULPHITE OF SODIUM.

Made by saturating a solution of Na_2CO_3 with sulphurous acid gas, and crystallizing.

$Na_2CO_3 + 2SO_2 + 2H_2O = 2NaHSO_3 + H_2O + CO_2.$
$\begin{pmatrix}\text{Sodium}\\\text{Carbonate.}\end{pmatrix}$ $\begin{pmatrix}\text{Sulphurous}\\\text{Acid Gas.}\end{pmatrix}$ (Water.) $\begin{pmatrix}\text{Sodium}\\\text{Bi-sulphite.}\end{pmatrix}$ (Water.) $\begin{pmatrix}\text{Carbon}\\\text{Dioxide.}\end{pmatrix}$

Description. Opaque crystals, or a crystalline or granular powder; faint, sulphurous odor and taste; alk. reaction. Sol. water (4), alc. (72).

Impurities and tests. *Sulphate:* + HCl + $BaCl_2$ = cloudiness.

Test to distinguish from hyposulphite: Aq. sol. $+$ HCl $=$ evolution of sulphurous vapors, but no cloudiness.

($Na_2B_4O_7.10H_2O$—382)   SODII BORAS.—BORATE OF SODIUM.

(Borax.   Biborate of Sodium.)

Found native as *tincal*, an incrustation on the shores of certain lakes, and as a crystalline deposit at the bottom of the borax lake in California.   Purification, by solution and re-crystallization, yields the officinal salt.

Description.   Colorless, transparent, shining crystals; efflorescent in dry air; odorless; mild, cooling, sweetish taste; alk. reaction. Sol. water (16), insol. alcohol.   *General Impurities.*

(H_3BO_3—62)   ACIDUM BORICUM.—BORIC ACID.   (Boracic Acid.)

Found native in the *lagoons* of the volcanic districts of Sicily and Tuscany, and converted into borax.   The boric acid is prepared for medicinal use, by adding HCl or H_2SO_4 to a solution of this salt; on standing the acid crystallizes out. .

$$Na_2B_4O_7.10H_2O + 2HCl = 2NaCl + 4H_3BO_3 + 5H_2O.$$
(Sodium Borate.)   (Hydrochloric Acid.)   (Sodium Chloride.)   (Boric Acid.)   (Water.)

Description.   Transparent, colorless plates; slightly unctuous to the touch; odorless; cooling, bitterish taste; feebly acid reaction in solution, and *turns turmeric paper brown*, which color is unaffected by HCl.   Sol. water (25), alcohol (15).

The alcoholic solution burns with green flame.   .

Impurities and tests.   *Sulphate:* $+$ $BaCl_2$ $=$ white ppt.   *Calcium:* $+$ oxalate of ammonium $=$ ppt.   *Chloride:* $+$ HNO_3 $+$ $AgNo_3$ $=$ white ppt.   *Metals:* $+$ $(NH_4)_2S$ $=$ dark ppt.   *Sodium Salt:* yellow flame.

($NaClO_3$—106.4)   SODII CHLORAS.—CHLORATE OF SODIUM.

Made by the mutual decomposition between sodium bitartrate and potassium chlorate, both in solution.

Reaction. $NaHC_4H_4O_6 + KClO_3 = KHC_4H_4O_6 + NaClO_3.$
(Sodium Bitartrate.)   (Potassium Chlorate.)   (Potassium Bitartrate.)   (Sodium Chlorate.)

Purified by re-crystallizing from alcoholic solution.

Description.   Colorless, transparent, crystals; odorless; cooling, saline taste; neutral reaction.   Sol. water (1.1), alcohol (40).

Impurities and tests. General impurities, and *Potassium:* + sol. bitartrate sodium = white cryst. ppt.

Precautions. Same as those given under Potassium Chlorate.

($Na_2S_2O_3 . 5H_2O$—248) SODII HYPOSULPHIS.—HYPOSULPHITE OF SODIUM. (Sodium Thiosulphate.)

Made by decomposing Na_2CO_3 with calcium thiosulphate. The latter salt is obtained commercially by oxidizing the *gas-lime* (mostly CaS_5) obtained in the purification of gas by dry lime.

Reaction. CaS_2O_3 + Na_2CO_3 = $Na_2S_2O_3$ + $CaCO_3$.
$\begin{pmatrix}\text{Calcium}\\\text{Thiosulphate.}\end{pmatrix}$ $\begin{pmatrix}\text{Sodium}\\\text{Carbonate.}\end{pmatrix}$ $\begin{pmatrix}\text{Sodium}\\\text{Thiosulphate.}\end{pmatrix}$ $\begin{pmatrix}\text{Calcium}\\\text{Carbonate.}\end{pmatrix}$

Description. Large, colorless crystals or plates; efflorescent; odorless; cooling, bitter and sulphurous taste; neutral or faintly alkaline reaction. Sol. water (1.5), insol. alcohol.

Test to distinguish from bisulphite and sulphite: + H_2SO_4 = odor of burning sulphur, and *white ppt.* of sulphur.

($NaNO_3$—85) SODII NITRAS.—NITRATE OF SODIUM.

(Cubic Nitre. Chili Saltpetre.)

A native salt, found in Chili and Peru, forming beds of vast extent. Purified by crystallization from its aqueous solution. By the aid of mechanical methods employing steam, it may be made to contain only 0.5 % of impurities.

Description. Colorless, transparent crystals; slightly deliquescent; odorless; cooling, saline and slightly bitter taste; neutral reaction. Sol. water (1.3), scarcely sol. in alcohol.

Impurities and tests. General impurities, and *Potassium:* + $NaHC_4H_4O_6$ = white crys. ppt. *Iodide:* + H_2S + gelat. starch + chlorine water = blue color.

($2NaC_7H_5O_3.H_2O$—338) SODII SALICYLAS.—SALICYLATE OF SODIUM.

Prepared by saturating salicylic acid with sodium bicarbonate, filtering and evaporating.

Reaction. $NaHCO_3$ + $H C_7H_5O_3$ = $NaC_7H_5O_3$ + H_2O + CO_2.
$\begin{pmatrix}\text{Sodium}\\\text{Bicarbonate.}\end{pmatrix}$ $\begin{pmatrix}\text{Salicylic}\\\text{Acid.}\end{pmatrix}$ $\begin{pmatrix}\text{Sodium}\\\text{Salicylate.}\end{pmatrix}$ (Water.) $\begin{pmatrix}\text{Carbon}\\\text{Dioxide.}\end{pmatrix}$

Description. Small, white, crystalline plates, or a crystalline powder; odorless; sweetish, saline and mildly alkaline taste; feebly acid reaction. Sol. water (1.5)—alcohol (6).

Impurities and tests. General impurities, and *Organic matter:*

$+ H_2SO_4 =$ coloration of acid. *Identification test :* $+$ ferric salts $=$ intense violet color.

$(Na_2SO_4.10H_2O)$ SODII SULPHAS.—SULPHATE OF SODIUM.

Found native, and also obtained as a by-product in the manufacture of many chemicals, including Na_2CO_3 (Leblanc's process), HCl, HNO_3, CO_2 (from $NaHCO_3$), etc.

Purified by repeated recrystallizations.

Description. Large, colorless, transparent crystals ; exceedingly efflorescent ; odorless ; cooling, saline, bitter taste ; neutral reaction. Sol. water (2.8)—ins. alcohol.

Impurities and tests. General impurities and *Ammonia :* $+$ $HNO_3 +$ soda $+$ heat $=$ alkaline vapors.

$(Na_2SO_3.7H_2O$—252) SODII SULPHIS.—SULPHITE OF SODIUM.

Formed by passing SO_2 into a solution of Na_2CO_3 till saturated, and *bisulphite of sodium* is formed ; an equal weight of Na_2CO_3 is dissolved in the liquid, which is evaporated to crystallization.

Reaction. $Na_2CO_3 + SO_2 = Na_2SO_3 + CO_2.$
$$\begin{pmatrix}\text{Sodium} \\ \text{Carbonate.}\end{pmatrix} \begin{pmatrix}\text{Sulphur} \\ \text{Dioxide.}\end{pmatrix} \begin{pmatrix}\text{Sodium} \\ \text{Sulphite.}\end{pmatrix} \begin{pmatrix}\text{Carbon} \\ \text{Dioxide.}\end{pmatrix}$$

Description. Colorless, transparent crystals ; efflorescent in dry air ; odorless ; cooling, saline and sulphurous taste ; neutral or feebly alkaline reaction. Sol. water (4)—sp. sol. alcohol.

Test.—(difference from hyposulphite) : Aq. sol. $+ HCl =$ odor of burning sulphur, and cloudiness of solution.

$(NaC_6H_5SO_4.2H_2O$—232) SODII SULPHOCARBOLAS.
(Sulphocarbolate (Sulphophenate) of Sodium.)

On dissolving crystal carbolic acid in strong H_2SO_4, a new acid results, *sulpho-carbolic* or *orthophenolsulphonic acid.*

Reaction. $C_6H_5OH + H_2SO_4 = HC_6H_5SO_4 + H_2O.$
$$\begin{pmatrix}\text{(Phenol.)}\end{pmatrix} \begin{pmatrix}\text{Sulphuric} \\ \text{Acid.}\end{pmatrix} \begin{pmatrix}\text{Sulphocarbolic} \\ \text{Acid.}\end{pmatrix} \begin{pmatrix}\text{(Water.)}\end{pmatrix}$$

The mixture is digested for three days at a temperature of 60° C. (140°F.), and diluted with water. It is now saturated with barium carbonate, barium sulphate (due to free H_2SO_4) precipitating, with barium sulphocarbolate in solution. The latter solution is used to decompose Na_2SO_4, the solution filtered and crystallized.

$$Ba(C_6H_5SO_4)_2 + Na_2SO_4 = 2NaC_6H_5SO_4 + BaSO_4$$
$$\begin{pmatrix}\text{Barium} \\ \text{Sulphocarbolate.}\end{pmatrix} \begin{pmatrix}\text{Sodium} \\ \text{Sulphate.}\end{pmatrix} \begin{pmatrix}\text{Sodium} \\ \text{Sulphocarbolate.}\end{pmatrix} \begin{pmatrix}\text{Barium} \\ \text{Sulphate.}\end{pmatrix}$$

Description. Colorless, transparent crystals ; odorless, or nearly so ; cooling, saline, bitter taste ; neutral reaction. Sol. water (5), alcohol (132). Impurity.—*Sulphate:* $+ HCl + BaCl_2 =$ white ppt.

LIQUOR SODII SILICATIS. SOLUTION OF SILICATE OF SODA.
(Liquid Glass. Soluble Glass.)

Made by fusing together 1 part of fine sand or powd. flint and 2 parts dried Na_2CO_3, dissolving the mass in boiling water, filtering and evaporating.

Description. A semi-transparent, yellowish, or pale-greenish yellow, viscid liquid—Sp. gr. 1.300–1.400—odorless ; sharp, saline and alkaline taste ; alk. reaction. Sol. in boiling water, insol. alc.

Impurity. *Excess of Alkali:* Caustic effect, when applied to the skin. Used for surgical dressings.

[*Note.* The following sodium salts are treated of elsewhere: Sodium arseniate (under *Arsenic*), bromide (*Bromine*), hypophosphite, phosphate and pyrophosphate (*Phosphorus*), iodide (*Iodine*), santoninate (*Glucosides*).]

AMMONIUM SALTS.

SOURCES : **Coal-gas Liquor,** and **Bone Spirit.** By-products from the manufacture of illuminating gas and bone-black.

AMMONIA (NH_3) is always a product of the putrefaction or destructive distillation of animal matter. It is a colorless gas, having a penetrating odor and an acrid, alkaline taste ; and its hydroxide, unlike potassa or soda, will not saponify the fats.

Properties and tests: The salts of ammonium are all colorless, very soluble in water, and have a neutral or faintly alkaline reaction. They are volatilized at high temperatures, and when heated with the hydroxide of sodium, potassium, or calcium, evolve the odor of ammonia, which changes the color of red litmus to blue ; darkens the color of sulphate of copper paper, and forms a white cloud with HCl. Platinic chloride yields a yellow precipitate in the presence of HCl, with ammonium salts.

General Impurities and tests : *Sulphate :* $+ BaCl_2 =$ white ppt. *Chloride* (limit) : $+ HNO_3 + AgNO_3 =$ white ppt. *Metals* : $+ H_2S$ or $+ (NH_4)_2S =$ ppt.

Derivation of Ammonium Salts. The so-called *coal-gas liquor* is a watery liquid condensed in the preparation and purification of coal gas, and contains principally carbonate of ammonium, besides some cyanide, sulphide and empyreumatic products. It is saturated with H_2SO_4, and on evaporation, brown crystals of ammonium sulphate are obtained, which are mixed with sodium chloride and sublimed from iron pots, the vapors of ammonium chloride condensing upon the inside of leaden or iron domes.

Reaction. $(NH_4)_2SO_4 + 2NaCl = 2NH_4Cl + Na_2SO_4.$
$\left(\begin{smallmatrix}\text{Ammonium}\\\text{Sulphate.}\end{smallmatrix}\right) \left(\begin{smallmatrix}\text{Sodium}\\\text{Chloride.}\end{smallmatrix}\right) \left(\begin{smallmatrix}\text{Ammonium}\\\text{Chloride.}\end{smallmatrix}\right) \left(\begin{smallmatrix}\text{Sodium}\\\text{Sulphate.}\end{smallmatrix}\right)$

The ammonia of the gas-liquor is sometimes converted directly to the chloride, by the addition of HCl or $CaCl_2$, and on evaporation, brown crystals of NH_4Cl result, which may be purified by sublimation. $(NH_4)_2CO_3 + CaCl_2 = 2NH_4Cl + CaCO_3.$

(NH_4Cl—53.4) AMMONII CHLORIDUM.—CHLORIDE OF AMMONIUM.
(Sal Ammoniac.)

Made by re-subliming the crude salt obtained from gas liquor, as above, and further purifying by granulation. Iron, a usual impurity, is removed by the addition of water of ammonia to a solution of the salt.

Reaction. $Fe_2Cl_6 + 6NH_4OH = 6NH_4Cl + Fe_2(OH)_6.$
$\left(\begin{smallmatrix}\text{Ferric}\\\text{Chloride.}\end{smallmatrix}\right) \left(\begin{smallmatrix}\text{Ammonium}\\\text{Hydroxide.}\end{smallmatrix}\right) \left(\begin{smallmatrix}\text{Ammonium}\\\text{Chloride.}\end{smallmatrix}\right) \left(\begin{smallmatrix}\text{Ferric}\\\text{Hydroxide.}\end{smallmatrix}\right)$

Description. A snow-white, crystalline powder; odorless; cooling, saline taste, and slight acid reaction; Sol. water (3), sp. sol. alc.

Impurities and tests : General impurities, and *Barium :* + dil. H_2SO_4 = white ppt. ; *Iron :* + ferrocyanide potass. = blue color.

Officinal Preparation. Trochisci Ammonii Chloridi. (Troches of Ammonium Chloride.). 2 grains in each.

(($NH_4)_2SO_4$—132) AMMONII SULPHAS.—SULPHATE OF AMMONIUM.

Preparation. Ammonical *gas-liquor*, or *fetid bone-spirit*, after saturation with H_2SO_4 is sublimed, and repeatedly submitted to solution and crystallization until pure. Also made by passing the *gas-liquor* through calcium sulphate.

Reaction. $CaSO_4 + (NH_4)_2CO_3 = CaCO_3 + (NH_4)_2SO_4.$
$\left(\begin{smallmatrix}\text{Calcium}\\\text{Sulphate.}\end{smallmatrix}\right) \left(\begin{smallmatrix}\text{Ammonium}\\\text{Carbonate.}\end{smallmatrix}\right) \left(\begin{smallmatrix}\text{Calcium}\\\text{Carbonate.}\end{smallmatrix}\right) \left(\begin{smallmatrix}\text{Ammonium}\\\text{Sulphate.}\end{smallmatrix}\right)$

$CaCO_3$ remains undissolved, while $(NH_4)_2SO_4$ is in solution.

Description. Colorless, transparent crystals; odorless; saline taste; neutral reaction. Sol. water (1.3) sl. sol. alcohol.

General impurities. Used only for preparing alum, and sulphate of iron and ammonium.

($NH_4HCO_3, NH_4NH_2CO_2$—157) AMMONII CARBONAS.—CARBONATE OF AMMONIUM. (Sal Volatile. Alkali Volatile.)

Made by sublimation of ammonium chloride or sulphate with an excess of calcium carbonate, and purified by re-sublimation.

$$2(NH_4)_2SO_4 + 2CaCO_3 = (NH_4HCO_3 + NH_4NH_2CO_2) + 2CaSO_4$$

(Ammonium Sulphate.) (Calcium Carbonate.) (Ammonium Bicarbonate.) (Ammonium Carbamate.) (Calcium Sulphate.)

$$+ NH_3 + H_2O.$$

(Ammonia.) (Water.)

Description. White, translucent masses consisting of acid carbonate, and carbamate of ammonium. On exposure becoming opaque, and finally converted into the bicarbonate (acid carbonate). Pungent ammoniacal odor, free from empyreuma; sharp, saline taste; alkaline reaction. Sol. water (4)—alcohol dissolves the *carbamate*, leaving the *bicarbonate*.

Impurities and tests. *General impurities*, and *Empyreumatic matter:* + excess of H_2SO_4, + H_2O + sol. potass. permanganate = bleaching of latter.

Officinal Preparation. Aromatic Spirit of Ammonia.

LIQUOR AMMONII ACETATIS. (Solution of Acetate of Ammonium. Spirit of Mindererus.) Made by saturating dilute acetic acid with ammonium carbonate, and should be freshly made when required. Also made by preparing separate solutions of the carbonate and acetic acid in water, and mixing equal weights when wanted.

$$(NH_4HCO_3 + NH_4NH_2CO_2) + 3HC_2H_3O_2 = 3NH_4C_2H_3O_2 + 2CO_2$$

(Ammonium Bicarbonate and Carbamate.) (Acetic Acid.) (Ammonium Acetate.) (Carbon Dioxide.)

$$+ H_2O.$$

(Water.)

This solution contains about 7.6% of ammonium acetate.

Officinal Preparation. Mistura Ferri et Ammonii Acetatis.

(NH_4NO_3—80) AMMONII NITRAS.—NITRATE OF AMMONIUM.

Made by neutralizing ammonium carbonate with nitric acid, and crystallizing.

$$(NH_4HCO_3 + NH_4NH_2CO_2) + 3HNO_3 = 3NH_4NO_3 + 2CO_2 + H_2O.$$

(Ammonium Bicarbonate and Carbamate.) (Nitric Acid.) (Ammonium Nitrate.) (Carbon Dioxide.) (Water.)

Description. Colorless crystals, or fused masses; deliquescent; odorless; sharp bitter taste; neutral reaction. Sol. water (0.5), alcohol (20). When gradually heated, it is decomposed into nitrous oxide gas and water.

Reaction. NH_4NO_3 (Ammonium Nitrate.) $+$ Heat $=$ N_2O (Nitrous Oxide, or Laughing Gas.) $+$ $2H_2O.$ (Water.)

This salt absorbes ammonia gas at a low temperature, evolving it again at a moderate heat. General impurities.

$(NH_4OH + H_2O)$ AQUA AMMONIÆ.—WATER OF AMMONIA.

Made by distilling a mixture of $NH_4Cl.$ milk of lime and water.

$2NH_4Cl$ (Ammonium Chloride.) $+$ $Ca(OH)_2$ (Calcium Hydroxide.) $=$ $2NH_3$ (Ammonia.) $+$ $CaCl_2$ (Calcium Chloride.) $+ 2H_2O.$ (Water.)

The ammonia gas, after passing through a wash-bottle, is passed into cold distilled water.

Description. Colorless, transparent liquid; pungent odor; acrid, alkaline taste; alkaline reaction. Sp. gr. .959—contains 10% by weight of ammonia.

Impurities and tests. General impurities, and *Carbonate:* + lime-water = cloudiness. *Calcium:* + ammon. oxalate = white ppt. *Empyreumatic matter:* + excess dilute H_2SO_4 = characteristic odor.

Officinal Preparations. Liniment, and Aromatic Spirits.

LINIMENTUM AMMONIÆ. (Ammonia Liniment. Volatile Liniment.) Mix aq. ammonia (30), and cotton-seed oil (70).

SPIRITUS AMMONIÆ AROMATICUS. (Aromatic Spirit of Ammonia.) Containing ammonium carbonate, water of ammonia, oils of lavender, fl's. lemon and pimento, alcohol and water. Sp. gr. 0.885.

Officinal Preparations. Tinctura Guaiaci Ammoniata. Tinctura Valerianæ Ammoniata—each containing 20% of the drug.

AQUA AMMONIÆ FORTIOR.—STRONGER WATER OF AMMONIA. An aqueous solution of ammonia (NH_3), containing 28% by weight. Sp. gr. 0.900.

Officinal Preparations. Spiritus Ammoniæ (Spirit of Ammonia.) An alcoholic solution of ammonia (NH_3) containing 10% by weight. Sp. gr. about 0.810.

Made by distilling aq. ammon. fortior with alcohol, which has been kept in glass vessels.

Examples. How much stronger water of ammonia must be mixed with water, to make 100 lbs. of the weaker? *Ans.* 35.7 lbs.

Explanation. One hundred lbs. of 10% water of ammonia is equivalent to 1000 lbs. at 1%; or as many lbs. of the 28%, as 28 is contained times in 1000 = 35.7. 28 : 100 :: 10 : x = 35.7.

Having several lots of water of ammonia of 10%, 14%, 16% and 20%

strength, and wishing them mixed to make a uniform mixture of 15%, how much of each must be used? *Ans.* 5 lbs. of 10%; 1 lb. 14%; 1 lb. 16%; 5 lbs. 20%. (See page 31, part I.)

5	⌐—10⌐		*Proof.*	5 lbs. at 10% =	50 lbs. at 1%
1	⌐14⌐	15		1 lb. at 14% =	14 lbs. at 1%
1	⌐16⌐			1 lb. at 16% =	16 lbs. at 1%
5	⌐—20⌐			5 lbs. at 20% =	100 lbs. at 1%

Total, 180 lbs. at 1%, or

as many lbs. at 15% as 15 is contained times in $180 = 12$ lbs.

$(NH_4C_7H_5O_2—139)$ AMMONII BENZOAS.—BENZOATE OF AMMONIUM.

Made by saturating benzoic acid with water of ammonia, evaporating and crystallizing.

Reaction. $NH_4OH + HC_7H_5O_2 = NH_4C_7H_5O_2 + H_2O.$
(Ammonium Hydroxide.) (Benzoic Acid.) (Ammonium Benzoate.) (Water.)

Description. Thin, white crystals; slight odor of benzoic acid; saline, bitter, acrid taste; neutral reaction. Sol. water (5), alcohol (28).

$(NH_4Br—97.8)$ AMMONII BROMIDUM.—BROMIDE OF AMMONIUM.

By several of the processes in use for preparing this salt, an unstable compound is obtained, but the following gives a more stable salt: viz., subliming a mixture of KBr and $(NH_4)_2SO_4$.

Reaction. $2KBr + (NH_4)_2SO_4 = K_2SO_4 + 2NH_4Br.$
(Potassium Bromide.) (Ammonium Sulphate.) (Potassium Sulphate.) (Ammonium Bromide.)

or, by the reaction between bromine and ammonia in the presence of water, concentrating the solution, and granulating or crystallizing.

Reaction. $8NH_4OH + 3Br_2 = 6NH_4Br + N_2 + 8H_2O.$
(Ammonium Hydroxide.) (Bromine.) (Ammonium Bromide.) (Nitrogen.) (Water.)

Description. White granular salt, or colorless, transparent crystals, becoming yellow on exposure to air; pungent, saline taste; neutral reaction. Sol. water (1.5), alcohol (150).

Impurities and Tests. General Impurities, and *Bromate :* + dil. $H_2SO_4 =$ yellow color. *Iodide :* Sol. + gelatinized starch + Cl = blue zone.

$(NH_4I—144.6)$ AMMONII IODIDUM.—IODIDE OF AMMONIUM.

Made by adding to boiling water, a mixture of potassium iodide and ammonium sulphate.

Reaction. $2KI + (NH_4)_2SO_4 = 2NH_4I + K_2SO_4.$
(Potassium Iodide.) (Ammonium Sulphate.) (Ammonium Iodide.) (Potassium Sulphate.)

On the addition of alcohol and the application of cold to the above mixture, potassium sulphate separates as a crystalline powder, and after filtration, the solution is evaporated to dryness.

This salt should not be made by the action of iodine on water of ammonia, as nitrogen iodide (a very explosive compound) is thus generated.

Reaction. $\underset{\left(\substack{\text{Ammonium} \\ \text{Hydroxide.}}\right)}{\text{NH}_4\text{OH}} + \underset{\text{(Iodine.)}}{6\text{I}} = \underset{\left(\substack{\text{Hydriodic} \\ \text{Acid.}}\right)}{3\text{HI}} + \underset{\left(\substack{\text{Nitrogen} \\ \text{Iodide.}}\right)}{\text{NI}_3} + \underset{\text{(Water.)}}{\text{H}_2\text{O.}}$

Description. White, granular salt, or in crystals; very deliquescent, and fast becoming yellow on exposure to air; odorless; sharp, alkaline taste; neutral reaction. Sol. water (1), alcohol (9).

When deeply colored, it should not be dispensed, but may be deprived of iodine by washing with stronger ether, and rapidly drying.

Impurities and tests. General impurities, and *Iron:* + Potass. Ferrocyanide = blue color. *Iodine* (free): + starch jelly = deep blue color. *Bromide* and *Chloride:* Dissolve in NH_4OH; + $AgNO_3$ + HNO_3 (excess) = white ppt.

($(NH_4)_2HPO_4$—132) Ammonii Phosphas.—Phosphate of Ammonium. (Diammonium Orthophosphate.)

Made by saturating phosphoric acid with water of ammonia.

Reaction. $\underset{\left(\substack{\text{Ammonium} \\ \text{Hydroxide.}}\right)}{2\text{NH}_4\text{OH}} + \underset{\left(\substack{\text{Phosphoric} \\ \text{Acid.}}\right)}{\text{H}_3\text{PO}_4} = \underset{\left(\substack{\text{Ammonium} \\ \text{Phosphate.}}\right)}{(\text{NH}_4)_2\text{HPO}_4} + \underset{\text{(Water.)}}{2\text{H}_2\text{O.}}$

Description. Colorless, translucent crystals, losing ammonia on exposure to dry air; odorless; cooling, saline taste; neutral or faintly alkaline reaction. General impurities.

Oxalate of Ammonium ($(NH_4)_2C_2O_4$) is a very poisonous salt; used in pharmacy only as a reagent for calcium salts, producing with them a white precipitate of calcium oxalate, insoluble in acetic acid,

Citrate of Ammonium ($(NH_4)_3C_6H_5O_7$), and Tartrate of Ammonium ($(NH_4)_2C_4H_4O_6$) are used as solvents for the iron salts, etc. The former is also a solvent for bismuth citrate, and its solution sometimes employed in the place of *Liq. Ammon. Acetatis.*

ALKALINE EARTHS AND THEIR COMPOUNDS.

Calcium, Magnesium, Barium and Strontium.

Points of Distinction from the Alkalies. The carbonates of the alkalis are soluble and have an alkaline reaction, while the alkaline earth carbonates are insoluble, and have a neutral reaction.

CALCIUM SALTS.

SOURCES. A very abundant natural production. Found as a *carbonate* in chalk, marble, calcareous spar, limestone and shells ; as a *sulphate* in the different kinds of gypsum ; as a *phosphate* in the bones of animals ; and *combined with silica* in a great variety of minerals.

Tests. Ammonium oxalate gives a white ppt. insoluble in acetic acid, but soluble in excess of HCl; the blowpipe flame is colored reddish-yellow. The alkaline carbonates, sulphuric acid, and phosphates also produce insoluble precipitates.

(CaO—56) CALX.—LIME. (Burned Lime. Quicklime. Calx usta.)

Made by calcining marble or limestone with a strong heat, until all of the CO_2 is expelled.

Reaction. $CaCO_3$ + Heat = CaO + CO_2
(Calcium Carbonate.) (Calcium Oxide.) (Carbon Dioxide.)

Description. Hard, white or grayish-white masses ; attracts moisture and CO_2 on exposure to air, and falls to a white powder; odorless; sharp, caustic taste; alkaline reaction. Sl. sol. water (750) insol. alcohol.

SLAKED LIME. When lime is treated with half its weight of water, it absorbs the latter, becomes heated, and gradually converted into a white powder. The addition of sufficient water to this powder to produce fluidity yields MILK OF LIME.

Impurities and tests. *Carbonate* (limit): + HNO_3 = effervescence. *Alkalies,* and their *carbonates:* + CO_2 to saturate = alkaline reaction. *Insoluble Matter:* Nitric acid solution leaves residue.

Officinal Preparations. 1. Liquor Calcis; 2. Potassa cum Calce (See *Potass.*); 3. Syrupus Calcis.

LIQUOR CALCIS. (Solution of Lime. Lime Water.) An aqueous solution containing 0.15% calcium hydroxide ($Ca(OH)_2$) — Sp. gr. 1.0015. Made by adding an excess of washed slaked lime to water.

Officinal Preparation. LINIMENTUM CALCIS, (Lime Liniment. Carron Oil.) Lime water and cotton-seed oil equal parts, mix.

SYRUPUS CALCIS. (Syrup of Lime. Saccharate of Calcium.) Lime (5) and sugar (30) are triturated and dissolved in boiling water, filtered and evaporated (to 100).

($CaBr_2$—199.6) CALCII BROMIDUM.—BROMIDE OF CALCIUM.

Made by saturating hydrobromic acid with calcium carbonate, and evaporating to dryness.

Reaction. $CaCO_3 + 2HBr = CaBr_2 + CO_2 + H_2O.$
$$\underset{\left(\substack{\text{Calcium} \\ \text{Carbonate.}}\right)}{} \underset{\left(\substack{\text{Hydrobromic} \\ \text{Acid.}}\right)}{} \underset{\left(\substack{\text{Calcium} \\ \text{Bromide.}}\right)}{} \underset{\left(\substack{\text{Carbon} \\ \text{Dioxide.}}\right)}{} \underset{\left(\text{Water.}\right)}{}$$

($CaCO_3$—100) CALCII CARBONAS PRÆCIPITATUS.

PRECIPITATED CARBONATE OF CALCIUM. (Precipitated Chalk.)

Made by the mutual decomposition between sodium carbonate and calcium chloride; washing and drying the ppt.

Reaction. $CaCl_2 + Na_2CO_3 = 2NaCl + CaCO_3.$
$$\underset{\left(\substack{\text{Calcium} \\ \text{Chloride.}}\right)}{} \underset{\left(\substack{\text{Sodium} \\ \text{Carbonate.}}\right)}{} \underset{\left(\substack{\text{Sodium} \\ \text{Chloride.}}\right)}{} \underset{\left(\substack{\text{Calcium} \\ \text{Carbonate.}}\right)}{}$$

Boiling solutions yield the most minute division of the particles. For ordinary use this salt is not superior to *Prepared Chalk.*

Description. Very fine, white, impalpable powder; odorless; tasteless; insol. water, and alcohol.

Impurities and tests. *Magnesium:* Make neutral solution in acetic acid; $+ NH_4Cl + (NH_4)_2CO_3 + NH_4OH$ (excess) $+$ heat; filtrate $+ Na_2HPO_4 =$ white ppt. *Aluminium, iron,* or *phosphate:* $+$ HCl (to dissolve) $+$ heat $+ NH_4OH$ (excess) $=$ ppt.

($CaCO_3$—100)   CRETA PRÆPARATA.—PREPARED CHALK.

Native friable calcium carbonate ($CaCO_3$) freed from most of its impurities by elutriation. Made on a large scale from *whiting.*

(Calcium carbonate exists in mineral and spring waters held in solution by CO_2, forming a *bicarbonate.* Waters containing $CaCO_3$ are said to possess *temporary hardness,* and are rendered *soft* by boiling, thereby driving off the excess of CO_2, while $CaCO_3$ ppts. If $CaSO_4$ is present, water possesses *permanent hardness;* unaffected by boiling, but made *soft* by the use of a fixed alkali carbonate or hydroxide.)

Preparation. *Native chalk* is pulverized and rubbed with water on a porphyry slab, by means of a muller of the same material. It is then agitated with water, which on standing deposits the coarser particles; on pouring off the liquid, the remainder slowly falls in an impalpable state. (This process combines *elutriation* and *levigation.*) This impalpable powder is made to fall on an absorbent surface in small portions, by means of a mechanical contrivance, and on drying assumes a conical shape.

Description. White, amorphous powder, or in the form of small cones; odorless, and tasteless; insoluble in water, or alcohol.

Impurities and tests. *Magnesium* (limit): (See Carbonate.) *Barium* and *Strontium:* $+$ Test sol. $CaSO_4 =$ ppt. *Iron* (a limit): $+$ Potass. ferrocyanide $=$ blue color.

Officinal Preparations. 1. Hydrargyrum cum Creta (See Mercury.) 2. Pulvis Cretæ Compositus. 3. Trochisci Cretæ.

PULVIS CRETÆ COMPOSITUS—COMPOUND CHALK POWDER.

Prepared chalk (30), powd. acacia (20), powdered sugar (50)—mix.
Officinal Preparation. MISTURA CRETÆ. (CHALK MIXTURE).
Compound chalk powder (20), cinnamon water (40), water (40).
Should be freshly made when wanted.

Trochisci Cretæ. (Chalk Troches.) 4 grs. in each.

($CaCl_2$—110.8) CALCII CHLORIDUM. (CHLORIDE OF CALCIUM.)

Obtained as a by-product in many chemical processes; or may be made by the action of HCl on marble or chalk, evaporating the solution to dryness, and fusing the salt at a red heat.

$$CaCO_3 + 2HCl = CaCl_2 + H_2O + CO_2.$$

$\begin{pmatrix}\text{Calcium} \\ \text{Carbonate.}\end{pmatrix}$ $\begin{pmatrix}\text{Hydrochloric} \\ \text{Acid.}\end{pmatrix}$ $\begin{pmatrix}\text{Calcium} \\ \text{Chloride.}\end{pmatrix}$ (Water.) $\begin{pmatrix}\text{Carbon} \\ \text{Dioxide.}\end{pmatrix}$

Description. Colorless, hard masses; very deliquescent, odorless; hot, sharp, saline taste; neutral or faint alkaline reaction. Soluble in water (1.5), alc. (8).

Impurities and Tests. *Aluminium, iron, etc:* $+ NH_4OH = $ ppt.
Sulphate: $+ BaCl_2 = $ white ppt. *Magnesium* (a limit): See Carbonate.

($Ca_3(PO_4)_2$—310) CALCII PHOSPHAS PRÆCIPITATUS.
PRECIPITATED PHOSPHATE OF CALCIUM.

Made by dissolving calcined bone in HCl, and treating the solution with water of ammonia, producing NH_4Cl in solution, while calcium phosphate precipitates.

1. $Ca_3(PO_4)_2 + 4HCl = CaH_4(PO_4)_2 + 2CaCl_2.$

$\begin{pmatrix}\text{Calcium} \\ \text{Phosphate.}\end{pmatrix}$ $\begin{pmatrix}\text{Hydrochloric} \\ \text{Acid.}\end{pmatrix}$ $\begin{pmatrix}\text{Calcium} \\ \text{Acid Phosphate.}\end{pmatrix}$ $\begin{pmatrix}\text{Calcium} \\ \text{Chloride.}\end{pmatrix}$

2. $\quad CaH_4(PO_4)_2 + 2CaCl_2 + 4NH_4OH = Ca_3(PO_4)_2$

$\begin{pmatrix}\text{Calcium} \\ \text{Acid-phosphate.}\end{pmatrix}$ $\begin{pmatrix}\text{Calcium} \\ \text{Chloride.}\end{pmatrix}$ $\begin{pmatrix}\text{Ammonium} \\ \text{Hydroxide.}\end{pmatrix}$ $\begin{pmatrix}\text{Calcium} \\ \text{Phosphate.}\end{pmatrix}$

$+ 4NH_4Cl + 4H_2O.$

$\begin{pmatrix}\text{Ammonium} \\ \text{Chloride.}\end{pmatrix}$ (Water.)

Also made by the mutual decomposition between calcium chloride and sodium phosphate.

Description. A light, white, amorphous powder; odorless, and tasteless; insol. water, or alc. Often used as a filtering media.

Impurities and tests. *Carbonate:* $+ HNO_3$, or HCl = effervescence; *Aluminium:* $+ KOH +$ boil = ppt.

Officinal Preparation. SYRUPUS CALCII LACTOPHOSPHATIS. (Syrup of Lactophosphate of Calcium.) A solution of re-precipitated calcium phosphate in lactic acid and water, flavored with orange-flower water, and protected by sugar.

CALX SULPHURATA. (SULPHURATED LIME.)

A mixture (commonly misnamed *Sulphide of Calcium*) consisting chiefly of calcium sulphide and sulphate (CaS, and $CaSO_4$), in varying proportions, but containing not less than 36% of absolute calcium sulphide. Made by heating lime and precipitated sulphur together in a crucible.

Reaction.　$\underset{\text{(Lime.)}}{4CaO} + \underset{\text{(Sulphur.)}}{2S_2} = \underset{\binom{\text{Calcium}}{\text{Sulphide.}}}{3CaS} + \underset{\binom{\text{Calcium}}{\text{Sulphate.}}}{CaSO_4}.$

Description. Grayish-white, or yellowish-white powder; gradually changed by exposure; faint H_2S odor; offensive, alkaline taste; alkaline reaction; v. sl. sol. water, insol. alc.

Calcium Sulphate is recognized only in the form of a *Test Solution*.

[*Note.*—For Calx Chlorata, see *Chlorine;* Calcis Hypophosphis, see *Phosphorus.*]

MAGNESIUM SALTS.

SOURCES. Found in the *serpentine rocks* of Pennsylvania, Ohio, and Hoboken, N. J., as *siliceous hydrate;* as *carbonate* in Magnesite, on the coast of Greece; as a *double carbonate of magnesium and calcium* in Dolomite; as impure *sulphate* in the Kieserite of the Stassfurt mines; also in soapstone, talc, asbestos, chrysolite, bitter spar, magnesian lime-stone, sea-water and mineral springs (chloride and sulphate), and the bittern of salt works.

The magnesium minerals are of a green color, and have a soft and unctuous feeling to the touch.

MAGNESIUM. The metal is produced by decomposing its chloride with potassium. They are fused together, ignited, and the KCl washed out with water, $MgCl_2 + K_2 = 2KCl + Mg$. It has a silvery appearance, is soft and malleable, and burns with an intense white light.

Tests. With magnesium salts, solution of *sodium phosphate* gives a white crystalline precipitate; K_2CO_3 or Na_2CO_3 produce white precipitates; and *caustic alkalies* yield a gelatinous precipitate.

General Impurities. Chloride: $+ AgNO_3 =$ white ppt. *Sulphate:* $+ BaCl_2 =$ white ppt.

($MgSO_4.7H_2O$—246) MAGNESII SULPHAS.—SULPHATE OF MAGNESIUM. (Epsom Salts.)

Originally obtained by the evaporation of the waters of the Epsom Springs (Eng.),—also made from the *Kieserite* deposits of Stassfurt.

At present, most extensively made from the *siliceous hydrate*, on account of the absence of lime. The mineral is powdered, and saturated with H_2SO_4, the mass dried and calcined at a red heat (to convert any ferrous sulphate present into red oxide), dissolved and crystallized. Purified by recrystallization.

Description. Small, colorless crystals; effloresceat in dry air; odorless; cooling, saline, bitter taste; neutral reaction. Sol. water (8), insol. alc.

Impurities and tests: *General impurities*, and *Metals:* $+ H_2S$, or $(NH_4)_2S = ppt$. Other *alkaline earths:* Sol. $+ NH_4Cl + (NH_4)_2CO_3 + NH_4OH = ppt$. *Alkali Sulphates* (over 1%): Sol $+ NH_4Cl + (NH_4)_3PO_4 + NH_4OH$; evap. filt. to dryness, ignite, $+ H_2O + HCl + alc.$ (or $BaCl_2) = ppt$.

Officinal Preparation. INFUSUM SENNÆ COMPOSITUM.

(Compound Infusion of Senna. Black Draught.) Contains Senna (6), manna (12), $MgSO_4$. (12), fennel (2), and water (to make 100).

$((MgCO_3)_4Mg(OH)_2 .5H_2O$—484) MAGNESII CARBONAS.—CARBONATE OF MAGNESIUM.

Made from *dolomite, magnesite*, the bittern of salt works, etc. The purest carbonate is made by obtaining a pure sulphate of magnesium, decomposing with a solution of pure sodium carbonate, washing and drying the precipitate.

Reaction.
$$5Na_2CO_3 + 5MgSO_4 + H_2O = 4MgCO_3$$
$$\begin{pmatrix}\text{Sodium}\\\text{Carbonate.}\end{pmatrix} \begin{pmatrix}\text{Magnesium}\\\text{Sulphate.}\end{pmatrix} \text{(Water.)} \begin{pmatrix}\text{Magnesium}\\\text{Carbonate.}\end{pmatrix}$$
$$+ Mg(OH)_2 + 5Na_2SO_4 + CO_2.$$
$$\begin{pmatrix}\text{Magnesium}\\\text{Hydroxide.}\end{pmatrix} \begin{pmatrix}\text{Sodium}\\\text{Sulphate.}\end{pmatrix} \begin{pmatrix}\text{Carbon}\\\text{Dioxide.}\end{pmatrix}$$

If the *Light Carbonate of Magnesium* (U. S. P.) is wanted, cold diluted solutions are used, and the mixture boiled for fifteen minutes, then the precipitate is washed and dried. If the *Heavy Carbonate* is desired, more concentrated solutions are employed, and the mixture evaporated to dryness on a sand bath; the residue is digested, washed and dried.

Description. Light, white, friable masses, or light, white powder; odorless; tasteless; insoluble in alcohol—alm. ins. water, to which it imparts a feebly alkaline reaction.

Impurities and tests. General impurities, and *Aluminium*, or *Calcium:* $+ HCl + (NH_4)_2CO_3$ (excess) = white ppt. *Metals:* acetic acid sol. $+ HCl$, or $(NH_4)_2CO_3$ and NH_4OH, or $(NH_4)_2S = ppt$.

Officinal Preparation. Mistura Magnesiæ et Asafœtidæ. (Mixture of Magnesia and Asafetida. Dewees' Carminative.) Contains MgCO$_3$, tinctures of asafetida, and opium, sugar and water.

(MgO—40) MAGNESIA.—LIGHT MAGNESIA.
(Calcined Magnesia. Magnesia Usta.)

Made by the calcination of *light* magnesium carbonate.

$$4MgCO_3 + Mg(OH)_2 + 5H_2O + Heat = 5MgO + 6H_2O + 4CO_2$$

$\left(\begin{array}{c}\text{Magnesium carbonate}\\\text{officinal.}\end{array}\right)$ (Water.) $\left(\begin{array}{c}\text{Magnesium}\\\text{Oxide.}\end{array}\right)$ (Water.) $\left(\begin{array}{c}\text{Carbon}\\\text{Dioxide.}\end{array}\right)$

Description. Light, white, odorless powder; having an earthy, but no saline taste; faint alkaline reaction when moistened with water, alm. insol. water, insol. alcohol.

Impurities and tests. General impurities, and *Carbonate:* + dil. H$_2$SO$_4$ = white ppt.

Officinal Preparations. 1. Ferri Oxidum Hydratum cum Magnesia (see Iron). 2. Pulvis Rhei Comp. 3. Trochisci Magnesiæ.

PULVIS RHEI COMPOSITUS. (Compound Powder of Rhubarb.) Contains powd. rhubarb (25), magnesia (65), and powd. ginger (10).

TROCHISCI MAGNESIÆ. (Troches of Magnesia.) Each contains magnesia (3 grs.), powd. nutmeg and sugar.

(MgO—40) MAGNESIA PONDEROSA.—HEAVY MAGNESIA.

Made by calcining *heavy* magnesium carbonate.

Description. White, dense, fine powder; in other respects resembling the *light* salt.

MAGNESII CITRATUS GRANULATUS. (Granulated Citrate of Magnesia.) Mg$_3$(C$_6$H$_5$O$_7$)$_2$, etc.

Magnesium carbonate (11), citric acid (48), sodium bicarbonate (37), powd. sugar (8), alcohol, and water ft. (100). Triturate the magnesium carbonate with part of the citric acid and distilled water q.s. to make a thick paste; dry and powder; mix with the powd. sugar, sodium bicarbonate, and the remainder of the citric acid (powdered). Dampen the mass with alcohol, and rub through a tinned iron sieve to form a coarse granular powder.

Description. White, coarse, granular salt; deliquescent on exposure; odorless; mildly acidulous refreshing taste; acid reaction. Soluble water (2), with copious effervescence.

Impurity (or adulteration) and test. *Tartaric acid:* + solution potass. acetate + acetic acid = white cryst. ppt.

LIQUOR MAGNESII CITRATIS. (Solution of Citrate of Magnesium). Made by dissolving magnesium carbonate in citric acid and water, flavoring with syrup of citric acid, and adding potassium bicarbonate to generate CO_2.

(MgSO₃.6H₂O—212) MAGNESII SULPHIS.—SULPHITE OF MAGNESIUM.

Made by passing SO_2 into a mixture of magnesium carbonate in water, until all of the CO_2 has been expelled.

$$Mg(OH)_2 + 4MgCO_3 + 5SO_2 = 5MgSO_3 + 4CO_2. + H_2O.$$
(Magnesium carbonate officinal.) (Sulphur Dioxide.) (Magnesium Sulphite.) (Carbon Dioxide.) (Water.)

Description. White, crystalline powder; bitter and sulphurous taste; neutral, or slightly alkaline reaction; sol. water (22), insol. alc.

BARIUM AND STRONTIUM SALTS.

SOURCE. Found as *Heavy Spar* ($BaSO_4$), *Witherite* ($BaCO_3$), *Baryta* (BaO).

Tests. The soluble salts are tests for sulphuric acid and sulphates, and *vice versa*, producing insoluble white precipitates; the color of its blowpipe flame is light green; white precipitates are produced by the soluble carbonates. There are no officinal salts of barium, but the following are often used. All are poisonous.

BARIUM SULPHATE. (Heavy Spar)—($BaSO_4$). The mineral from which the compounds of barium are prepared. The impure sulphate is first converted into a sulphide by igniting with charcoal.

Reaction. $BaSO_4 + C_2 = BaS + 2CO_2.$
(Barium Sulphate.) (Carbon.) (Barium Sulphide.) (Carbon Dioxide.)

The BaS is dissolved and treated with dil. H_2SO_4, thus forming $BaSO_4$. Called *permanent white*, or *blanc fix*, and used for glazing cards; also as an adulterant of white lead.

BARIUM CHLORIDE ($BaCl_2$). Made by dissolving $BaCO_3$ in HCl, or BaS in HCl.

Reaction. $BaS + 2HCl = BaCl_2 + H_2S.$
(Barium Sulphide.) (Hydrochloric Acid.) (Barium Chloride.) (Hydrogen Sulphide.)

The *Test Solution* contains 10% of the salt.

BARIUM CARBONATE ($BaCO_3$). Found native as *Witherite*. May be made by the double decomposition between a soluble barium salt, and an alkaline carbonate.

BARIUM PEROXIDE (BaO_2). Made by passing oxygen or atmospheric air over the oxide or hydroxide, heated to dull redness. By treating with HCl this salt yields *peroxide of hydrogen.*

Reaction. $BaO_2 + 2HCl = H_2O_2 + BaCl_2.$
(Barium Peroxide.) (Hydrochloric Acid.) (Hydrogen Peroxide.) (Barium Chloride.)

The barium chloride is removed by the addition of silver sulphate.

BARIUM HYDROXIDE ($Ba(OH)_2$). Made by calcining the nitrate, or a mixture of the nitrate and sulphate, thereby forming an oxide, to which is added water, causing it to slake like lime, forming $Ba(OH)_2$.

Reaction. $BaO + H_2O = Ba(OH)_2.$
(Barium Oxide.) (Water.) (Barium Hydroxide.)

STRONTIUM SALTS. There are no *officinal* salts of strontium; some of its compounds are used as tests, or for making colored fires. Strontium nitrate ($Sr(NO_3)_2$) is the most common salt.

Tests. The blowpipe flame has a bright crimson color; solutions of the salts produce precipitates with carbonates and sulphates.

LITHIUM SALTS.

SOURCE. Lithium is found in the mineral springs of Carlsbad, Marienbad and Franzensbrun. Met with as phosphate in *monte-brasite*, as fluoride, or silicate, in lepidolite or spodumene. It is the lightest of all metals. Sp. gr. 0.6, and burns with a *carmine* flame. Its salts are precipitated white, by sodium phosphate and ammonium carbonate.

General impurities and tests: *Salts of Alkalies:* Ignite; residue + dil. HCl + evap. to dryness; residue (1) + abs. alc. (3) = sol. + ether = ppt. *Salts of alkaline earths:* Aqueous sol. of above residue in water + $(NH_4)_2 C_2O_4$ = white ppt. *Metals:* + H_2S, or $(NH_4)_2S$ = ppt.

(Li_2CO_3—74) LITHII CARBONAS.—CARBONATE OF LITHIUM.

This salt is the origin of the other lithium compounds. *Lepidolite* is heated with H_2SO_4, and the aqueous solution, containing impure Li_2SO_4, treated with lime—to separate metallic oxides and earths—and with $BaCl_2$ to remove H_2SO_4, and $(NH_4)_2C_2O_4$ to remove calcium, leaving impure lithium chloride in solution. Evaporate to dryness, and dissolve the residue in a mixture of alcohol and ether (to remove the chlorides of rubidium, cæsium, sodium and potassium, which are present in *lepidolite*). Evaporate again, dissolve residue in water, and add $(NH_4)_2CO_3$, when Li_2CO_3 precipitates. Wash with alcohol to remove LiCl.

Reaction. $2LiCl + (NH_4)_2CO_3 = Li_2CO_3 + 2NH_4Cl.$
$\begin{pmatrix}\text{Lithium}\\\text{Chloride.}\end{pmatrix} \begin{pmatrix}\text{Ammonium}\\\text{Carbonate.}\end{pmatrix} \begin{pmatrix}\text{Lithium}\\\text{Carbonate.}\end{pmatrix} \begin{pmatrix}\text{Ammonium}\\\text{Chloride.}\end{pmatrix}$

Description. Light, white powder; odorless; alkaline taste, and reaction. Sol. water (130), insol. alc. General impurities.

($Li_7CH_5O_2$—128) LITHII BENZOAS.—BENZOATE OF LITHIUM.

Made by treating a mixture of Li_2CO_3 and boiling water, with benzoic acid, evaporating or crystallizing.

$Li_2CO_3 + 2HC_7H_5O_2 = 2LiC_7H_5O_2 + CO_2 + H_2O.$
$\begin{pmatrix}\text{Lithium}\\\text{Carbonate.}\end{pmatrix} \begin{pmatrix}\text{Benzoic}\\\text{Acid.}\end{pmatrix} \begin{pmatrix}\text{Lithium}\\\text{Benzoate.}\end{pmatrix} \begin{pmatrix}\text{Carbon}\\\text{Dioxide.}\end{pmatrix} \begin{pmatrix}\text{Water.}\end{pmatrix}$

Description. A white powder, or small, shining scales; faintly benzoin-like odor; cooling, sweetish taste; faintly acid reaction. Sol. water (4), alc. (12). General impurities.

(LiBr—86.8) LITHII BROMIDUM.—BROMIDE OF LITHIUM.

Made by dissolving Li_2CO_3 in HBr, or by the mutual decomposition between Li_2CO_3 and ferrous bromide; filtration and evaporation.

Reaction. $FeBr_2 + Li_2CO_3 = 2LiBr + FeCO_3.$
$\begin{pmatrix}\text{Ferrous}\\\text{Bromide.}\end{pmatrix} \begin{pmatrix}\text{Lithium}\\\text{Carbonate.}\end{pmatrix} \begin{pmatrix}\text{Lithium}\\\text{Bromide.}\end{pmatrix} \begin{pmatrix}\text{Ferrous}\\\text{Carbonate.}\end{pmatrix}$

Description. A white, granular salt; very deliquescent; odorless; sharp, bitter taste; neutral reaction. General impurities.

($Li_3C_6H_5O_7$,—210.). LITHII CITRAS.—CITRATE OF LITHIUM.

Made by saturating a solution of citric acid with Li_2CO_3, and evaporating.

$$3Li_2CO_3 + 2H_3C_6H_5O_7 = 2Li_3C_6H_5O_7 + 3CO_2 + 3H_2O.$$
$$\begin{pmatrix}\text{Lithium}\\\text{Carbonate.}\end{pmatrix} \begin{pmatrix}\text{Citric}\\\text{Acid.}\end{pmatrix} \begin{pmatrix}\text{Lithium}\\\text{Citrate.}\end{pmatrix} \begin{pmatrix}\text{Carbon}\\\text{Dioxide.}\end{pmatrix} (\text{Water.})$$

Description. White powder; deliquescent; odorless; cooling, faintly alkaline taste; neutral reaction. Sol. water (5.5), sl. sol. alc.

($2LiC_7H_5O_3.H_2O$—306) LITHII SALICYLAS.—SALICYLATE OF
LITHIUM.

Made by saturating salicylic acid with Li_2CO_3, and evaporating.

Reaction. $Li_2CO_3 + 2HC_7H_5O_3 = (2LiC_7H_5O_3 + H_2O) + CO_2.$
$$\begin{pmatrix}\text{Lithium}\\\text{Carbonate.}\end{pmatrix} \begin{pmatrix}\text{Salicylic}\\\text{Acid.}\end{pmatrix} (\text{Lithium Salicylate.}) \begin{pmatrix}\text{Carbon}\\\text{Dioxide.}\end{pmatrix}$$

Description. White powder; deliquescent; odorless; sweetish taste; faintly acid reaction; very soluble in water, alcohol and ether.

Impurities and tests. General impurities, and *Carbonate:* $+ HCl$ = effervescence. *Foreign organic matters:* $+$ conc. H_2SO_4 = color.

CERIUM SALTS.

SOURCE. The metal Cerium is found in the minerals *cerite* and *allanite*, as silicates of cerium, lanthanum and didymium.

($Ce_2(C_2O_4)_3.9H_2O$) CERII OXALAS.—OXALATE OF CERIUM.

Preparation. The powdered mineral is heated with conc. H_2SO_4 to decompose the silicates, the dried mass ignited, and dissolved in HNO_3 and treated with H_2S to remove copper, etc. A little HCl is added to hold in solution the calcium salts present, and the *cerite* metals are precipitated by oxalic acid. The oxalates are *purified* by calcining with $MgCO_3$, thereby decomposing them; the residue dissolved in HNO_3, and the solution poured into water containing about ½% of H_2SO_4; *ceric sulphate* is precipitated yellow, while the lanthanum, didymium, and magnesium salts remain in solution. The ceric sulphate is dissolved in H_2SO_4, and reduced to *cerous* sulphate by the aid of sodium hyposulphite; by treating the solution with oxalic acid, cerium oxalate precipitates.

Description. White, granular powder; odorless; tasteless; insol. in water, and alc.; sol. in HCl. Dose, grs. i–iv.

Impurities. Carbonate, metals and aluminium.

CERIUM NITRATE. $Ce_2(NO_3)_6$, *not officinal.* Made by the double decomposition between barium nitrate and cerium sulphate.

Reaction. $3Ba(NO_3)_2 + Ce_2(SO_4)_3 = Ce_2(NO_3)_6 + 3BaSO_4.$
$$\begin{pmatrix}\text{Barium}\\\text{Nitrate.}\end{pmatrix} \begin{pmatrix}\text{Cerium}\\\text{Sulphate.}\end{pmatrix} \begin{pmatrix}\text{Cerium}\\\text{Nitrate.}\end{pmatrix} \begin{pmatrix}\text{Barium}\\\text{Sulphate.}\end{pmatrix}$$

Description. Colorless crystals; very deliquescent; *freely soluble in water or alcohol.* Dose, grs. i–iv.

ALUMINIUM SALTS.

SOURCE. Exist as a silicate in the ordinary clays; as a fluoride in *cryolite* ($Al_2F_6.6NaF$); also found in the minerals *alum-stone, alunite* (of Italy), and *alum-slate ;* as native hydroxide in *gibbsite* $Al_2(OH)_6$ of North America, and *diaspore* ($Al_2(OH)_2O$) of Europe; as oxide in the *ruby, sapphire, corundum,* and *emery.*

Aluminium is a very light (sp. gr. 2.67) silvery white metal. Used as an alloy, and in making *aluminium-bronze,* which bears the color and appearance of gold, and is much more durable than that metal. The propelling-screw of many of the largest ocean steamers is made of this alloy.

Tests. Hydroxide of sodium or potassium produce *white precipitates* ($Al_2(OH)_6$) *soluble in excess* of the alkali. Water of ammonia yields a like precipitate, *insoluble in excess.* Alkaline carbonates give a similar reaction, with the evolution of CO_2. Ammonium sulphide also precipitates $Al_2(OH)_6$, but with evolution of H_2S.

General Impurities and tests. *Iron* (limit): $+$ Potass. ferrocyanide $=$ blue color. *Zinc,* or *lead:* $+ NaOH + (NH_4)_2S =$ ppt.

ALUMS. An alum is the double sulphate of a monad and *pseudo-triad* element, crystallizing in cubes and octahedra, with twenty-four molecules of water.

Examples. Alums containing Aluminium :

$$K_2SO_4 \ + \ Al_2(SO_4)_3 \ + \ 24H_2O \ = \ K_2Al_2(SO_4)_4 \,.\, 24H_2O.$$
$$\begin{pmatrix}\text{Potassium}\\\text{Sulphate.}\end{pmatrix} \qquad \begin{pmatrix}\text{Aluminium}\\\text{Sulphate.}\end{pmatrix} \qquad \text{(Water.)} \qquad \text{(Potassium Alum.)}$$

($NH_4)_2Al_2(SO_4)_4 \,.\, 24H_2O$ (Ammonium alum); $Na_2Al_2(SO_4)_4 \,.\, 24H_2O$ (Sodium alum); $Al_2Cs_2(SO_4)_4 \,.\, 24H_2O$ (Cæsium alum), $Al_2Rb_2(SO_4)_4 \,.\, 24H_2O$ (Rubidium alum), $Ag_2Al_2(SO_4)_4 \,.\, 24H_2O$ (Silver alum), etc.

Alums not containing Aluminium : ($NH_4)_2Fe_2(SO_4)_4 \,.\, 24H_2O$ (Ammonio-ferric alum), ($NH_4)_2Cr_2(SO_4)_4 \,.\, 24H_2O$ (Chromium alum), $K_2Fe_2(SO_4)_4 \,.\, 24H_2O$ (Potassio-ferric alum), etc.

($K_2Al_2(SO_4)_4 \,.\, 24H_2O$—948)   ALUMEN.—POTASSA ALUM.

(Sulphate of Aluminium and Potassium.)

Preparation. Clays (Pipe clay) are selected as free from iron and $CaCO_3$ as possible, and calcined to oxidize the iron, as well as to render them pulverizable. They are then treated with dilute H_2SO_4 and heated. The resulting solution of aluminium sulphate is mixed with K_2SO_4; and on concentration and cooling, crystals of alum are obtained. Also made from *cryolite* by the same method.

Description. Large, colorless, octahedral crystals; odorless; sweet, astringent taste; acid reaction; sol. water (10.5), insol. alc.

Impurities and tests. *General impurities,* and *Ammonia alum :* $+ KOH +$ Heat $=$ odor of NH_3, or the same reaction if powder is dropped on slaking lime.

Officinal Preparations. ALUMEN EXSICCATUM. (DRIED ALUM. Burnt Alum.) ($K_2Al_2(SO_4)_4$—516.) Made by driving off the water of crystallization from alum (184) at a temperature below 401° F., and heating until the mass becomes porous and weighs (100).

Description. A white, granular powder; attracts moisture from air; v. sl. sol. in water (20); other characteristics like the crystal.

Alum is often used as a mordant (*mordeo*—to bite) for *fixing* colors in fabrics, and other material; also forms *lakes* (compounds of alumina with coloring matter), by adding alum to the solution containing coloring matter, when the *lake* precipitates.

AMMONIA-ALUM. $((NH_4)_2Al_2(SO_4)_4 . 24H_2O.)$ Not officinal; but extensively used. Made by treating a solution of $Al_2(SO_4)_3$ with $(NH_4)_2SO_4$ and crystallizing.

$(Al_2(OH)_6$—156) ALUMINII HYDRAS.—HYDRATED ALUMINA.
(Hydroxide of Aluminium.)

Made by mixing boiling hot solutions of alum and sodium carbonate. The precipitate is well washed and dried.

Reaction. $\underset{\text{(Potassa-alum.)}}{K_2Al_2(SO_4)_4} + \underset{\substack{\text{Sodium} \\ \text{Carbonate.}}}{3Na_2CO_3} + \underset{\text{(Water.)}}{3H_2O} = \underset{\substack{\text{Aluminium} \\ \text{Hydroxide.}}}{Al_2(OH)_6}$

$+ \underset{\substack{\text{Potassium} \\ \text{Sulphate.}}}{K_2SO_4} + \underset{\substack{\text{Sodium} \\ \text{Sulphate.}}}{3Na_2SO_4} + \underset{\substack{\text{Carbon} \\ \text{Dioxide.}}}{3CO_2.}$

Description. White, light, amorphous powder; odorless; tasteless; insol. water, or alcohol.

Impurities and tests. *General impurities*, and *sulphate:* $+ HCl + BaCl_2 =$ white ppt. *Alkaline earths* (a limit): Boil with $H_2O +$ evap. = residue.

$(Al_2(SO_4)_3.18H_2O$—666) ALUMINII SULPHAS.—SULPHATE OF ALUMINIUM.

Made by dissolving $Al_2(OH)_6$ in dilute H_2SO_4, and evaporating to dryness.

Reaction. $\underset{\substack{\text{(Aluminium} \\ \text{Hydroxide.)}}}{Al_2(OH)_6} + \underset{\substack{\text{(Sulphuric} \\ \text{Acid.)}}}{3H_2SO_4} = \underset{\substack{\text{(Aluminium} \\ \text{Sulphate.)}}}{Al_2(SO_4)_3} + \underset{\text{(Water.)}}{6H_2O.}$

Description. White crystalline powder; odorless; sweet, astringent taste; acid reaction; sol. water (1.2), insol. alc.

THE HALOGENS AND THEIR SALTS.

CHLORINE, IODINE, BROMINE AND FLUORINE.

The above are called *halogens* (salt producers), and their salts termed *haloid* salts (άλς—*sea salt*, ειδος—*like*, resembling sea-salt).

CHLORINE.

Discovered 1774, by Scheele.

Description. A heavy, yellowish-green gas, having an irritating and suffocating odor; Sp. gr. 2.450. A great bleaching agent and disinfectant.

Preparation. Made by the action of H_2SO_4 on NaCl and MnO_2; the mixture is heated, and the gas evolved.

Reaction. $4NaCl$ + MnO_2 + $2H_2SO_4$ = $MnCl_2$
           (Sodium   (Manganese   (Sulphuric   (Manganese
           Chloride.)   Dioxide.)   Acid.)   Chloride.)

           + Cl_2 + $2Na_2SO_4$ + $2H_2O$.
           (Chlorine.)   (Sodium   (Water.)
                          Sulphate.)

Other methods: $MnO_2 + 4HCl = MnCl_2 + Cl_2 + 2H_2O$

or, $K_2Cr_2O_7$ + $14HCl$ = $3Cl_2$ + $2KCl$ + Cr_2Cl_6 + $7H_2O$.
   (Potassium   (Hydrochloric (Chlorine.) (Potassium)   (Chromium)   (Water.)
   Bichromate.)   Acid.   Chloride.)   Chloride.)

or, $\begin{cases} 4KClO_3 + 12HCl = Cl_{12}O_6 + 4KCl + 6H_2O. \\ \qquad\qquad\qquad\qquad \text{(Euchlorine), a very explosive gas.} \\ \text{Euchlorine (+ water)} = Cl_9 + 3ClO_2. \end{cases}$

Tests for Chlorides and Hydrochloric Acid: A curdy white precipitate is produced with $AgNO_3$, soluble in NH_4OH, but insol. in HNO_3.

AQUA CHLORI.—CHLORINE WATER.

By the action of HCl on MnO_2 (as shown above) Cl. is evolved, and passed into cold distilled water until the latter is saturated.

Description. A greenish-yellow liquid; suffocating odor; disagreeable taste. Contains 0.4% of Cl. Should leave no residue on evaporation; and is decomposed by exposure to air or sunlight, forming HCl. $2Cl + H_2O = 2HCl + O$.

Impurity. *Hydrochloric Acid:* Shake with mercury in excess, until the odor of Cl. disappears; the remaining liquid gives an acid reaction.

The Assay Process is based upon the amount of volumetric solution of sodium hyposulphite required to decolorize the iodine liberated from a solution of potassium iodide, by a definite quantity of Cl. water.

Extemporaneous preparation of Chlorine Water. 1. NaCl—60 grs., lead oxide (red)—350 grs., triturate and introduce into a bottle; add water f ℥ viij and H_2SO_4 f ℨ ij and let stand; $PbSO_4$ precipitates, while Cl. and Na_2SO_4 are in solution.

2. $KClO_3$—60 grs., is put into an 8-oz. bottle; add HCl f ℨ ij; let stand till reaction ceases, and add water to make one pint.

CALX CHLORATÆ.—CHLORINATED LIME. (Chloride of Lime.)

Made by the action of Cl. on milk of lime.

$2Ca(OH)_2$ + $4Cl$ = $(CaCl_2$ + $Ca(ClO)_2$ + $2H_2O)$.
(Calcium   (Chlorine.)   (Calcium   (Calcium   (Water.)
Hydroxide.)   Chloride.)   Hypochlorite.)

$CaCl_2 + Ca(ClO)_2 = 2(CaO)Cl_2$; the supposed composition of this salt; hence the name " *Chloride of Lime.*"

Description. White, or grayish-white powder (slightly damp); —or friable lumps; becoming moist, and gradually decomposing on exposure to air; feeble, chlorine-like odor; disagreeable, saline taste. Partially soluble in water, and in alcohol; completely sol. in HCl. evolving Cl., the solution having an alkaline reaction.

$2(CaO)Cl_2$ + $4HCl$ = $2CaCl_2$ + $2Cl_2$ + $2H_2O$.
(Chloride of Lime.) (Hydrochloric) (Calcium)   (Chlorine.)   (Water.)
                     Acid.   Chloride.)

The aqueous solution quickly bleaches the color of litmus or indigo. *Chlorinated Lime should contain at least 25% of available chlorine.*

Assay Process. Mix 0.71 Gm. $CaOCl_2$ with sol. KI (1.25 Gm. in 122 cm³ water) and dilute HCl 9 Gms.; the red-brown solution should require not less than 50 cm³ of volumetric solution of sodium hyposulphite for complete decoloration.

Explanation. The *available chlorine* is derived from the $Ca(ClO)_2$ (one of the portions of this salt), as the $CaCl_2$ cannot give up its Cl. In the first part of the assay process, iodine is liberated from the potassium salt, producing the red-brown solution (or in the case of the presence of gelatinized starch, as in Liq. Sodæ Chloratæ, a blue color); the hyposulphite causes the formation of tetrathionate and iodide of sodium, the red or blue color disappearing as soon as all of the free iodine has been converted into the iodide.

Reaction. $2Na_2S_2O_3 + I_2 = 2NaI + Na_2S_4O_6.$

$\begin{pmatrix}\text{Sodium} \\ \text{Hyposulphite.}\end{pmatrix}$ $\begin{pmatrix}\text{Iodine.}\end{pmatrix}$ $\begin{pmatrix}\text{Sodium} \\ \text{Iodide.}\end{pmatrix}$ $\begin{pmatrix}\text{Sodium} \\ \text{Tetrathionate.}\end{pmatrix}$

Properties. A great bleaching agent and disinfectant.

LIQUOR SODÆ CHLORATÆ.—SOLUTION OF CHLORINATED SODA.

(Labarraque's Solution.)

Made by decomposing a mixture of chlorinated lime and water, with a boiling hot solution of Na_2CO_3; $CaCO_3$ precipitates, and the clear solution is decanted.

Reaction. $Ca(ClO)_2 + CaCl_2 + 2Na_2CO_3 =$

$\begin{pmatrix}\text{Calcium} \\ \text{Hypochlorite.}\end{pmatrix}$ $\begin{pmatrix}\text{Calcium} \\ \text{Chloride.}\end{pmatrix}$ $\begin{pmatrix}\text{Sodium} \\ \text{Carbonate.}\end{pmatrix}$

$2CaCO_3 + 2NaCl + 2NaClO.$

$\begin{pmatrix}\text{Calcium} \\ \text{Carbonate.}\end{pmatrix}$ $\begin{pmatrix}\text{Sodium} \\ \text{Chloride.}\end{pmatrix}$ $\begin{pmatrix}\text{Sodium} \\ \text{Hypochlorite.}\end{pmatrix}$

or $CaOCl_2 + Na_2CO_3 = Na_2OCl_2 + CaCO_3.$

Description. Clear, colorless liquid ; faint odor of Cl ; alkaline taste and reaction ; decolorizes indigo. Sp. gr. 1.044. HCl causes effervescence of Cl and CO_2. *Sol. Chlorinated Soda should contain at least 2% of available chlorine.*

Assay Process. 8.88 Gm. of the solution + sol. KI (2.6 Gm. in 200 cm³ water) + 18 Gm. HCl and a little gelatinized starch, should require for complete decoloration not less than 50 cm³ of vol. sol. sodium hyposulphite.

JAVELLE WATER.—(Solution Chlorinated Potassa.) Not officinal. Made by substituting an equal quantity of K_2CO_3 for Na_2CO_3 in the above formula.

IODUM (Iodine).

This non-metallic element is obtained from *kelp*, the ashes of certain sea-weeds, and from the mother liquor left on crystallizing Chili nitre ($NaNO_3$); also found in many mineral springs, in sea-water, cod-liver oil, sponge, coal, etc.

Preparation. The sea-weeds are charred at as low a temperature as possible to avoid loss of I. The ash is lixiviated with water, and the solution concentrated. During evaporation Na_2SO_4 separates out, and on cooling KCl deposits. The uncrystallizable mother liquor contains I in the form of iodide and iodate of sodium. On mixing with excess of H_2SO_4 and heating with MnO_2, the I, distils, leaving sodium and manganous sulphates in the retort.

Reaction.
$$2NaI \ + \ MnO_2 \ + \ 2H_2SO_4 \ = \ I_2$$
(Sodium Iodide.) (Manganese Dioxide.) (Sulphuric Acid.) (Iodine)
$$+ \ Na_2SO_4 \ + \ MnSO_4 \ + \ 2H_2O.$$
(Sodium Sulphate.) (Manganous Sulphate.) (Water.)

Purification. In its crude state I is contaminated with water, and sometimes ICN or ICl. Purify by drying, and then subliming; ICN and ICl (the more volatile compounds) sublime first; then the receiver is changed and the heat raised till the iodine has all distilled over. The presence of water may be detected by shaking with chloroform, when a limpid, unclean liquid results.

Description. Heavy, bluish-black, dark and friable, rhombic plates, of a metallic lustre, resembling iron; distinctive odor; sharp, acrid taste, and neutral reaction. Imparts a deep brown, slowly evanescing stain to the skin, and destroys vegetable colors; sp. sol. water, sol. alc. (1)—very sol. ether, CS_2, chloroform, and KI solution.

Should contain 100% of absolute iodine, the quantitative test dependent upon the amount of a volumetric solution of hyposulphite of sodium required to decolorize a solution of a definite quantity of iodine in solution of potassium iodide.

Tests for Iodine and Iodides. *Iodine:* With gelatinized starch in a cold solution, *iodine* gives a dark, blue color. *Iodides:* 1. Add chlorine water to liberate free iodine, and apply the above starch test; or if the colored liquid be agitated with ether, benzin, CS_2, or chloroform, the iodine dissolves. 2. With soluble salts of lead, the neutral iodides produce a yellow precipitate. 3. With mercuric chloride, a red precipitate. 4. With silver nitrate, a white precipitate, sl. sol. in NH_4OH, insol. in HNO_3.

Officinal Preparations. 1. Liquor Iodi Compositus (Lugol's Solution) contains I (5), KI, (10), Water (85)—about $3\frac{1}{4}$ grs. I in f ʒ j. 2. Tinctura Iodi—8% Iodine. 3. Unguentum Iodi—contains I (4), KI (1), Water (2), Benz. Lard (93).

SYRUPUS ACIDI HYDRIODICI.—SYRUP OF HYDRIODIC ACID.

Made by passing H_2S into an alcoholic solution of I mixed with syrup, until the latter becomes light yellow in color, heating to drive off H_2S, flavoring with spirit of orange and dissolving more sugar in the liquid.

Reaction.
$$I_2 \ + \ H_2S \ = \ 2HI \ + \ S.$$
(Iodine.) (Hydrogen Sulphide.) (Hydriodic Acid.) (Sulphur.)

Description. A transparent, colorless, or pale, straw-colored liquid; odorless; sweet, acidulous taste; acid reaction; sp. gr. 1.300—contains 1% of absolute HI.

(KI—165.6) Potassii Iodidum.—Iodide of Potassium.

Made by adding Iodine to a hot solution of KOH, until the liquid remains slightly colored from excess of iodine, when iodide and iodate of potassium are formed.

Reaction. $6KOH + 6I = 5KI + KIO_3 + 3H_2O.$
(Potassium Hydroxide.) (Iodine) (Potassium Iodide.) (Potassium Iodate.) (Water.)

The solution is evaporated to dryness, powdered charcoal is added, and the mixture heated to redness, in order to deoxidize the *iodate*, thereby converting it to the *iodide*.

Reaction. $KIO_3 + 3C + Heat = KI + 3CO.$
(Potassium Iodate.) (Charcoal.) (Potassium Iodide.) (Carbon Monoxide.)

Dissolve, evaporate and crystallize.

Description. When *pure* it occurs in colorless, translucent, cubical crystals, slightly deliquescent, having a peculiar faint odor; a pungent, saline, bitter taste; neutral reaction; sol. water (0.8), alc. (18). The *commercial salt* appears in white, opaque crystals, having a faintly alkaline reaction (due to crystallization from an alkaline solution, thus producing a more stable salt), but single crystals placed on moistened red litmus paper should not at once produce a violet-blue stain (showing the absence of more than 0.1% of alkali).

Impurities and tests. *Iodate:* + gelatinized starch + dilute H_2SO_4 (or $H_2C_4H_4O_6$) = *blue* color. *Chloride*, or *bromide:* Sol. in $NH_4OH + AgNO_3$; filt. + HNO_3 (excess) = cloudiness. *Sulphate* (limit): + $Ba(NO_3)_2$ = white ppt.

A *simple test* to distinguish between KI and KBr is their solubility:

KI (1) in water (0.8)—KBr (1) in water (1.6).
KI (1) in alcohol (18)—KBr (1) in alcohol (200).

Officinal Preparations. Unguentum Potassii Iodidi (Ointment of Iodide of Potassium). Contains KI (12), $Na_2S_2O_3$ (1), boiling water (6), and benz. lard (81). The hyposulphite of sodium is added to prevent the liberation of free iodine, which would change the color of the ointment from white to yellow or brown.

(NaI—149.6) Sodii Iodidum.—Iodide of Sodium.

Made by a process analogous to that by which KI is produced—

(1) $6NaOH + 6I = 5NaI + NaIO_3 + 3H_2O.$
(Sodium Hydroxide.) (Iodine.) (Sodium Iodide.) (Sodium Iodate.) (Water.)

(2) $NaIO_3 + 3C = NaI + 3CO.$

or made by the double decomposition between ferrous iodide and sodium carbonate.

Reaction. $FeI_2 + Na_2CO_3 = 2NaI + FeCO_3.$
(Ferrous Iodide.) (Sodium Carbonate.) (Sodium Iodide.) (Ferrous Carbonate.)

This salt is little used on account of its great deliquescent nature.

Description. Minute, colorless, or white, monoclinic crystals, or a crystalline powder; very deliquescent; odorless; having a saline and slightly bitter taste; neutral or faintly alkaline reaction; sol. water (0.6), alc. (1.8). Impurities, same as KI.

(CHI₃—392.8) IODOFORMUM.—IODOFORM. (Methenyl Iodide.)

Made by the action of I. on alcohol in the presence of a fixed alkali or alkali carbonate; also true regarding the action of I on certain ethers, aldchyd, acetone, amylene; butyl, capryl, and propyl alcohols, kinic, lactic, meconic acids, and other compounds.

Process. Iodine, KHCO₃, water, and alcohol are mixed in a flask and heated until the color has disappeared, then more iodine is added in portions as long as the liquid remains colorless on heating; set aside to cool and crystallize.

Reaction.

$$C_2H_5OH + 8I + 6KHCO_3 = CHI_3$$

$$\begin{pmatrix} \text{Ethyl} \\ \text{Hydroxide.} \end{pmatrix} \quad \text{(Iodine.)} \quad \begin{pmatrix} \text{Potassium} \\ \text{Bicarbonate.} \end{pmatrix} \quad \text{(Iodoform.)}$$

$$+ 5KI + KCHO_2 + 6CO_2 + 5H_2O.$$

$$\begin{pmatrix} \text{Potassium} \\ \text{Iodide.} \end{pmatrix} \quad \begin{pmatrix} \text{Potassium} \\ \text{Formate.} \end{pmatrix} \quad \begin{pmatrix} \text{Carbon} \\ \text{Dioxide.} \end{pmatrix} \quad \text{(Water.)}$$

Both iodide and formate of potassium are always produced, but additional crystals of CHI₃ may be obtained by passing Cl into the mother liquor, by which the KI becomes decomposed, I being set free, which in turn decomposes the alcohol, producing more CHI₃.

Description. Small, lemon-yellow, lustrous crystals of the hexagonal system; saffron-like and almost insuppressible odor; unpleasant iodine-like taste; neutral reaction in solution. Insol. water; sol. in alcohol (80), ether (5.2), chloroform, CS₂, benzol, benzin, fixed and volatile oils.

Impurities and tests. *Iodide,* or *iodate:* Shake with water = no change of color to litmus paper; and filtrate + AgNO₃ = *white ppt.*

Officinal Preparation. UNGUENTUM IODOFORMI (Iodoform Ointment) contains iodoform (10), incorporated with benzoinated lard (90).

Note.—To disguise the unpleasant odor of iodoform, in mixtures and ointments, add 3-5 drops of oil of peppermint to the ounce; balsam peru, coumarin, oils of fennel, anise and thyme are also employed for the same purpose.

BROMUM (Bromine).

A liquid non-metallic element obtained from sea-water, and from saline springs.

Occurrence. It is found as magnesium or calcium bromide, and obtained in considerable quantities from the mother liquors of many salt works in the United States and Europe.

Preparation. These mother liquors (bittern), which have been freed by crystallization as much as possible from alkaline chlorides and sulphates, contain the bromine usually in combination, as MgBr₂ or CaBr₂. After evaporation, the concentrated solution is heated with HCl and MnO₂, and Br. distils. The neck of the retort is plunged into cold water, and the Br. collects in drops at the bottom of the receiver.

Reaction. $MgBr_2 + 4HCl + MnO_2 = MgCl_2$

$$\begin{pmatrix}\text{Magnesium}\\\text{Bromide.}\end{pmatrix} \begin{pmatrix}\text{Hydrochloric}\\\text{Acid.}\end{pmatrix} \begin{pmatrix}\text{Manganese}\\\text{Dioxide.}\end{pmatrix} \begin{pmatrix}\text{Magnesium}\\\text{Chloride.}\end{pmatrix}$$

$$+ MnCl_2 + Br_2 + 2H_2O.$$

$$\begin{pmatrix}\text{Manganese}\\\text{Chloride.}\end{pmatrix} \text{(Bromine.)} \quad \text{(Water.)}$$

The $MgBr_2$ is sometimes decomposed by passing Cl. directly into the solution.

Reaction. $MgBr_2 + 2Cl = MgCl_2 + Br_2.$

$$\begin{pmatrix}\text{Magnesium}\\\text{Bromide.}\end{pmatrix} \text{(Chlorine.)} \begin{pmatrix}\text{Magnesium}\\\text{Chloride.}\end{pmatrix} \text{(Bromine.)}$$

Description. Dark, brownish-red mobile liquid, evolving at all temperatures a yellowish-red vapor, very corrosive and suffocating, and highly irritating to the eyes and lungs, and having a peculiar suffocating odor, resembling chlorine. Sp. gr. 2.990—sol. water (33), v. sol. alcohol and ether, gradually decomposing these two liquids, also very soluble in chloroform, CS_2; destroys color of litmus and sulphate of indigo.

Impurities. Chlorine, and Iodine; a limit of each allowed.

Tests for Bromine and Bromides. *Bromine:* With gelatinized starch, gives a yellow color. *Bromides:* 1. Add chlorine to strong solution, bromine is liberated, and apply the above starch test; or if the colored liquid be agitated with ether, chloroform, CS_2 or benzine, the bromine dissolves. 2. With silver nitrate a yellowish-white precipitate results, insoluble in HNO_3, slightly soluble in NH_4OH. 3. Concentrated H_2SO_4 added to the salt, yields reddish vapors of bromine.

(KBr—118.8) POTASSII BROMIDUM.—BROMIDE OF POTASSIUM.

PREPARATION. Made by three processes. 1. The double decomposition between ferrous bromide and K_2CO_3:

Reaction. $FeBr_2 + K_2CO_3 = 2KBr + FeCO_3.$

$$\begin{pmatrix}\text{Ferrous}\\\text{Bromide.}\end{pmatrix} \begin{pmatrix}\text{Potassium}\\\text{Carbonate.}\end{pmatrix} \begin{pmatrix}\text{Potassium}\\\text{Bromide.}\end{pmatrix} \begin{pmatrix}\text{Ferrous}\\\text{Carbonate.}\end{pmatrix}$$

2. The double decomposition between calcium bromide and potassium sulphate:

Reaction. $CaBr_2 + K_2SO_4 = CaSO_4 + 2KBr.$

$$\begin{pmatrix}\text{Calcium}\\\text{Bromide.}\end{pmatrix} \begin{pmatrix}\text{Potassium}\\\text{Sulphate.}\end{pmatrix} \begin{pmatrix}\text{Calcium}\\\text{Sulphate.}\end{pmatrix} \begin{pmatrix}\text{Potassium}\\\text{Bromide.}\end{pmatrix}$$

3. The action of bromine on a solution of potash, thereby producing bromide and bromate of potassium, calcining with charcoal, solution, filtration and crystallization:

(a) $6KOH + 6Br = 5KBr + KBrO_3 + 3H_2O.$

$$\begin{pmatrix}\text{Potassium}\\\text{Hydroxide.}\end{pmatrix} \text{(Bromine.)} \begin{pmatrix}\text{Potassium}\\\text{Bromide.}\end{pmatrix} \begin{pmatrix}\text{Potassium}\\\text{Bromate.}\end{pmatrix} \text{(Water.)}$$

(b) $KBrO_3 + 3C = KBr + 3CO.$

$$\begin{pmatrix}\text{Potassium}\\\text{Bromate.}\end{pmatrix} \text{(Charcoal.)} \begin{pmatrix}\text{Potassium}\\\text{Bromide.}\end{pmatrix} \begin{pmatrix}\text{Carbon}\\\text{Monoxide.}\end{pmatrix}$$

The latter step may also be accomplished as follows: $KBrO_3 + 3H_2S = KBr + 3H_2O + S_3.$

Description. When *pure:* colorless, translucent, cubical crystals, permanent in dry air, odorless, having a pungent, saline taste, and a neutral reaction. Soluble in water (1.6), alcohol (200). The *commercial salt* appears in white opaque, or semi-transparent crystals; faintly alkaline reaction (due to crystallization from an alkaline liquid), but single crystals laid on moistened red litmus paper should not at once produce a violet-blue stain (absence of more than 0.1% alkali).

Impurities and tests. *Bromate :* Drop dil. H_2SO_4 on crushed crystals = yellow color. *Iodide :* Sol. + starch jelly + Cl. water = blue zone. *Sulphate* (a limit): + $Ba(NO_3)_2$ = white ppt. *Chloride :* (more than 3%): Volumetric test for chlorides, using potass. bichromate as an indicator, and $AgNO_3$ as the precipitant.

(NaBr—102.8) Sodii Bromidum.—Bromide of Sodium.

Made by processes identical with those for KBr., substituting a sodium salt for the potassium compound.

Description. Small, colorless or white, monoclinic crystals, or a crystalline powder; permanent in dry air; odorless; saline, slightly bitter taste; neutral or faintly alkaline reaction. Sol. water (1.2), alcohol (13).

Impurities, and tests for their presence, are identical with those found under Potassium Bromide.

(HBr—80.8) Acidum Hydrobromicum Dilutum.—Diluted Hydrobromic Acid.

Preparation. Several methods. 1. The action of H_2SO_4 on KBr; the crystals of K_2SO_4 are allowed to crystallize out, the mother liquor distilled, and the distillate diluted to the proper degree :

Reaction. $2KBr + H_2SO_4 = K_2SO_4 + 2HBr.$
$\begin{pmatrix}\text{Potassium}\\\text{Bromide.}\end{pmatrix}$ $\begin{pmatrix}\text{Sulphuric}\\\text{Acid.}\end{pmatrix}$ $\begin{pmatrix}\text{Potassium}\\\text{Sulphate.}\end{pmatrix}$ $\begin{pmatrix}\text{Hydrobromic}\\\text{Acid.}\end{pmatrix}$

2. The decomposition of KBr by tartaric acid; potassium bitartrate precipitates, while HBr is left in solution :

Reaction. $KBr + H_2C_4H_4O_6 = KHC_4H_4O_6 + HBr.$
$\begin{pmatrix}\text{Potassium}\\\text{Bromide.}\end{pmatrix}$ $\begin{pmatrix}\text{Tartaric}\\\text{Acid.}\end{pmatrix}$ $\begin{pmatrix}\text{Potassium}\\\text{Bitartrate.}\end{pmatrix}$ $\begin{pmatrix}\text{Hydrobromic}\\\text{Acid.}\end{pmatrix}$

3. By the action of Br. on phosphorus, pentabromide of phosphorus is formed; this taking place in the presence of water, the latter decomposes, as is shown below :

Reaction. $PBr_5 + 4H_2O = H_3PO_4 + 5HBr.$
$\begin{pmatrix}\text{Phosphorus}\\\text{Pentabromide.}\end{pmatrix}$ (Water.) $\begin{pmatrix}\text{Phosphoric}\\\text{Acid.}\end{pmatrix}$ $\begin{pmatrix}\text{Hydrobromic}\\\text{Acid.}\end{pmatrix}$

The HBr is distilled off, and H_3PO_4 remains in the retort.

Description. A clear, colorless liquid; odorless; strongly acid taste; acid reaction; contains 10% absolute HBr and 90% water. Sp. gr. 1.077. *Test.* Same as for *bromides.*

Impurities and tests. *Organic matter :* discolored by age. *Sulphuric acid :* + $BaCl_2$ = white ppt.

CYANOGEN SALTS.

CYANOGEN. (CN) is a gas obtained by heating mercuric cyanide ($Hg(CN)_2$) or silver cyanide ($AgCN$).

($K_4Fe(CN)_6.3H_2O$—421.9) POTASSII FERROCYANIDUM.—FERRO-CYANIDE OF POTASSIUM. (Yellow Prussiate of Potash.)

Prepared by heating in suitable iron vessels K_2CO_3 (free from sulphate, to prevent the formation of sulphocyanide) until melted, and introducing a mixture composed of iron filings and charcoal obtained from refuse animal matter rich in nitrogen. When CO_2 and inflammable gases cease to be evolved, the liquid mass is ladled out, cooled, lixiviated with water, and the resulting solution crystallized. Purified by re-crystallization.

[*Note.* This process is one of pure synthesis; the nitrogenous bodies produce the N and C, which combine with the Fe and K.]

Description. Large, coherent, lemon-yellow, translucent, soft crystals; slightly efflorescent in dry air; odorless; sweet, saline taste; neutral reaction. Sol. water (4), insol. alcohol.

Tests. Aqueous solution with *ferric* salts gives a *dark-blue* precipitate (Prussian Blue); with *ferrous* salts *bluish-white* gradually turning darker; with *copper* salts, *red-brown* (chocolate); with *lead* acetate, *white ;* with *mercuric* salts, *white.*

Impurities and tests. *Carbonate :* + dil. H_2SO_4 = effervescence. *Sulphate* (a limit): + HCl + $BaCl_2$ = cloudiness, or white ppt. *Chloride* (a limit): Fuse with KNO_3 + H_2O; filt. + $AgNO_3$ = white ppt. This salt is the source of the other compounds of cyanogen.

FERRICYANIDE OF POTASSIUM.—Red Prussiate of Potash. ($K_6Fe_2(CN)_{12}$).—*Officinal as Test-solution.*

Made by passing Cl into a cold solution of the ferrocyanide; the liquid changes in color from yellow to red, and when it ceases to produce a blue precipitate or blue color with ferric chloride, it is concentrated to crystallization.

Reaction. $2K_4Fe(CN)_6$ + Cl_2 = $K_6Fe_2(CN)_{12}$ + $2KCl.$
$\begin{pmatrix}\text{Potassium}\\\text{Ferrocyanide.}\end{pmatrix}$ (Chlorine.) $\begin{pmatrix}\text{Potassium}\\\text{Ferricyanide.}\end{pmatrix}$ $\begin{pmatrix}\text{Potassium}\\\text{Chloride.}\end{pmatrix}$

On exposure to air, this salt decomposes into the ferrocyanide.

The *fresh* aqueous solution is used as a test; with *ferrous* salts, it gives a *dark-blue* precipitate (Turnbull's Blue); with *copper* salts, *brownish-yellow ;* *mercurous* salts, *red-brown ;* *silver* salts, *orange colored ;* but *no precipitates*, with *ferric, mercuric,* or *lead salts.*

FERROCYANIDE OF IRON.—PRUSSIAN BLUE. (Paris Blue. Williamson's Blue. $Fe_43Fe(CN)_6$.) *Not officinal.*

Made by double decomposition between ferrocyanide of potassium and a ferric salt, washing and drying the precipitate.

$3K_4Fe(CN)_6$ + $2Fe_2(SO_4)_3$ = $Fe_4(FeC_6N_6)_3$ + $6K_2SO_4.$
$\begin{pmatrix}\text{Potassium}\\\text{Ferrocyanide.}\end{pmatrix}$ $\begin{pmatrix}\text{Ferric}\\\text{Sulphate.}\end{pmatrix}$ $\begin{pmatrix}\text{Ferric}\\\text{Ferrocyanide.}\end{pmatrix}$ $\begin{pmatrix}\text{Potassium}\\\text{Sulphate.}\end{pmatrix}$

Also made by precipitating ferrous sulphate with potass. ferro-cyanide, and exposing the bluish-white precipitate to the air, till it has acquired the proper color.

(KCN—65) POTASSII CYANIDUM.—CYANIDE OF POTASSIUM.

Made by fusing exsiccated potassium ferrocyanide with K_2CO_3; pour the liquid mass from the sediment of iron, and allow the former to cool and solidify.

$$2K_4Fe(CN)_6 + 2K_2CO_3 = 10KCN + 2KCNO + Fe_2 + 2CO_2.$$
$\begin{pmatrix}\text{Potassium} \\ \text{Ferrocyanide.}\end{pmatrix}$ $\begin{pmatrix}\text{Potassium} \\ \text{Carbonate.}\end{pmatrix}$ $\begin{pmatrix}\text{Potassium} \\ \text{Cyanide.}\end{pmatrix}$ $\begin{pmatrix}\text{Potassium} \\ \text{Cyanate.}\end{pmatrix}$ (Iron.) $\begin{pmatrix}\text{Carbon} \\ \text{Dioxide.}\end{pmatrix}$

The cyanate is dissolved out with CS_2.

Another method. HCN is passed into an alcoholic solution of KOH, and the crystalline precipitate washed with alcohol and dried.

May also be made by heating the ferrocyanide.

$$K_4Fe(CN)_6 + \text{Heat} = 4KCN + N_2 + FeC_2.$$

The KCN is dissolved out with water, while carbide of iron remains undissolved.

Description. White, opaque, amorphous pieces, or a white, granular powder; deliquescent in damp air; odorless when perfectly dry, but generally of a peculiar, characteristic odor; sharp, alkaline, and bitter almond taste; strong alkaline reaction; sol. water (2), sp. sol. alcohol. Should contain at least 90% of pure KCN, determined by the amount of volumetric solution of silver nitrate it will precipitate.

Impurity. *Carbonate :* + acid = brisk effervescence.

Most poisonous salt known; rarely given internally. *Dose,* $\frac{1}{16}$ to $\frac{1}{8}$ gr.

(HCN—27) ACIDUM HYDROCYANICUM DILUTUM.—DILUTED HYDROCYANIC ACID. (Prussic Acid.)

Two methods given in the U. S. Pharmacopœia.

First Method. Made by distilling a mixture of H_2SO_4, ferrocyanide of potassium, and water; the condensed vapor is dissolved in diluted alcohol, and sufficient water is added to bring the product to the proper degree of strength.

The equation for the reaction taking place in the above process may be written as follows:

$$2K_4Fe(CN)_6 + 3H_2SO_4 = 3K_2SO_4 + Fe_2K_2(CN)_6$$
$\begin{pmatrix}\text{Potassium} \\ \text{Ferrocyanide.}\end{pmatrix}$ $\begin{pmatrix}\text{Sulphuric} \\ \text{Acid.}\end{pmatrix}$ $\begin{pmatrix}\text{Potassium} \\ \text{Sulphate.}\end{pmatrix}$ $\begin{pmatrix}\text{Potassium Ferrous} \\ \text{Ferrocyanide (Everitt's Salt).}\end{pmatrix}$
$$+ 6HCN.$$
$\begin{pmatrix}\text{Hydrocyanic} \\ \text{Acid.}\end{pmatrix}$

The intermediate reactions are as follows:

(1) $K_4Fe(CN)_6 + 2H_2SO_4 = 2K_2SO_4 + H_4Fe(CN)_6.$
(Hydroferrocyanic acid.)

(2) $H_4Fe(CN)_6 + K_4Fe(CN)_6 + H_2SO_4 = 6HCN + K_2SO_4 + K_2Fe_2(CN)_6$
(Everitt's salt—
a white salt rapidly turning green and then blue in the presence of oxygen.)

Extemporaneous Method. Mix HCl (5) with dist. water (55), add AgCN (6) and shake; let the precipitate subside, and pour off the clear liquid.

Reaction. $AgCN + HCl = AgCl + HCN.$
$\begin{pmatrix}\text{Silver} \\ \text{Cyanide.}\end{pmatrix}$ $\begin{pmatrix}\text{Hydrochloric} \\ \text{Acid.}\end{pmatrix}$ $\begin{pmatrix}\text{Silver} \\ \text{Chloride.}\end{pmatrix}$ $\begin{pmatrix}\text{Hydrocyanic} \\ \text{Acid.}\end{pmatrix}$

Description. A colorless liquid, having odor and taste of bitter almonds; slightly acid reaction; completely volatilized by heat.

Test for identity. Acid + KOH (excess) + FeSO$_4$ + Fe$_2$Cl$_6$ + HCl = *blue ppt.* Should contain 2% absolute HCN.

Assay Process. 6.75 gms. diluted HCN + 30 cm^3 water, mixed with sufficient aqueous suspension of magnesia to make the mixture quite opaque, and afterwards with a few drops of a dilute solution of potassium chromate, should require 50 cm^3 of the volumetric sol. of AgNO$_3$, before the red color caused by the latter ceases to disappear on stirring. *Explanation.* The magnesia is added not only to prevent the volatilization of the acid, but also because the double cyanides of silver with alkali-metals are very permanent; and to produce a white background to show the red precipitate. Chromate of potassium is used as an *indicator*, as all of the cyanide will be precipitated white, before the red silver chromate forms.

Diluted hydrocyanic acid becomes discolored on keeping, due to the formation of paracyanogen. It has been suggested that, if kept in cork-stoppered bottles, this change can be prevented or retarded, but such appears not to be the case.

Dose. Two to four drops. *Extremely poisonous.*

Antidotes. Mild inhalations of ammonia or chlorine, and the application of cold water to the head and spine, or take the following three solutions, in order, viz.:

No. 1. K$_2$CO$_3$, 20 grs. in water f ℥ j.
No. 2. FeSO$_4$, 10 grs. in water f ℥ j.
No. 3. Tinct. Fe$_2$Cl$_6$, f ʒ j.

The object of the above being to form, *first*, potassium cyanide; *second*, potassium ferrocyanide; *third*, ferrocyanide of iron (insoluble Prussian Blue).

AMMONIUM SULPHOCYANIDE. (NH$_4$CNS.) Made by dissolving CS$_2$ in alcohol and heating in the presence of ammonia. CS$_2$ + 2NH$_3$ = NH$_4$CNS + H$_2$S.

POTASSIUM SULPHOCYANIDE. (KCNS.) Made by heating K$_2$CO$_3$, sulphur and K$_4$Fe(CN)$_6$, treating the cooled mass with alcohol, and crystallizing.

The two salts just treated of are very delicate *tests for ferric salts*, giving a *blood-red precipitate*, which is not discharged by HCl (difference from acetates and formates), but disappears on the addition of mercuric chloride (difference from meconates).

SULPHUR.

OCCURRENCE. Found native in great abundance in volcanic regions, beds of which have been discovered in the Western United States, Mexico, West Indies, etc. The chief supply however, comes from Italy. Sulphur is also a constituent of the volatile oils of mustard, garlic and horseradish; and of albumen and other proteids; also found in mineral waters as H$_2$S and sulphates; in *iron pyrites* (FeS$_2$), *galena* (PbS), *blende* (ZnS), *black antimony* (Sb$_2$S$_3$), *cinnabar* (HgS), *gypsum* (CaSO$_4$), *heavy spar* (BaSO$_4$), etc.

Recovery. Obtained by melting it from the ore, running into moulds and solidifying, forming the *rough-sulphur* of commerce.

Sulphur is officinal in three forms, viz.: *sublimed, washed* and *precipitated.*

SULPHUR SUBLIMATUM.—SUBLIMED SULPHUR. (Flowers of Sulphur.)

Made by subliming the *rough sulphur* from iron retorts. It condenses in the form of a fine powder, which is removed from time to time, before the condensing chamber becomes too hot. If however, the operation is not interrupted, the brick walls of the condenser become hot enough to melt the sulphur, which is then conducted into moulds, and constitutes *brimstone* or *roll-sulphur.*

Description. Fine, citron-yellow powder, of a slight characteristic odor; faintly acid taste; acid reaction; insol. water, or alcohol.

Officinal Preparations. 1. Sulphur lotum. 2. Sulphur præcipitatum. 3. Unguentum sulphuris (Sulphur Ointment). Contains sublimed sulphur (30), benzoinated lard (70).

SULPHUR LOTUM.—WASHED SULPHUR.

Made by washing sublimed S. with a dilute water of ammonia (to remove H_2SO_4 and other impurities) until the washings cease to precipitate $BaCl_2$, then draining and drying and passing through a 30-mesh sieve. The ammonia neutralizes the acid, forming $(NH_4)_2SO_4$, which is washed out.

Description. Fine, citron-yellow powder; odorless; almost tasteless; insoluble in water and alcohol; sol. in boiling solution NaOH, or in CS_2.

Impurities and tests. *Free acid:* litmus paper = red color. *Arsenious sulphide:* + NH_4OH (2); filt. + HCl (excess) = ppt. *Arsenious acid:* filtrate from above + H_2S = yellow ppt.

Officinal Preparations. 1. Pulv. glycyrrhizæ compositus (Compound licorice powder). Contains senna (18), glycyrrhiza (16), fennel (8), washed S (8), sugar (50). 2. Ung. sulphuris alkalinum (See K_2CO_3). 3. Sulphuris iodidum.

SULPHURIS IODIDUM.—IODIDE OF SULPHUR.
Subiodide of Sulphur. (S_2I_2.)

Made by fusing together, in a flask, washed sulphur (1) and iodine (4). Used in ointments.

SULPHUR PRÆCIPITATUM.—PRECIPITATED SULPHUR.
(Milk of Sulphur.)

Slaked lime is boiled with sublimed S (forming calcium penta sulphide and thiosulphate), then enough HCl is added to neutralize the mixture; sulphur precipitates, and is thoroughly washed with water and dried.

First reaction. $3Ca(OH)_2$ + $6S_2$ = $2CaS_5$ + CaS_2O_3

(Calcium Hydroxide.) (Sulphur.) (Calcium Pentasulphide.) (Calcium Thiosulphate.)

+ $3H_2O.$

(Water.)

Second reaction. $2CaS_5$ + CaS_2O_3 + $6HCl$ = $6S_2$
(Calcium Pentasulphide.) (Calcium Thiosulphate.) (Hydrochloric Acid.) (Sulphur.)
+ $3CaCl_2$ + $3H_2O$.
(Calcium Chloride.) (Water.)

Lac sulphuris, made by adding H_2SO_4 to the solution obtained by the first step of the above process; contains a large quantity of $CaSO_4$, which is most objectionable, thus:

Reaction. $2CaS_5$ + CaS_2O_3 + $3H_2SO_4$ = $3CaSO_4$
(Calcium Pentasulphide.) (Calcium Thiosulphate.) (Sulphuric Acid.) (Calcium Sulphate.)
+ $6S_2$ + $3H_2O$.
(Sulphur.) (Water.)

Description. Fine, yellowish-white, amorph. powder; odorless; almost tasteless; insol. water, or alcohol; soluble boiling sol. NaOH, or in CS_2.

Impurities and tests. *Free acid :* + blue litmus paper = red color. *Calcium sulphate :* Boil with dil. HCl; filt. + $BaCl_2$ or $(NH_4)_2CO_3$ = ppt. *Alkalies, alkaline earths,* or *sulphide :* Digest successively with water, HCl, and NH_4OH; evap. filt. from each = residue. *Arsenious acid :* same test as under Washed Sulphur.

HYDROSULPHURIC ACID. (H_2S.)

Made by the action of dil. H_2SO_4 on ferrous sulphide (FeS): the gas H_2S (*Hydrogen sulphide*, or sulphuretted hydrogen) is washed and passed into water and dissolved. $FeS + H_2SO_4 = H_2S + FeSO_4$.

Used as a test for the metals, yielding with their salts characteristic precipitates.

(CS_2—76) CARBONEI BISULPHIDUM.—BISULPHIDE, OR DISULPHIDE OF CARBON.

Made by heating fragments of charcoal or coke to redness, and dropping through a tube to the bottom of the retort, pieces of sulphur, which vaporize and unite with the red-hot charcoal. The condensed liquid contains S in solution, and other impurities.

Purification. Agitation with $Ca(OH)_2$, litharge, mercury, mercuric chloride, or copper sulphate, and distilling the decanted liquid with a bland fixed oil or beeswax, and rectifying repeatedly in a water-bath.

Used as a solvent for fats, essential oils, rubber, etc.

Description. Clear, colorless, highly refractive, very diffusive liquid; strong, characteristic odor; sharp, aromatic taste; neutral reaction; insol. water, sol. in alc., ether, chloroform, fixed and volatile oils. Sp. gr. 1.272. Vaporizes at ordinary temperatures; highly inflammable, burns with blue flame.

Impurities and tests. *Sulphurous acid :* + blue litmus paper = red color. *Sulphur:* + evap. spontaneously = residue. *Hydrogen sulphide:* + lead acetate (sol.) = black ppt.

PHOSPHORUS.

OCCURRENCE. This non-metallic element exists as phosphates in all plants and animals.

Preparation. Calcined bones containing calcium phosphate are treated with H_2SO_4, thereby converting the salt into acid calcium phosphate, while $CaSO_4$ is also formed, thus:

$$Ca_3(PO_4)_2 + 2H_2SO_4 = CaH_4(PO_4)_2 + 2CaSO_4.$$

(Calcium Phosphate.) (Sulphuric Acid.) (Acid Calcium Phosphate.) (Calcium Sulphate.)

The solution of the acid phosphate is evaporated to dryness, after having added charcoal, and the residue distilled in a stoneware retort. The distilled P is condensed under water and run into tubes, and congealed.

Reaction.

$$3CaH_4(PO_4)_2 + 16C = Ca_3(PO_4)_2 + 2P_2$$

(Acid Calcium Phosphate.) (Carbon.) (Calcium Phosphate.) (Phosphorus.)

$$+ 16CO + 12H.$$

(Carbon Monoxide.) (Hydrogen.)

Description. Translucent, nearly colorless solid, of a waxy lustre; of about the consistency of beeswax at ordinary temperatures; distinctive and disagreeable taste and odor (the latter due to *ozone* produced by the decomposition of the air by P), melts at 111.2° F.— Sp. gr. 1.830 at 50° F.; insol. water; sol. in abs. alc. (350), abs. ether (80), fatty oils (50), CS_2, chloroform. Emits white fumes on exposure to air, which are luminous in the dark, with an odor resembling that of garlic. On long exposure to air it takes fire spontaneously. Should be kept under water in a moderately cool, dark place.

Impurities. *Arsenic* (due to the H_2SO_4 used in making it being made from iron pyrites) and *sulphur*. *Dose:* $\frac{1}{60}$ to $\frac{1}{20}$ grain.

Officinal Preparations. 1. Acidum phosphoricum. 2. Oleum phosphoratum. 3. Pilulæ phosphori.

AMORPHOUS PHOSPHORUS, or *red phosphorus*. Made by heating ordinary or vitreous phosphorus for a long time to near its boiling point, in an atmosphere of CO_2. *Non-luminous* and *non-poisonous*.

Oxides of Phosphorus. *Hypophosphorus oxide* (P'_2O) producing *hypophosphorous* acid (H_3PO_2) mono-basic; *phosphorous oxide* (P'''_2O_3), yielding *phosphorous* acid (H_3PO_3) di-basic; and *phosphoric oxide* ($P^v_2O_5$) the source of *orthophosphoric* acid (H_3PO_4), tribasic. *Metaphosphoric* acid is derived by taking one molecule of H_2O from phosphoric acid, thus: H_3PO_4 less $H_2O = HPO_3$; *pyrophosphoric* acid by removing from two molecules of phosphoric acid, one of water, thus: $2H_3PO_4$ less $H_2O = H_4P_2O_7$.

Phosphorous acid and phosphites are rarely, if ever, employed in pharmacy.

(H_3PO_4) ACIDUM PHOSPHORICUM.—PHOSPHORIC ACID.

Preparation. Phosphorus in small pieces is added to a mixture of equal weights of HNO_3 and water, and the mixture gradually heated until reaction commences, the heat being regulated in order to keep the reaction under control. When the phosphorus is entirely dissolved, the excess of HNO_3 is driven off by heating till an odorless, syrupy liquid remains, and on cooling diluted with water to the proper degree of strength. The phosphorus is oxidized by the nitric acid, and with the water forms phosphoric acid.

$$6P_2 + 20HNO_3 + 8H_2O = 12H_3PO_4 + 10N_2O_2.$$
(Phosphorus.) (Nitric Acid.) (Water.) (Phosphoric Acid.) (Nitrogen Dioxide.)

Description.—Colorless, odorless liquid, of a strong acid taste and reaction; sp. gr. 1.347; contains 50% orthophosphoric acid, and 50% water. When heated loses water, and at 392°F. gradually becomes converted into pyro- and meta-phosphoric acids, which may be volatized at a red heat.

If the acid is saturated with NH_4OH, the addition of test mixture of magnesium gives a *white, crystalline* precipitate; this precipitate dissolved in dil. acetic acid yields a yellow precipitate with $AgNO_3$.

Impurities and tests. *Phosphorous acid:* Dil. acid $+ AgNO_3 =$ blk.; or $+ HgCl_2 =$ whitish ppt. *Arsenic acid:* Heat to 158°F. $+ H_2S$, and cool $=$ lemon yellow ppt. *Nitric acid:* $+ FeSO_4$ and H_2SO_4 $=$ brown or reddish zone. *Sulphuric acid:* $+ BaCl_2 =$ white ppt. *Hydrochloric acid:* $+ AgNO_3 =$ white ppt. *Meta-* or *Pyro-phosphoric acid:* $+$ tincture chloride of iron $=$ ppt. after several hours.

The impurities *nitric, phosphorous* and *arsenic acids* may be removed in the following manner: NITRIC ACID: Evaporate till no reaction for nitric acid can be obtained, cool, and replace the loss of water. PHOSPHOROUS ACID: Add nitric acid and distilled water and evaporate till no reaction for phosphorous or nitric acids can be obtained; restore original weight with water. $3H_3PO_3 + 2HNO_3 = 3H_3PO_4 + H_2O + N_2O_2.$ ARSENIC ACID: Dilute, heat to 158°F. and pass H_2S into it for one half-hour; remove the heat, and continue passing the gas into the liquid until cold; filter, heat to drive off excess of H_2S, filter and evaporate to proper degree of strength.

REAGENT.

Tests for:	Solution Albumen.	BaCl₂	CaCl₂	AgNO₃
Pyrophosphoric Acid..	*White ppt.*	*White ppt.*	*White ppt.*	*Transparent gelatinous ppt.*
Metaphosphoric Acid..	*No reaction.*	*No reaction.*	*No reaction.*	*White ppt.*
Orthophosphoric Acid.	*No reaction.*	*No reaction.*	*No reaction.*	*Yellow ppt. Sol. in* NH₄OH.

Officinal Preparations. ACIDUM PHOSPHORICUM DILUTUM.— DILUTED PHOSPHORIC ACID.—Phosphoric acid (20) water (80)—Sp. gr. 1.057—contains 10% orthophosphoric acid. Should be tested for the impurities common to the stronger acid. Unless free from pyrophosphoric acid, a gelatinous precipitate results on adding to tincture of chloride of iron.

OLEUM PHOSPHORATUM.—PHOSPHORATED OIL. Made by dis-

solving 1% P. in expressed almond oil.   The expressed oil of almond
is first heated to 482°F., cooled, and filtered, for the purpose of
removing air and moisture, also certain organic matters are volatilized or destroyed, the oil becoming nearly colorless, separating
a little flocculent matter which is removed by filtration.   The P. is
dissolved by the aid of heat, and on cooling, stronger ether (9) is
added to prevent phosphorescence in the dark.

PILULÆ PHOSPHORI.—PILLS OF PHOSPHORUS.   A solution of P.
in chloroform is added to a mixture of powdered althæa and acacia,
and the mass completed with glycerin and water; after rolling the
pills, they are coated with a solution of tolu in ether, to protect
them from moisture and oxidation.   Chloroform used as a solvent
here, because it is non-inflammable, while its vapor prevents oxidation of P. $\frac{1}{100}$ gr. P. in each pill.   Dose, 1-2 pills.

($Na_2HPO_4.12H_2O-358$)   SODII PHOSPHAS.—PHOSPHATE OF SO-
                                          DIUM.

Preparation.   *Bone-ash* (calcined bones) is treated with H_2SO_4
as in the preparation of phosphorus (see page 114), and the heated
solution of acid calcium phosphate, freed from the precipitated
$CaSO_4$, treated with Na_2CO_3; mono-calcic phosphate precipitates,
CO_2 is given off, and sodium phosphate is in solution; the filtered
liquid is evaporated to crystallization.

Reaction. $CaH_4(PO_4)_2$ + Na_2CO_3 = Na_2HPO_4
(Acid Calcium   (Sodium   (Di-sodic
Phosphate.)   Carbonate.)   Phosphate.)
         + $CaHPO_4$ + CO_2 + H_2O.
(Mono-calcic)   (Carbon   (Water.)
Phosphate.)   Dioxide.)

Description.—Large, colorless, transparent crystals; very effflores-
cent; odorless; cooling, saline and feebly alkaline taste, and a
slightly alkaline reaction; sol. in water (6), insol. alcohol.

Impurities and tests.   *Carbonate:* + acid = effervescence.   *Metals:*
+ H_2S or $(NH_4)_2S$ = ppt.   *Sulphate:* + HNO_3 + $Ba(NO_3)_2$ = ppt.
Chloride: + HNO_3 + $AgNO_3$ = ppt.

($Na_4P_2O_7.10H_2O-446$)   SODII PYROPHOSPHAS.—(PYROPHOSPHATE
                                      OF SODIUM.)

Made by heating sodium phosphate to dull redness, until its solution gives a white precipitate, free from yellow tint, with $AgNO_3$;
dissolve and crystallize.

Reaction. $2Na_2HPO_4$ + Heat = $Na_4P_2O_7$ + H_2O.
Di-sodic   Sodium   (Water.)
(Phosphate.)   (Pyrophosphate.)

Description.—Colorless, translucent prisms; odorless; sweetish,
saline and mildly alkaline taste; feeble acid reaction; sol. in water
(12), insol. alcohol.

Impurities and tests, same as under Sodii Phosphas.

($CaH_4(PO_3)_2-170$)   CALCII HYPOPHOSPHIS.—HYPOPHOSPHITE OF
                                     CALCIUM.

Made by boiling P. with milk of lime ; phosphoretted hydrogen is evolved, and the solution containing calcium hypophosphite is evaporated to crystallization.

$$3Ca(OH)_2 + 4P_2 + 6H_2O = 3CaH_4(PO_2)_2 + 2PH_3.$$
(Calcium Hydroxide.) (Phosphorus.) (Water.) (Calcium Hypophosphite.) (Phosphoretted Hydrogen.)

Description. Colorless, or white crystals, or in scales of a pearly lustre; odorless; nauseous, bitter taste; neutral reaction; soluble in water (6.8), insol. alcohol.

Test for Hypophosphites. 1. When heated they give off water, then evolve spontaneously inflammable PH_3. 2. Mercury is precipitated on adding a solution of mercuric chloride. 3. An acid solution of potassium permanganate is decolorized.

Impurities and tests. *Insoluble calcium salts:* Should be entirely soluble in water. *Soluble phosphates:* + Lead acetate = ppt., or + $BaCl_2$ = ppt. *Magnesium:* See test under Calcium Salts.

Officinal Preparation. SYRUPUS HYPOPHOSPHITUM. (Syrup of Hypophosphites). Contains the hypophosphites of calcium, sodium and potassium; citric acid. sugar, and water—flavored with spirit of lemon. *Dose*, ½ to 1 fluidrachm.

Officinal Preparation. SYRUPUS HYPOPHOSPHITUM CUM FERRO. (Syrup of Hypophosphites with Iron.) Made by dissolving lactate of iron (1) in syrup of hypophosphites (100) by trituration. *Dose* ½ to 1 fluidrachm.

($NaH_2PO_2.H_2O$—106) SODII HYPOPHOSPHIS.—HYPOPHOSPHITE OF SODIUM.

Made by double decomposition of sodium carbonate and calcium hypophosphite: calcium carbonate precipitates, while sodium hypophosphite is in solution, and is obtained by evaporation at a low temperature, and crystallization.

$$CaH_4(PO_2)_2 + Na_2CO_3 = 2NaH_2PO_2 + CaCO_3.$$
(Calcium Hypophosphite.) (Sodium Carbonate.) (Sodium Hypophosphite.) (Calcium Carbonate.)

Description. Small, colorless, or white, rectangular plates, or a white, granular powder; deliquescent; odorless; sweetish, saline taste, and neutral reaction. Sol. in water (1), alcohol (30). On triturating or heating with an oxidizing agent, the mixture explodes.

Impurities and tests. *Carbonate:* + Acid = effervescence. *Calcium:* + $(NH_4)_2C_2O_4$ = white ppt. *Potassium:* + $NaHC_4H_4O_6$ = ppt. *Sulphate:* + $BaCl_2$ = ppt. *Phosphate* (a limit): + test sol. magnesium = white ppt.

(KH_2PO_2—104) POTASSII HYPOPHOSPHIS.—HYPOPHOSPHITE OF POTASSIUM.

Made similar to sodium hypophosphite, by substituting K_2CO_3 for Na_2CO_3 in the preceding process.

Description. White, opaque, confused—crystalline masses, or a white, granular powder; very deliquescent; odorless; sharp, saline, bitterish taste; neutral reaction; sol. in water (0.6), alc. (7.8).

IMPURITIES; same as under Sodium Hypophosphite.

Hypophosphorous Acid (H_3PO_2).   Not officinal.   Used as a solvent for hypophosphites.

Made by the action of oxalic acid on calcium hypophosphite in solution.

Reaction. $CaH_4(PO_2)_2 + H_2C_2O_4 = CaC_2O_4 + 2H_3PO_2.$

$$\underset{\substack{\text{Calcium}\\\text{Hypophosphite.}}}{} \qquad \underset{\substack{\text{Oxalic}\\\text{Acid.}}}{} \qquad \underset{\substack{\text{Calcium}\\\text{Oxalate.}}}{} \qquad \underset{\substack{\text{Hypophosphorous}\\\text{Acid.}}}{}$$

FERRUM.—(FE.—55·9.)

Ferri Chloridum, Fe_2Cl_6 (*grs.* i·v.)
Liquor—S. G. 1.⁴²⁵ (♏. i-v, *in syrup.*)
Tinctura $\begin{cases} \text{Liq. } Fe_2Cl_6 & 35 \\ \text{Alcohol,} & 65 \\ \text{Mix,} & \overline{100} \end{cases}$ (*gtts.* x-xxx)
Mistura Ferri et Ammonii Acet. (f ℥ ss-i.)
Ferri Iodidum Sacch. 20% Fe I_2(*grs.* ii-v.)

Syr. Ferri Iodidi, 10% FeI₂ (*gtts.* x-xl.)
Syr. Ferri Bromidi, 10% FeBr₂ (*gtts.* x-xl.)
Ferri Lactas, $Fe(C_3H_5O_3)_2$ (1 *gr. upwards.*)
Syr. Hypophos. cum Ferro (f ℥ i-ii.)
Ferri Sulphas, $FeSO_4.7H_2O$ (*grs.* i-ii.)

FERRI SULPHAS, $FeSO_4.7H_2O.$

Ferri Sulphas Exsiccatus, $FeSO_4.H_2O.$ Pil. Aloe et Ferri—(*grs.* v-xv.)
Ferri Sulphas Præcipitatus. $FeSO_4.7H_2O.$
Mistura Ferri Comp—f ℥ ss-iss.)
Liq. Ferri Subsulphatis, Fe_4O ($SO_4)_5.$ S. G. 1⁵⁵⁵ (*grs.* v-xv.)

Ferri Carbonas Sacch. 15% $FeCO_3.$ (*grs.* v. *upwards.*)
Massa Ferri Carbonatis (*grs.* iii-v.)
Pilulæ Ferri Comp.—(*pil.* ii-vi.)
Ferri Oxalas, FeC_2O_4—(*grs.* ii-iii.)
Liq. Ferri Tersulph. $Fe_2(SO_4)_3$—S. G. 1.³²⁰.

LIQUOR FERRI TERSULPHATIS, $FE_2(SO_4)_3.$

Ferri Oxidum Hydratum, $Fe_2(OH)_6.$
Ferrum Reductum—(*grs.* iii-v.)
Pil. Ferri Iodidi—(*grs.* iii-viii.)
Emplastrum Ferri—10% $Fe_2(OH)_6.$
Trochisci Ferri—5% $Fe_2(OH)_6$ (i-vi.)
Ferri Oxidum Hydratum cum Magnesia.
Ferri et Ammon. Sulph. $Fe_2(NH_4)_2$ ($SO_4)_4.24H_2O$ (*grs.* v-xv.)
Ferri et Ammon. Tartras (*grs.* x-xxx.)
Ferri et Potassii Tartras (*grs.* x-xxx.)
Ferri Hypophosphis, $Fe_2(H_2PO_2)_6$ (*grs.* iv-xii.)
Liq. Ferri Nitratis, $Fe_2(NO_3)_6$ S. G. 1.²⁵² contains 6% salt (*gtts.* vii-viii.)
Liq. Ferri Acetatis, $Fe_2(C_2H_3O_2)_6$— S. G. 1.¹⁶⁰ (♏ ii-vi.)
Tinctura—(*gtts.* xx-f ℥ i.)
Ferri Valerianas, $Fe_2(C_3H_9O_2)_6.$ (1 *gr. upwards.*)

Liq. Ferri Citratis, $Fe_2(C_6H_5O_7)_2$ S. G. 1.²⁵² (*grs.* v-xx.)
Ferri et Ammon. Citras (*grs.* v *upwards.*)
Vinum Ferri Citratis—(f ℥ i.)
Liq. Ferri et } 6% Quinine.
Quin. Cit. } Dose: (♏.x-xx.)
Vinum Ferri Amarum (f ℥ ii-iv.)
Ferriet Strych. } 1% Strychnine.
Citras, } Dose: (*grs.* iii-v.)
Ferri Citras, $Fe_2(C_6H_5O_7)_26H_2O$ (*grs.* v.)
Ferri et Quini- } 12% Quinine
næ Citras } (*grs.* v-vi.)
Ferri Phosphas, $Fe_2(PO_4)_2$ (*grs.* v-x.)
Syr. Ferri et Quin. et Strych. Phos. (f ℥ i.)
Ferri Pyrophosphas, $Fe_4(P_2O_7)_3$ (*grs.* ii-v.)

FERRUM—IRON.

Metallic iron in the form of fine, bright and non-elastic wire.

CARD-TEETH, represents iron in one of its purest forms, and is extensively employed in the manufacture of its preparations.

TESTS FOR IRON SALTS. 1. *Ferric* salts with potassium ferrocyanide produce a deep blue color (Prussian Blue) at once; *ferrous* salts yield a bluish-white precipitate gradually changing to a pale blue. 2. *Ferrous* salts give a deep blue color (Turnbull's Blue) with potassium ferricyanide; *ferric* salts strike a greenish or olive color. 3. Water of ammonia with *ferrous* salts gives a white precipitate of *ferrous* hydroxide, gradually becoming green, then black and brown; with *ferric* salts, a brown precipitate of *ferric* hydroxide results. 4. Ammonium sulphide give a black precipitate with iron salts. 5. Sulphocyanide of potassium strikes a blood-red color with *ferric* salts. 6. With *ferric* salts, tannic acid produces a greenish black precipitate (ink); no reaction with *ferrous* salts, that have not been oxidized.

$(Fe_2Cl_6.12H_2O—540.2)$ FERRI CHLORIDUM.—CHLORIDE OF IRON.

(Ferric Chloride. Sesqui-chloride of Iron.)

Made by treating iron wire with dilute HCl, allowing the mixture to stand till effervescence ceases, boiling and filtering, thus producing a solution of ferrous chloride ($FeCl_2$), hydrogen being evolved.

Reaction. $Fe + 2HCl = FeCl_2 + 2H.$
(Iron.)   (Hydrochloric Acid.)   (Ferrous Chloride.)   (Hydrogen.)

The ferrous chloride is oxidized to ferric chloride by adding more HCl, and pouring into HNO_3.

$6FeCl_2 + 6HCl + 2HNO_3 = 3Fe_2Cl_6 + N_2O_2 + 4H_2O.$
(Ferrous Chloride.)   (Hydrochloric Acid.)   (Nitric Acid.)   (Ferric Chloride.)   (Nitrogen Dioxide.)   (Water.)

The nitric oxide vapors are driven off by heat, and the solution tested for ferrous salt with ferricyanide of potassium; if a blue color results, HNO_3 is added and the excess evaporated off as before. An excess of HCl is added and the solution set aside till a solid crystalline mass is obtained.

Description. Orange yellow crystalline pieces; very deliquescent; odorless, or faint odor of HCl; styptic taste; freely soluble in water, alc. and ether.

Impurities and tests. *Nitric acid:* $+ FeSO_4 + H_2SO_4 =$ brown zone. *Ferrous chloride :* $+$ potass. ferricyanide = blue color. *Oxychloride:* 1% sol. in water $+$ boil $=$ cloudiness.

LIQUOR FERRI CHLORIDI.—SOLUTION OF FERRIC CHLORIDE.

(Solution Sesqui chloride of Iron.)

Made by the process used for Ferri Chloridum, retaining the salt in the form of a solution.

Description. Reddish-brown liquid; faint odor of HCl; acid styptic taste; acid reaction. Sp. gr. 1.045—contains 37.8% of anhydrous Fe_2Cl_6, and some free HCl. If red brown ppt. forms in this solution, add a few drops of HCl and heat. If colored black, add few drops of HNO_3 and heat to the boiling point.

Impurities and tests, same as given under Ferri Chloridum.

Officinal Preparation. TINCTURA FERRI CHLORIDI. (Tincture of Chloride of Iron.) Contains solution chloride of iron (35), and alcohol (65). Mix, and let stand for three months. During that time several ethereal compounds are produced by the action of the chloride and free HCl on the alcohol. A red-brown ppt. in this preparation denotes a deficiency of HCl; this ppt. is very slowly dissolved on adding HCl.

Officinal Preparation. MISTURA FERRI ET AMMONII ACETATIS. (Mixture of Acetate of Iron and Ammonium. Basham's Mixture.) Contains tinct. chloride iron (2), dil. acetic acid (3), solution ammonium acetate (20), (slightly acid to prevent formation of carbonate of iron) elixir of orange (10), syrup (15), water (50).

FERRI IODIDUM SACCHARATUM. (SACCHARATED IODIDE OF IRON.)

Iodine (17) and iron (6), are combined in the presence of water, forming a green solution of ferrous iodide, which when it has lost its odor of iodine is filtered into a capsule containing sugar of milk (40); evaporate the mixture to dryness, add sugar of milk (40) and powder.

Description. Yellowish-white, or grayish powder; very hygroscopic; odorless; sweet ferruginous taste; slightly acid reaction; soluble in water, partially soluble in alcohol. Contains at least 20% of ferrous iodide (FeI_2), determined by volumetric solution of $AgNO_3$.

Impurity. *Free iodine :* + starch jelly = blue color.

SYRUPUS FERRI IODIDI. (SYRUP OF IODIDE OF IRON.)

A solution of ferrous iodide made as above, is filtered upon sugar, which is disolved in it by the aid of heat, and the finished syrup kept in a place accessible to sunlight. The reaction between iodine and iron is feeble at first, but on the formation of a small quantity of FeI_2, the latter acts as a solvent for more iodine, which combines with the iron so rapidly as to cause a brisk reaction. If violet vapors are given off, the reaction should be somewhat retarded to prevent loss of iodine.

Description. Transparent, pale-green syrupy liquid; ferruginous taste; neutral reaction; contains 10% ferrous iodide (FeI_2), estimated by volumetric solution $AgNO_3$.

SYRUPUS FERRI BROMIDI. (SYRUP OF BROMIDE OF IRON.)

Made in the same manner as syrup of iodide of iron, substituting Br. for I. Resembles syrup of iodide of iron, and contains 10% ferrous bromide ($FeBr_2$).

(Fe $(C_3H_5O_3)_2.3H_2O$—287.9) FERRI LACTAS. LACTATE OF IRON. (Ferrous Lactate.)

Made by the double decomposition between calcium lactate and ferrous sulphate in solution.

Reaction. $Ca(C_3H_5O_3)_2 + FeSO_4 = CaSO_4 + Fe(C_3H_5O_3)_2.$
(Calcium Lactate.) (Ferrous Sulphate.) (Calcium Sulphate.) (Ferrous Lactate.)

Also made by the action of diluted lactic acid on iron, and the subsequent evaporation of the solution to crystallization.

Reaction. Fe + $2HC_3H_5O_3$ = $Fe(C_3H_5O_3)_2$ + H_2.
(Iron.) (Lactic Acid.) (Ferrous Lactate.) (Hydrogen.)

Description. Pale, greenish-white crystalline crusts or grains; odorless ; sweet, ferruginous taste ; feeble acid reaction ; soluble in water, and solution of sodium citrate, alm. ins. alcohol.

Impurities and tests. *Sulphate, tartrate, citrate* (a limit of each): + lead acetate = white cloudiness.

Officinal Preparation. Syr. Hypophosphitum cum Ferro.

($FeSO_4.7H_2O$—277.9) FERRI SULPHAS.—SULPHATE OF IRON. (Ferrous Sulphate.)

Made by the action of diluted H_2SO_4 on iron ; evaporating and crystallizing. The commercial *copperas*, or *green vitriol*, is obtained by the use of an impure H_2SO_4, obtained during the purification of kerosene and other petroleum hydrocarbons, but for pharmaceutical purposes a pure H_2SO_4 should be employed.

Reaction. Fe + H_2SO_4 = $FeSO_4$ + H_2.
(Iron.) (Sulphuric Acid.) (Ferrous Sulphate.) (Hydrogen.)

Description. Large, bluish-green, monoclinic prisms ; efflorescent and absorbing oxygen on exposure to air; odorless ; saline, styptic taste ; acid reaction ; sol. in water (1.8), ins. alcohol.

Impurities and tests. *Copper :* + H_2SO_4 = colored ppt. *Ferric salt* ; + H_2S = white turbidity.

Officinal Preparations. 1. Ferri sulphas exsiccatus. 2. Ferri sulphas præcipitatus.

($FeSO_4.H_2O$—169.99) FERRI SULPHAS EXSICCATUS.—DRIED SULPHATE OF IRON. (Dried Ferrous Sulphate.)

Made by exposing $FeSO_4$ crystals to a moderate heat till effloresced, then heating to 300° F., maintaining at that temperature till it ceases to lose weight, and powdering. 100 parts of the crystal yield 61 parts dried salt.

Description. Grayish-white powder, not entirely soluble in water.

Officinal Preparation. PILULÆ ALOES ET FERRI. (Pills of Aloes and Iron.) Each contains powd. purified aloes 1 gr., dried $FeSO_4$ 1 gr., aromatic powder and confection of roses.

($FeSO_4.7H_2O$—277.9) FERRI SULPHAS PRÆCIPITATUS.—(PRECIPITATED SULPHATE OF IRON. (Precipitated Ferrous Sulphate.)

Made by dissolving $FeSO_4$ in water containing H_2SO_4 (to dissolve any oxidized portion) and pouring into an equal volume of alcohol ; drain the precipitated crystals, wash with alcohol till the washings cease to redden litmus, and dry.

Description. Pale, bluish-green crystalline powder, efflorescent in dry air; gradually oxidized in moist air ; odorless ; styptic, saline taste ; acid reaction.—Solubility, etc., as Ferri Sulphas.

MISTURA FERRI COMPOSITA. COMPOUND IRON MIXTURE. (Griffith's Mixture.)

Contains $FeSO_4$ (6), powd. myrrh (18), sugar (18), K_2CO_3(8), spirit of lavender (50), rose water (900). Should be freshly made when wanted for use. The reaction between the iron and potassium salts produce insoluble ferrous carbonate and potassium sulphate, the former being held in suspension in the myrrh emulsion.

Reaction. $FeSO_4 + K_2CO_3 = FeCO_3 + K_2SO_4.$
(Ferrous Sulphate.) (Potassium Carbonate.) (Ferrous Carbonate.) (Potassium Sulphate.)

($FeCO_3$ + Sugar) FERRI CARBONAS SACCHARATUS.—SACCHARATED FERROUS CARBONATE.

Made by the mutual decomposition between $FeSO_4$ and $NaHCO_3$ both in solution; the precipitated ferrous carbonate, freed from Na_2SO_4 by repeated washings with boiled water, is preserved by mixing with powd. sugar, quickly evaporated to dryness and powdered. The following reaction occurs:

$FeSO_4 + 2NaHCO_3 = FeCO_3 + Na_2SO_4 + H_2O + CO_2.$
(Ferrous Sulphate.) (Acid Sodium Carbonate.) (Ferrous Carbonate.) (Sodium Sulphate.) (Water.) (Carbon Dioxide.)

This process should be conducted with the exclusion of air (as far as possible), hence the occasion for using boiled water in washing the precipitate, and the subsequent quick evaporation.

Description: Greenish-gray powder; oxidizing on contact with air; odorless; sweetish, ferruginous taste; neutral reaction; partially sol. in water, wholly in dilute HCl, giving off CO_2; should contain at least 15% of $FeCO_3$.

Impurity. *Sulphate* (a limit): $+BaCl_2$ = white ppt.

MASSA FERRI CARBONATIS. (Mass of Carbonate of Iron. Vallet's Mass.) Precipitated $FeCO_3$ is obtained by the double decomposition between $FeSO_4$ and Na_2CO_3 (both in solution); the precipitate is washed with syrup and water to prevent oxidation, then mixed with honey and sugar and evaporated to the required weight.

Reaction. $FeSO_4 + Na_2CO_3 = FeCO_3 + Na_2SO_4.$
(Ferrous Sulphate.) (Sodium Carbonate.) (Ferrous Carbonate.) (Sodium Sulphate.)

Description. Greenish-gray mass, changing on exposure to greenish-black. Contains about 40% $FeCO_3$

PILULÆ FERRI COMPOSITÆ. (Compound Pills of Iron. Griffith's Pills.) Each pill contains powd. myrrh 1½ grs., Na_2CO_3, ⅔ gr., $FeSO_4$, ⅔ gr., and syrup. $FeCO_3$ is produced in this pill by the reaction between the two chemical salts present.

($FeC_2O_4 . H_2O$—161.9) FERRI OXALAS.—OXALATE OF IRON. (Ferrous Oxalate.)

Made by decomposing a solution of ferrous sulphate with oxalic acid in solution, collecting, washing and drying the precipitate.

Reaction. $H_2C_2O_4 + FeSO_4 = FeC_2O_4 + H_2SO_4.$
(Oxalic Acid.) (Ferrous Sulphate.) (Ferrous Oxalate.) (Sulphuric Acid.)

Description. Yellow, crystalline powder; odorless; decomposed by heat in contact with air; slightly sol. in hot and cold water.

Liquor Ferri Subsulphatis.—Solution of Subsulphate of Iron. (Solution of Basic Ferric Sulphate. Monsel's Solution.)

Preparation. A mixture of H_2SO_4, HNO_3 and water, is heated to the boiling-point, and $FeSO_4$ crystals added in portions; a black color results from the combination of N_2O_2 (nitric oxide) with $FeSO_4$, which disappears as fast as the latter dissolves in the liquid, with effervescence and the evolution of reddish-brown fumes of N_2O_2. Boiling is continued until the latter is driven off and the liquid assumes a ruby-red tint; water is added to make the required weight.

Description. Dark, reddish-brown, almost syrupy liquid. Sp. gr. 1.555, containing 43.7% of basic ferric sulphate or oxysulphate $(Fe_4O(SO_4)_5$ or $5(Fe_2(SO_4)_3Fe_2(OH)_6$. Almost odorless; extremely astringent taste; free from causticity; acid reaction; miscible in all proportions with water and alcohol.

Test to distinguish from solution tersulphate of iron. Mix with one half its volume of conc. H_2SO_4; the mixture becomes a solid white mass on standing. Solution of tersulphate of iron yields a clear liquid with conc. H_2SO_4.

Impurities and tests. *Nitric acid:* $+ FeSO_4 + H_2SO_4 =$ brown-black zone. *Ferrous salt:* $+$ potass. ferricyanide = blue color.

Solution of Subsulphate of Iron is to be dispensed when Solution of Persulphate of Iron is ordered by the physician. The *tersulphate* or *normal ferric sulphate* is, however, the *true* persulphate.

Liquor Ferri Tersulphatis.—Solution of Tersulphate of Iron. (Solution of Normal Ferric Sulphate.)

Preparation. The only difference in the method of preparation and product obtained, between this solution and solution of subsulphate of iron, is in the quantity of H_2SO_4 employed; this preparation containing more, in order to form a normal ferric sulphate.

$$6FeSO_4 + 2HNO_3 + 3H_2SO_4 = 3Fe_2(SO_4)_3 + N_2O_2 + 4H_2O.$$
$\begin{pmatrix}\text{Ferrous}\\\text{Sulphate.}\end{pmatrix}$ $\begin{pmatrix}\text{Nitric}\\\text{Acid.}\end{pmatrix}$ $\begin{pmatrix}\text{Sulphuric}\\\text{Acid.}\end{pmatrix}$ $\begin{pmatrix}\text{Ferric}\\\text{Sulphate.}\end{pmatrix}$ $\begin{pmatrix}\text{Nitrogen}\\\text{Dioxide.}\end{pmatrix}$ (Water.)

Description. Dark, reddish-brown liquid. Sp. gr. 1.320. Miscible with water and alcohol in any proportions; contains 28.7% of normal ferric sulphate $Fe_2(SO_4)_3$.

Impurities. Same as under Liq. Ferri Subsulphatis.

$(Fe_2(OH)_6$—213.8) Ferri Oxidum Hydratum.—Hydrated Oxide of Iron. (Ferric Hydroxide.)

Prepared by precipitation from diluted solution of tersulphate of iron, by pouring it into water of ammonia, and after washing the precipitate till the washings give no reaction with $BaCl_2$, drain and mix with water, the latter preventing decomposition for a time.

$$Fe_2(SO_4)_3 + 6NH_4OH = 3(NH_4)_2SO_4 + Fe_2(OH)_6.$$
$\begin{pmatrix}\text{Ferric}\\\text{Sulphate}\end{pmatrix}$ $\begin{pmatrix}\text{Ammonium}\\\text{Hydroxide.}\end{pmatrix}$ $\begin{pmatrix}\text{Ammonium}\\\text{Sulphate.}\end{pmatrix}$ $\begin{pmatrix}\text{Ferric}\\\text{Hydroxide.}\end{pmatrix}$

Description. Brown-red magma, soluble in HCl without effervescence.

On account of the occasional use of this preparation as an **Antidote for arsenical poisoning**, the ingredients for preparing it should always be kept on hand in bottles holding respectively 10 Troy ozs. of solution of tersulphate of iron, and 8 Troy ozs. water of ammonia.

Officinal Preparations. 1. Trochisci Ferri (Iron Troches), each containing 5 grs. dry $Fe_2(OH)_6$, flavored with vanilla.

2. Emplastrum Ferri (Chalybeate pl., Strengthening pl., Iron pl., Emplastrum Roborans) contains dried $Fe_2(OH)_6$ (10), Canada turpentine (10), Burgundy pitch (10), and lead plaster (70).

FERRUM REDUCTUM.—REDUCED IRON.

Made by heating $Fe_2(OH)_6$ in a reduction-tube so arranged that a stream of dry hydrogen gas is constantly passed over it. The high temperature attained changes the iron salt to ferric oxide, and the H takes away its oxygen, leaving almost pure iron in powder.

Reactions. 1. $\underset{\left(\substack{\text{Ferric} \\ \text{Hydroxide.}}\right)}{Fe_2(OH)_6}$ + Heat = $\underset{\left(\substack{\text{Ferric} \\ \text{Oxide.}}\right)}{Fe_2O_3}$ + $\underset{\text{(Water.)}}{3H_2O.}$

2. $\underset{\left(\substack{\text{Ferric} \\ \text{Oxide.}}\right)}{Fe_2O_3}$ + $\underset{\text{(Hydrogen.)}}{3H_2}$ = $\underset{\text{(Iron.)}}{Fe_2}$ + $\underset{\text{(Water.)}}{3H_2O.}$

Description. Very fine, grayish-black, lustreless powder; odorless; tasteless; insol. in water or alc. Should contain at least 88% of metallic iron.

PILULÆ FERRI IODIDI.—PILLS OF IODIDE OF IRON.

Contain reduced iron, iodine, powdered licorice, sugar, extract of glycyrrhiza, acacia, and water. Coated with balsam tolu from an ether solution to prevent oxidation. Each pill contains ferrous iodide 1 gr. and reduced iron 0.2 gr.

FERRI OXIDUM HYDRATUM CUM MAGNESIA.—HYDRATED OXIDE OF IRON WITH MAGNESIA.

Dilute solution of tersulphate of iron 65 Gms., with twice its weight of water; make a thin mixture of magnesia by rubbing 10 Gms. with one liter of water. The liquids are to be kept separate, and when the preparation is wanted for use, add the magnesia mixture to the iron solution, shaking until a homogeneous mass results.

$\underset{\left(\substack{\text{Ferric} \\ \text{Sulphate.}}\right)}{Fe_2(SO_4)_3}$ + $\underset{\text{(Magnesia.)}}{3MgO}$ + $\underset{\text{(Water.)}}{3H_2O}$ = $\underset{\left(\substack{\text{Ferric} \\ \text{Hydroxide.}}\right)}{Fe_2(OH)_6}$ + $\underset{\left(\substack{\text{Magnesium} \\ \text{Sulphate.}}\right)}{3MgSO_4.}$

Use as an Antidote. If freshly made and quickly administered in large doses, this preparation is without doubt a better antidote for arsenic than ferric hydroxide alone, as the $MgSO_4$ formed in the double decomposition acts as a cathartic to remove the arseniate of iron produced, and is less irritating than $(NH_4)_2SO_4$ formed in the other preparation.

$(Fe_2(NH_4)_2(SO_4)_4.24H_2O—963.8)$ FERRI ET AMMONII SULPHAS.— AMMONIO-FERRIC SULPHATE. (Ammonio-ferric Alum.)

Made by dissolving ammonium sulphate in a boiling-hot solution of ferric sulphate, cooling the liquid and crystallizing (see Alums).

Reaction. $Fe_2(SO_4)_3 + (NH_4)_2SO_4 = Fe_2(NH_4)_2(SO_4)_4.$
(Ferric Sulphate.) (Ammonium Sulphate.) (Ammonio-Ferric Sulphate.)

Description. Pale-violet octahedral crystals, efflorescent; odorless; acid, styptic taste; slight acid reaction; sol. in water, ins. alcohol.

Impurity (or adulteration). *Aluminium:* + KOH to ppt. iron; filt.+ NH_4Cl (excess) + Heat = white, gelatinous ppt.

$(Fe_2(H_2PO_2)_6—501.8)$ FERRI HYPOPHOSPHIS.—HYPOPHOSPHITE OF IRON. (Ferric Hypophosphite.)

Made by the double decomposition between sodium hypophosphite (free from carbonate to prevent the formation of $Fe_2(OH)_6$) and solution of ferric chloride or sulphate (free from excess of acid to prevent the hypophosphite from remaining in solution). The precipitate is washed and dried at a moderate heat.

$Fe_2(SO_4)_3 + 6NaH_2PO_2 = Fe_2(H_2PO_2)_6 + 3Na_2SO_4.$
(Ferric Sulphate.) (Sodium Hypophosphite.) (Ferric Hypophosphite.) (Sodium Sulphate.)

May also be made from $FeSO_4$ and $CaH_4(PO_2)_2$, forming *ferrous* hypophosphite in solution, and converted by heat to the *ferric* salt.

Description. White, or grayish-white powder; odorless; nearly tasteless; sl. sol. in water; more so in the presence of hypophosphorous acid; freely sol. in HCl and sodium citrate, forming a green solution with the latter.

Impurities and tests. *Ferric phosphate:* + acetic acid=residue. *Calcium:* + acetic acid (ft. sol.)+$(NH_4)_2C_2O_4$ = white ppt. sol. in HCl.

LIQUOR FERRI NITRATIS. — SOLUTION OF NITRATE OF IRON. (Solution of Ferric Nitrate.)

Made by preparing $Fe_2(OH)_6$, dissolving it in HNO_3 and adding water.

Reaction. $Fe_2(OH)_6 + 6HNO_3 = Fe_2(NO_3)_6 + 6H_2O.$
(Ferric Hydroxide.) (Nitric Acid.) (Ferric Nitrate.) (Water.)

Description. Transparent, amber-colored, or reddish liquid; odorless; having an acid, strongly styptic taste; acid reaction. Sp. gr. 1.050; contains 6% of anhydrous $Fe_2(NO_3)_6$.

LIQUOR FERRI ACETATIS. — SOLUTION OF ACETATE OF IRON. (Solution of Ferric Acetate.)

Prepare $Fe_2(OH)_6$, and after removing water by powerful expression, dissolve in glacial acetic acid.

Reaction. $Fe_2(OH)_6 + 6HC_2H_3O_2 = Fe_2(C_2H_3O_2)_6 + 6H_2O$
(Ferric Hydroxide.) (Acetic Acid.) (Ferric Acetate.) (Water.)

Description. Dark, red-brown, transparent liquid; sp. gr. 1.160; contains 33% anhydrous $Fe_2(C_2H_3O_2)_6$; acetous odor; sweetish, styptic taste; acid reaction.

Impurities and tests. *Zinc:* Precip. iron from sol.: filt. $+ H_2S =$ white ppt. *Fixed Alkalies:* Precip. iron by NH_4OH; filt.$+$ evap. $+$ ignition $=$ residue.

Officinal Preparation. TINCTURA FERRI ACETATIS. (Tinct. Ferric Acetate.) Solution acetate of iron (50), add to a mixture of alcohol (30) and acetic ether (20). Sp. gr. 0.950. Liable to decompose, giving a red-brown ppt. insol. in acetic acid.

$Fe_2(C_5H_9O_2)_6$—717.8) FERRI VALERIANAS.—VALERIANATE OF IRON. (Ferric Valerianate.)

Made by double decomposition, employing solutions of ferric sulphate and sodium valerianate; the iron salt precipitating, with sodium sulphate in solution.

$$6NaC_5H_9O_2 + Fe_2(SO_4)_3 = 3Na_2SO_4 + Fe_2(C_5H_9O_2)_6.$$
$$\begin{pmatrix}\text{Sodium}\\\text{Valerianate.}\end{pmatrix} \quad \begin{pmatrix}\text{Ferric}\\\text{Sulphate.}\end{pmatrix} \quad \begin{pmatrix}\text{Sodium}\\\text{Sulphate.}\end{pmatrix} \quad \begin{pmatrix}\text{Ferric}\\\text{Valerianate.}\end{pmatrix}$$

Description. Dark, tile-red, amorph. powder; faint odor of valerianic acid; mildly, styptic taste; insol. in water. sol. in alcohol; decomposed by boiling water, setting free valerianic acid, leaving $Fe_2(OH)_6$. Rarely used in pharmacy.

LIQUOR FERRI CITRATIS.—SOLUTION OF CITRATE OF IRON. (Solution of Ferric Citrate.)

Freshly prepared $Fe_2(OH)_6$ is dissolved by the addition of citric acid crystals heating to 140° F.; the liquid is filtered and concentrated by evaporation.

Reaction. $Fe_2(OH)_6 + 2H_3C_6H_5O_7 = Fe_2(C_6H_5O_7)_2 + 6H_2O.$
$$\begin{pmatrix}\text{Ferric}\\\text{Hydroxide.}\end{pmatrix} \quad \begin{pmatrix}\text{Citric}\\\text{Acid.}\end{pmatrix} \quad \begin{pmatrix}\text{Ferric}\\\text{Citrate.}\end{pmatrix} \quad \text{(Water.)}$$

Description. Dark-brown liquid; odorless; slight ferruginous taste; acid reaction. Sp. gr. 1.260; contains about 35.5% anhydrous $Fe_2(C_6H_5O_7)_2$.

Impurity (or adulteration). *Tartaric acid:* $+ HCl +$ conc. sol. potass. acetate $=$ cryst. ppt.

Officinal Preparations. 1. Ferri et Ammonii Citras. 2. Ferri Citras.

The Scale Salts of Iron, and their Officinal Preparations.

The interesting and popular compounds comprising the **Scale Salts** (so-called on account of their appearance), may properly be considered as a class, from the fact that the general processes of manufacture are somewhat similar.

They are eight in number, viz.: 1. Ferri et ammonii tartras; 2. Ferri et potassii tartras; 3. Ferri citras; 4. Ferri et ammonii citras; 5. Ferri et quininæ citras; 6. Ferri et strychninæ citras; 7. Ferri phosphas; 8. Ferri pyrophosphas.

Characteristics. The two last occur in bright green scales, while the others are garnet-red, or yellow-brown. With but two exceptions, they are all compound salts, having present besides the iron salt, some alkali salt of citric or tartaric acid which has the property of increasing their solubility; the exceptions are Ferri citras, and Ferri et quininæ citras, these are *very slowly* soluble, while the others are *very* soluble in water, and are deliquescent.

Preparation. Solution of tersulphate of iron is really the starting-point with each salt, the former being the source of the ferric hydroxide, which is employed in its freshly precipitated state for subsequent solution. After obtaining the desired salt in solution, the latter is evaporated at a temperature below 140° F. (*to prevent conversion to ferrous compounds*) to a syrupy consistence, and spread on plates of glass so that when dry, the salt may be obtained in scales. Failure in scaling is usually due to the incomplete saturation of the acid with ferric hydroxide, or to the presence of sulphates in the imperfectly washed hydroxide.

FERRI ET AMMONII TARTRAS.—TARTRATE OF IRON AND AMMONIUM. (Ammonio-ferric Tartrate.)

After preparing ferric hydroxide, it is dissolved in a solution of acid tartrate of ammonium (made by neutralizing tartaric acid with ammonium carbonate and adding another equivalent of tartaric acid), and scaled by the usual method. The possible composition of the double salt may be shown by the following reaction:

$$3Fe_2(OH)_6 + 6NH_4HC_4H_4O_6 = 3Fe_2(NH_4)_2(C_4H_4O_6)_2 + 6H_2O.$$

(Ferric Hydroxide.)   (Acid Ammonium Tartrate.)   (Ammonio-ferric Tartrate.)   (Water.)

Description. Transparent, garnet-red, or yellow-brown scales; slightly deliquescent; odorless; sweet, ferruginous taste; neutral reaction; very sol. in water, insol. alcohol. When deprived of iron by boiling with an excess of solution of potash,* a white crystalline precipitate of potassium bitartrate will be produced on supersaturating the concentrated and cooled filtrate with acetic acid.

Impurities. *Fixed alkalies:* + incineration = residue having alkaline reaction.

FERRI ET POTASSII TARTRAS. TARTRATE OF IRON AND POTASSIUM. (Potassio-ferric Tartrate.)

Made by dissolving potassium bitartrate in a mixture of freshly-prepared ferric hydroxide and water by the aid of heat; a small amount of NH_4OH is added to produce a perfectly and readily soluble salt, scaled by the usual method.

$$Fe_2(OH)_6 + 6KHC_4H_4O_6 = Fe_2K_6(C_4H_4O_6)_6 + 6H_2O.$$

(Ferric Hydroxide.)   (Potassium Bitartrate.)   (Potassio-ferric Tartrate.)   (Water.)

Description. Properties, solvents, etc., resemble tartrate of iron and ammonium.

FERRI ET AMMONII CITRAS.—CITRATE OF IRON AND AMMONIUM. (Ammonio-ferric Citrate.)

Made by adding NH_4OH to a solution of citrate of iron, and scaling by usual method.

---

* *Note.*—The text of the U. S. P. states *solution of soda*, which is doubtless an error.

In composition, it is probably a mixture of ammonio-ferric citrate with ferric oxycitrate.

Description. Transparent, garnet-red scales; deliquescent on exposure to damp air; odorless; saline, mild ferruginous taste; neutral reaction; sol. in water, insol. alcohol.

Impurities. *Fixed alkalies:* + incineration = ash with alkaline reaction.

Officinal Preparations. 1. Vinum ferri citratis; 2. Liquor ferri et quininæ citratis; 3. Ferri et strychninæ citras.

VINUM FERRI CITRATIS.—WINE OF CITRATE OF IRON.

Contains ammonio-ferric citrate (4), tincture of sweet orange-peel (12), syrup (12), and stronger white wine (72).

LIQUOR FERRI ET QUININÆ CITRATIS.—SOLUTION OF CITRATE OF IRON AND QUININE.

Made by adding to a solution of citrate of iron and ammonium, citric acid and quinine, concentrating and adding alcohol.

Description. Dark, greenish-yellow liquid; transparent in thin layers; odorless; bitter, mildly ferruginous taste; slight acid reaction. Contains 6% quinine.

Reaction. On supersaturating the diluted solution with a slight excess of NH_4OH the color deepens and a white curdy precipitate deposits, soluble in ether and answering to the reaction of quinine.

Assay. To 8 grams of solution, add water ft. 30 cm³; introduce it into a glass separator, add a solution of 0.5 grams tartaric acid, then NaOH in excess. Extract the alkaloid by agitation with four successive portions of chloroform, each of 15 cm³. Separate the chloroformic layers, mix them, evaporate and dry residue at 212° F.; it should weigh 0.48 grams.

Explanation. The tartaric acid combining with the soda produces a tartrate of soda which holds the iron in solution, while the excess of soda solution precipitates the quinine, for which chloroform is a ready solvent, not mixing with the watery liquid.

Officinal Preparations. VINUM FERRI AMARUM (Bitter Wine of Iron). Contains solution of citrate of iron and quinine (8); tincture of sweet orange-peel (12), syrup (36), and stronger white wine (44). Each drachm contains nearly one grain of citrate of iron and ammon.

FERRI ET STRYCHNINÆ CITRAS. (Citrate of Iron and Strychnine.)

Preparation. Strychnine dissolved in water with the aid of citric acid (thus producing citrate of strychnine) is added to a solution of citrate of iron and ammonium, and scaled by the usual method.

Description. Similar to ammonio-ferric citrate, except that it has a bitter taste and produces a white precipitate with NH_4OH. Contains 1% of strychnine.

Assay. Dissolve one gram of the salt in 4 cm³ water in a test tube; add one cm³ of liquor potassa, and shake with chloroform; the residue left on evaporating the chloroformic layer will answer to the reaction for strychnine, and weigh about 0.01 gram.

($Fe_2(C_6H_5O_7)_2.6H_2O-597.8$) FERRI CITRAS.—CITRATE OF IRON.
(Ferric Citrate.)

Made by evaporating the officinal solution of citrate of iron, and scaling by the usual method.

Description. Transparent, garnet red scales; not deliquescent; odorless; faint ferruginous taste; acid reaction; very slowly sol. in cold water but readily in boiling water, insol. in alcohol.

Impurities and tests. *Fixed alkalies:* + incineration = ash with alkaline reaction. *Tartaric acid* (adulteration): acidulate with HCl; + $KC_2H_3O_2$ = white ppt.

Officinal Preparations.—FERRI ET QUININÆ CITRAS (CITRATE OF IRON AND QUININE). Made by dissolving citrate of iron in water below 140° F., and dissolving quinine in the solution; subsequently evaporating and scaling.

No definite compound is formed, the quinine not entering into any chemical combination with the iron salt.

Description. Transparent, odorless, thin scales; varying in color from red-brown to yellow-brown; slowly deliquescent; bitter ferruginous taste; acid reaction; slowly but wholly soluble in cold water, more readily so in hot water, insol. in alcohol. Contains 12% of dry quinine.

Assay process, same as for solution of citrate of iron and quinine, except that the same result is derived by the use of one half as much salt as the required amount of solution.

REMARKS. The above salt on account of its exceedingly slow solubility in cold water, is a very undesirable preparation for the use of pharmacists except when desired in pill form, and consequently but little used.

Citrate of Iron and Quinine, containing 10% of quinine, is a *better* preparation. It contains a small amount of ammonium citrate, which renders the salt exceedingly soluble and of a greenish, golden-yellow color.

CITRATE OF IRON, QUININE AND STRYCHNINE.

A soluble non-officinal scale salt, extensively used; containing quinine 10%, strychnine 1%. Color same as the soluble citrate of iron and quinine.

FERRI PHOSPHAS.—PHOSPHATE OF IRON. (Ferric Phosphate.)

Preparation. Citrate of iron is dissolved in water by the aid of heat, and sodium phosphate dissolved in the solution, which is evaporated and scaled. Ferric phosphate and acid citrate of sodium are formed, the latter acting as a solvent for the former.

Reaction.

$$2Na_2HPO_4 + Fe_2(C_6H_5O_7)_2 + 6H_2O$$
(Di-sodic Phosphate.) (Ferric Citrate.) (Water.)

$$= Fe_2(PO_4)_2, 2Na_2H(C_6H_5O_7), 6H_2O.$$
(Ferric Phosphate.) (Acid Sodium Citrate.) (Water.)

The name of this preparation gives no idea as to its composition, ferric phosphate being a white, amorphous, insoluble powder. A better name for the officinal salt might be one of the following, viz.: citro-sodic ferric-phosphate, sodio-ferric citro-phosphate, or, *soluble* ferric phosphate.

Description. Thin, bright green, transparent scales, turning dark on exposure to light; odorless; saline taste; slight acid reaction; sol. in water, insol. alcohol.

Officinal Preparations. Syrupus Ferri, Quininæ et Strychninæ Phosphatum. (Syrup of phosphate of iron, quinine and strychnine. Eaton's Syrup.) Contains phosphate of iron (1.33) quinine (1.33) strychnine (.04) phosphoric acid (8) sugar (60) and water ft. 100.

FERRI PYROPHOSPHAS.—PYROPHOSPHATE OF IRON.
(Ferric Pyrophosphate.)

Made by dissolving sodium pyrophosphate in a solution of citrate of iron, evaporating and scaling.

Reaction.
$$3Na_4P_2O_7 + 2Fe_2(C_6H_5O_7)_2 + 12H_2O$$
(Sodium Pyrophosphate.) (Ferric Citrate.) (Water.)

$$= Fe_4(P_2O_7)_3 . 4Na_3C_6H_5O_7 . 12H_2O.$$
(Ferric Pyrophosphate.) (Sodium Citrate.) (Water.)

This salt like the phosphate is incorrectly named, pyrophosphate of iron being an insoluble white salt, the sodium citrate acting as its solvent. A better name would be *soluble* pyrophosphate of iron; or, sodio-ferric citro-pyrophosphate.

Description. Reactions, and its behavior to solvents, are identical with phosphate of iron, with the following exception: *Test to distinguish from phosphate.* Remove the iron from a solution of the salt by boiling with KOH (in excess); ferric hydroxide precipitates; supersaturate the filtrate with acetic acid, and add solution of silver nitrate,—result a *white ppt.*; under similar conditions the phosphate gives a *yellow ppt.*

DIALYSED IRON. (*Unofficinal.*)

Made by treating solution of ferric chloride with water of ammonia, and dissolving the precipitated magma in solution of ferric chloride; by placing the mixture on a dialysator and subjecting to dialysis, it is freed from ammonium chloride and any free HCl that may be present, a solution of oxychloride of iron remaining, the latter is diluted with water to the sp. gr. 1.047.

Description. A dark-brown liquid, transparent in thin layers; permanent; odorless; tasteless, or slightly acid taste; slightly acid reaction; miscible with water and alcohol in all proportions.

MANGANUM. Manganese. (Mn.—54.)

OCCURRENCE. Found in Nature as an impure oxide; or, in combination with iron, calcium, silica, baryta, zinc, etc., as *pyrolusite, braunnite, franklinite,* and *manganite.*

Tests *for Manganese salts in solution:* 1. Ammonium sulphide solution produces a flesh-colored precipitate (MnS) soluble in acetic acid. 2. Water of ammonia yields a white precipitate ($Mn(OH)_2$) changing to brown.

(MnO_2—86) MANGANI OXIDUM NIGRUM.—BLACK OXIDE OF MANGANESE. (Di- or Per-oxide of Manganese.)

Native crude binoxide of manganese, containing at least 66% of the pure oxide.

Description. Heavy, grayish-black, gritty powder; odorless; tasteless; insol. in water, or alc. Oxygen is evolved at a high heat, and in the presence of HCl with heat, chlorine is given off.

Used in the preparation of Aq. chlori.

($MnSO_4 . 4H_2O$—222) MANGANI SULPHAS.—SULPHATE OF MANGANESE.

Preparation. Binoxide of manganese is heated with charcoal, converting it into a monoxide (MnO), then treated with strong H_2SO_4, heated and evaporated to dryness, then heated to redness to decompose iron sulphate; the residue is dissolved in water, the solution filtered and crystallized.

Description. Colorless, or pale rose-colored crystals; odorless; slightly bitter and astringent taste; faint acid reaction; sol. in water (0.7), insol. in alcohol.

Impurities, to be tested for, are zinc, iron, copper, alkalies and magnesium.

($K_2Mn_2O_8$—314) POTASSII PERMANGANAS.—PERMANGANATE OF POTASSIUM.

Made by fusing KOH with MnO_2 and $KClO_3$.

Reaction.
$$6KOH + 3MnO_2 + KClO_3 = 3K_2MnO_4$$
$$\text{(Potassium Hydroxide.)} \quad \text{(Manganese Dioxide.)} \quad \text{(Potassium Chlorate.)} \quad \text{(Potassium Manganate.)}$$
$$+ KCl + 3H_2O.$$
$$\text{(Potassium Chloride.)} \quad \text{(Water.)}$$

The resulting green mass is boiled in water to decompose the potassium manganate formed, yielding a purple solution containing potassium permanganate and KOH, while MnO_2 is deposited.

$$3K_2MnO_4 + 2H_2O = K_2Mn_2O_8 + MnO_2 + 4KOH.$$
$$\text{(Potassium Manganate.)} \quad \text{(Water.)} \quad \text{(Potassium Permanganate.)} \quad \text{(Manganese Dioxide.)} \quad \text{(Potassium Hydroxide.)}$$

The KOH is neutralized by the addition of H_2SO_4, MnO_2 removed by filtration through asbestos, and on crystallizing the $K_2Mn_2O_8$ is obtained, while KCl and K_2SO_4 remain in the mother liquor.

Description. Deep, purple-violet, needle-shaped rhombic prisms: unchangeable in air; neutral reaction; odorless; sweet, astringent taste; Sol. in water (20); decomposed by alcohol. When heated to redness, oxygen is given off. The rose color of its solution is destroyed by the addition of organic substances, with the formation of a brown precipitate, soluble in dilute H_2SO_4 forming a colorless liquid. On mixing a solution of the salt with glycerin, syrup, or other solutions of organic matter in a closed vessel, a similar decomposition results followed by explosion.

Impurities and test. *Nitrate:* Make colorless solution by addition of oxalic acid, and dil. H_2SO_4 and treat with solution $FeSO_4$ in H_2SO_4 = brown zone. *Chloride:* The above colorless solution + $AgNO_3$ = white ppt. *Sulphate* (a limit allowed).

Properties. Permanganate of potassium is a great disinfectant, deodorizer, and oxidizing agent, and hence *should not be triturated nor combined in solution with organic or readily oxidizable substances.*

When desired in pill form the following excipients may be employed with safety; vaseline, cocoa butter, kaolin, kaolin with resin cerate, etc. This salt is often used for purifying water, and rendering it palatable by adding the solution by drops until its color ceases to be destroyed.

Other Salts of Manganese. (unofficinal) Iodide of manganese; occasionally employed in the form of a syrup, and the Hypophosphite in certain preparations of Syrup Hypophosphites Co.

ARGENTUM. Silver. (Ag.—107.7).

Occurrence. Found native as *silver glance* (sulphide); *horn-silver* (chloride), and combined with lead in *galena.*

Description. A brilliant, white metal; very ductile, and malleable; Sp. gr. 10.5; soluble in HNO_3 forming silver nitrate, which is the starting-point of the other salts. Metallic silver is used in the form of *silver leaf* for coating pills.

The salts are so easily decomposed and reduced to the metallic state, that their preservation in dark, amber-colored vials should be observed.

Test *for Silver salts.* With hydrochloric acid a white precipitate of silver chloride results, soluble in NH_4OH, and re-precipitated by HNO_3.

($AgNO_3$—169.7) Argenti Nitras.—Nitrate of Silver.

Made by dissolving silver in nitric acid, and crystallizing.

Reaction. $\underset{\text{(Silver.)}}{6Ag} + \underset{\substack{\text{(Nitric} \\ \text{Acid.)}}}{8HNO_3} = \underset{\substack{\text{(Silver} \\ \text{Nitrate.)}}}{6AgNO_3} + \underset{\substack{\text{(Nitrogen} \\ \text{Dioxide.)}}}{N_2O_2} + \underset{\text{(Water.)}}{4H_2O}.$

Description. Colorless, transparent crystals; becoming grayish-black on exposure to light in the presence of organic matter; sol. in water (0.8), alcohol (26).

It has a very caustic action on the skin, and is a highly corrosive poison when taken internally. *Dose.* One eighth to one fourth grain.

Antidote. NaCl, which produces an insoluble chloride.

Impurities and tests. *Copper:* + NH_4OH = blue color. *General foreign metallic impurities:* Solution + HCl; filtrate + evap. = residue.

Officinal Preparations. Argenti nitras dilutus. Argenti nitras fusus.

ARGENTI NITRAS DILUTUS.—MITIGATED NITRATE OF SILVER.
(Diluted Nitrate of Silver.)
Made by melting together equal parts of $AgNO_3$ and KNO_3, casting into suitable moulds and cooling.
Description. White, hard solid, in the form of pencils or cones.

ARGENTI NITRAS FUSUS.—MOULDED NITRATE OF SILVER.
(Lunar Caustic.)
Made by melting $AgNO_3$ (100) and adding HCl (4), heating until nitrous vapors cease to be evolved, and casting into suitable moulds. The resulting product contains 5% of silver chloride, which renders it less fragile.
Impurities and tests. *Copper:* $+ NH_4OH =$ blue color.
Possible adulterations. KNO_3 or other alkaline salts: On reducing to a fine powder with twice its weight of sugar and igniting, the ash produced will impart a saline or alkaline taste.

(Ag₂O—231.4). ARGENTI OXIDUM. (OXIDE OF SILVER.)
Made by precipitating a solution of silver nitrate with KOH, washing and drying the precipitate.
Reaction. $2AgNO_3 + 2KOH = Ag_2O + 2KNO_3 + H_2O.$
$\begin{pmatrix} \text{Silver} \\ \text{Nitrate.} \end{pmatrix}$ $\begin{pmatrix} \text{Potassium} \\ \text{Hydroxide.} \end{pmatrix}$ $\begin{pmatrix} \text{Silver} \\ \text{Oxide.} \end{pmatrix}$ $\begin{pmatrix} \text{Potassium} \\ \text{Nitrate.} \end{pmatrix}$ (Water.)
Description. Brown, or brownish black powder; feeble alkaline reaction; sl. sol. in water, insol. in alcohol; when freshly prepared soluble in NH_4OH, leaving a black powder called *fulminating silver*, which is violently explosive. *Caution:* Should not be triturated with readily oxidizable or combustible substances, and should not be brought in contact with ammonia; hence the use of any saccharine substance as an excipient (when the oxide is desired in pill form) is not allowable.

(AgCN—133.7) ARGENTI CYANIDUM.—CYANIDE OF SILVER.
Made by passing HCN gas into a solution of silver nitrate, or by the double decomposition between KCN and $AgNO_3$ in solution; in either case AgCN precipitates, is washed and dried.
Reactions. 1. $HCN + AgNO_3 = AgCN + HNO_3.$
$\begin{pmatrix} \text{Hydrocyanic} \\ \text{Acid.} \end{pmatrix}$ $\begin{pmatrix} \text{Silver} \\ \text{Nitrate.} \end{pmatrix}$ $\begin{pmatrix} \text{Silver} \\ \text{Cyanide.} \end{pmatrix}$ $\begin{pmatrix} \text{Nitric} \\ \text{Acid.} \end{pmatrix}$
2. $KCN + AgNO_3 = AgCN + KNO_3.$
$\begin{pmatrix} \text{Potassium} \\ \text{Cyanide.} \end{pmatrix}$ $\begin{pmatrix} \text{Silver} \\ \text{Nitrate.} \end{pmatrix}$ $\begin{pmatrix} \text{Silver} \\ \text{Cyanide.} \end{pmatrix}$ $\begin{pmatrix} \text{Potassium} \\ \text{Nitrate.} \end{pmatrix}$
Description. White powder, gradually becoming brown on exposure; odorless; tasteless; insol. in water and alcohol.
Officinal Preparation. Diluted hydrocyanic acid.

(AgI—234.3) ARGENTI IODIDUM.—IODIDE OF SILVER.
Made by precipitating a solution of $AgNO_3$ with KI.
Reaction. $AgNO_3 + KI = AgI + KNO_3.$
$\begin{pmatrix} \text{Silver} \\ \text{Nitrate.} \end{pmatrix}$ $\begin{pmatrix} \text{Potassium} \\ \text{Iodide.} \end{pmatrix}$ $\begin{pmatrix} \text{Silver} \\ \text{Iodide.} \end{pmatrix}$ $\begin{pmatrix} \text{Potassium} \\ \text{Nitrate.} \end{pmatrix}$
Description. Heavy, amorphous, light-yellow powder; odorless; tasteless; insol. in water or alcohol.

CUPRUM.—Copper. (Cu—632.).

Occurrence. Found native on the borders of Lake Superior, also as an oxide, phosphate, arseniate, carbonate (*malachite*) and sulphides (*copper pyrites*—Cu_2S, Fe_2S_3). A brilliant metal of reddish color; sp. gr. 8.92; very ductile and malleable.

Tests for Copper Compounds. 1. Water of ammonia produces an intense blue color with dilute solutions of copper salts, or a pale blue precipitate with conc. solutions. 2. Potassium ferrocyanide gives a red-brown precipitate. 3. H_2S and $(NH_4)_2S$ give black precipitates. 4. If a piece of bright steel or zinc is introduced into the solution of a copper salt, it becomes coated with metallic copper. 5. Color of blowpipe flame is green.

Antidote. Albumen.

($Cu(C_2H_3O_2)H_2O$—199.2) CUPRI ACETAS.—ACETATE OF COPPER. (Crystallized Verdigris.)

Made by dissolving verdigris in dilute acetic acid. (Verdigris is the subacetate of copper ($Cu_2O(C_2H_3O_2)_2$)—made by allowing the marc obtained from the wine or cider-press, to undergo acetic fermentation, and placing it between sheets of copper; after a time the verdigris is scraped off) or, by the mutual decomposition between acetate of lead and copper sulphate, subsequently filtering and evaporating to crystallization.

Reaction. $Pb(C_2H_3O_2)_2 + CuSO_4 = Cu(C_2H_3O_2)_2 + PbSO_4.$
    (Lead Acetate.)   (Copper Sulphate.)   (Copper Acetate.)   (Lead Sulphate.)

Description. Deep-green, prismatic crystals; efflorescent; odorless; metallic taste; acid reaction; sol. in water (15), alcohol (135).

($CuSO_4, 5H_2O$—249.2) CUPRI SULPHAS.—SULPHATE OF COPPER. (Blue Vitriol. Blue Stone.)

Prepared from copper pyrites; also by evaporating the water that collects in the copper mines; and by oxidation of the artificially prepared sulphide obtained by placing sulphur upon red-hot sheets of copper. Also formed during the purification of silver; or by dissolving the black scales obtained in coppersmithing in weak sulphuric acid; and by the action of *hot* sulphuric acid on the metal.

Reaction. $Cu + H_2SO_4 = CuSO_4 + H_2.$
    (Copper.)   (Sulphuric Acid.)   (Copper Sulphate.)   (Hydrogen.)

Description. Large, translucent, deep-blue, triclinic crystals; efflorescent; odorless; nauseous metallic taste; acid reaction; sol. in water (2.6), insol. alcohol.

Impurities and tests. *Foreign metals : alkalies,* and *alk. earths :* 5% solution + HCl + H_2SO_4, precip. with H_2S; filt. + evap. = residue.

Test for iron (ferrous) by oxidizing with chlorine, and adding NH_4OH, which precipitates $Fe_2(OH)_6$.

Properties. Astringent, emetic, and poisonous in large doses.

AMMONIATED COPPER, or Ammoniated Sulphate of Copper.

Made by dissolving $CuSO_4$ in NH_4OH; on mixing the solution with alcohol, the blue salt precipitates.

Reaction. $CuSO_4 + 4NH_4OH = Cu(NH_3)_4SO_4 + 4H_2O.$
$\begin{pmatrix}\text{Copper}\\\text{Sulphate.}\end{pmatrix}$ $\begin{pmatrix}\text{Ammonium}\\\text{Hydroxide.}\end{pmatrix}$ $\begin{pmatrix}\text{Ammoniated}\\\text{Copper Sulphate.}\end{pmatrix}$ $\begin{pmatrix}\text{Water.}\end{pmatrix}$

PLUMBUM.—Lead. (Pb.—206.5).

OCCURRENCE. Found in the United States as oxide, carbonate (white lead ore), and most abundantly as *galena*, a sulphide (PbS). The metal is obtained from *galena* by roasting; at first a sulphate is formed through oxidation by the oxygen from air; by the action of more galena on this sulphate, the latter splits up into lead and SO_2.

First reaction. $PbS + Heat + 2O_2 = PbSO_4.$
$\begin{pmatrix}\text{Lead}\\\text{Sulphide.}\end{pmatrix}$ $\begin{pmatrix}\text{Oxygen,}\\\text{from air.}\end{pmatrix}$ $\begin{pmatrix}\text{Lead}\\\text{Sulphate.}\end{pmatrix}$

Second reaction. $PbSO_4 + PbS = Pb_2 + 2SO_2.$
$\begin{pmatrix}\text{Lead}\\\text{Sulphate.}\end{pmatrix}$ $\begin{pmatrix}\text{Lead}\\\text{Sulphide.}\end{pmatrix}$ (Lead.) $\begin{pmatrix}\text{Sulphur}\\\text{Dioxide.}\end{pmatrix}$

Description. A bluish-gray metal; malleable; ductile; sp. gr. 11.4
Tests for Lead Salts. 1. Solutions of the lead salts yield white precipitates, with HCl, H_2SO_4, or potassium ferrocyanide. 2. Yellow precipitates result when tested with iodide or chromate of potassium. 3. H_2S and $(NH_4)_2S$ yield black precipitates. 4. The introduction of metallic zinc or tin into the solution of a lead salt, causes a deposition of metallic lead.
Antidote. Soluble sulphates, producing an insoluble lead sulphate.

(PbO —222.5) PLUMBI OXIDUM.—OXIDE OF LEAD. (Litharge.)

Made by heating the metal in contact with air to a white heat.
Description. Heavy, reddish-yellow powder or scales; odorless; tasteless; insoluble in water or alcohol.
Impurities and tests. *Carbonate:* $+ HNO_3 = $ effervescence. *Zinc, alkalies,* and *alk. earths* (a limit): solution in $HNO_3 + H_2S$; filt. + evap. = residue.
Officinal Preparations. 1. Liquor plumbi subacetatis. 2. Emplastrum plumbi.
RED LEAD. (PbO_4.) This is a higher oxide, made by exposing litharge which has not been fused, to a dull red heat.

EMPLASTRUM PLUMBI.—LEAD PLASTER. (Diachylon Plaster.)

Made by boiling olive oil, litharge, and water together; saponification takes place, producing an insoluble lead soap.
Officinal Preparation. Unguentum Diachylon. Also used as a base in making the following-named plasters: Ammoniac with mercury, asafetida, iron, galbanum, mercurial, opium, resin, and soap.
UNGUENTUM DIACHYLON. (Diachylon Ointment. Hebra's Ointment.) Made by dissolving lead plaster (60) in olive oil (39) by the aid of heat, and adding oil of lavender (1).

$(Pb(C_2H_3O_2)_2.3H_2O—378.5)$　PLUMBI ACETAS.—ACETATE OF LEAD.
(Sugar of Lead.)

Made by dissolving litharge in acetic acid, evaporating, crystallizing, purifying, and re-crystallizing.

Reaction.　PbO　+　$2HC_2H_3O_2$　=　$Pb(C_2H_3O_2)_2$　+　H_2O.
(Lead Oxide.)　　(Acetic Acid.)　　　(Lead Acetate.)　　(Water.)

The *impure brown acetate of lead* is made by suspending sheet-lead in pyroligneous acid.

Description.　Colorless, transparent crystals or scales; efflorescent, and attracting CO_2 on exposure to air; faint acetous odor; sweet astringent, afterward metallic taste; faint acid reaction; sol. in water (1.8), alcohol (8).

Solution of this salt should be effected with *distilled water* only, otherwise a slight turbidity results, due to the formation of carbonate, by the action of the dissolved CO_2 in alimentary waters.

Impurities and tests.　General impurities.　*Copper :* + H_2SO_4; filt. + NH_4OH (excess) = blue color. *Zinc, alkalies, and alk. earths :* Sol. + H_2S; filt. + evap. = residue.

Officinal Preparation.　LIQUOR PLUMBI SUBACETATIS. (Solution of Subacetate of Lead. Goulard's Extract.)　Made by boiling litharge with solution of lead acetate.

Description.　A clear, colorless liquid; sweet, astringent taste; alkaline reaction; precipitates slightly on exposure to air; incompatible with mucilage of acacia; sp. gr. 1.228; contains about 25% subacetate of lead $(Pb_2O(C_2H_3O_2)_2)$.

Officinal Preparations.　1. Liquor Plumbi Subacetatis Dilutus. 2. Ceratum Plumbi Subacetatis.　3. Linimentum Plumbi Subacetatis.

LIQUOR PLUMBI SUBACETATIS DILUTUS. (Diluted Solution of Subacetate of Lead.　Lead Water.)　Made by diluting Goulard's Extract (3) with distilled water (97) previously boiled (to remove air and CO_2) and cooled.

CERATUM PLUMBI SUBACETATIS.　(Cerate of Subacetate of Lead. Goulard's Cerate.)　Made by incorporating Goulard's Extract (20) with camphor cerate (80).　Should be freshly made when needed.

LINIMENTUM PLUMBI SUBACETATIS.　(Liniment of Subacetate of Lead.　Contains Goulard's Extract (40), and Cotton-seed Oil (60) thoroughly mixed.

$((PbCO_3)_2 . Pb(OH)_2—773.5)$　PLUMBI CARBONAS.—CARBONATE
OF LEAD.　(White Lead.)

Made by passing CO_2 into a solution of lead acetate, or by the mutual decomposition between an alkali carbonate and a neutral lead salt, both in solution.

First method.　$3Pb(C_2H_3O_2)_2$　+　$2CO_2$　+　$4H_2O$
(Lead Acetate.)　　　(Carbon Dioxide.)　　(Water.)

$= (PbCO_3)_2 . Pb(OH)_2$　+　$6HC_2H_3O_2$.
(Officinal Lead Carbonate.)　　(Acetic Acid.)

Second method. $3Pb(NO_3)_2$ + $3Na_2CO_3$ + $2H_2O$
$\begin{pmatrix}\text{Lead}\\\text{Nitrate.}\end{pmatrix}$ $\begin{pmatrix}\text{Sodium}\\\text{Carbonate.}\end{pmatrix}$ (Water.)

= $(PbCO_3)_2 . Pb(OH)_2$ + CO_2 + H_2O + $6NaNO_3$.
$\begin{pmatrix}\text{Lead Carbonate.}\\\text{U. S. P.}\end{pmatrix}$ $\begin{pmatrix}\text{Carbon}\\\text{Dioxide.}\end{pmatrix}$ (Water.) $\begin{pmatrix}\text{Sodium}\\\text{Nitrate.}\end{pmatrix}$

Also made by the action of CO_2 from decaying vegetable matter, and acetous vapors, on lead.

Description. Heavy, white powder; odorless; tasteless; insol. in water, or alcohol.

Impurities: *Zinc, alkalies, and alk. earths.* (See Acetate.)

Officinal Preparations. Unguentum Plumbi Carbonatis. (Ointment of Carbonate of Lead.) Contains lead carbonate (10) incorporated with benzoinated lard (90).

(PbI_2—459.7) PLUMBI IODIDUM.—IODIDE OF LEAD.

Made by mutual decomposition between potassium iodide and lead nitrate in solution; the precipitate is collected, washed and dried.

Reaction. $Pb(NO_3)_2$ + $2KI$ = PbI_2 + $2KNO_3$.
$\begin{pmatrix}\text{Lead}\\\text{Nitrate.}\end{pmatrix}$ $\begin{pmatrix}\text{Potassium}\\\text{Iodide.}\end{pmatrix}$ $\begin{pmatrix}\text{Lead}\\\text{Iodide.}\end{pmatrix}$ $\begin{pmatrix}\text{Potassium}\\\text{Nitrate.}\end{pmatrix}$

Lead acetate cannot be substituted for the above nitrate, inasmuch as the double iodide of lead and potassium is formed, which dissolves in the potassium acetate formed in the supernatant liquid.

Description. A heavy, bright yellow powder; odorless; tasteless; neutral reaction; alm. insol. in water and alcohol; sol. in acetates of the alkalies, and NH_4Cl.

Impurities: Same as other lead salts.

Officinal Preparations. Unguentum Plumbi Iodidi. (Ointment of Iodide of Lead.) Incorporate powd. iodide of lead (10), with benzoinated lard (90).

($Pb(NO_3)_2$—330.5) PLUMBI NITRAS.—NITRATE OF LEAD.

(Slow process.) Dissolve lead in warm diluted HNO_3.

(Quick process.) Dissolve litharge or lead carbonate in dil. HNO_3.

First. $3Pb$ + $8HNO_3$ = $3Pb(NO_3)_2$ + N_2O_2 + $4H_2O$.
(Lead.) $\begin{pmatrix}\text{Nitric}\\\text{Acid.}\end{pmatrix}$ $\begin{pmatrix}\text{Lead}\\\text{Nitrate.}\end{pmatrix}$ $\begin{pmatrix}\text{Nitrogen}\\\text{Dioxide.}\end{pmatrix}$ (Water.)

Second. PbO + $2HNO_3$ = $Pb(NO_3)_2$ + H_2O.
$\begin{pmatrix}\text{Lead}\\\text{Oxide.}\end{pmatrix}$ $\begin{pmatrix}\text{Nitric}\\\text{Acid.}\end{pmatrix}$ $\begin{pmatrix}\text{Lead}\\\text{Nitrate.}\end{pmatrix}$ (Water.)

Description. Colorless, transparent, or white crystals; odorless; sweet, astringent, afterwards metallic taste; acid reaction; sol. in water (2), alm. ins. alcohol. Impurities: Same as under Acetate.

CHROMIUM. (Cr.—552.4).

OCCURRENCE. Found in United States and Russia as a mineral, chromate of lead, also as *chrome iron ore* (FeO,Cr_2O_3).

Tests for Chromium Salts. 1. $(NH_4)_2$ S, NaOH, and KOH give green precipitates of chromic hydroxide with solution of chromium salts. 2. Soluble lead salts precipitate yellow chromate of lead.

($K_2Cr_2O_7$—294.8) Potassii Bichromas.—Bichromate of Potassium.

Preparation. *Chrome iron ore* is roasted, powdered and mixed with K_2CO_3 and $CaCO_3$, and the mixture strongly heated in a current of air, thereby oxidizing the iron and chromium oxides to ferric oxide and chromic acid, the latter combining with K_2CO_3 to make neutral potassium chromate, CO_2 being evolved.

Reaction. $2(FeO, Cr_2O_3)$ + $4K_2CO_3$ + $7O$ = $4K_2CrO_4$
(Chrome Iron Ore.) (Potassium Carbonate.) (Oxygen) (Potassium Chromate.)

+ Fe_2O_3 + $4CO_2$.
(Ferric Oxide.) (Carbon Dioxide.)

The above mass is lixiviated with water, which dissolves out the potassium salt, and on adding H_2SO_4 to the solution and evaporating, potassium bichromate crystallizes out.

$2K_2CrO_4$ + H_2SO_4 = $K_2Cr_2O_7$ + K_2SO_4 + H_2O.
(Potassium Chromate.) (Sulphuric Acid.) (Potassium Bichromate.) (Potassium Sulphate.) (Water.)

Description. Large, orange-red, transparent crystals; odorless; bitter, disagreeable, metallic taste; acid reaction; sol. in water (10), insol. in alcohol.

Impurities. *Sulphate :* sol. + HNO_3 + $BaCl_2$ = ppt.

(CrO_3—100.4) Acidum Chromicum.—Chromic Acid.
(Chromic Anhydride.)

Made by the action of H_2SO_4 on potassium bichromate in solution; on standing crystals of chromic acid separate.

$K_2Cr_2O_7$ + $2H_2SO_4$ = $2KHSO_4$ + $2CrO_3$ + H_2O
(Potassium Bichromate.) (Sulphuric Acid.) (Acid Potassium Sulphate.) (Chromic Acid.) (Water.)

Description. Small, crimson, needle-shaped crystals, deliquescent; odorless; having a caustic effect on the skin and other animal tissues; acid reaction; very soluble in water; decomposes with alcohol.

Caution. On contact, triturating or warming with strong alcohol, glycerin, spirit of nitrous ether, or other easily oxidizable substances, it is liable to cause sudden combustion or explosion. At a moderately high temperature it rapidly dissolves all animal tissues immersed in it, including even hair, bone, and teeth.

Impurities: *Sulphuric acid :* 1% sol. + HCl + $BaCl_2$ = white ppt.

CADMIUM. (Cd.—111.8).

Occurrence. Found as a sulphide (*greenochite*), but more frequently combined with zinc ore.

Description. A malleable and ductile metal, having the color of tin; sp. gr. 8.7

There are no officinal preparations of cadmium; the salts are used extensively in photography, and often in medicine. The more important salts follow.

CADMIUM SULPHATE. $(3CdSO_4.8H_2O—767.4)$

Made by the action of dilute H_2SO_4 on cadmium in the presence of HNO_3.

Reaction. $\underset{\text{(Cadmium.)}}{3Cd_2}$ $+$ $\underset{\substack{\text{(Sulphuric} \\ \text{Acid.)}}}{6H_2SO_4}$ $+$ $\underset{\substack{\text{(Nitric} \\ \text{Acid.)}}}{4HNO_3}$ $=$ $\underset{\substack{\text{(Cadmium} \\ \text{Sulphate.)}}}{6CdSO_4}$

$+$ $\underset{\text{(Water.)}}{8H_2O}$ $+$ $\underset{\substack{\text{(Nitrogen} \\ \text{Dioxide.)}}}{2N_2O_2}.$

Description. Colorless crystals; efflorescent; astringent taste; acid reaction; sol. in water or alcohol.

CADMIUM IODIDE. $(CdI_2—365.8)$

Made by the mutual decomposition between potassium iodide and cadmium sulphate.

Reaction. $\underset{\substack{\text{(Cadmium} \\ \text{Sulphate.)}}}{CdSO_4}$ $+$ $\underset{\substack{\text{(Potassium} \\ \text{Iodide.)}}}{2KI}$ $=$ $\underset{\substack{\text{(Potassium} \\ \text{Sulphate.)}}}{K_2SO_4}$ $+$ $\underset{\substack{\text{(Cadmium} \\ \text{Iodide.)}}}{CdI_2}.$

Description. White, flat crystals of a pearly lustre; sol. in water and alcohol.

ZINCUM.—Zinc. $(Zn.—64.9)$.

Occurrence. Found in combination as a silicate (*calamine*), carbonate (*Smithsonite*), or sulphide (*blende*).

Made by roasting the impure carbonate with charcoal in iron retorts, when the zinc distils and is condensed.

Description. A bluish-white metal: sp. gr. 6.9 Officinal in the form of thin sheets, or irregular, granulated pieces.

Impurities and tests: *Arsenic:* $+$ dil. H_2SO_4, the gas evolved blackens paper wet with $AgNO_3$. *Lead iron,* or *copper:* $+ NH_4OH$ (excess) $=$ ppt.

Reactions of the Zinc Salts in Solution:
With ammonium sulphide $=$ a white precipitate (sulphide).
" water of ammonia $=$ white precipitate.
" potassium ferrocyanide $=$ green precipitate.
" potassium ferricyanide $=$ orange precipitate.
" alkali carbonates $=$ white precipitate.

Antidotes. Na_2CO_3; tannic acid: albumen.

General impurities of the zinc salts and tests for their presence: *Lead* or *copper:* Sol. $+ HCl + H_2S =$ dark ppt. *Iron, aluminium, alkaline earths:* Sol. $+ (NH_4)_2CO_3$ (excess) $=$ ppt. *Salts of alkalies* or *alk. earths:* Sol. $+ (NH_4)_2S$; filt. $+$ evap. $+$ ignition $=$ fixed residue.

LIQUOR ZINCI CHLORIDI.—SOLUTION OF CHLORIDE OF ZINC.
(Burnett's Disinfecting Fluid.)

Made by dissolving granulated zinc in HCl, straining the liquid, adding HNO_3 (to oxidize the ferrous chloride formed, due to the iron usually present in zinc) evaporating to dryness and fusing. By re-dissolving in distilled water, and agitating the solution with $ZnCO_3$

the iron is precipitated as a carbonate together with the excess of $ZnCO_3$ added, both of which are removed by filtration.

Reaction. Zn_2 + $4HCl$ = $2ZnCl_2$ + $2H_2$.

      (Zinc.)   (Hydrochloric Acid.)   (Zinc Chloride.)   (Hydrogen.)

Reactions representing the removal of iron :

1. $6FeCl_2$ + $6HCl$ + $2HNO_3$ = $3Fe_2Cl_6$ + N_2O_2

    (Ferrous Chloride.) (Hydrochloric Acid.) (Nitric Acid.) ('Ferric Chloride.) (Nitrogen Dioxide.)

             + $4H_2O$.

              (Water.)

2. Fe_2Cl_6 + $3ZnCO_3$ = $3ZnCl_2$ + $Fe_2(CO_3)_3$.

    (Ferric Chloride.) (Zinc Carbonate.) (Zinc Chloride.) (Ferric Carbonate.)

Description. Clear, colorless, odorless liquid; astringent, sweetish taste; acid reaction; sp. gr. 1.555, contains about 50% of $ZnCl_2$.

($ZnCl_2$—135.7) ZINCI CHLORIDUM.—CHLORIDE OF ZINC.

Made by evaporating a solution of zinc chloride, which has been made in accordance with the requirements for the officinal solution.

Description. White, crystalline powder, or opaque pieces; very deliquescent; odorless; astringent, caustic, saline and metallic taste; acid reaction; very sol. in water or alcohol. General impurities.

(ZnO—80.9) ZINCI OXIDUM.—OXIDE OF ZINC.

Made by driving off the CO_2 from $ZnCO_3$ by heat.

Description. Pale-yellowish, nearly white powder; odorless; tasteless; insol. in water or alcohol; sol. in acids, without effervescence. General impurities.

Officinal Preparations. Unguentum Zinci Oxidi (Ointment of Oxide of Zinc). Contains ZnO (10), thoroughly incorporated with benzoinated lard (90).

($ZnSO_4.7 H_2O$—286.9) ZINCI SULPHAS.—SULPHATE OF ZINC.

(White Vitriol.)

Made by dissolving zinc in dilute H_2SO_4, oxidizing and precipitating any iron salt that may be present, as a carbonate, by the addition of chlorine and $ZnCO_3$.

Reaction. Zn_2 + $2H_2SO_4$ = $2ZnSO_4$ + $2H_2$.

     (Zinc.)   (Sulphuric Acid.)   (Zinc Sulphate.)   (Hydrogen.

Description. Small, colorless, needle-shaped crystals; slowly efflorescent in dry air; sharp, saline, nauseous, metallic taste; acid reaction; sol. in water (0.6), insol. in alcohol. General impurities, and *Chloride:* + $AgNO_3$ = white ppt.

This salt is often confounded with magnesium sulphate, which it somewhat resembles in appearance.

(($ZnCO_3$)$_2$.3Zn(OH)$_2$—546.5) ZINCI CARBONAS PRÆCIPITATUS.—

PRECIPITATED CARBONATE OF ZINC.

Made by precipitating a boiling solution of $ZnSO_4$ with a boiling solution of Na_2CO_3, washing and drying the precipitate. The precipitated $ZnCO_3$ is soluble in excess of Na_2CO_3, also in a solution of

CO_2, hence *boiling* solutions are used to drive off the excess of the latter.

$$5ZnSO_4 + 5Na_2CO_3 + 3H_2O = (ZnCO_3)_2 . 3Zn(OH)_2$$
$$\underset{\left(\substack{Zinc \\ Sulphate.}\right)}{} \quad \underset{\left(\substack{Sodium \\ Carbonate.}\right)}{} \quad \underset{(Water.)}{} \quad \underset{(Zinc\ Carbonate.)}{}$$
$$+ 5Na_2SO_4 + 3CO_2.$$
$$\underset{\left(\substack{Sodium \\ Sulphate.}\right)}{} \quad \underset{\left(\substack{Carbon \\ Dioxide.}\right)}{}$$

Description. White, impalpable powder; odorless; tasteless; insol. in water or alcohol; sol. in acids with copious effervescence. General impurities.

$(ZnC_2H_3O_2)_2.3H_2O$—236.9) ZINCI ACETAS.—ACETATE OF ZINC.

Made by digesting the commercial oxide or carbonate of zinc in diluted acetic acid, boiling the solution, and crystallizing.

Reaction. $\underset{\left(\substack{Zinc \\ Oxide.}\right)}{ZnO} + \underset{(Acetic\ Acid.)}{2HC_2H_3O_2} = \underset{(Zinc\ Acetate.)}{Zn(C_2H_3O_2)_2} + \underset{(Water.)}{H_2O.}$

Description. Soft, white, pearly octahedral tablets or scales; faint acetous odor; sharp, metallic taste; slight acid reaction; sol. in water (3), alcohol (30). General impurities.

$(ZnBr_2$—224.5) ZINCI BROMIDUM.—BROMIDE OF ZINC.

Made by digesting zinc in HBr, or by the mutual decomposition between $ZnSO_4$ and KBr; zinc bromide and potassium sulphate are both formed in solution, and the latter removed by adding alcohol and filtering through asbestos.

First method. $\underset{(Zinc.)}{Zn} + \underset{\left(\substack{Hydrobromic \\ Acid.}\right)}{2HBr} = \underset{\left(\substack{Zinc \\ Bromide.}\right)}{ZnBr_2} + \underset{(Hydrogen.)}{H_2.}$

Second method. $\underset{\left(\substack{Zinc \\ Sulphate.}\right)}{ZnSO_4} + \underset{\left(\substack{Potassium \\ Bromide.}\right)}{2KBr} = \underset{\left(\substack{Zinc \\ Bromide.}\right)}{ZnBr_2} + \underset{\left(\substack{Potassium \\ Sulphate.}\right)}{K_2SO_4.}$

Description. White, granular powder; very deliquescent; odorless; sharp, alkaline, metallic taste; neutral reaction; very sol. in water, or alcohol. General impurities.

$(ZnI_2$—318.1) ZINCI IODIDUM.—IODIDE OF ZINC.

Made by dissolving zinc oxide or carbonate, in hydriodic acid, or by digesting zinc with iodine in water, until the liquid becomes colorless; filter through powdered glass and evaporate.

First reaction. $\underset{(Zinc\ Carbonate.)}{(ZnCO_3)_2 . 3Zn(OH)_2} + \underset{\left(\substack{Hydriodic \\ Acid.}\right)}{10HI} = \underset{\left(\substack{Zinc \\ Iodide.}\right)}{5ZnI_2}$
$$+ \underset{\left(\substack{Carbon \\ Dioxide.}\right)}{2CO_2} + \underset{(Water.)}{8H_2O.}$$

Second reaction. $\underset{(Zinc.)}{Zn} + \underset{(Iodine.)}{I_2} = \underset{(Zinc\ Iodide.)}{ZnI_2.}$

Description. White, granular powder; *very* deliquescent; odorless; sharp, saline taste; acid reaction; very sol. in water, or alcohol. General impurities.

(Zn₃P₂—256.7) ZINCI PHOSPHIDUM.—PHOSPHIDE OF ZINC.

Made by fusing zinc in a current of hydrogen, and introducing vapors of phosphorus.

Description. Small, crystalline, friable fragments of metallic lustre; or a grayish-black powder having faint odor and taste of phosphorus; insol. in water, or alcohol; sol. in HCl, or H_2SO_4.

General impurities.

(Zn(C₅H₉O₂)₂.H₂O—284.9) ZINCI VALERIANAS.—VALERIANATE OF ZINC.

Made by the mutual decomposition between sodium valerianate and zinc sulphate, both in hot solutions; on cooling, the zinc salt crystallizes out; also by dissolving fresh moist zinc carbonate in valerianic acid.

$$2NaC_5H_9O_2 + ZnSO_4 = Zn(C_5H_9O_2)_2 + Na_2SO_4$$

$$\begin{pmatrix}\text{Sodium}\\\text{Valerianate.}\end{pmatrix} \quad \begin{pmatrix}\text{Zinc}\\\text{Sulphate.}\end{pmatrix} \quad \begin{pmatrix}\text{Zinc}\\\text{Valerianate.}\end{pmatrix} \quad \begin{pmatrix}\text{Sodium}\\\text{Sulphate.}\end{pmatrix}$$

or, $(ZnCO_3)_2 . 3Zn(OH)_2 + 10HC_5H_9O_2 = 5Zn(C_5H_9O_2)_2$

(Zinc Carbonate.) (Valerianic Acid.) (Zinc Valerianate.)

$$+ 2CO_2 + 8H_2O.$$

$$\begin{pmatrix}\text{Carbon}\\\text{Dioxide.}\end{pmatrix} \quad \text{(Water.)}$$

Description. Soft, white, pearly scales; odor of valerianic acid; sweet, styptic, and metallic taste; acid reaction; sol. in water 100, alcohol 40.

General impurities, and *Butyrate:* Sol. + copper acetate = ppt.

ARSENIUM.—Arsenic. (As.—74.9)

OCCURRENCE. The metalloid arsenic is found as *native arsenic,* also as *cobaltum* or *fly-stone,* but more frequently as sulphides, *red orpiment,* or *realgar* (As_2S_2), *yellow orpiment* (As_2S_3), *mispickel* ($Fe_2S_2,FeAs_2$).

Preparation. Made by roasting mispickel (*arsenical pyrites*), or by roasting arsenious oxide with charcoal.

Description. Steel-gray, crystalline mass; volatile; sp. gr. 5.73–5.96. When heated in the air it absorbes oxygen and forms arsenious oxide (As_2O_3).

Reactions of Arsenic and its salts.

1. H_2S; with acid solutions of arsenic or its salts, gives a *bright yel'ow precipitate,* soluble in alkalies, but insoluble in HCl.

2. Ammoniacal solution of copper sulphate; produces a *grass-green precipitate* (Scheele's Green), soluble in excess of NH_4OH.

3. Ammoniacal solution of silver nitrate; yields a *lemon-yellow precipitate* (silver arsenite), soluble in excess of NH_4OH.

4. Berzelius' test : On heating in a test tube with charcoal, an *iron-gray mirror of metallic arsenic,* having an alliaceous odor, *deposits* on the tube.

5. Reinch's test: If a strip of bright copper foil is boiled with a solution of arsenic acidulated with HCl, a *deposition of gray metallic arsenic takes place on the copper,* accompanied by bluish spots.

6. Marsh's test: Arseniuretted hydrogen (AsH₃) is evolved on treating test-zinc with the arsenic solution (acidulated with H₂SO₄); *the gas on ignition deposits a brown-black spot of metallic arsenic* upon a piece of porcelain held in the flame, which *dissolves on adding moist chlorinated lime* or solution of chlorinated soda. Antimony compounds yield a similar spot, which remains *unaffected by the hypochlorites.* If the delivery tube through which the gas passes is heated, arseniuretted hydrogen is decomposed and *metallic arsenic is deposited just beyond the point of flame;* antimony deposits just *at the point* of flame.

If *dry H₂S is passed through the tube* after the formation of the mirror, and the tube heated, *the volatilized metal* (arsenic or antimony) *again deposits as a sulphide* with its characteristic color, *yellow* or *orange-red.*

7. Fleitmann's test: Also depends upon the generation of AsH₃, *substituting for the dilute acid, a strong solution of potassa* or *soda* (which prevents the formation of antimoniuretted hydrogen); the evolved AsH₃ produces a black stain on filter paper moistened with silver nitrate solution. Aluminium wire is often used in the above, in place of zinc.

Antidotes for Arsenic poison. After evacuating the stomach by means of emetics or the stomach pump, give freshly precipitated hydrated oxide of iron, hydrated oxide of iron with magnesia, dialysed iron, saccharated carbonate of iron, or, solution of ferric chloride. The following *reaction* with ferric hydroxide is possible:

$$2Fe_2(OH)_6 + As_2O_3 = Fe_3(AsO_4)_2 + Fe(OH)_2 + 5H_2O.$$
(Ferric Hydroxide.) (Arsenious Oxide.) (Ferrous Arseniate.) (Ferrous Hydroxide.) (Water.)

The strength of all officinal arsenical solutions is equivalent to about 1% arsenious acid. Dose, 5–8 minims.

(As₂O₃—197.8) ACIDUM ARSENIOSUM.—ARSENIOUS ACID. (White Arsenic. Arsenious Anhydride. Arsenious Oxide.)

Made from the arsenical ores by roasting; purified by sublimation. The action of water on As₂O₃ produces the true arsenious acid:

$$As_2O_3 + 3H_2O = 2H_3AsO_3.$$

[*Arsenic Oxide* (As₂O₅) is made by the oxidation of As₂O₃ by HNO₃. It is but little used.]

Description.—A heavy white solid, occurring either as an opaque powder, or in glass-like, transparent pieces (when freshly made); odorless; tasteless; faint acid reaction; sol. in water 30–80, dependent on its physical condition; sp. sol. in alcohol. Should contain at least 97% of As₂O₃.

Assay, dependent on the quantity of volumetric solution of iodine it decolorizes, after being dissolved in boiling water by the aid of sodium bicarbonate.

$$As_2O_3 + 2I_2 + 5H_2O = 2H_3AsO_4 + 4HI.$$
(Arsenious Oxide.) (Iodine.) (Water.) (Arsenic Acid.) (Hydriodic Acid.)

Officinal Preparations. 1. Liquor acidi arseniosi. 2. Liquor potassii arsenitis.

LIQUOR ACIDI ARSENIOSI.—SOLUTION OF ARSENIOUS ACID.

Formerly termed Solution of Arsenic Chloride. Made by dissolving arsenious acid (1), in boiling water containing HCl (2), filtering and adding water ft. 100.

No chemical action takes place, as the HCl is merely added as solvent for As_2O_3.

Description. A colorless solution; sp. gr. 1.009; contains 1% As_2O_3, or 4 grs. to each fluid ounce.

[*Valangin's Solution* contains 0.88%, or 1¼ grs. in the fluid ounce.]

Assay, dependent on quantity of volumetric solution of iodine it decolorizes.

LIQUOR POTASSII ARSENITIS.—SOLUTION OF ARSENITE OF POTASSIUM. (Fowler's Solution. Arsenical Solution.)

Made by boiling white arsenic with acid potassium carbonate, and flavoring with compound tincture of lavender.

Reaction. $As_2O_3 + 2KHCO_3 + H_2O = 2KH_2AsO_3 + 2CO_2.$
(Arsenious Oxide.) (Acid Potassium Carbonate.) (Water.) (Potassium Arsenite.) (Carbon Dioxide.)

Description. A reddish liquid, somewhat opalescent; alkaline reaction; sp. gr. 1.009; contains 1% As_2O_3.

Assay. The amount of As_2O_3 is ascertained with iodine, using starch jelly as an indicator, which does not become permanently blue until the *arsenious* is oxidized to *arsenic* acid. (See reaction for assay under *Arsenic.*)

(AsI_3—454.7) ARSENII IODIDUM.—ARSENIOUS IODIDE. (Iodide of Arsenic.)

Made by combining iodine and metallic arsenic by heating gently until liquefied; also made by dissolving As_2O_3 in HI.

Reaction. $As_2O_3 + 6HI = 2AsI_3 + 3H_2O.$
(Arsenious Oxide.) (Hydriodic Acid.) (Arsenious Iodide.) (Water.)

Description. Glossy, orange-red crystalline masses, or scales; neutral reaction; odor and taste of iodine; sol. in water (8.5), alcohol (10), ether, and CS_2.

Officinal Preparation. LIQUOR ARSENII ET HYDRARGYRI IODIDI. (Solution of Iodide of Arsenic and Mercury. Donovan's Solution.)

Contains AsI_3 (1) and HgI_2 (1), dissolved in water ft. 100. No chemical combination takes place between the two iodides.

Description. A light, yellow-colored liquid, becoming darker by age; original color may be restored by agitation with a small quantity each of mercury and arsenic.

($Na_2HAsO_4.7H_2O$—311.9) SODII ARSENIAS.—ARSENIATE OF SODIUM.

Made by heating arsenious acid, exsiccated sodium carbonate, and sodium nitrate to fusion; dissolving, filtering, and crystallizing.

Reaction. $As_2O_3 + 2NaNO_3 + Na_2CO_3 = Na_4As_2O_7$
(Arsenious Oxide.) (Sodium Nitrate.) (Sodium Carbonate.) (Sodium Pyro-arseniate.)
$+ CO_2 + N_2O_3.$
(Carbon Dioxide.) (Nitrogen Trioxide.)

On dissolving the pyro-arseniate in water, ortho-arseniate is formed.

Reaction. $Na_4As_2O_7 + H_2O = 2Na_2HAsO_4.$

$\underset{\text{(Pyro-arseniate.)}}{\underset{\text{Sodium}}{\Big(}} \qquad \underset{\text{(Water.)}}{} \qquad \underset{\text{(Arseniate.)}}{\underset{\text{Sodium}}{\Big)}}$

Description. Colorless, transparent crystals; odorless; feeble alkaline taste and reaction; sol. in water (4), alcohol (slightly).—*Impurity, Arsenite:* Cold aq. sol. $+ HCl + H_2S =$ yellow color, or ppt.

Officinal Preparation. LIQUOR SODII ARSENIATIS.—SOLUTION OF ARSENIATE OF SODIUM. Made by dissolving anhydrous sodium arseniate (1), in distilled water (99).

Pearson's Solution. Contains *crystallized* arseniate of sodium 1 gr., dissolved in water 600 grs. or, one tenth the strength of the officinal solution.

Clemen's Solution. A solution of arsenious bromide in distilled water. Dose, 1–4 drops.

Scheele's Green. $3CuO, As_2O_3, 2H_2O.$

Paris Green. (Schweinfurth's Green. Vienna Green.) An aceto-arsenite of copper. Formula of best variety is:

$$3CuO, As_2O_3 + 2Cu(C_2H_3O_2)_2 + 5H_2O.$$

STIBIUM—Antimony. (Sb.—120)

OCCURRENCE. Found *native*, but more abundantly as sulphide (black antimony or *stibnite*), oxide, or oxysulphide. Metallic antimony is not used in pharmacy, its chief use being for type metal.

Description. A brilliant, brittle metal, of crystalline structure, having a silver-white color; sp. gr. 6.7

Reactions of Antimony and its Salts.

1. H_2S; yields an *orange-red precipitate* soluble in $(NH_4)_2S$, and in boiling HCl.

2. On introducing a piece of bright iron or zinc into the solution, *metallic antimony precipitates* as a black powder.

For other tests, see Arsenic.

(Sb₂S₃—336) ANTIMONII SULPHIDUM.—SULPHIDE OF ANTIMONY. (Black Antimony.)

Native sulphide of antimony, purified by fusion and as nearly free from arsenic as possible.

Description. Steel-gray masses, of a metallic lustre, and crystalline fracture; forming a dull, blackish powder; odorless; tasteless; insol. in water or alcohol; sol in boiling HCl.

Often adulterated with coal dust, and clay.

Officinal Preparation. Antimonii Sulphidum Purificatum.

ANTIMONII SULPHIDUM PURIFICATUM.—PURIFIED SULPHIDE OF ANTIMONY.

Preparation. Sulphide of antimony is powdered, and the coarser particles separated by elutriation; after allowing the finely divided sulphide to deposit, the water is removed, and the sulphide macerated for five days with NH_4OH, which dissolves out the arsenious sulphide; the powder is then washed with water and dried.

Description. Dark-gray powder; odorless; tasteless; insol. in water or alcohol; sol. in boiling HCl.

Impurities: Other metallic sulphides.

Officinal Preparation. Antimonium Sulphuratum.

ANTIMONIUM SULPHURATUM.—SULPHURATED ANTIMONY.
(Golden Sulphur.)

Chiefly antimonious sulphide (Sb_2S_3) with a very small amount of antimonious oxide. Made by boiling the purified sulphide with dilute solution of soda, then straining and slowly adding H_2SO_4 to the liquid as long as a precipitate is produced, wash, dry and powder.

(1) $4Sb_2S_3 + 8NaOH = 3Na_2Sb_2S_4 + 2NaSbO_2$
(Antimony Sulphide.) (Sodium Hydroxide.) (Sodium Sulphantimonite.) (Sodium Antimonite.)
$+ 4H_2O.$
(Water.)

(2) $3Na_2Sb_2S_4 + 2NaSbO_2 + 4H_2SO_4 = 4Sb_2S_3$
(Sodium Sulphantimonite.) (Sodium Antimonite.) (Sulphuric Acid.) (Antimony Sulphide.)
$+ 4Na_2SO_4 + 4H_2O.$
(Sodium Sulphate.) (Water.)

Description. A reddish-brown, amorphous powder; odorless; tasteless; insol. in water, or alcohol; sol. in hot HCl.

Impurities and tests. *Sulphate* (a limit): $+ H_2O +$ boil; filt. $+ BaCl_2 =$ white ppt.

Officinal Preparation. PILULÆ ANTIMONII COMPOSITÆ. (Compound Pills of Antimony. Plummer's Pill.) Each pill contains ½ grain each of sulphurated antimony and calomel, and 1 gr. guaiac.

(Sb_2O_3—288) ANTIMONII OXIDUM.—OXIDE OF ANTIMONY.
(Antimonious Oxide.)

Made by dissolving sulphurated antimony in hot HCl, and pouring the antimonious chloride solution thus formed into water; the oxy-chloride precipitates, is allowed to subside, and washed with water, then with NH_4OH (forming the oxide), again washed with water and dried.

$Sb_2S_3 + 6HCl = 2SbCl_3 + 3H_2S.$
(Antimony Sulphide.) (Hydrochloric Acid.) (Antimonious Chloride.) (Hydrogen Sulphide.)

$12SbCl_3 + 15H_2O = 2SbCl_3 . 5Sb_2O_3 + 30HCl.$
(Antimonious Chloride.) (Water.) (Antimony Oxychloride.) (Hydrochloric Acid.)

$2SbCl_3 . 5Sb_2O_3 + 6NH_4OH = 6Sb_2O_3 + 6NH_4Cl + 3H_2O.$
(Antimony Oxychloride.) (Ammonium Hydroxide.) (Antimony Oxide.) (Ammonium Chloride.) (Water.)

Description. Heavy, grayish-white powder; alm. insol. in water; insol. alcohol; sol. in HCl and warm solution of tartaric acid.

Impurities and tests. *Chloride:* Sol. $+ AgNO_3 =$ white ppt. *Sulphate:* Sol. $+ BaCl_2 =$ white ppt. *Iron and other metals:* Sol. $+$ potass. ferrocyanide $=$ ppt.

Officinal Preparation. PULVIS ANTIMONIALIS. (Antimonial Powder. James' Powder. Pulvis Jacobi.) Contains antimonious oxide (33), diluted with precipitated calcium phosphate (67).

$(2KSbOC_4H_4O_6.H_2O)$ ANTIMONII ET POTASSII TARTRAS.—
TARTRATE OF ANTIMONY AND POTASSIUM. (Tartar Emetic.)
Made by boiling potassium bitartrate and antimonious oxide with
water, filtering and crystallizing.

Reaction. $2KHC_4H_4O_6 + Sb_2O_3 = 2KSbOC_4H_4O_6, H_2O.$

$$\underset{\substack{\text{(Potassium} \\ \text{Bitartrate.)}}}{} \quad \underset{\substack{\text{(Antimonious} \\ \text{Oxide.})}}{} \quad \underset{\substack{\text{(Antimoniated Potassium} \\ \text{Tartrate.})}}{}$$

Description. Small, transparent crystals, becoming white on
exposure to air; sweet, afterward disagreeable taste; feebly acid
reaction; sol. in water 17, boiling water 3, insol. in alcohol.

Properties. Very poisonous. Most powerful emetic known.
Dose: one grain.

Impurities and tests. Besides those given under Antimonii Oxidum,
the following, viz.: *Calcium:* $+ (NH_4)_2C_2O_4 =$ white ppt. *Arsenic:*
Fleitmann's test (see Arsenic).

Officinal Preparation. 1. Syrupus scillæ compositus. 2. Vinum
antimonii.

SYRUPUS SCILLÆ COMPOSITUS. (Compound Syrup of Squill.
Hive Syrup. Croup Syrup.) The active ingredients are squill,
seneka, and tartar emetic; three parts of the last mentioned in 2000
parts, or 0.15%. *Dose,* 10–30 drops.

VINUM ANTIMONII.—WINE OF ANTIMONY. Made by dissolving
tartar emetic (4), in boiling water (60), and adding to stronger
white wine ft. 1000. Contains 0.4% tartar emetic. *Dose.* 10 drops.

Officinal Preparation. MISTURA GLYCYRRHIZÆ COMPOSITA.
(Compound Licorice Mixture. Brown Mixture.) Contains purified
extract licorice, sugar, acacia, paregoric, wine of antimony, spirit of
nitrous ether, and water. Contains 6% wine of antimony. *Dose*
four fluid-drachms.

BISMUTHUM.—Bismuth. (Bi.—210)

OCCURRENCE. Found in the metallic state associated with cobalt,
nickel and silver ores; occasionally found as sulphide.

Description. Brilliant, grayish-white metal, of a crystalline
texture; sp. gr. 9.83; sol. in HNO_3. Usually contaminated with arsenic.

Reactions of Bismuth and its salts. 1. H_2S: gives *black
precipitate,* soluble in HNO_3.

2. Water of Ammonia: yields a white precipitate, insoluble in
excess. 3. Potassium chromate: produces a yellow precipitate.

$((BiO)_2CO_3.H_2O—580)$ BISMUTHI SUBCARBONAS.—SUBCARBONATE
OF BISMUTH.

Preparation. Metallic bismuth is dissolved in dilute nitric acid,
forming a solution of bismuthous nitrate, which is diluted with
water and filtered, then still further diluted and poured into water
of ammonia. The resulting precipitate is drained, washed and dissolved in nitric acid; the solution, diluted with water, is filtered and
added to a cold solution of sodium carbonate, when bismuth subcarbonate precipitates, which is drained, washed and dried.

Explanation of above process. Most metallic bismuth contains some arsenic, which is oxidized by the nitric acid, so that *arseniate* of bismuth is formed, most of which deposits on diluting. The clear liquid still retaining small quantities of arsenic, is deprived of it by pouring into an excess of NH_4OH, producing nitrate and arseniate of ammonium (both soluble) while bismuthous hydroxide precipitates, and is further converted into the subcarbonate by dissolving in nitric acid and pouring into a solution of sodium carbonate.

First step. $\underset{\text{(Bismuth.)}}{2Bi} + \underset{\substack{\text{(Nitric} \\ \text{Acid.)}}}{8HNO_3} = \underset{\substack{\text{(Bismuth} \\ \text{Nitrate.)}}}{2Bi(NO_3)_3} + \underset{\substack{\text{(Nitrogen} \\ \text{Dioxide.)}}}{N_2O_2} + \underset{\text{(Water.)}}{4H_2O}.$

Second step. $\underset{\substack{\text{(Bismuth} \\ \text{Nitrate.)}}}{2Bi(NO_3)_3} + \underset{\substack{\text{(Ammonium} \\ \text{Hydroxide.)}}}{6NH_4OH} = \underset{\substack{\text{(Bismuthous} \\ \text{Hydroxide.)}}}{2Bi(OH)_3} + \underset{\substack{\text{(Ammonium} \\ \text{Nitrate.)}}}{6NH_4NO_3}.$

Third step. $\underset{\substack{\text{(Bismuthous} \\ \text{Hydroxide.)}}}{2Bi(OH)_3} + \underset{\substack{\text{(Nitric} \\ \text{Acid.)}}}{6HNO_3} = \underset{\substack{\text{(Bismuth} \\ \text{Nitrate.)}}}{2Bi(NO_3)_3} + \underset{\text{(Water.)}}{6H_2O}.$

Fourth step. $\underset{\substack{\text{(Bismuth} \\ \text{Nitrate.)}}}{2Bi(NO_3)_3} + \underset{\substack{\text{(Sodium} \\ \text{Carbonate.)}}}{3Na_2CO_3} = \underset{\substack{\text{(Bismuthous} \\ \text{Subcarbonate.)}}}{(BiO)_2CO_3}$
$+ \underset{\substack{\text{(Sodium} \\ \text{Nitrate.)}}}{6NaNO_3} + \underset{\substack{\text{(Carbon} \\ \text{Dioxide.)}}}{2CO_2}.$

Description. Pale, yellowish-white powder; odorless; tasteless; insol. in water or alcohol; sol. in nitric acid with effervescence.

Impurities and tests. *Insoluble foreign matter :* $+ HNO_3 =$ solution with residue. *Lead :* Solution $+ H_2O$; filt. $+ H_2SO_4 =$ cloudiness. *Copper :* Solution $+ NH_4OH =$ blue color. *Chlorides :* Solution $+ AgNO_3 =$ white ppt. *Sulphates :* Solution $+ Ba(NO_3)_2 =$ white ppt. *Silver :* Solution $+ HCl =$ white ppt. *Alkalies, and Alk. earths :* $+$ dil. $HC_2H_3O_2 +$ boil; filt. $+ H_2S$; filt. $+$ evap. $=$ fixed residue. *Antimony, arsenic,* and *tin :* $+$ solution soda $+$ boil $+ H_2O$; filt. $+ HCl + H_2S =$ yellow, or orange ppt. *Arsenic :* Fleitmann's test. (See *Arsenic.*)

($BiONO_3.H_2O$—306) BISMUTHI SUBNITRAS.—SUBNITRATE OF BISMUTH.

Preparation. After preparing the washed bismuthous subcarbonate, as shown above, dissolve in diluted nitric acid, filter and pour into water containing a small amount of NH_4OH to partly neutralize the HNO_3, in order to precipitate the greater part of the bismuth, some of which would still remain held in solution by the nitric acid of the supernatant liquid. The subnitrate deposits, is washed and dried.

$\underset{\substack{\text{(Bismuthous} \\ \text{Subcarbonate.)}}}{(BiO)_2CO_3} + \underset{\substack{\text{(Nitric} \\ \text{Acid.)}}}{6HNO_3} = \underset{\substack{\text{(Bismuth} \\ \text{Nitrate.)}}}{2Bi(NO_3)_3} + \underset{\substack{\text{(Carbon} \\ \text{Dioxide.)}}}{CO_2} + \underset{\text{(Water.)}}{3H_2O}.$

$\underset{\substack{\text{(Bismuth} \\ \text{Nitrate.)}}}{6Bi(NO_3)_3} + \underset{\text{(Water.)}}{10H_2O} = \underset{\substack{\text{(Bismuth} \\ \text{Subnitrate.)}}}{5BiONO_3.H_2O} + \underset{\substack{\text{(Bismuth} \\ \text{Nitrate.)}}}{Bi(NO_3)_3} + \underset{\text{(Nitric Acid.)}}{10HNO_3}.$

Description. Heavy, white powder; odorless; almost tasteless; slight acid reaction; insol. in water or alcohol.

Impurities and tests. *Carbonate :* $+ HNO_3 =$ effervescence ; and those found under the Subcarbonate.

($BiC_6H_5O_7$—399) BISMUTHI CITRAS.—CITRATE OF BISMUTH.

Made by boiling bismuth subnitrate in a solution of citric acid, until a drop of the mixture yields a clear solution with water of ammonia; on adding water, the citrate deposits, is drained, washed and dried.

$$BiONO_3 \ + \ H_3C_6H_5O_7 \ = \ BiC_6H_5O_7 \ + \ HNO_3 \ + \ H_2O.$$

$\binom{\text{Bismuth}}{\text{Subnitrate.}}$ (Citric Acid.) $\binom{\text{Bismuth}}{\text{Citrate.}}$ $\binom{\text{Nitric}}{\text{Acid.}}$ (Water.)

Description. White, amorphous powder; odorless; tasteless; insol. in water or alcohol; soluble in NH_4OH.

Impurity. *Nitrate :* $+ NH_4OH + H_2S$; filt. $+ FeSO_4 =$ brown zone.

Officinal Preparation. BISMUTHI ET AMMONII CITRAS.—CITRATE OF BISMUTH AND AMMONIUM. Made by dissolving bismuth citrate in diluted water of ammonia, evaporating to a syrupy consistence and scaling.

Description. Small, shining, pearly or translucent scales, becoming opaque on exposure; odorless; acidulous, metallic taste; neutral or faintly alkaline reaction; *very* soluble in water; sp. sol. in alcohol. Impurity; same as in the *Citrate.*

HYDRARGYRUM.—Mercury. (Quicksilver.) Hg.

OCCURRENCE. Found in nature most abundantly as *cinnabar* (HgS), in California, Peru, China, and Spain.

Preparation. Obtained by roasting the ore. Conducted in such a manner, that the sulphur is burned into SO_2, while the metal volatilizes and is condensed in a series of chambers called *aludels;* the incondensable gases escaping.

Reaction. $2HgS \ + \ 2O_2 \ = \ Hg_2 \ + \ 2SO_2.$

$\binom{\text{Mercury}}{\text{Sulphide.}}$ $\binom{\text{Oxygen.}}{\text{(from Air)}}$ (Mercury.) $\binom{\text{Sulphur}}{\text{Dioxide.}}$

Description. Shining, silver-white metal; liquid between $-40°$ and $662°$ F. ($-40°$ and $350°$ C.); sp. gr. 13.5; insoluble in ordinary solvents; sol. in nitric acid; odorless; tasteless. Forms two kinds of salts, *mercuric* and *mercurous.*

Impurities and Tests. The presence of other metals is indicated by the shape of the globule, which should be *round* and not *elongated ;* it should not adhere to paper, nor leave a dark streak upon it, nor fail to have a bright surface.

PURIFICATION. Accomplished by re-distillation, or by digesting with diluted nitric acid, washing well, drying, and passing forcibly through chamois; the contaminating metals become oxidized, and only a small portion of the mercury passes into solution. Also purified by agitation with solution of ferric chloride, or conc. H_2SO_4.

Subdivision. The subdivision of mercury is termed *extinguishing* or *killing*, and is accomplished by trituration with foreign substances; the minute globules becoming coated with the substance used, thus preventing them from cohering. The *officinal* degree of *extinction* is reached, when globules are no longer visible under a magnifying power of ten diameters.

Reactions of Mercury Salts.

Reagent.	With mercurous salts gives;	With mercuric salts gives;
Potassium Iodide	Green ppt.	Red ppt.
Potassium Hydroxide	Black ppt.	Yellow ppt.
Hydrogen Sulphide	Black ppt.	Black ppt.
Stannous Chloride	Gray-black ppt.	Gray-black ppt.
Bright Copper Wire	Coating of Mercury.	Coating of Mercury.
Hydrochloric Acid	White ppt.	No reaction.

Antidote. Albumen in the form of egg, flour or milk, followed by emetics.

Officinal Preparations. 1. Emplastrum Ammoniaci cum hydrargyro. 2. Emplastrum hydrargyri. 3. Hydrargyrum cum creta. 4. Massa hydrargyri. 5. Unguentum hydrargyri.

Emplastrum Ammoniaci cum Hydrargyro.—Ammoniac Plaster with Mercury. Made by dissolving sulphur (1) in hot olive oil (8) and triturating mercury (180) with it till extinguished; incorporate with a hot emulsion of ammoniac (720), (made by digestion with diluted acetic acid and evaporation) and lead plaster ft. 1000 parts. *Contains* 18% *mercury.*

Emplastrum Hydrargyri.—Mercurial Plaster. Made by extinguishing mercury (30) with a mixture of rosin (10) and olive oil (10), and incorporating with it melted lead plaster (50). *Contains* 30% *mercury.*

Hydrargyrum cum Creta.—Mercury with Chalk. Made by the extinction of mercury (38) with milk sugar (12) and chalk (50), using ether and alcohol to moisten the mass.

Description. Gray, non-gritty, odorless and tasteless powder. *Contains* 38% *mercury.*

Caution. On exposure to light or air, oxidation takes place; the *mercurous oxide* being identified by dissolving out with diluted acetic acid, and treating with HCl, which produces a cloudiness; *mercuric oxide*, after dissolving out with the aid of HCl, a black precipitate is produced with H_2S, or gray with stannous chloride. *Dose*, 3–10 grs.

Massa Hydrargyri.—Blue Mass. (Blue Pill.) Made by extinguishing mercury (33) with honey of roses (34) and glycerin (3), and incorporating with powdered licorice (5) and marshmallow (25). *Contains* 33% *mercury. Dose*, 3–10 grs.

Unguentum Hydrargyri.—Mercurial Ointment. (Blue Ointment.) Made by extinguishing mercury (450) with tinct. benzoin comp. (40), and mercurial ointment (100), and incorporating with a previously melted mixture of lard and suet. The storax in tincture benzoin comp. aids in readily extinguishing the mercury, while the balsamic matter of tolu and benzoin after evaporation of the alcohol, act as preservative agents. *Contains* 50% *mercury.*

($HgCl_2$—270.5) HYDRARGYRI CHLORIDUM CORROSIVUM.—CORROSIVE CHLORIDE OF MERCURY. (Bi- or Perchloride of Mercury. Mercuric Chloride. Corrosive Sublimate.)

Made by boiling mercury with H_2SO_4 until a dry mass (mercuric sulphate) remains, which is mixed with sodium chloride and sublimed; mercuric chloride volatilizes.

$$1. \quad \underset{\text{(Mercury.)}}{Hg_2} + \underset{\left(\substack{\text{Sulphuric} \\ \text{Acid.}}\right)}{4H_2SO_4} = \underset{\left(\substack{\text{Mercuric} \\ \text{Sulphate.}}\right)}{2HgSO_4} + \underset{\left(\substack{\text{Sulphur} \\ \text{Dioxide.}}\right)}{2SO_2} + \underset{\text{(Water.)}}{4H_2O.}$$

$$2. \quad \underset{\left(\substack{\text{Mercuric} \\ \text{Sulphate.}}\right)}{HgSO_4} + \underset{\left(\substack{\text{Sodium} \\ \text{Chloride.}}\right)}{2NaCl} = \underset{\left(\substack{\text{Sodium} \\ \text{Sulphate.}}\right)}{Na_2SO_4} + \underset{\left(\substack{\text{Mercuric} \\ \text{Chloride.}}\right)}{HgCl_2.}$$

Description. Heavy, colorless rhombic crystals, or crystalline masses; odorless, acrid and persistent metallic taste; acid reaction; sol. in water 16, alcohol 3, ether 4, and very soluble in ammonium chloride solution. *Dose*, $\frac{1}{16} - \frac{1}{4}$ grain.

Impurities and tests. *Arsenic:* Fleitmann's test, using aluminium wire in the place of zinc.

(Hg_2Cl_2—470.2) HYDRARGYRI CHLORIDUM MITE.—MILD CHLORIDE OF MERCURY. (Sub- or Protochloride of Mercury. Mercurous Chloride. Calomel.)

Preparation. Mercuric sulphate (as made by the process given under *mercuric chloride*) is mixed with the requisite quantity of mercury to form mercurous sulphate.

Reaction. $\quad \underset{\text{(Mercury)}}{Hg_2} + \underset{\left(\substack{\text{Mercuric} \\ \text{Sulphate.}}\right)}{2HgSO_4} = \underset{\left(\substack{\text{Mercurous} \\ \text{Sulphate.}}\right)}{2Hg_2SO_4.}$

Sodium chloride is added to the mercurous salt, and the mixture heated, when Hg_2Cl_2 sublimes.

Reaction. $\quad \underset{\left(\substack{\text{Mercurous} \\ \text{Sulphate.}}\right)}{Hg_2SO_4} + \underset{\left(\substack{\text{Sodium} \\ \text{Chloride.}}\right)}{2NaCl} = \underset{\left(\substack{\text{Mercurous} \\ \text{Chloride.}}\right)}{Hg_2Cl_2} + \underset{\left(\substack{\text{Sodium} \\ \text{Sulphate.}}\right)}{Na_2SO_4.}$

The vaporized Hg_2Cl_2 passes into a suitable condenser, falling as a powder, while Na_2SO_4 remains. Some *mercuric* chloride also forms, but may be removed by washing with water, or by injecting steam into the condenser as sublimation proceeds. *Dose*, 5–20 grains.

Description. White, impalpable powder; odorless; tasteless; insol. in water, alcohol or ether; blackened by NH_4OH.

Impurities and tests. *Mercuric chloride:* Treat with water or alcohol; filt. $+ H_2S =$ black ppt.; or filt. $+ AgNO_3 =$ white ppt. *Ammoniated mercury:* $+ KOH +$ Heat = odor of NH_3, besides above reactions.

Officinal Preparations. 1. Pilulæ antimonii comp. (See Antimony.)

2. PILULÆ CATHARTICÆ COMPOSITÆ.—COMPOUND CATHARTIC PILLS. (Anti-bilious Pills.) Each pill contains comp. extract of colocynth 1.3 gr.; abstract jalap, 1 grain; calomel, 1 gr.; powd. gamboge, 0.25 grain. *Dose*, 1–3 pills.

(HgI$_2$—452.9)   HYDRARGYRI IODIDUM RUBRUM.   RED IODIDE OF MERCURY.

(Biniodide, or Deutoiodide of Mercury.   Mercuric Iodide.)

Made by the mutual decomposition between mercuric chloride and potassium iodide, both in solution.   Wash and dry the precipitate.

Reaction. $2KI$ + $HgCl_2$ = HgI_2 + $2KCl.$

$\begin{pmatrix}\text{Potassium}\\\text{Iodide.}\end{pmatrix}$ $\begin{pmatrix}\text{Mercuric}\\\text{Chloride.}\end{pmatrix}$ $\begin{pmatrix}\text{Mercuric}\\\text{Iodide.}\end{pmatrix}$ $\begin{pmatrix}\text{Potassium}\\\text{Chloride.}\end{pmatrix}$

The precipitated iodide is soluble in excess of either of the chemicals used.

Description.   Scarlet-red, crystalline powder; odorless; tasteless; almost insol. in water; sol. in alcohol (130), and in solution of KI, or HgCl$_2$, also in a hot solution of NaCl, from which it crystallizes on cooling.   *Dose,* $\frac{1}{16}-\frac{1}{8}$ grain.

Impurities and tests.   *Soluble iodides* and *chlorides :* $+$ H$_2$O; filt. $+$ AgNO$_3$ = white ppt.

Officinal Preparation.   Liquor arsenii et hydrargyri iodidi.   (See Arsenic.

(Hg$_2$I$_2$—652.6)   HYDRARGYRI IODIDUM VIRIDE.—GREEN IODIDE OF MERCURY.   Protoiodide of Mercury.   Mercurous Iodide.)

Made by triturating together mercury (8) and iodine (5) (using alcohol to keep down the temperature) until a greenish yellow color is acquired.   Some HgI$_2$ is also produced which is removed by washing with alcohol till the washings are not affected by H$_2$S. Keep in *dark-colored bottles.*

Description.   Dull green, to greenish yellow powder; becoming more yellow by exposure to light; odorless; tasteless; alm. insol. in water; insol. alcohol or ether.   On exposure to light, it decomposes into mercuric iodide.   *Dose,* $\frac{1}{4}-1$ grain.

Impurities and tests.   *Mercuric Iodide :* $+$ alc.; filt. $+$ H$_2$O = opalescence; or, on evaporating on white porcelain, only a faint red stain remains.

(HgO—215.7)   HYDRARGYRI OXIDUM FLAVUM.—YELLOW OXIDE OF MERCURY.   (Mercuric Oxide.)

Made by the mutual decomposition between mercuric chloride in solution, and solution of potash, pouring the *former into* the *latter* (to prevent the formation of *red oxide*).

Reaction. $HgCl_2$ + $2KOH$ = HgO + $2KCl$ + $H_2O.$

$\begin{pmatrix}\text{Mercuric}\\\text{Chloride.}\end{pmatrix}$ $\begin{pmatrix}\text{Potassium}\\\text{Hydroxide.}\end{pmatrix}$ $\begin{pmatrix}\text{Mercuric}\\\text{Oxide.}\end{pmatrix}$ $\begin{pmatrix}\text{Potassium}\\\text{Chloride.}\end{pmatrix}$ (Water.)

Description.   Light, orange-yellow, impalpable powder; becoming darker on exposure; odorless; tasteless; insol. in water, or alcohol; sol. in HNO$_3$ or HCl.

Difference from red oxide :   When digested with solution of oxalic acid, it forms a *white* mercuric oxalate.

Officinal Preparations.   1. Oleatum hydrargyri.   2. Ung. hydrargyri oxidi flavi.

OLEATUM HYDRARGYRI.—MERCURIC OLEATE. Made by dissolving yellow oxide of mercury (10) in oleic acid (90), with the aid of heat, below 165° F.

UNGUENTUM HYDRARGYRI.—OXIDI FLAVI. (Ointment of Yellow Oxide of Mercury.) Yellow HgO (10), incorporated with ointment (90).

(HgO—215.7) HYDRARGYRI OXIDUM RUBRUM.—RED OXIDE OF MERCURY.

(Red Precipitate. Peroxide of Mercury. Red Mercuric Oxide.)

Made by first forming a mercuric nitrate, by treating the metal with diluted HNO_3, and evaporating to dryness, when another equivalent of mercury is added, and the mixture heated till nitrous fumes cease to be evolved.

(1) $\underset{\text{(Mercury.)}}{3Hg} + \underset{\left(\substack{\text{Nitric} \\ \text{Acid.}}\right)}{8HNO_3} = \underset{\left(\substack{\text{Mercuric} \\ \text{Nitrate.}}\right)}{3Hg(NO_3)_2} + \underset{\left(\substack{\text{Nitrogen} \\ \text{Dioxide.}}\right)}{N_2O_2} + \underset{\text{(Water.)}}{4H_2O.}$

(2) $\underset{\left(\substack{\text{Mercuric} \\ \text{Nitrate.}}\right)}{2Hg(NO_3)_2} + \underset{\text{(Mercury.)}}{Hg_2} + Heat = \underset{\left(\substack{\text{Mercuric} \\ \text{Oxide.}}\right)}{4HgO} + \underset{\left(\substack{\text{Nitrogen} \\ \text{Tetroxide.}}\right)}{2N_2O_4.}$

Description. Heavy, orange-red crystalline scales, or a crystalline powder, becoming yellow by trituration; odorless; tasteless; insol. in water or alcohol; sol. in HNO_3, or HCl.

Impurities and tests. *Nitrate:* $+$ Heat $=$ dark color, and reddish fumes.

Difference from yellow oxide: Digest with strong solution oxalic acid $=$ no change in color in two hours.

Officinal Preparations. UNGUENTUM HYDRARGYRI OXIDI RUBRI. (Ointment of Red Oxide of Mercury.) Contains red HgO (10), incorporated with ointment (90).

($Hg(CN)_2$—251.7) HYDRARGYRI CYANIDUM.—CYANIDE OF MERCURY. (Mercuric Cyanide.)

Made by dissolving HgO in HCN, also by boiling potassium ferrocyanide with solution of mercuric sulphate, and separating the cyanide by crystallization from alcohol.

(1) $\underset{\left(\substack{\text{Hydrocyanic} \\ \text{Acid.}}\right)}{2HCN} + \underset{\left(\substack{\text{Mercuric} \\ \text{Oxide.}}\right)}{HgO} = \underset{\left(\substack{\text{Mercuric} \\ \text{Cyanide.}}\right)}{Hg(CN)_2} + \underset{\text{(Water.)}}{H_2O.}$

(2) $\underset{\left(\substack{\text{Potassium} \\ \text{Ferrocyanide.}}\right)}{2K_4Fe(CN)_6} + \underset{\left(\substack{\text{Mercuric} \\ \text{Sulphate.}}\right)}{7HgSO_4} = \underset{\left(\substack{\text{Mercuric} \\ \text{Cyanide.}}\right)}{6Hg(CN)_2} + \underset{\text{(Mercury.)}}{Hg}$

$+ \underset{\left(\substack{\text{Potassium} \\ \text{Sulphate.}}\right)}{4K_2SO_4} + \underset{\left(\substack{\text{Ferric} \\ \text{Sulphate.}}\right)}{Fe_2(SO_4)_3.}$

Description. Colorless, or white crystals, becoming dark on exposure to light; odorless; bitter, metallic taste; neutral reaction; sol. in water (12.8), alc. (15).

Impurities and tests. *Mercuric chloride:* $+$ KI $=$ red ppt. soluble in excess.

(Hg(HgO)$_2$SO$_4$—727.1) HYDRARGYRI SUBSULPHAS FLAVUS.—
YELLOW SUBSULPHATE OF MERCURY.

(Basic Mercuric Sulphate. Turpeth Mineral.)

Made by dissolving mercury in a mixture of H$_2$SO$_4$, HNO$_3$ and water, forming a solution of normal mercuric sulphate (Hg$_2$ + 2H$_2$SO$_4$ + 2HNO$_3$ = 2HgSO$_4$ + 3H$_2$O + N$_2$O$_3$), which on being poured into boiling water, yields a precipitate of mercury subsulphate, while acid mercuric sulphate remains in solution.

Description. Heavy, lemon-yellow powder; odorless; almost tasteless; insol. in water, or alcohol; sol. in HNO$_3$, or HCl.

(NH$_2$HgCl—251.1) HYDRARGYRUM AMMONIATUM.—AMMONIATED
MERCURY. (White Precipitate. Mercur-ammonium Chloride.)

Made by pouring a solution of HgCl$_2$ into NH$_4$OH, keeping the latter in slight excess; wash and dry the precipitate.

$$\underset{\substack{\text{(Mercuric}\\\text{Chloride.)}}}{\text{HgCl}_2} + \underset{\substack{\text{(Ammonium}\\\text{Hydroxide.)}}}{\text{2NH}_4\text{OH}} = \underset{\substack{\text{(Mercur-Ammonium}\\\text{Chloride.)}}}{\text{NH}_2\text{HgCl}} + \underset{\substack{\text{(Ammonium}\\\text{Chloride.)}}}{\text{NH}_4\text{Cl}} + \underset{\text{(Water).}}{\text{2H}_2\text{O.}}$$

Description. White, pulverulent pieces; or, a white powder; odorless; tasteless; insol. in water or alcohol.

Impurities and tests. *Mercurous salt :* + HCl = not wholly soluble. *Carbonate :* + HCl = effervescence. *Lead :* + acetic acid = Sol. + H$_2$SO$_4$ = white ppt.

Officinal Preparation. UNGUENTUM HYDRARGYRUM AMMONIATUM. (Ointment of Ammoniated Mercury.) Made by incorporating ammoniated mercury (10) with benzoinated lard (90).

LIQUOR HYDRARGYRI NITRATIS—SOLUTION OF NITRATE OF
MERCURY. (Solution of Pernitrate of Mercury.)

Made by dissolving mercury in diluted HNO$_3$. (See Reaction under *Red Oxide*).

Description. Colorless liquid; strong acid reaction; odor of HNO$_3$; sp. gr. 2.100, contains about 50% Hg(NO$_3$)$_2$.

UNGUENTUM HYDRARGYRI NITRATIS. (Ointment of Nitrate of
Mercury. Citrine Ointment.)

Made by treating lard oil at 158° F. with HNO$_3$ and heating till effervescence ceases; when cool, it is incorporated with solution of mercuric nitrate, made by the action of nitric acid on mercury. A very complex reaction takes place in this preparation; the fat is oxidized, N$_2$O$_2$ and N$_2$O$_4$ are evolved, and the *olein* of the oil converted to solid *elaidin.*

(HgS—231.7) HYDRARGYRI SULPHIDUM RUBRUM.—RED SULPHIDE
OF MERCURY. (Cinnabar. Vermilion. Paris Red. Red Mercuric Sulphide.)

Made by melting mercury (40) with sulphur (8), and subliming. It has the same composition as *native cinnabar.*

Description. Brilliant, dark-red, crystalline masses; or fine, bright, scarlet powder; odorless; tasteless; insol. in water, alcohol, HNO$_3$ or HCl.

PART III.

ORGANIC PHARMACY.

Relations of Pharmacy to Organic Chemistry.

ORGANIC CHEMISTRY is the science which treats of carbon compounds.

The term organic chemistry originally referred to the chemistry of compounds formed only in the bodies of animals and plants, but this erroneous idea was overthrown by the result of the experiments of Wöhler in 1828, who produced *urea* by artificial means.

Composition of Plants. All plants are composed mainly of woody fibre termed *Cellulose* or *Cellulin*, which represents the framework or cells (these cells are lined with a material called *Lignin*, which tends to harden them), also certain organic *proximate principles*, which, when further resolved, are found to consist of carbon, hydrogen and oxygen. When hydrogen and oxygen are present in the proportion in which they unite to form water, they are termed *Carbo-hydrates*.

Some proximate principles are distinguished by containing *nitrogen*, and some *phosphorus* or *sulphur*.

Points of Similarity. The existence of one or more proximate principles in excess, in any group of animal or vegetable products, generally adapts its individual members to certain methods of manipulation and uses in medicine, and constitute strong features of resemblance among them. Substances in which a starchy matter predominates, to which their utility is due, are classified as *Farinaceous;* the *Gums* are associated with each other; the *Narcotics*, containing alkaloidal principles; the *Aromatics*, containing essential oils; the *Resins*, etc.

The Proximate Principles of Plants may be divided into two classes, viz.:

I. **Nutritious or Inert.** Comprising cellulose; starch; gums; sugars; fixed oils; fats, etc.

II. **Non-Nutritious and Poisonous.** Comprising crystallizable and non-crystallizable neutral principles; vegetable acids; vegetable alkalies; essential oils; resins, etc.

THE CELLULIN GROUP.

CELLULOSE.—CELLULIN.   ($C_6H_{10}O_5$)^n

CELLULIN in a nearly pure condition constitutes cotton, linen, and the best kinds of unsized paper, since the processes to which the woody fibre is subjected in these materials, separate the *lignin* and bodies which accompany it.

Description. An inert, colorless (sometimes translucent), tasteless, odorless, organized substance; insol. in water, dilute acids, or alkalies. Its only solvent is Schweizer's Solution, an ammoniacal solution of copper sulphate, made by dissolving $CuSO_4$ (10) in water (100) and adding solution of potash (5-50); wash the precipitate, and dissolve in a 20% sol. NH_4OH. On treating with conc. H_2SO_4, cellulose is converted into *soluble cellulose* or *Dextrin*, and on diluting and boiling this solution with water *Glucose* is obtained; by fusing with KOH it is changed into oxalic acid.

Cellulose is official in the form of Gossypium.

GOSSYPIUM.—COTTON.
(Purified Cotton. Absorbent Cotton.)

The hairs of the seeds of Gossypium herbaceum, and other species of Gossypium, freed from adhering impurities and deprived of fatty matter.

Method of Purification. Cotton is boiled with solution potash or soda, and washed to remove the soap formed, expressed and immersed in a 5% solution of chlorinated soda to bleach it, then washed again and treated with water acidulated with HCl, washed, expressed and dried. Loses 7% of its weight.

Properties. When thrown on water, it absorbs moisture readily and sinks; the water should have a neutral reaction; inodorous, tasteless; insoluble except in Schweizer's Solution.

Tests to distinguish between Cotton and Linen fibre. 1. Boil with KOH; *linen* partakes of a deep yellow color within two minutes, *cotton* remains white. 2. Tincture of Madder: With *linen* = yellowish red color, with *cotton* = light yellow. 3. Conc. H_2SO_4; chars and destroys cotton in $\frac{1}{2}$-2 minutes, linen not as readily. 4. Olive oil; renders *cotton* transparent, *linen* is unchanged. 5. Microscopical examination; *cotton* fibres appear as flat, ribbon-like joints, *linen* fibres like long, straight, slender tubes. 6. *Wool* and *silk* may be distinguished from cotton and linen and all other carbohydrates, by treating with perchloride of tin, which bleaches the latter, while wool and silk are unchanged.

Officinal Preparation. Pyroxylinum.

PYROXYLINUM.—SOLUBLE GUN COTTON. (COLLODION COTTON.)

Cotton (1) is macerated with a mixture of HNO_3(10) and H_2SO_4 (12) for about ten hours, and washed with cold water to remove acid, then with boiling water, and finally drained and dried. It should be soluble in a mixture of alcohol one volume, and stronger ether three volumes.

The following reactions show the important kinds of pyroxylin that may be formed:

(Cellulin.)	(Nitric Acid.)	(Nitro-Cellulin.)	(Water.)
(1) $C_{12}H_{20}O_{10}$	$+ \; 2HNO_3$	$= \; C_{12}H_{18}(NO_2)_2O_{10}$	$+ \; 2H_2O.$
(2) $C_{12}H_{20}O_{10}$	$+ \; 4HNO_3$	$= \; C_{12}H_{16}(NO_2)_4O_{10}$	$+ \; 4H_2O.$
(3) $C_{12}H_{20}O_{10}$	$+ \; 6HNO_3$	$= \; C_{12}H_{14}(NO_2)_6O_{10}$	$+ \; 6H_2O.$

(1) Non-explosive; insoluble in ether-alcohol.
(2) *Officinal.* Slightly explosive; soluble in ether-alcohol.
(3) Highly explosive; insoluble in ether-alcohol.
Officinal Preparation. Collodium.

COLLODIUM.—COLLODION. (Contractile Collodion.)

Made by dissolving pyroxylin (4) in a mixture of stronger ether (70) and alcohol (26).
Description. Colorless, slightly yellow liquid of a syrupy consistence, and ethereal odor. Leaves a thin, transparent, closely adhering film on evaporation.
Officinal Preparations. 1. Collodium flexile. 2. Collodium stypticum.

COLLODIUM FLEXILE.—FLEXIBLE COLLODION. Canada turpentine (5) and castor oil (3) are dissolved in collodion (92).
Description. Appearance like *collodium;* produces a flexible, opaque film on evaporation, afterwards becoming transparent.

COLLODIUM STYPTICUM.—STYPTIC COLLODION. (Xylostyptic Ether.) Made by dissolving tannic acid (20) in a mixture of alcohol (5), ether (20) and collodion (55). *Prop.* Styptic and hæmostatic.

COLLODIUM CUM CANTHARIDE.—CANTHARIDAL COLLODION. (Blistering Fluid.)

Made by exhausting powd. cantharides (60) by percolating with chloroform, distilling the percolate to (15), and dissolving in flexible collodion ft. (100).
Description. A transparent, brownish-green liquid.
Properties. Vesicant, and epispastic.

PAPER.

Paper, another form of cellulin, is made from wood (spruce or poplar), straw, cotton, linen, hemp, jute, etc.
Ledger paper, and the finest grades of *writing paper* are made entirely from linen rags; many of the cheaper grades of *printing* and *wall papers* contain clay, added to increase their weight, which however, renders them brittle. This admixture may be detected by ignition, when a heavy ash remains.
PREPARATION. **Wood** is converted into a pulp as follows: After chipping and heating with steam at 120 lbs. pressure for 12 hours, it is blown upon a strainer by means of live steam, and washed with hot water; it is next boiled with soda, to remove all resinous and fatty matter, then washed and ground with water, drained, and treated as rag pulp.
Rags are treated as follows: They are cut into small pieces, put

into a revolving iron cylinder and boiled with lime and water, resulting in the removal of all adhering impurities, and loosening of coloring matter; they are next placed in "beating-engines," and while mixed with water, are finely cut by revolving knives and at the same time bleached by the addition of chlorinated lime, and the lime fixed with H_2SO_4. After draining the mass, it is passed into a Jordan engine (composed of an iron cylinder in which a conical wheel of knives revolves) where the mass is ground to a smooth pulp with water, forming a milky mixture which is repeatedly washed and drained upon a belt of wire-gauze, and passed between rollers which press the pulp down to the thickness of paper desired; it is then caught upon an endless sheet of felt, and by means of the latter carried over heated, revolving, iron cylinders, till completely dry, when it is cut into sheets of the desired size. [B.H.S.]

MEDICATED PAPERS.—CHARTÆ.

There are three officinal medicated papers, viz.: Charta cantharidis, Charta potassii nitratis, and Charta sinapis. These are made by impregnating paper with the medicinal ingredient in the form of mixture or solution. (See Part I. page 61.)

PARCHMENT PAPER.

Made by immersing unsized paper made from rags, in sulphuric acid (sp. gr. 1.56–1.60) for a short time, and washing with diluted water of ammonia to neutralize any adhering acid, and finally with water. Parchment, parchment-paper, bladder, skin, etc., have the property of separating *crystalloid* bodies from *colloids* by a process called Dialysis. (See Part I. page 43.)

($H_2C_2O_4 . 2H_2O$—126) OXALIC ACID.

Occurs combined with ammonium in *guano*, with calcium in a large number of plants, in rhubarb, curcuma, ginger, squill, orris, valerian, quassia, etc.

Preparation. May be made by the action of nitric acid on sugar, molasses, or starch; but usually made from sawdust (cellulin) by heating with potash and soda on iron plates, forming oxalates of potassium and sodium; on treating with Na_2CO_3 the potassium salt is washed out as K_2CO_3, the less soluble sodium oxalate remaining. Milk of lime is then added, and $NaOH$ and CaC_2O_4 are formed, the latter precipitating, and on treating with H_2SO_4, oxalic acid is set free in solution and obtained by crystallization.

(1) $2K_2C_2O_4 + Na_2C_2O_4 + 2Na_2CO_3 = 2K_2CO_3 + 3Na_2C_2O_4.$
(Potassium Oxalate.) (Sodium Oxalate.) (Sodium Carbonate.) (Potassium Carbonate.) (Sodium Oxalate.)

(2) $Na_2C_2O_4 + Ca(OH)_2 = 2NaOH + CaC_2O_4.$
(Sodium Oxalate.) (Calcium Hydroxide.) (Sodium Hydroxide.) (Calcium Oxalate.)

(3) $CaC_2O_4 + H_2SO_4 = CaSO_4 + H_2C_2O_4.$
(Calcium Oxalate.) (Sulphuric Acid.) (Calcium Sulphate.) (Oxalic Acid.)

Description. Colorless, transparent, odorless crystals; strong, acid taste, and reaction; sol. in water, or alcohol.

Impurities and tests. *Sulphuric acid:* Ba(NO$_3$)$_2$ = white ppt. *Organic impurities:* + H$_2$SO$_4$ + boil = black color.
Officinal as a Volumetric Solution.
Antidote. Magnesia, chalk or some other calcium salt.

Destructive Distillation of Cellulin.

ACIDUM ACETICUM. See Part II, page 68.

(CH$_3$OH) METHYLIC ALCOHOL.—WOOD ALCOHOL. (Methyl Alcohol. Wood Naphtha. Pyroxylic, or Pyroligneous Spirit.)

Found in the aqueous distillate obtained by the destructive distillation of wood, to the extent of 1%, together with acetic acid, acetone, etc. Separated by distilling with chalk to fix the acetic acid. Purified by distilling with calcium chloride, and again with water; rectified by carefully distilling with lime. *Properties.* A good solvent for shellac, etc.

Methylated Spirit. A mixture of ethyl and methyl alcohol containing 10% of the latter, and called Methylated Spirit is not held for duty in England.

PIX LIQUIDA.—TAR.

An empyreumatic oleoresin obtained by the destructive distillation of the wood of *Pinus Palustris*, and other species of Pinus.

Preparation. Billets of wood are piled in conical furnaces, and covered with a layer of earth and ignited above, with a draft regulated to keep up a slow combustion without flame; the tarry products collect in a ditch at the bottom of the pile. The pyroligneous acid and volatile oils of the wood are allowed to escape, thereby leaving charcoal and tar of a better quality than if the above were recovered.

Description. Thick, viscid, semi-fluid; blackish-brown; heavier than water; transparent in thin layers; becoming granular (due to the presence of pyro-catechin) or opaque by age; acid reaction; unpleasant, empyreumatic odor and taste. Slightly sol. in water, sol. in alcohol, ether or chloroform, fixed and volatile oils, and solutions of soda or potash.

Officinal Preparations. 1. Syrupus picis liquidæ. 2. Unguentum picis liquidæ.

SYRUPUS PICIS LIQUIDÆ.—SYRUP OF TAR. Tar is washed with cold water by maceration, to remove acetic acid. The soluble constituents of tar are then extracted by boiling water, and sugar is dissolved in the filtered liquid. *Dose:* f ℥ ss—f ℥ ij.

UNGUENTUM PICIS LIQUIDÆ. (Ointment of Tar.) Incorporate tar (50) with suet (50), using heat.

OLEUM PICIS LIQUIDÆ.—OIL OF TAR.

A volatile oil distilled from tar.

Description. An almost colorless liquid when fresh, but soon acquires a dark, reddish-brown color; strong tarry odor and taste; acid reaction; sp. gr., about 0.970; sol. in alcohol.

Pitch. Black Pitch. Pix navalis. The residue left after distilling the oil from tar.

CARBO LIGNI.—CHARCOAL.　WOOD CHARCOAL.

Charcoal prepared from soft wood. Made by heating wood to about 572° F., out of contact with air. Used as an ingredient in dentifrices. *Prop.* A great deoxidizer, absorbent and disinfectant.

CARBO ANIMALIS.—ANIMAL CHARCOAL.
(Bone black. Ivory black.)

Animal charcoal prepared from bone. Made by roasting bones deprived of fat in iron cylinders; an ammoniacal liquid called *bone-spirit*, and a dark tar called *bone-oil* distil over, the charcoal and inorganic constituents remaining.

Description. Dull-black powder, or granular fragments; odorless; nearly tasteless; insol. in water or alcohol.

Officinal Preparation. CARBO ANIMALIS PURIFICATUS.—PURIFIED ANIMAL CHARCOAL. Made by digesting animal charcoal with diluted HCl, decanting the liquid, and again digesting with water, washing thoroughly, draining and drying.

This process removes calcium phosphate and carbonate, and magnesium compounds.

Description. Dull black powder: odorless; tasteless; insoluble.

Impurities and tests. *Phosphates:* + HCl (dil.); filtrate + NH_4OH + test sol. magnesium = white ppt.

Properties: Removes organic coloring matters from solution, also tannin, alkaloids, and some metallic salts.

CREASOTUM.—CREASOTE.　(κρέας--flesh; σωξω—I save.)
(Oil of Smoke).

A product of the distillation of wood tar. The distillate separates into a heavy and light oily layer; the heavy oil is treated with Na_2CO_3 and distilled, that portion of the distillate which is heavier than water is treated with KOH, which dissolves the creasote, separating *eupion*. By repeated fractional distillations of the solution, alternately treating with H_2SO_4 and KOH, a pure product is obtained.

Description. An almost colorless, or yellowish, oily, inflammable liquid, becoming reddish yellow or brown on exposure to light; penetrating, smoky odor; burning caustic taste; neutral reaction; sp. gr. 1.035–1.085; sol. in water (80), abs. alcohol, ether, chloroform, benzin.

Impurities. *Carbolic acid.* See page 161.

Officinal Preparation. AQUA CREASOTI (Creasote Water). A one per cent solution in distilled water.

ACIDUM CARBOLICUM CRUDUM.—CRUDE CARBOLIC ACID.

A liquid obtained during the distillation of coal tar between the temperatures of 170°–190° C. (338°–378° F.), containing *carbolic* and *cresylic* acids in variable proportions, together with other substances. Obtained *directly* by distillation of the *dead oil* derived from coal tar.

Description. A nearly colorless or reddish-brown liquid; strong, disagreeable, empyreumatic odor, having a benumbing, blanching, and caustic effect on the skin or mucous membrane; neutral reaction.

Impurities. *Water:* + equal vol. chloroform = separation; *alkalies:* + litmus = blue color.

(C_6H_5OH — 94)   ACIDUM CARBOLICUM. — CARBOLIC ACID.
(Phenol. Phenic Acid. Phenylic Acid.)

A product of the distillation of coal tar between the temperatures of 180°-190° C. (356°-374° F.).

Description. Colorless, needle-shaped crystals, acquiring a pinkish tint, and becoming deliquescent on exposure; action on the skin same as the *crude* acid; neutral reaction; slightly aromatic odor resembling creasote; sweet taste (when diluted) with a slight burning aftertaste. Forms 5% and 95% solutions with water, other proportions producing turbidity. Sol. in alcohol, ether, chloroform, glycerin, benzol, CS_2, and oils. Crystals melt at 97°-107° F.; boil at 357°-366° F.

Characteristic reactions of Creasote and Carbolic Acid. *Creasote:* + collodion (or albumen solution) = transparent solution. *Carbolic acid:* + collodion (or albumen solution) = gelatinous mass. *Creasote:* Sol. + sol. Fe_2Cl_6 = blue color changing to green and brown, with brown ppt. *Carbolic acid:* Sol. + sol. Fe_2Cl_6 = red solution, becoming violet-blue. *Creasote:* Splinter of fir wood dipped into the solution, and then into HNO_3 or HCl = no reaction. *Carbolic acid:* Under similar circumstances = first blue, then brown.

On mixing equal volumes of 95% carbolic acid and glycerin, a clear mixture results, which remains clear on the addition of three volumes of water. (Creasote and cresylic acid produce turbidity.) Water is detected by the chloroform test.

Officinal Preparations. UNGUENTUM ACIDI CARBOLICI.—(Ointment of Carbolic Acid.) Made by incorporating carbolic acid (10) with ointment ft. 100.

($HC_7H_5O_3$—138)   ACIDUM SALICYLICUM.—SALICYLIC ACID.

Formerly prepared from oil of wintergreen, but at present from carbolic acid, which is converted into sodium carbolate and evaporated to dryness at a high heat in an atmosphere of CO_2, with the following reaction:

$$2NaC_6H_5O + CO_2 = Na_2C_7H_4O_3 + C_6H_5(OH).$$
$$\left(\begin{smallmatrix}\text{Sodium}\\\text{Carbolate.}\end{smallmatrix}\right) \quad \left(\begin{smallmatrix}\text{Carbon}\\\text{Dioxide.}\end{smallmatrix}\right) \quad \left(\begin{smallmatrix}\text{Normal Sodium}\\\text{Salicylate.}\end{smallmatrix}\right) \quad \text{(Phenol.)}$$

The residue after solution, is decomposed by HCl, forming impure salicylic acid.

Reaction: $Na_2C_7H_4O_3 + 2 HCl = HC_7H_5O_3 + 2 NaCl.$

The acid is purified by solution in alcohol, filtration through animal charcoal, and crystallization, or by subliming with steam.

Description. Fine, white, light acicular crystals; free from carbolic acid odor, but having a slight aromatic odor; sweetish and acrid taste; acid reaction; sol. in water (450), alcohol (2.5), ether (2), chloroform (80). *Test:* With iron salts it produces a violet red color.

Impurities and tests *Hydrochloric acid:* + $AgNO_3$ = white ppt. *Organic matter*, and *iron:* Evaporate solution = colored residue. *Foreign organic matter:* + conc. H_2SO_4 = color. *Carbolic acid:* Sol. + $KClO_3$ + HCl + NH_4OH = red or brown tint.

OLEUM SUCCINI.—OIL OF AMBER.

A volatile oil obtained by the destructive distillation of amber and purified by subsequent rectification. [*Amber* is a fossil resin obtained from a number of extinct coniferous trees found in Europe, Greenland and N. A.].

Description. Colorless, or pale-yellow, thin liquid; becoming dark and thick by age, and on exposure; empyreumatic and balsamic odor; sp. gr. 0.920; sol. in alcohol; produces with fuming HNO_3, a brown resinous mass called *artificial musk* on account of its odor.

COAL.

A fossil formation produced by a peculiar decomposition or fermentation of buried vegetable matter, found below the surface of the earth.

Theory of formation. $2C_6H_{10}O_5 = 5CH_4 + 5CO_2 + C_2.$
(Cellulin.)   (Methane.) $\left(\begin{smallmatrix} \text{Carbon} \\ \text{Dioxide.} \end{smallmatrix}\right)$ (Carbon.)

COAL TAR.

The residue obtained as one of the secondary products of coal gas manufacture. By the action of various acids and alkalies on coal tar, the beautiful *aniline* colors are produced.

AMYLACEOUS PRINCIPLES AND THEIR PRODUCTS.

AMYLUM.—STARCH.—WHEAT STARCH.

The fecula of the seed of *Triticum vulgare*. (N. O. Graminaceæ.)

Starch has the same chemical composition as *cellulose*, $C_6H_{10}O_5$, but differs widely from it in physical properties. It exists in various parts of plants during some period of their growth, in tuberous and bulbous roots, but especially in the seed in minute cells which may be distinguished by the aid of the microscope.

Its usefulness in the seed as a storehouse of food for the plant, depends upon its conversion into grape-sugar by the action of the moisture and warmth of the soil, when it is readily assimilated by the developing plantlet.

OCCURRENCE. Starch occurs most abundantly in the following plants: Potato, barley, indian corn, rye, wheat, arrow-root, salep, Iceland-moss, sago and tapioca.

Preparation. Made by macerating potatoes, wheat, or other grain in warm water (to which an alkali is sometimes added) until the outer coat softens; it is then ground or grated under water. The resulting soft mass is washed upon a sieve, when the starch granules pass through with the water, from which they separate on standing; finally drained and dried. The alkali water acts as a solvent for the gluten, but the latter is often removed by allowing the grain to undergo a slight fermentation. The quality of the starch depends upon the purity and quantity of the water used in washing.

The envelope of the starch granule is insoluble in cold water, but is ruptured on the application of heat, so that the contents are exposed and become dissolved, hence starch is said to be *insoluble* in *cold*, but *soluble* in *hot water*.

Restoration. Musty and mouldy starch may be restored by washing well with water, and re-drying.

Description. Irregular, angular, white masses, easily reduced to powder; odorless; tasteless; insol. in ether, alcohol or cold water. On triturating with cold water, the filtrate should have a neutral reaction.

Test. On boiling with water, it yields a white jelly, having a bluish tinge, which on cooling acquires a deep blue color on the addition of a solution of *iodine* (with *bromine*, a yellow or brown color results).

Officinal Preparations. 1. Amylum Iodatum. 2. Glyceritum Amyli.

AMYLUM IODATUM.—IODIZED STARCH. (Iodide of Starch.) Made by triturating iodine (5) with a small amount of water, gradually adding the starch under trituration till a uniform dark-blue color results, drying below 104° F. and powdering. Better results may be obtained by using ether in the place of water. This preparation decolorizes by the action of sunlight.

Often used as a general antidote for poisons.

SYRUP OF IODIDE OF STARCH. (Unofficinal.) Made by dissolving iodized starch in water, adding sugar, and heating till dissolved.

GLYCERITUM AMYLI. — GLYCERITE OF STARCH. (Plasma.) Made by rubbing starch (10) to a fine powder, then with glycerin (90) and heating to 284° F. (not above 291°) till the starch granules dissolve and form a translucent jelly.

Use. An excellent excipient for most pill masses, and a valuable substitute for lard or ointment in compound ointments.

DEXTRIN.—BRITISH GUM. ($C_6H_{10}O_5$)

Made by baking starch at about 500° F., or, by boiling starch with water acidulated with sulphuric or oxalic acid.

Reaction. $C_{18}H_{30}O_{15}$ + H_2O + H_2SO_4 = $C_6H_{12}O_6$
(Starch.)   (Water.)   (Sulphuric Acid.)   (Glucose.)
+ $2C_6H_{10}O_5$ + H_2SO_4.
(Dextrin.)   (Sulphuric Acid.)

A small quantity of glucose is also formed, which may be removed by treating with dilute alcohol, while the acid is neutralized by $CaCO_3$.

Description. Exists in granular form, or an amorphous gummy mass; sol. in water, insol. in alcohol or ether.

The solution is often used as a mucilage, and is employed for that purpose on postage stamps by the U. S. P. O. Dept.

($C_6H_{12}O_6$) GLUCOSE.—GRAPE-SUGAR.—STARCH-SUGAR.

Exists naturally in the grape, and other fruit.

Preparation. Made by boiling starch (100) with water (400) and sulphuric acid (5), until iodine ceases to produce a blue coloration. The free acid is neutralized with chalk, the filtrate clarified and decolorized (by treating with clay and animal charcoal) and concentrated in a vacuum pan.

Solid Grape Sugar occurs in whitish, granular powder, or masses; glucose also occurs as a syrupy liquid. When made directly from corn it is termed *Corn Syrup*.

Test for identity. Test-Solution of Potassio-Cupric Tartrate (similar to Fehling's Solution), which on boiling with a solution containing glucose, deposits a brick-red precipitate (*cuprous oxide*).

Fehling's Solution. Dissolve 34.64 grams $CuSO_4$ in 200 cm³ distilled water, and mix with a cold solution of 200 grams tartrate of sodium and potassium in 600 cm³ solution of soda (sp. gr. 1.20) and dilute with water to one liter. Ten (10) cm³ of this solution are reduced by 0.5 grams of grape-sugar.

SACCHARINE PRINCIPLES.

($C_{12}H_{22}O_{11}$—342) SACCHARUM.—REFINED SUGAR.—CANE SUGAR.

The refined sugar of *Saccharum officinarum.*

Cane-sugar exists in the sugar-cane, sugar maple, beet root, birch, palm, honey, sorghum, etc.

Preparation. Made by crushing the sugar-cane and expressing its juice, then clarifying by boiling—a little lime being added to neutralize free acid,—straining, and concentrating by rapid evaporation, then cooling and transferring to perforated casks, to drain off the liquid portion. The solid portion is called *raw* or *muscovado sugar*, and the liquid product *treacle* or *molasses.*

Refining. The raw sugar is dissolved in water, and the solution heated with blood, which acts as a mechanical clarifier. After straining, the liquid is filtered through animal charcoal. The colorless filtrate is concentrated in a vacuum pan (boiling at about 120° F.), and when of the proper density, cooled to crystallize, and placed in centrifugal machines to remove the mother-liquor from the crystals. The product constitutes the *refined* or *loaf sugar*, and the uncrystallizable mother-liquor is known as *sugar-house molasses.* Slightly discolored (yellow) sugar is made whiter by the addition of Prussian Blue, thereby producing a bluish white.

Description. White, dry, hard, crystalline granules; odorless; purely sweet taste; neutral reaction. Soluble in water (0.5), alcohol (175), insol. ether.

Impurities and tests. *Insoluble salts, foreign matter, ultramarine, prussian blue*, etc.: Aq. or alc. solution deposits sediment on long standing. *Grape-sugar*, and *inverted sugar :* Sol. $+ AgNO_3$ $+ NH_4OH +$ boil $=$ black ppt.

Use. As a preservative for liquid preparations, and to mask the taste of unpleasant medicines.

Officinal Preparation. Syrupus (and compound syrups).

SYRUPUS.—SYRUP. Sugar (65) is dissolved in water (35) using heat, and strained. Sp. gr. 1.310.

Officinal Preparation. Syrupus Acaciæ (see Acacia.)

Caramel.—Burnt Sugar. ($C_{12}H_{18}O_9$).

Made by heating cane-sugar to 392° F.; also prepared from inferior qualities of sugar, molasses or glucose. Used as a coloring agent.

($C_{12}H_{22}O_{11}.H_2O$—360) Saccharum Lactis.—Milk Sugar. (Lactose.)

A peculiar crystalline sugar, obtained from the whey of cow's milk.

Preparation. Made by removing the cream from milk, then on the addition of an acid the caseine is removed in a coagulated condition called *curds*. The liquid portion (or *whey*) is concentrated and allowed to crystallize on sticks or cords suspended in large tanks. Whiter crystals are derived by re-crystallization from an aqueous solution.

Description. White, hard, crystalline masses, yielding a white powder, feeling gritty on the tongue; odorless; faint, sweet taste; neutral reaction; sol. in water (7), insol. alcohol, ether or chloroform.

Impurities and tests. *Cane-sugar:* $+ H_2SO_4 =$ brown or black color, within an hour.

Mel.—Honey.

A saccharine secretion deposited in the honey-comb by *Apis mellifica* (Honey Bee) (Class, *Insecta ;* Order, *Hymenoptera*). Obtained by draining the comb, thus producing *virgin honey* the purest article. A darker-colored honey is obtained by the use of pressure or heat.

Composition. Contains about 80% sugar, representing about equal quantities of grape-sugar or *dextrose* (which renders honey granular) and fruit-sugar or *levulose*, which remains liquid.

Description. A syrupy liquid, light-yellow or brown-yellow in color; gradually becoming crystalline by age or reduction of temperature; sweet, faintly acrid taste.

Impurities and tests. Any admixture of *glucose* may be detected by testing for calcium sulphate. *Starch:* Boiled solution $+ I =$ blue color. *Chlorides:* $+ AgNO_3 =$ white ppt.

Officinal Preparation. Mel Despumatum.—Clarified Honey.

Heat honey on water-bath, and add a small quantity of cold water; the scum which arises and floats on the water can be poured off, free from all honey.

Officinal Preparations. 1. Confectio rosæ. 2. Mel rosæ. [J. A.]

Confectio Rosæ.—Confection of Rose. Contains powd. red rose (8), powd. sugar (64), clarified honey (12). and rose-water (16).

Mel Rosæ.—Honey of Rose. Powd. red rose is percolated with diluted alcohol, and mixed with clarified honey.

Cera Flava.—Yellow Wax. Beeswax.

A peculiar, concrete substance prepared by *Apis mellifica*—Honey bee (Class, *Insecta ;* Order, *Hymenoptera*.) Wax is secreted in thin scales about the abdomen of the honey bee, and is used in the formation of the hexagonal cells of the comb, in which the honey is afterwards deposited.

How Obtained. By draining off the honey, and expressing the comb, or separating by means of centrifugal machines, melting in water, and running into moulds.

Composition. *Myricin, cerotic acid* or *cerin, cerolein,* and aromatic and coloring matter.

Description. Yellowish, or brownish yellow solid; agreeable, honey-like odor; faint, balsamic taste; brittle when cold, becoming plastic by the heat of the hand; fusing at 145°–147° F., insol. in water, sol. in boiling alcohol (300), partly sol. in cold alcohol, sol. in ether (35), chloroform (11), turpentine and oils; sp. gr. 0.955–0.967.

Impurities, adulterations and tests. *Paraffin:* 1. When melted *wax* congeals, it presents a *smooth level surface;* while the surface of *paraffin,* or of wax adulterated with paraffin, is *concave.* 2. When heated with H_2SO_4, *wax is completely destroyed,* while *paraffin* (also *mineral,* or *earth wax*) *is unaffected.* *Fats, fatty acids, Japan wax, resin:* $+$ sol. $NaOH +$ boil: filt. $+ HCl =$ ppt. *Soap:* $+ H_2O +$ boil: filt. $+ HCl =$ ppt.

Officinal Preparations. 1. Ceratum Resinæ (and compound cerates). 2. Unguentum.

CERATUM RESINÆ. — RESIN CERATE. (Basilicon ointment.) Contains resin (35), yellow wax (15), lard (50), incorporated by heat.

Officinal Preparation. LINIMENTUM TEREBINTHINÆ. (Turpentine Liniment.) Melted resin cerate (65), oil of turpentine (35), are thoroughly incorporated.

UNGUENTUM.—OINTMENT. Contains lard (80), yellow wax (20), thoroughly incorporated by heat.

CERA ALBA.—WHITE WAX.

Yellow wax, bleached. *Method.* Melted wax is run through a trough upon wet revolving cylinders, where it congeals in thin ribbon-like sheets (or it is granulated) and is exposed to light and air, being frequently turned and moistened. The process is repeated until the wax is white. Sometimes bleached by the aid of chlorine, which is objectionable.

Description. A yellowish-white solid, generally in the form of circular cakes; translucent in thin layers; slightly rancid odor; insipid taste; melts at 149° F.; sp. gr. 0.965–0.975.

Impurities: Same as mentioned under yellow wax.

Officinal Preparation. Ceratum (and compound cerates).

CERATUM. (Cerate. Simple cerate.) Incorporate white wax (30), and lard (70), with heat.

EXUDATIONS OF PLANTS.

The Exudations of Plants represent the moisture derived from the soil and atmosphere, holding in solution some peculiar medicament found in the plant.

GUMS.

The *gums* are concrete substances that flow from trees and harden by spontaneous evaporation; nearly or wholly soluble in water, but the insoluble portion is also insoluble in alcohol.

Gums are divided into two classes:

True Gums. 1. Arabins: wholly soluble in water. 2. Bassorins: insoluble in, but swelling with water.

Ceracins (cherry gums, etc.). Insoluble in water.

Solutions of gums are called *mucilages.*

ACACIA.—GUM ARABIC.

A gummy exudation from *Acacia Verek*, and from other species of *Acacia* (N. O. *Leguminosæ. Mimosæ*). *Hab.* Egypt, Smyrna, Turkey.

Collection. The gum exudes spontaneously during the hot summer months, but is hastened by incisions.

Description. Roundish tears, or angular fragments, having a glass-like fracture; opaque from numerous fissures, but transparent in thin pieces. The best quality is colorless or white, while inferior varieties have more or less of a yellowish or brownish tint; odorless; insipid mucilaginous taste; insol. in alcohol; sol. in water, forming a thick mucilaginous liquid, having an acid reaction.

Incompatibles. Its solution yields gelatinous precipitates with solution subacetate of lead (*but not with acetate of lead*), and soluble silicates, ferric salts, and borax. Sp. gr. 1,355–1.525.

Composition. A compound of *arabic* or *gummic acid*, with calcium, magnesium or potassium.

Impurities and adulterations. *Flour:* Boil with water = gelatinous mass. *Starch:* + test-sol. iodine = blue color. *Dextrin:* Fehling's Solution = red ppt.,due to the presence of glucose, always found in dextrin.

The best test for purity and quality may be said to be the absence of color in the mucilage. Acacia is used in the preparation of many of the officinal mixtures and troches.

Officinal Preparation. MUCILAGO ACACIÆ. (Mucilage of Acacia.) Made by washing acacia (34) with *cold* water; and dissolving in water (66) by agitation. Best made by circulatory displacement. Used as a vehicle and an emulsifying agent.

Officinal Preparation. SYRUPUS ACACIÆ. (Syrup of Acacia.) Mucilage acacia (25), syrup (75), mix. Should be freshly made when required for use.

TRAGACANTHA.—TRAGACANTH.

A gummy exudation from *Astragalus gummifer*, and from other species of *Astragalus.* (N. O. *Leguminosæ. Papilionaceæ.*)

Hab. Asia Minor, Persia.

Composition. Contains a large amount of soluble gum (not identical with *arabin*) and an insoluble gum, *bassorin*, and *pectin*.

Description. Narrow, or broad ribbons; more or less curved or contorted, marked by parallel lines or ridges; color white or faintly yellowish; translucent, hornlike, tough, swelling in water to a gelatinous mass (which is tinged blue by test-solution iodine), the fluid portion of which is not precipitated by alcohol.

Used as an excipient in pill masses and troches.

Officinal Preparation. MUCILAGO TRAGACANTHÆ. (Mucilage of Tragacanth.) Tragacanth is digested in a boiling mixture of glycerin (18) and water (76) and strained forcibly through muslin. The glycerin prevents it from drying out and rendering pills insoluble, when used as an excipient.

MUCILAGINES.—MUCILAGES.

Beside the mucilages of acacia and tragacanth already referred to, three others are officinal.

MUCILAGO CYDONII. (Quince-Seed Mucilage. Bandolin.) Made by macerating cydonium (2) with distilled water, and straining. Not precipated by borax.

MUCILAGO SASSAFRAS MEDULLÆ. (Mucilage of Sassafras-Pith.) Sassafras-pith (2), water (100), made by maceration. Not precipitated by alcohol.

MUCILAGO ULMI. (Mucilage of Slippery Elm Bark.) Digest sliced elm bark (6) with boiling water (100). Precipitated by alcohol, and lead acetate.

Flaxseed also produces a mucilage with water, but there is no officinal preparation. The mucilage is precipitated by alcohol, and lead subacetate.

SYRUPUS ALTHÆÆ.—SYRUP OF ALTHÆA. A mucilage is obtained by macerating cut althæa (4) with cold water. In forty parts of the drained mucilage, sugar (60) is dissolved by agitation.

GUM RESINS.

The *gum-resins* are exudations partly soluble in water, and partly in alcohol, soluble in diluted alcohol, and form emulsions when triturated with water.

AMMONIACUM.—AMMONIAC.

A gum resin obtained from *Dorema ammoniacum* (N. O. *Umbelliferæ.*) *Hab.* Persia, Tartary.

Composition. Contains about 4% of volatile oil, 70% resin, 22% gum, and 4% bassorin or gluten. When fused with KOH, resorcin, oxalic acid and a fatty acid result.

Description. Roundish tears; externally pale yellowish-brown, internally milk-white, of a peculiar odor; bitter, acrid, nauseous taste; yields a milk-white emulsion.

Officinal Preparations. 1. Mistura ammoniaci. 2. Emplastrum ammoniaci. 3. Emp. ammoniaci cum hydrargyro. (See Mercury.)

MISTURA AMMONIACI. (Ammoniac Mixture.) Rub ammoniac (4) with water (100), in portions; when thoroughly mixed, strain.

EMPLASTRUM AMMONIACI. (Ammoniac plaster.) Digest ammoniac (100) in dilute acetic acid (140), until entirely emulsionized; strain and evaporate to plaster consistence.

ASAFŒTIDA.—ASAFETIDA.

A gum resin obtained from the root of *Ferula scorodosma* (N. O. *Umbelliferæ. Orthospermæ.*) *Hab.* Africa.

Composition. 9% volatile oil (sulphide of ferulyl or lasseryl C_6H_{11}), 65% resin, and 25% gum.

Description. Masses of whitish tears, imbedded in a yellowish gray, or brownish-gray sticky mass; internally, the tears are of a milk-white color, which changes to pink, and gradually to brown; persistent, alliaceous odor; bitter, acrid taste. When triturated with water, it yields a milk-white emulsion.

Officinal Preparations. 1. Emplastrum asafœtidæ. 2. Mistura asafœtidæ. 3. Pilulæ aloes et asafœtidæ. 4. Pil. asafœtidæ. 5. Pil. galbani compositæ. 6. Tinctura asafœtidæ(20%).

EMPLASTRUM ASAFŒTIDÆ. (Asafetida Plaster.) Asafetida (35), lead plaster (35), galbanum (15), and yellow wax (15), are thoroughly incorporated by the aid of alcohol and heat.

MISTURA ASAFŒTIDÆ. (Asafetida mixture. Milk of asafetida.) Rub asafetida (4) with water (100) gradually added.

PILULÆ ALOES ET ASAFŒTIDÆ. (Pills of aloes and asafetida.) Each pill contains 1⅓ grains, each, of purified aloes, asafetida, and soap.

PILULÆ ASAFŒTIDÆ. (Pills of asafetida.) Each pill contains galbanum 1½ gr., myrrh 1½ gr., asafetida ½ gr., and syrup.

CAMBOGIA.—GAMBOGE.

A gum resin obtained from *Garcinia Hanburii.* (N. O. *Guttiferæ.*) *Hab.* China, Siam.

Description. Solid or hollow cylindrical sticks, called *pipes* (on account of the juice being conveyed into bamboo canes, drying out in the above form). Orange-red, or in powder bright yellow; odorless; acrid taste; the powder, sternutatory; yields bright yellow emulsion with water, and forms an orange-red solution with KOH, from which HCl precipitates a yellow resin.

Composition. Contains *gambogic acid*, which precipitates yellow with lead acetate, and brown with iron, or copper salts.

Officinal Preparation. Pil. catharticæ comp. (See Calomel.)

MYRRHA.—MYRRH.

A gum resin obtained from *Balsamodendron Myrrha.* (N. O. *Burseraceæ.*) *Hab.* Arabia, Africa. Contains 60% gum, 35% resin, and 2½% vol. oil.

Description. Roundish, or irregular tears, or masses; brownish yellow or reddish-brown; balsamic odor; bitter, acrid taste. Yields a brownish-yellow emulsion, with HNO_3.

Officinal Preparations. Mistura ferri compositæ (see *Iron*). 2. Pil. aloes et myrrhæ. 3. Pil. ferri comp. (see *Iron*). 4. Pil. galbani comp. (see *Asafetida*). 5. Tinct. aloes et myrrhæ (10% of each). 6. Tinct. Myrrhæ (20%). 7. Pilulæ Aloes et Myrrhæ (Pills of aloes and myrrh. Rufus' Pills). Each contains purified aloes 2 grs., myrrh 1 gr., aromatic powder ½ gr.

RESINS.

Resins are solid or semi-solid exudations, insoluble in water, generally soluble in alcohol, ether, chloroform and light hydrocarbons.

Natural Resins.

MASTICHE.—MASTIC.

A concrete resinous exudation from *Pistacia Lentiscus.* (N. O. *Terebinthaceæ. Anacardieæ.*) *Hab.* Grecian Archipelago.

Composition. Volatile oil, *mastichic acid* 90% (a resin soluble in alcohol.)

Description. Globular or elongated tears; about the size of a pea; pale-yellow, transparent; brittle, becoming plastic when chewed; resinous odor; turpentine taste.

Officinal Preparation. Pilulæ Aloes et Mastiches. (Pills of Aloes and Mastic. Lady Webster's Dinner Pills.) Each contains purified aloes 2 grs., mastic ½ gr., and powd. red rose ½ gr.

PIX BURGUNDICA.—BURGUNDY PITCH.

The prepared resinous exudation of *Abies excelsa.* (N. O. *Coniferæ.*) *Hab.* N. Asia, N. Europe.

Contains. A vol. oil and resin (*abietic acid.*)

Description. Hard, gradually taking the form of the vessel in which it is kept; brittle, opaque or translucent; reddish-brown color; aromatic, not bitter taste; almost entirely insoluble in glacial acetic acid.

Officinal Preparations. 1. Emplastrum Picis Burgundicæ. 2. Emp. Picis cum Cantharide.

Emplastrum Picis Burgundicæ. (Burgundy Pitch Plaster.) Burgundy pitch (90), and yellow wax (10), incorporated with heat.

Emplastrum Picis cum Cantharide. (Pitch Plaster with Cantharides. Warming Plaster.) Burg. Pitch (92), and cerate cantharides (8); incorporate, using heat.

PIX CANADENSIS.—CANADA PITCH. (Hemlock Pitch.)

The prepared resinous exudation of *Abies Canadensis* (N. O. *Coniferæ.*). *Hab.* Canada and No. U. S. Contains one or more resins and a small quantity of volatile oil (called *oil of spruce,* or *oil of hemlock.*

Description. Resembles Burgundy Pitch.

Officinal Preparation. Emplastrum Picis Canadensis. (Canada, or Hemlock Pitch Plaster.) Canada pitch (90), yellow wax (10); incorporate, using heat.

GUAIACI RESINA.—GUAIAC.

The resin of the wood of *Guaiacum officinale* (N. O. *Zygophyllaceæ*.)
The heart-wood is officinal also, under the name of *Guaiaci Lignum*, and is used in the form of raspings. Contains 20–25% resin.
Hab. W. Indies, and coast of S. A. and Florida.

Composition of Resin. Contains three acids (*guaiacic* 10%, *guaiaretic* 10%, and *guaiaconic* 70%), gum 4%, and impurities.

Description. In masses, or sub-globular pieces; greenish, or reddish-brown color, depending on the age of the trees; feebly aromatic and acrid; powder grayish, becoming green on exposure; sol. in solution potash, and in alcohol. The alcoholic solution is colored blue by tincture of ferric chloride.

Officinal Preparations. 1. Tinctura Guaiaci (20%). 2. Tinctura Guaiaci Ammoniata (20%).

GUTTA PERCHA.

The concrete exudation of *Isonandra Gutta.* (N. O. *Sapotaceæ*.)
Hab. Malayan Peninsula, and Archipelago.

Contains a white crystalline resin, called *Albane*, and yellow amorphous *fluavil*.

Description. Grayish, or yellowish, hard, somewhat flexible, but scarcely elastic mass; plastic above 140° F., and very soft at 212° F. Insoluble in water or alcohol; sol. in chloroform, oil of turpentine, CS_2, benzin or benzol.

Officinal Preparation. Liquor Gutta-Perchæ. (Solution of gutta-percha.) Made by dissolving gutta-percha (9) in chloroform (91), and clarifying by means of lead carbonate in fine powder (10), which carries the impurities to the bottom.

SCAMMONIUM.—SCAMMONY.

A resinous exudation from the root of *Convolvulus Scammonia* (N. O. *Convolvulaceæ.*) *Hab.* Asia Minor. The root yields about 5% of resin. Scammony should contain 80–90% of resin; the finest grade is known in commerce as *virgin scammony*, the *pure* resin is termed *scammonin*.

Description. Irregular, angular pieces, or circular cakes; greenish-gray, or blackish; peculiar cheese-like odor; slightly acrid taste; yields a greenish emulsion with water.

Ether should dissolve at least 75%, and on evaporating the ether, the residue dissolved in hot solution of potash is not precipitated by dil. H_2SO_4.

Adulterations. *Chalk :* + dil. HCl = effervescence. *Starch :* Cooled decoction + test-sol. iodine = blue color.

Officinal Preparation. Resina Scammonii. (See Artificial Resins.)

Artificial Resins.

Artificial resins are extracted from the drug by means of a simple solvent, the resulting solution after concentration being poured into water, when the resin separates, falling to the bottom of the vessel; or, made by distilling the volatile oil from an oleo-resin.

RESINA.—RESIN. (COLOPHONY.)

The residue left after distilling off the volatile oil from Turpentine.

Composition. The anhydride of *abietic acid,* which is converted into the acid on agitation with warm diluted alcohol.

Description. A transparent, amber-colored substance; hard, brittle, with a glossy and shallow conchoidal fracture; turpentine odor and taste: sp. gr. 1.07–1.08; sol. in alcohol, ether, fixed and volatile oils.

Officinal Preparations. 1. Ceratum resinæ (see *Wax*). 2. Emplastrum resinæ. (Resin Plaster. Adhesive Plaster.) Resin (14), lead plaster (80), and yellow wax (6); incorporate, using heat.

RESINA COPAIBA.—RESIN OF COPAIBA. (Copaivic Acid.)

The residue left after distilling of the volatile oil from Copaiba.

RESINA JALAPÆ.—RESIN OF JALAP.

Obtained from *Jalapa,* the tuberous root of *Exegonium Purga,* which should assay not less than 12% resin. Powdered Jalap is percolated with alcohol till exhausted, and the percolate reduced to a syrupy consistence and poured into cold water. The resin subsides, while the water holds in solution the sugar and other principles.

Description. Partly soluble in ether; insol. in CS_2, soluble in NH_4OH (50), and on evaporation the residue dissolves in water. The ammoniacal solution should not gelatinize on cooling, and should not be precipitated by an acid.

RESINA PODOPHYLLI.—RESIN OF PODOPHYLLUM.

Process identical with that for resin of jalap, except that the water employed is acidulated with 1% of HCl.

Description. Grayish white, with a tinge of yellow. Partly soluble in ether; the residue after solution in KOH is precipitated by HCl.

RESINA SCAMMONII.—RESIN OF SCAMMONY.

Powd. scammony is exhausted by digestion, using boiling alcohol, but otherwise treated like jalap. Soluble in ether.

Officinal Preparation. Extractum colocynthidis compositum. (Compound extract of colocynth.) Contains extract of colocynth (16), purif. aloes (50), cardamom (6), resin scammony (14), and powd. soap, thoroughly incorporated, dried and powdered.

Officinal Preparation. Pil. catharticæ comp. (See Calomel.)

OLEO-RESINS.

The *Oleo-Resins* are resins combined with a volatile oil; obtained either as an exudation, or derived from the portion of the plant in which they exist, by means of a solvent.

Natural Oleo-resins.

TEREBINTHINA.—TURPENTINE. (Crude Turpentine.)

A concrete oleo-resin obtained from *Pinus Australis,* and from other species of *Pinus.* (N. O. Coniferæ.) *Hab.* Southern United States.

OLEUM TEREBINTHINÆ. (Oil of Turpentine.)

A volatile oil distilled from turpentine.

Description. Thin, colorless liquid; characteristic odor and taste; neutral, or faint acid reaction, sp. gr. 0.855–0.870; sol. in alcohol (6); explodes with bromine or iodine, and takes fire if brought in contact with a mixture of HNO_3 and H_2SO_4.

Officinal Preparations. 1. Linimentum Cantharidis. 2. Linimentum Terebinthinæ.

Linimentum Cantharidis. (Cantharides Liniment.) Digest cantharides (60) with oil turpentine (100) for three hours; strain and add q.s. oil turpentine ft. (100).

Linimentum Terebinthinæ. (Turpentine Liniment.) Made by mixing resin cerate (65), and oil of turpentine (35).

TEREBINTHINA CANADENSIS. (Canada Turpentine. Balsam Fir. Canada Balsam.)

The liquid oleo-resin obtained from *Abies Balsamea.* (N.O. *Coniferæ.*) *Hab.* N. A.

Description. Yellowish, or faintly greenish, transparent, viscid liquid of an agreeable terebinthinate odor; bitterish, slightly acrid taste; soluble in ether, chloroform, or benzol.

COPAIBA.—COPAIBA BALSAM. (Copaiva.)

The oleo-resin of *Copaifera Langsdorfii,* and other species of Copaifera. (N. O. *Leguminosæ.*) *Hab.* So. America.

Description. A transparent or translucent, viscid liquid; pale yellow to brownish yellow; peculiar, aromatic odor; bitter and acrid taste; sp. gr. 0.940–0.993. Soluble in abs. alcohol.

Impurities and tests. *Fixed oils:* + heat = turpentine odor; or, after distillation, a resin not hard or friable remains. *Gurjun balsam :* solution in CS_2 + mixture of H_2SO_4 and HNO_3 = purple, or violet color.

Officinal Preparation. MASSA COPAIBÆ.—MASS OF COPAIBA. (Pill Copaiba.) Copaiba (94), magnesia (6); mix intimately and set aside to form a pilular mass. If a pilular consistence does not result in 8 or 10 hours, a deficiency of water in the copaiba may be inferred. This difficulty may be avoided by shaking the oleo-resin with 5% of water, and after standing for a time, decant from the uncombined water.

Derived Oleo-resins.

The Derived Oleo-resins are made by percolating the powdered drug with stronger ether till exhausted; the residue left on evaporation of the solvent is the *oleo-resin.*

The following six are officinal: Oleoresina Aspidii (yield 10–15%); Capsici (yield about 4%); Cubebæ (yields 18–25%); Lupulin (yield 50%); Piperis (yield 5%); Zingiberis (yield 5–7%).

EMPLASTRUM CAPSICI. (Capsicum Plaster.) Melted resin plaster is thinly spread on muslin, and when cooled, a thin coating of oleo-resin capsicum is applied by means of a brush. Each sq. inch should contain one grain oleo-resin.

TROCHISCI CUBEBÆ. (Troches of Cubeb.) Each contains ½ grain oleo-resin cubeb, combined with oil of sassafras, extract of glycyrrhiza, powdered acacia and syrup tolu.

BALSAMS.

Balsams are oleo-resins or gum-resins, containing either benzoic or cinnamic acid, or both.

BALSAMUM PERUVIANUM.—BALSAM PERU.

A balsam obtained from *Myroxylon Pareiræ.* (N. O. *Leguminosæ.*) *Hab.* Cent. America.

Constituents. Cinnamic and benzoic acids, resin 32%, benzylic benzoate and cinnamate 60 %, and stilbene.

Description. A thick, brownish-black liquid; syrupy consistence; smoky, but agreeable balsamic odor; warm, bitter and acrid taste; sp. gr. 1.135–1.150; sol. in alcohol (5); miscible with absolute alcohol, chloroform, and glacial acetic acid.

Impurities and tests. *Fixed oils,* and *alcohol:* $+$ equal vol. benzin or water=diminished volume. Other adulterations: copaiba, gurjun balsam, rosin, turpentines, storax and alcohol.

BALSAMUM TOLUTANUM.—BALSAM OF TOLU.

A balsam obtained from *Myroxylon Toluifera* (N.O. *Leguminosæ.*) *Hab.* So. America.

Constituents. Cinnamic and benzoic acids, amorphous resin, benzylic ether of cinnamic and benzoic acids, *toluene* 1%, and toluol.

Description. Yellowish or brownish-yellow semi-fluid or nearly solid mass; brittle when cold; agreeable balsamic odor; mild aromatic taste. Its alcoholic solution has an acid reaction; almost insol. in water and benzine.

Adulterations. Turpentines (sol. in CS_2), copaiba and castor oil.

Officinal Preparations. 1. Syrupus Tolutana. 2. Tinctura Tolutana (10%).

SYRUPUS TOLUTANA (Syrup of Tolu). Digest Tolu (4) with sugar and water at 180° F. for two hours; cool and strain ft. 100. [An objectional method, yielding an unsightly preparation.]

STYRAX.—STORAX. (LIQUID STORAX).

A balsam prepared from the inner bark of *Liquidambar orientalis.* (N. O. *Hamamelaceæ.*) *Hab.* Asia Minor.

Constituents. *Styrole* (or *cinnamin*), *styracin,* cinnamic acid, benzoic acid, *storesin,* and two resins.

Description. Semi-liquid, gray, sticky, opaque; agreeable odor; balsamic taste; sol. in warm alcohol.

Officinal Preparation. Tinct. benzoinii composita.

BENZOINUM.—GUM BENZOIN. (Gum Benjamin.)

A balsamic resin obtained from *Styrax Benzoin.* (N. O. *Styraceæ.*) *Hab.* E. Indies and China.

Constituents. Benzoic acid (12–20%), but no cinnamic acid; volatile oil, and several resins.

Description. Masses of yellowish-brown tears (internally milk white) or reddish-brown mass mottled from the presence of whitish tears (the number of whitish tears diminishing as the trees become old). Almost wholly soluble in warm alcohol (5), and solution of potassa. When heated, fumes of benzoic acid are given off; slight aromatic taste, agreeable balsamic odor.

To detect Cinnamic Acid: Boil with milk of lime; the hot filtrate should not evolve the odor of HCN on adding test solution of potass. permanganate.

Officinal Preparations. 1. Adeps benzoinatus. 2. Tinct. benzoinii (20%). 3. Tinct. benzoinii compositæ.

ADEPS BENZOINATUS.—BENZOINATED LARD. (Ointment of Benzoin.) Made by suspending powdered benzoin (2) in melted lard (100), for two hours at 140° F., straining and stirring while cooling. Used in preparing many of the compound ointments.

($HC_7H_5O_2$—122) ACIDUM BENZOICUM.—BENZOIC ACID.
(Flowers of Benzoin.)

Occurrence. Found in benzoin, balsams tolu and peru, storax and other resinous exudations.

Preparation. Made by subliming benzoin, and allowing the vapors to pass through a cone of filter paper into a condenser, or by decomposing a solution of benzoate of sodium or calcium with HCl, and purifying the resulting crystals.

Most of the benzoic acid of commerce is, however, derived from urine or tar products.

The urine of cattle or horses is treated with lime in excess and evaporated; the resulting calcium hippurate is decomposed with HCl, forming impure hippuric acid, which after purification and subsequent boiling with HCl, produces the following result.

Reaction. $C_9H_9NO_3 + H_2O = C_7H_6O_2 + C_2H_5NO_2$.
$\underset{\text{(Hippuric Acid.)}}{} \quad \underset{\text{(Water.)}}{} \quad \underset{\text{(Benzoic Acid.)}}{} \quad \underset{\text{(Glycocoll.)}}{}$

When made from *Naphthalene* $C_{10}H_8$ (a derivative of coal tar), this substance is treated with HNO_3, producing *phthalic acid*, $C_8H_6O_4$, which is converted into a calcium salt, and on mixing with excess of $Ca(OH)_2$ is decomposed into calcium carbonate and benzoate; from the latter, benzoic acid is liberated by treating with HCl.

Description. White, lustrous scales or friable needles, permanent in air; slight aromatic odor of benzoin; warm, acid taste and reaction; sol. in water (500), alcohol (3), ether (3), chloroform (7) and CS_2.

Test. The neutral salts produce flesh-colored precipitates with dilute solutions of ferric sulphate.

Impurities and tests. *Chlorobenzoic acid:* On igniting in a loop of platinum wire with cuprous oxide = greenish color. *Cinnamic Acid:* See Benzoin for test.

MALTUM.—MALT. (BARLEY MALT.)

The seed of *Hordeum distichum,* caused to enter the incipient stage of germination by artificial means, and dried.

Made by soaking barley in water and placing in heaps, when heat is spontaneously generated and germination takes place; the germ, (or sprout) having acquired the desired length, the grain is quickly dried, and becomes malt.

During the germination of all seeds, either by natural or artificial means, a peculiar substance is developed, known as *diastase*, a body which, like *ptyalin*, possesses the properties of converting starch into dextrin and glucose.

Officinal Preparation. EXTRACTUM MALTI. (Extract of Malt.) Made by macerating malt with water and digesting with more water below 130° F., expressing, and evaporating the liquid to a thick honey consistence.

FERMENTATION.

The term *fermentation* refers to several processes of decomposition dependent on the presence of a certain substance or a compound called a *ferment*, which does not enter into any chemical composition with the fermenting body. and is capable of producing an unlimited quantity of products.

Kinds. There are various kinds of fermentation; the conversion of starch into dextrin or sugar by *diastase* is called *saccharine fermentation;* the transformation of milk sugar into lactic acid by *casein* is termed lactic fermentation; the changing of cane-sugar into mucus and mannit by proteids is known as *mucic fermentation;* the production of butyric acid from milk sugar and lactic acid is designated *butyric fermentation;* the production of alcohol from grape- or fruit-sugar by the action of yeast signifies *alcoholic* or *vinous fermentation;* the oxidation of alcohol into acetic acid is *acetic fermentation.*

Other kinds of fermentation may be represented by the action of *pepsin* on albumen, *ptyalin* on starch, *pancreatin* on fats, *emulsin* on glucosides, etc.

ALCOHOL.

Alcohol is produced by the fermentation of grape sugar. Cane-sugar is unfermentable until it has been inverted by the action of diluted acids or a *ferment*.

Preparation. Nearly all alcohol is derived from amylaceous substances, such as corn, rye. potatoes, etc., which are *mashed* with water, and on the addition of malt, by the influence of its *diastase*, the starch of the grain is converted into *maltose*.

Reaction. $\underset{\text{(Starch.)}}{3C_6H_{10}O_5} + \underset{\text{(Water.)}}{H_2O} = \underset{\text{(Maltose.)}}{C_{12}H_{22}O_{11}} + \underset{\text{(Starch.)}}{C_6H_{10}O_5}.$

Then by the action of maltose upon more starch, glucose is obtained.

Reaction. $\underset{\text{(Maltose.)}}{C_{12}H_{22}O_{11}} + \underset{\text{(Starch.)}}{C_6H_{10}O_5} + \underset{\text{(Water.)}}{2H_2O} = \underset{\text{(Glucose.)}}{3C_6H_{12}O_6}.$

On the addition of yeast to the mixture, which must be kept at a temperature of 64°-82° F., the *yeast-plant* (*saccharomyces cerevisiæ*) converts the grape-sugar into alcohol and carbonic anhydride.

Reaction. $C_6H_{12}O_6 = 2C_2H_5OH + 2CO_2.$
(Glucose.)   (Alcohol.)   (Carbon Dioxide.)

There is also produced at the same time glycerin, fusel oil, succinic acid, etc.

On distilling the fermented liquid, a weak spirit called *crude whiskey* is obtained.

Preparation of Liquors.—If the mash is made of potatoes or grain, the distilled spirit is termed *whiskey*, and contains amylic alcohol, œnanthic and other ethers, to which the odor is due; if distilled from wine, *brandy* is obtained—odor due to œnanthic, propylic and other ethers; when distilled from fermented molasses, *rum* is obtained —odor due to butyric acid; on distilling spirits with juniper berries, *gin* is obtained.

Purification of Alcohol. To obtain pure alcohol, the crude whiskey is leached through charcoal which absorbs most of its fusel oil, and sometimes distilled with certain chemicals ($AgNO_3$, $K_2Mn_2O_8$, etc.) with a view to further destroying the remaining fusel oil. The spirit is concentrated by distillation in a column-still, thereby removing the last traces of fusel oil, and most of the water.

Absolute Alcohol. To obtain absolute alcohol, the strong alcohol is treated for some time with lime, chloride of calcium, or some other deliquescent salt for the purpose of removing water, and afterwards carefully distilled. Absolute alcohol must be kept in well-corked bottles, on account of its great affinity for moisture of the atmosphere.

(C_2H_5OH—46) Alcohol.—Ethyl Alcohol.

A liquid composed of 91%, by weight, (94% by volume) of ethyl alcohol, and 9% weight, (6% by volume) of water. Sp. gr. 0.820 at 60° F., or 0.812 at 77° F.

Description. A transparent, colorless, volatile liquid, with a characteristic, pungent and agreeable odor, and burning taste; neutral reaction; boils at 78° C. (172.4° F.), burns with blue flame, without smoke.

Impurities and tests. *Fusel oil:* + equal volume water + ⅙ vol. glycerin; on wetting a piece of blotting paper with the mixture, and allowing the alcohol vapor to disappear, an irritating or foreign odor remains. *Amyl alcohol:* Evap. to ⅓ its vol.; add equal vol. H_2SO_4 = reddish color. *Methyl alcohol, aldehyd* and *oak-tannin:* + equal vol. liq. potassa = dark color. *Methyl alcohol:* Digest with lead carbonate and filter; distil filtrate on water-bath; first distillate + $K_2Mn_2O_8$ = no color. *Foreign organic matter, fusel oil,* etc.: + test solution $AgNO_3$ and exposure to direct sunlight for one day = opalescence.

Officinal Preparations. Alcohol Dilutum,—Dilute Alcohol. Mix alcohol (50) with water (50).—Sp. gr. 0.928 at 60° F., or 0.920 at 77° F. Contains ethyl alcohol 45% by weight, or 53% by volume. To prepare diluted alcohol from alcohol of any higher per cent, divide the percentage by weight of the stronger by 45.5 and subtract one from the quotient. The remainder represents the number of parts of water to be added to one part alcohol.

Proof Spirits. Dilute alcohol differs from the United States

Proof Spirits, the latter containing only 50% alcohol by volume. Sp. gr. 0.936 at 60° F.

($C_5H_{11}OH$—88) FUSEL OIL.—AMYLIC ALCOHOL.

A peculiar alcohol derived from fermented grain or potatoes, by continuing the process of distillation after the ethyl alcohol has ceased to distil.

Use. Used in the manufacture of certain alkaloids, on account of its great solvent power, also as a source of valerianic acid and various flavoring ethers.

VINUM ALBUM.—WHITE WINE.

A pale-amber, or straw-colored alcoholic liquid, made by fermenting the unmodified juice of the grape, free from seeds, stems and skins.

During the fermentation of grape-juice, if the latter contains only a limited amount of sugar, sufficient to produce by its decomposition 16% or less of alcohol, a *dry wine* is obtained; but if fermentation ceases before the sugar is entirely decomposed, a *sweet wine* results, and if the wine is bottled before fermentation is completed a *sparkling wine* will be obtained, effervescence being due to the presence of CO_2.

During grape juice fermentation, as the alcohol increases, the tartrates of potassium and calcium becomes less soluble and are deposited in crusts, called *argols* (see Tartaric Acid).

Description. A full, fruity, agreeable taste, without excess of sweetness or acidity; pleasant odor. Should contain 10–12% of absolute alcohol by weight.

Impurities and tests. *Tannin:* Dilute and add Sol. Fe_2Cl_6 = dark brown color. On evaporating and drying, it should leave not less than 1.5% nor more than 3% residue.

Officinal Preparation VINUM ALBUM FORTIOR.—STRONGER WHITE WINE. Mix white wine (7). alcohol (1). Contains 20–25% absolute alcohol (weight). Used in preparing the eleven officinal medicated wines.

VINUM RUBRUM.—RED WINE.

A deep-red, alcoholic liquid, made by fermenting the juice of colored grapes in the presence of their skins.

Description. A full, fruity, moderately astringent taste, without decided sweetness, or excessive acidity; pleasant odor. Contains 10–12% alcohol (weight). Should yield 1.6–3.5% dried residue. *Impurities:* aniline colors.

($H_2C_4H_4O_6$—150) ACIDUM TARTARICUM.—TARTARIC ACID.

OCCURRENCE. Found either *free* or in combination with bases, in grapes, tamarinds, sumach berries, pineapples, and other acidulous fruits.

Preparation. Acid tartrate of potassium is deposited in wine casks during the fermentation of grape juice; in crystalline crusts called *crude tartar* or *argols*, composed of neutral calcium tartrate, acid potassium tartrate, coloring and extractive matter, yeast and other vegetable fragments. This *crude tartar* is dissolved in water, chalk is added, forming calcium tartrate which precipitates, leaving neutral potassium tartrate in solution.

Reaction. $2KHC_4H_4O_6$ (Acid Potassium Tartrate.) $+$ $CaCO_3$ (Calcium Carbonate.) $=$ $K_2C_4H_4O_6$ (Neutral Potassium Tartrate.) $+$ $CaC_4H_4O_6$ (Calcium Tartrate.) $+$ H_2O (Water.) $+$ CO_2. (Carbon Dioxide.)

The calcium tartrate is decomposed with H_2SO_4.

Reaction. $CaC_4H_4O_6$ (Calcium Tartrate.) $+$ H_2SO_4 (Sulphuric Acid.) $=$ $CaSO_4$ (Calcium Sulphate.) $+$ $H_2C_4H_4O_6$. (Tartaric Acid.)

Calcium sulphate subsides, tartaric acid remaining in solution. The neutral potassium tartrate remaining in solution in the early stage of the process, is converted to $CaC_4H_4O_6$ by the addition of $CaCl_2$.

Reaction. $K_2C_4H_4O_6$ (Potassium Tartrate.) $+$ $CaCl_2$ (Calcium Chloride.) $=$ $CaC_4H_4O_6$ (Calcium Tartrate.) $+$ $2KCl$. (Potassium Chloride.)

The precipitated calcium tartrate is decomposed by H_2SO_4 as above, tartaric acid remaining in solution, and obtained by crystallization.

Purified by re-crystallization, yielding colorless crystals.

Description. Nearly or entirely colorless, transparent crystals; odorless; purely acid taste; acid reaction; sol. in water (0.7), alcohol (2.5), ether (23).

Test for identity. Aqueous solution + sol. potassium acetate + alcohol = white crystalline ppt.

Impurities and tests. *Lead* or *copper:* $+ H_2S$ = black coloration. *Copper:* Ash $+ NH_4OH$ = blue color. *Lead, copper, iron:* $+ (NH_4)_2S$ = black coloration. *Sulphuric acid:* $+ HCl + BaCl_2$ = ppt. within five mins.

$(H_3C_6H_5O_7.H_2O$—210) Acidum Citricum.—Citric Acid.

Source. Lemon, lime and other fruits of the Citrus family.

Preparation. The expressed juice of the fruit is clarified by ebullition, but if decayed fruit is used, it is allowed to undergo vinous fermentation. After decantation and straining, chalk is added in excess, also some milk of lime. Calcium citrate is formed, and being less soluble in hot than in cold water, the mixture is heated to boiling, and while hot the clear liquid is drawn off from the precipitated salt, which is washed with boiling water to remove extractive matter. The calcium citrate is then decomposed by diluted H_2SO_4 in slight excess; calcium sulphate precipitates, citric acid remaining in solution. The solution is decanted, concentrated by evaporation, and allowed to crystallize in lead-lined tanks.

(1) $2H_3C_6H_5O_7$ (Citric Acid.) $+$ $3CaCO_3$ (Calcium Carbonate.) $=$ $Ca_3(C_6H_5O_7)_2$ (Calcium Citrate.) $+$ $3H_2O$ (Water.) $+$ CO_2. (Carbon Dioxide.)

(2) $Ca_3(C_6H_5O_7)_2$ (Calcium Citrate.) $+$ $3H_2SO_4$ (Sulphuric Acid.) $=$ $3CaSO_4$ (Calcium Sulphate.) $+$ $2H_3C_6H_5O_7$. (Citric Acid.)

The crystals are purified by re-dissolving, filtering through animal charcoal and re-crystallizing.

Description. Colorless crystals, deliquescent in moist air; efflorescent in warm air; odorless; agreeable, purely acid taste; acid reaction; sol. in water (0.75), alcohol (1), ether 48.

Test. On adding an aqueous solution to lime-water, a clear mixture results until boiled, when a white precipitate separates which is nearly all re-dissolved on cooling.

Impurities and tests. *Tartaric* and *oxalic acids:* Sol. acid + sol. potass. acetate + equal volume alcohol = cloudy mixture. *Tartaric acid* (1% or more): Sol. acid + sol. potass. bichromate = dark color within 5 mins.; also, potass. permanganate gives dark ppt. of peroxide of manganese. *Lead* and *copper:* + H_2S = dark ppt. *Copper:* ash + NH_4OH = blue color. *Lead, copper, iron:* + $(NH_4)_2S$ = black color. *Sulphuric acid:* + $BaCl_2$ = white ppt.

Official Preparation. SYRUPUS ACIDI CITRICI. (Syrup of Citric Acid.) Contains spirit of lemon (4), syrup (980), citric acid (8), water (8).

SPIRITUS VINI GALLICI.—BRANDY.

An alcoholic liquid obtained by the distillation of fermented grapes, and at least four years old. During the *ageing* process, the fusel oil becomes converted into several fragrant ethers, principally œnanthic, acetic and propylic.

Description. Pale-amber color; distinctive taste and odor. Contains 39–47% (weight) alcohol, 46–55% (volume).

Impurities and tests. *Fusel oil:* By evaporating on a water bath, the last portions have a harsh disagreeable odor. *Excess of solid matter:* Yields more than 0.25% dry residue. *Sugars, glycerine, spices:* Taste.

SPIRITUS FRUMENTI.—WHISKEY.

An alcoholic liquid obtained by the distillation of fermented grain, usually corn, wheat, or rye, and at least two years old.

PROCESS. Raw whiskey (see alcohol) is kept in barrels for two years, when it acquires mellowness and improves in flavor, due to the formation of certain compound ethers, by the oxidation of the fusel oil.

Description. Amber color; distinctive taste, and odor. Contains 44–50% (weight) alcohol, 50–58% (volume).

Impurities: same as under brandy.

ALCOHOL DECOMPOSITION PRODUCTS.

$((C_2H_5)_2O)$ ÆTHER.—ETHER. SULPHURIC ETHER.

Preparation. On mixing alcohol with H_2SO_4 in a still, and heating between 266°–280° F., the following decomposition takes place:

Reaction. $\underset{\text{(Alcohol)}}{C_2H_5OH} + \underset{\begin{smallmatrix}\text{(Sulphuric} \\ \text{Acid.)}\end{smallmatrix}}{H_2SO_4} = \underset{\begin{smallmatrix}\text{(Ethyl-sulphuric or} \\ \text{Sulphovinic Acid.)}\end{smallmatrix}}{C_2H_5HSO_4} + \underset{\text{(Water.)}}{H_2O.}$

More alcohol is then added and heat applied, when ether forms and H_2SO_4 is reproduced.

Reaction. $\quad C_2H_5HSO_4 \; + \; C_2H_5OH \; = \; (C_2H_5)_2O \; + \; H_2SO_4.$
$\quad\begin{pmatrix}\text{Ethyl-sulphuric}\\\text{Acid.}\end{pmatrix} \quad\quad \text{(Alcohol.)} \quad\quad\quad \text{(Ether.)} \quad\quad \begin{pmatrix}\text{Sulphuric}\\\text{Acid.}\end{pmatrix}$

The distillate is carried through a solution of potash to neutralize any acidulous vapors, and finally through a series of fractional condensers where alcohol vapors are condensed and returned by a tube into the still, while the ether vapors pass into a final condenser.

Description. Sp. gr. 0.750; contains about 74% ethyl oxide ($(C_2H_5)_2O$) and about 26% alcohol, containing a little water; sol. in water (5 vols.) See Æther fortior.

Officinal Preparation.—SPIRITUS ÆTHERIS. (Spirit of Ether.) Contains ether (30), and alcohol (70). Represents the Compound Spirit of Ether of the German Pharmacopœia.

ÆTHER FORTIOR.—STRONGER ETHER. (Washed Ether.)

Made by washing ether with water to remove alcohol, decanting and distilling the ethereal layer with lime and calcium chloride, thereby removing the remaining water and most of the alcohol.

Description. A thin, very diffusive, clear, colorless liquid; characteristic odor; burning, sweetish taste; neutral reaction; sol. in water (8), alcohol, chloroform, and the light hydrocarbons; boils at 98.6° F.; highly inflammable; contains 94% of ethyl oxide and 6% alcohol; sp. gr. 0.725.

Impurities and tests. *Acids:* +litmus = red color: *Foreign matter:* Leaves fixed residue with odor. *Alcohol:* 10 cm³ ether fort. +10 cm³ glycerine; the ethereal layer = less than 8.6 cm³. Stronger ether should boil actively in a test tube, when held in the hand, on addition of pieces of broken glass.

Officinal Preparation. SPIRITUS ÆTHERIS COMPOSITUS.—COMPOUND SPIRIT OF ETHER (Hoffmann's Anodyne). Contains, stronger ether (30), alcohol (67), and ethereal oil (3).

Often adulterated with *light* oil of wine, or castor oil.

OLEUM ÆTHEREUM.—ETHEREAL OIL. (Heavy Oil of Wine.)
$(C_2H_5)_2SO_4, (C_2H_4)_2SO_3 = C_8H_{16}S_2O_7.$

Made by distilling a mixture of alcohol and H_2SO_4 between 150°-157° C., (302°-314.6° F.), until the yellow liquid ceases to come over, and a black froth forms in the retort. The ethereal layer of the distillate is separated and exposed to air for 24 hours in a capsule, drained on a wet filter and washed with water, again drained and mixed with an equal volume of stronger ether.

Reactions. On heating· alcohol with sulphuric acid, *sulphovinic acid* is produced (as shown under Ether), and on distilling at the temperature designated in the presence of uncombined H_2SO_4 and alcohol, ether and water are volatilized, followed by SO_2, ethylene or olefiant gas (C_2H_4), and heavy oil of wine. The distillate finally contains an aqueous solution of SO_2, and a yellowish ethereal layer of heavy oil of wine.

By exposing the ethereal portion of the distillate to the air, ether evaporates, while the oil with some acid watery liquid remains. After properly washing the oil, it is dissolved in an equal volume of stronger ether, to avoid spontaneous decomposition, and a separation into two liquids.

Description. Transparent, nearly colorless, volatile liquid; peculiar, aromatic, ethereal odor; pungent, refreshing, bitterish taste; neutral reaction. Sp. gr. 0.910

Officinal Preparation. Spiritus aetheris comp. (see *Æther fortior.*)

($C_2H_5C_2H_3O_2$) Æther Aceticus.—Acetic Ether.
(Acetate of Ethyl.)

Made by distilling a mixture of alcohol and H_2SO_4 with dehydrated sodium acetate. The distillate contains acetic ether, alcohol, water and acetic acid; the latter is removed by treatment with chalk, forming calcium acetate in solution. Dried calcium chloride is added, and the mixture distilled; acetic ether separates from the distillate, is decanted and rectified by re-distillation.

Reaction. Sulphovinic acid is first formed, and on rectifying with sodium acetate, the following results:

$$C_2H_5HSO_4 + NaC_2H_3O_2 = NaHSO_4 + C_2H_5C_2H_3O_2.$$

$\begin{pmatrix}\text{Sulphovinic}\\\text{Acid.}\end{pmatrix}$ $\begin{pmatrix}\text{Sodium}\\\text{Acetate.}\end{pmatrix}$ $\begin{pmatrix}\text{Acid Sodium}\\\text{Sulphate.}\end{pmatrix}$ (Ethyl Acetate.)

Description. Transparent and colorless liquid; strong, fragrant, ethereal, acetous odor; refreshing taste; neutral reaction; sol. in water (17), ether, chloroform, and alcohol; sp. gr. 0.889–0.897.

Officinal Preparations. 1. Tinctura Ferri Acetatis (see Iron). 2. Spiritus Odoratus. (Perfumed Spirit. Cologne Water.) A solution of oils of bergamot, lemon, rosemary, lavender and orange flowers, and acetic ether in alcohol and water.

Spiritus Ætheris Nitrosi.—Spirit of Nitrous Ether.
(Sweet Spirit of Nitre.)

An alcoholic solution of ethyl nitrite ($C_2H_5NO_2$) containing 5% of the crude ether.

Made by mixing H_2SO_4 with alcohol, and when cool adding HNO_3 and distilling through well-cooled condensers into a receiver surrounded by broken ice, which is connected by means of a glass tube with a small vial containing water to absorb the incondensable vapors. The distillate obtained between 176°–180° F., is shaken with ice-cold water (to remove various acid products that may be present), the ethereal layer separated and mixed with 19 times its weight of alcohol.

Explanation. In the above process H_2SO_4 acts merely to dehydrate the nitric acid as well as to absorb the water formed during the process; by the action of nitric acid on alcohol, *aldehyd* is formed as well as *ethyl nitrite.*

$$2C_2H_5OH + HNO_3 = C_2H_4O + C_2H_5NO_2 + 2H_2O.$$

(Alcohol.) $\begin{pmatrix}\text{Nitric}\\\text{Acid.}\end{pmatrix}$ (Aldehyd.) $\begin{pmatrix}\text{Ethyl}\\\text{Nitrite.}\end{pmatrix}$ (Water.)

Preservation. By age, or on exposure to direct sunlight, the aldehyd formed in the above process oxidizes into acetic acid.

Reaction. $\quad C_2H_4O + O = HC_2H_3O_2.$

(Aldehyd.) $\begin{pmatrix}\text{Oxygen}\\\text{from Air.}\end{pmatrix}$ (Acetic Acid.)

The free acid may be neutralized by keeping a small quantity of magnesia or potassium bicarbonate in contact with the spirit.

The *German Pharmacopœia* suggests that crystals of potassium tartrate be kept in the bottle, thereby neutralizing any free acid and forming a proportionate amount of potassium bitartrate which ppts.

Description. A transparent, mobile, volatile, inflammable liquid; greenish-yellow tint; agreeable fruit-like odor; sharp and burning taste; sp. gr. 0.823–0.825; slightly reddens litmus, but should not effervesce when a crystal of $KHCO_3$ is placed into it; mixes with water in all proportions.

Assay. (*Showing at least 4% of ethyl nitrite.*) Macerate 10 grams with 1.5 gram KOH for 12 hours with agitation, add an equal vol. of water, and set aside till the alcohol odor has disappeared, then acidulate with dil. H_2SO_4, add 0.335 grams test-sol. potass. permanganate, when the color of the latter disappears.

Officinal Preparation. Mistura Glycyrrhizæ Composita.

($C_5H_{11}NO_2$—117) AMYL NITRIS.—NITRITE OF AMYL.
(AMYLO-NITROUS ETHER.)

Made by the action of HNO_3 on purified amylic alcohol and distilling; purified by washing with water and an alkali and carefully re-distilling.

$$2C_5H_{11}OH + HNO_3 = C_5H_{11}NO_2 + C_5H_{10}O + 2H_2O.$$
(Amylic Alcohol.) (Nitric Acid.) (Amylic Nitrite.) (Valerianic Aldehyd.) (Water.)

Description. Pale-yellowish liquid; ethereal, fruity odor; aromatic taste; neutral or slightly acid reaction; sp. gr. 0.872–0.874; insol. in water, sol. in alcohol, ether, chloroform, etc.

Usually put up in glass "tears" containing five drops; the glass to be crushed in the handkerchief, and its contents inhaled.

Dose, 3–5 drops.

(C_2HCl_3O,H_2O—165.2) CHLORAL.—HYDRATE OF CHLORAL.

Made by the long continued action of *dry* chlorine (dried by passing through H_2SO_4 or $CaCl_2$) on *absolute* alcohol; the crude chloral obtained is purified by treating with H_2SO_4 and distilling over a mixture of lime and chalk. To the distillate the necessary quantity of water is added, forming a solid mass, chloral hydrate.

When dry chlorine gas is passed into alcohol, aldehyd and HCl are formed.

Reaction. $C_2H_5OH + Cl_2 = C_2H_4O + 2HCl$
(Alcohol.) (Chlorine.) (Aldehyd.) (Hydrochloric Acid.)

and by the *continued* action of dry chlorine, chloral is produced:

$$C_2H_4O + 3Cl_2 = C_2HCl_3O + 3HCl.$$
(Aldehyd.) (Chlorine.) (Chloral.) (Hydrochloric Acid.)

If water is present in either chlorine or alcohol, chloral is not formed, but the following reactions result:

$$C_2H_4O + H_2O + Cl_2 = C_2H_4O_2 + 2HCl.$$
(Aldehyd.) (Water.) (Chlorine.) (Acetic Acid.) (Hydrochloric Acid.)

and, $C_2H_4O_2$ + C_2H_5OH = $C_2H_3C_2H_3O_2$ + $H_2O.$
　　(Acetic Acid.)　　　(Alcohol.)　　　(Acetic Ether.)　　　(Water.)

The acetic ether thus formed cannot be further converted into chloral.

Description. Separate, rhomboidal, colorless, transparent crystals; evaporating when exposed to air; aromatic, penetrating, slightly acrid odor; bitterish caustic taste; neutral reaction; sol. in water, alcohol, ether, chloroform (4), glycerin, and the light hydrocarbons. Liquefies when mixed with carbolic acid or camphor. When a hot aqueous solution is treated with solution of potash, soda or ammonia, a vaporous milky mixture of chloroform is obtained with a formate in solution.

Impurities and tests. *Acids :* + litmus paper = red color. *Hydrochloric acid :* + HNO_3 + $AgNO_3$ = white ppt. *Chloral alcoholate :* Dissolves in less than 4 p. chloroform. Boiling-point higher than 206° F. Aq. solution warmed with KOH; filt. + test sol. potass. iodide = yellow ppt. (iodoform).

Camphorated Chloral. The liquid mixture of camphor and chloral is said to be a true chemical compound called *camphorated chloral*, but is decomposed by water, chloral dissolving while camphor precipitates. *Dose* of Chloral, ten to twenty grains.

BUTYL CHLORAL HYDRATE. (Croton Chloral Hydrate.)

Made by passing chlorine into acetic aldehyd, and subjecting the mass to repeated fractional distillations; the distillate on dissolving in water is converted into the hydrate.

Dose. Three to ten grains.

CHLOROFORMUM VENALE.—COMMERCIAL CHLOROFORM.

Made by distilling a mixture of alcohol, chlorinated lime and water. The distillate is washed with water, and the aqueous layer poured off, *crude chloroform* remaining. By the action of the chlorine present in the lime compound on the alcohol, aldehyd is formed, which by the further action of chlorine is converted into chloral and finally into chloroform.

(1) C_2H_5OH + $CaOCl_2$ = C_2H_4O + $CaCl_2$ + $H_2O.$
　　(Alcohol.)　　(Chlorinated Lime.)　　(Aldehyd.)　　(Calcium Chloride.)　　(Water.)

(2) $2C_2H_4O$ + $6CaOCl_2$ = $2C_2HCl_3O$ + $3CaCl_2$ + $3Ca(OH)_2.$
　　(Aldehyd.)　　(Chlorinated Lime.)　　(Chloral.)　　(Calcium Chloride.)　　(Calcium Hydroxide.)

(3) $2C_2HCl_3O$ + $Ca(OH)_2$ = $2CHCl_3$ + $Ca(CHO_2)_2$
　　(Chloral.)　　(Calcium Hydroxide.)　　(Chloroform.)　　(Calcium Formate.)

Description. (See Chloroformum Purif.) Sp. gr. 1.470; containing at least 98% chloroform; when shaken with an equal vol. H_2SO_4, the acid layer should not become quite black within 24 hours.

Officinal Preparations. 1. Linimentum Chloroformi. 2. Chloroformum Purificatum.

LINIMENTUM CHLOROFORMI. (Chloroform Liniment.) Contains commercial chloroform (40), and soap liniment (60).

($CHCl_3$—119.2) CHLOROFORMUM PURIFICATUM. (PURIFIED CHLOROFORM.)

Made by agitating crude chloroform with H_2SO_4 which destroys the impurities in the former, the lighter chloroformic layer is separated, and further agitated with solution of sodium carbonate for the purpose of removing any adherent acid, the chloroform is then separated from the supernatant liquid, mixed with 1% of alcohol, and distilled over lime to remove water, at a temperature below 152° F., thereby leaving behind all impurities which have escaped the action of the acid and that have a higher boiling-point than chloroform; the alcohol is added to prevent decomposition and the formation of dangerous chlorine compounds.

Description. A heavy, clear, colorless, diffusive liquid; characteristic, pleasant ethereal odor; burning, sweet taste; neutral reaction; sol. in water (200), alcohol, ether, etc. Sp. gr. 1.485–1.490; contains 0.75 to 1% alcohol. On agitating with conc. H_2SO_4 and allowing to stand for 24 hours, both liquids should remain colorless.

Impurities and tests. *Acids:* Agitate with water; washings + litmus paper = red color. *Chlorides:* Above washings + $AgNO_3$ = white ppt. *Chlorine:* Above washings + KI = coloration. *Aldehyd:* Digest with KOH = dark color.

Officinal Preparations: 1. Mistura Chloroformi. 2. Spiritus Chloroformi.

MISTURA CHLOROFORMI. (Chloroform Mixture. Chloroform Emulsion.) Contains purif. chloroform (8), camphor (2), fresh yolk of egg (10), water (80), made into a uniform mixture, by the use of a mortar.

SPIRITUS CHLOROFORMI. (Spirit of Chloroform. Chloric Ether.) Contains purif. chloroform (10), and alcohol (90).

VOLATILE OILS.—ESSENTIAL OILS.

Volatile oils are the proximate principles to which the odor of most plants is due. They are odorous, volatile, inflammable liquids, freely soluble in alcohol, ether, chloroform, CS_2, benzol, and the fixed oils, slightly soluble in water. When dropped on paper they leave a fatty stain which disappears on the application of heat.

Source. Found in the majority of plants, existing in every part from root to seed; in some instances produced by the action of a ferment.

Color. Colorless when pure, but acquiring certain colors on exposure to air and light, the color developed being due to the presence of distinct compounds.

Specific Gravity. Their Specific Gravities range between 0.850 to 0.990, while a few are even heavier than water. The lightest are oils of lemon and erigeron (0.850), the heaviest, oil of wintergreen (1.180).

Reactions. Rapidly decomposed by strong HNO_3; certain oils produce explosive fulminates with iodine; H_2SO_4 yields characteristic color reactions.

Composition. Hydrocarbons (mostly *terpenes*) and hydrocarbons with oxygen represent the elements found in the majority, but some contain sulphur (*Ex.* Oils of mustard, asafetida, horse-radish, etc.), and are characterized by a disagreeable, penetrating odor, while a few others contain nitrogen in the form of hydrocyanic acid. (*Ex.* Oils of bitter almond, cherry laurel, etc.)

All volatile oils contain at least *two proximate principles* having different boiling and congealing points; *elæopten* ($C_{10}H_{16}$ or $C_{10}H_{14}$) has the lowest boiling-point, *stearopten* or "camphor" as it is termed (an oxide or hydroxide of the terpene) is that portion which volatilizes last and congeals in crystals near the ordinary temperatures, and is isomeric with common camphor.

METHODS OF PREPARATION.

I. Simple Distillation. This process is employed in obtaining oils of turpentine, copaiba, tar, amber (by destructive distillation), etc.

II. Distillation with Water. The substance either in fresh or dried state, is cut up and macerated with water, then the mass is placed in a suitable still and mixed with more water, which prevents the burning and decomposition of the vegetable matter and facilitates the vaporizing of the oil, which readily distils with the steam produced on applying heat. Salt is sometimes added to raise the temperature of the boiling-point in making some of the heavier oils.

The milky distillate on cooling separates into two layers, one being a solution of oil in water, the other the pure oil, which may be separated by means of a separating funnel, or other convenient contrivance. *Examples.* Oils of *orange flowers, cinnamon, cloves,* and *wintergreen.*

III. Expression. This process avoids the use of heat (which injures the odor of certain delicate oils) and produces the most fragrant odors: such oils are however, cloudy in appearance, due to the presence of albuminous matter. *Examples.* .Oils of *almond, lemon, orange, bergamot, etc.*

IV. Solution. Comprising several processes: *Percolation,* using purified CS_2 or petroleum benzin for a menstruum, and the subsequent distillation of the solvent from the oil. *Maceration,* or *digestion* with some inodorous fixed oil.

Enfleurage. Several trays are covered with a layer of purified tallow, or some inodorous fat, and then with a layer of flowers, the latter being replaced by fresh flowers from time to time. The resulting product after separating the flowers, represents the *pommades* employed by perfumers, the commercial strengths of which are denoted by the numbers, 6, 12, 18, 24, 30 and 36.

To obtain the volatile oil, the *pommade* is melted and macerated with cologne spirits, the latter dissolving the odorous principles, the solution obtained constituting the *extracts* of perfumers, the small portion of dissolved fat being removed by chilling and filtering.

Preservation. When the volatile oils are exposed to air and light, ozone is developed, causing them to become viscid, or occasionally forming a solid resin; hence, they should be kept in a cool place, in well-stoppered, amber-colored vials, to prevent rancidity and oxidation. Many of the oils are preserved by the addition of 5% of alcohol.

Restoration. Some old and resinified oils may be restored by rectification with water to which an alkali has been added or, by agitation with borax solution and animal charcoal; the oil separates free from resin, having its original odor. Also purified by agitation with potassium permanganate and decanting.

ADULTERATIONS. Fixed oils, alcohol, cheaper volatile oils, water, chloroform or camphene.

Specific gravity is no test for purity.

TESTS FOR IMPURITIES. **Fixed oils:** 1. Leaves a permanent greasy stain on paper.

2. The residue left on distilling with water is saponifiable.

3. Strong alcohol dissolves out the volatile oil, leaving the fixed oil undissolved (true of all except castor oil).

Alcohol. 1. A separation with fixed oils (except castor oil), the alcoholic solution of volatile oil being above, and the fixed oil beneath.

2. A diminution of the volume of volatile oil, when agitated with an equal bulk of water or glycerin in a graduated tube.

3. Fused potassium acetate or calcium chloride are insoluble in the volatile oils, but become soft or liquid in the presence of alcohol.

4. Red aniline is insoluble in the oil, but becomes soluble if alcohol is present, producing a red color.

5. On heating potassium acetate and H_2SO_4 with the oil, if alcohol is present, acetic ether is produced.

Cheap volatile oils: Difficult to detect in many instances, but such adulterations are often indicated by the odor remaining after partial evaporation from bibulous paper.

Oils Derived by the Action of a Ferment.

OLEUM AMYGDALÆ AMARÆ.—OIL OF BITTER ALMOND.

A volatile oil obtained from bitter almond by maceration with water and subsequent distillation. The oil does not pre-exist in the almond, but is produced by the decomposition of amygdalin by *emulsin.*

Preparation. After extracting the fixed oil, the residue is treated with water, and *emulsin* or *synaptase* is set free, which decomposes the amygdalin, producing the oil which is separated by distillation.

$$C_{20}H_{27}NO_{11} + 2H_2O = C_7H_6O + 2C_6H_{12}O_6 + HCN.$$

(Amygdalin.) (Water.) (Oil of Almond, Benzyl Aldehyd.) (Glucose.) (Hydrocyanic Acid.)

OLEUM SINAPIS VOLATILE. (Volatile Oil of Mustard.) A volatile oil obtained from black mustard by maceration with water and subsequent distillation.

A peculiar ferment *myrosin*, becomes active in the presence of water, converting the potassium myronate into sulphocyanide of allyl (C_3H_5CNS).

OFFICINAL VOLATILE OILS.

NAME.	Source.	Natural Order.	Method of Extraction.	Sp. Gr.
Oleum Amygdalæ Amaræ (Oil of Bitter Almonds)	Seeds (*Amygdalus comunis var. amara*)	*Rosaceæ.*	Maceration and Distillation.	1.043–1.049
Oleum Anisi (Oil of Anise)	Fruit (*Pimpinella anisum* or *P. illicium*)	*Umbelliferæ, Magnoliaceæ.*	Distillation	0.976–0.990
Oleum Aurantii Corticis (Oil of Orange Peel)	Fresh peel (*Citrus vulgaris* or *C. aurantium*)	*Aurantiaceæ.*	Mechanical Means.	0.860
Oleum Aurantii Florum (Oil of Orange Flowers)	Fresh Flowers (*Citrus vulgaris*)	*Aurantiaceæ.*	Distillation	0.850–0.890
Oleum Bergamii (Oil of Bergamot)	Fresh peel (*Citrus Bergamia, var. vulgaris*)	*Aurantiaceæ.*	Mechanical Means.	0.860–0.890
Oleum Cajuputi (Oil of Cajuput)	Leaves (*Melaleuca Cajuputi*)	*Myrtaceæ.*	Distillation	0.920
Oleum Cari (Oil of Caraway)	Fruit (*Carum carui*)	*Umbelliferæ.*	Distillation	0.920
Oleum Caryophylli (Oil of Cloves)	Flower Buds (*Eugenia Caryophyllata*)	*Myrtaceæ.*	Distillation	1.050
Oleum Chenopodii (Oil of American Wormseed)	Fruit (*Chenopodium anthelminticum*)	*Chenopodiaceæ.*	Distillation	0.920
Oleum Cinnamomi (Oil of Cinnamon (Ceylon); Oil of Cinnamon (Chinese)	Bark of Shoots (*Cinnamomum, Zelanycum* and Chinese *Cinnamon*)	*Lauraceæ.*	Distillation	Ceylon, 1.040 Chinese, 1.160
Oleum Copaibæ (Oil of Copaiba)	Oleo Resin (Copaiba)	*Leguminosæ.*	Distillation	0.890
Oleum Coriandri (Oil of Coriander)	Fruit (*Coriandrum sativum*)	*Umbelliferæ.*	Distillation	0.870
Oleum Cubebæ (Oil of Cubeb)	Unripe Fruit (*Cubeba officinalis*)	*Piperaceæ.*	Distillation	0.920
Oleum Erigerontis (Oil of Fleabane)	Fresh Fl. Herb (*Erigeron Canadensis*)	*Compositæ.*	Distillation	0.850
Oleum Eucalypti (Oil of Eucalyptus)	Fresh Leaves (*Eucalyptus globulus,* etc.)	*Myrtaceæ.*	Distillation	0.900
Oleum Fœniculi (Oil of Fennel)	Fruit (*Fœniculum vulgare*)	*Umbelliferæ.*	Distillation	0.960
Oleum Gaultheriæ (Oil of Wintergreen)	Leaves (*Gaultheria procumbens*)	*Ericaceæ.*	Distillation	1.180
Oleum Hedeomæ (Oil of Pennyroyal)	Fresh Herb (*Hedeoma pulegioides*)	*Labiatæ.*	Distillation	0.940
Oleum Juniperi (Oil of Juniper Berries)	Fruit (*Juniperus communis*)	*Coniferæ.*	Distillation	0.870
Oleum Lavendulæ (Oil of Lavender)	Fl. Top or whole Herb (*Lavendula vera*)	*Labiatæ.*	Distillation	0.890

OFFICINAL VOLATILE OILS—*Continued.*

NAME.	Source.	Natural Order.	Method of Extraction.	Sp. Gr.
Oleum Lavendulæ Florum (Oil of Lavender Flowers)	Fresh Flowers (*Lavendula vera*)	*Labiatæ.*	Distillation	0.890
Oleum Limonis (Oil of Lemon)	Fresh peel (*Citrus limonum*)	*Aurantiaceæ.*	Mechanical Means.	0.850
Oleum Menthæ Piperitæ (Oil of Peppermint)	Leaves and Tops (*Mentha piperita*)	*Labiatæ.*	Distillation	0.900
Oleum Menthæ Viridis (Oil of Spearmint)	Leaves and Tops (*Mentha viridis*)	*Labiatæ.*	Distillation	0.900
Oleum Myrciæ (Oil of Bay)	Leaves (*Myrcia acris*)	*Myrtaceæ.*	Distillation	1.040
Oleum Myristicæ (Oil of Nutmeg)	Seed (*Myristica fragrans*)	*Myristicaceæ.*	Distillation	0.900
Oleum Picis Liquidæ (Oil of Tar)	Oleo Resin (*Pix liquida*)	*Coniferæ*	Distillation	0.970
Oleum Pimentæ (Oil of Pimento)	Fruit (*Eugenia pimenta*)	*Myraceæ.*	Distillation	1.040
Oleum Rosæ (Oil of Rose)	Fresh Fls. (*Rosa damascena*)	*Rosaceæ.*	Distillation	0.860
Oleum Rutæ (Oil of Rue)	Herb (*Ruta graveolens*)	*Rutaceæ.*	Distillation	0.880
Oleum Rosmarini (Oil of Rosemary)	Herb (*Rosmarinus officinalis*)	*Labiatæ.*	Distillation	0.950
Oleum Sinapis Volatile (Oil of Mustard)	Seed (*Sinapis nigra*)	*Cruciferæ.*	Maceration & Distill.	1.017–1 021
Oleum Succini (Oil of Amber)	Fossil (Amber)	*Coniferæ.*	Destructive Distillat'n	0.920
Oleum Terebinthinæ (Oil of Turpentine)	Oleo Resin (*Pinus australis*, etc.)	*Coniferæ.*	Distillation	0.855–0.870
Oleum Thymi (Oil of Thyme)	Herb (*Thymus vulgaris*)	*Labiatæ.*	Distillation	0.880
Oleum Valerianæ (Oil of Valerian)	Root (*Valeriana officinalis*)	*Valerianaceæ.*	Distillation	0.950

STEAROPTENS.

($C_{10}H_{16}O$—152) CAMPHORA.—CAMPHOR.

A stearopten (or concrete volatile oil) derived from *Cinnamomum Camphora*, and purified by sublimation. (N. O. *Lauraceæ.*) *Hab.* Asia, China and Japan.

Preparation. Obtained from the root, trunk and branches of the Camphor Laurel. The wood is cut into chips and boiled with water in a still, the camphor sublimes and the oil is drained from it. Camphor may be obtained as an impalpable powder by careful sublimation and a skilful arrangement of the temperature of the condensing chamber.

Description. White, translucent masses of a tough consistence and crystalline structure. Readily powdered by the aid of a little alcohol, ether or chloroform. Penetrating odor; pungent taste; sol. in alcohol, ether, chloroform, CS_2, etc., sp. sol. in water.

Officinal Preparations. 1. Aqua camphoræ (0.8%). 2. Linimentum camphoræ. 3. Linimentum saponis. 4. Spiritus camphoræ (10%). 5. Tinctura opii camphorata.

LINIMENTUM CAMPHORÆ. (Camphor Liniment.) Contains camphor (20), dissolved in cotton-seed oil (80).

LINIMENTUM SAPONIS. (Liquid Opodeldoc. Soap Liniment.) Contains soap (10), camphor (5), and oil of rosemary (1), dissolved in alcohol (70) and water ft. 100.

($C_{10}H_{15}BrO$—230.8) CAMPHORA MONOBROMATA.
(Bromated, or Mono-bromated Camphor.)

Made by uniting camphor and bromine with the aid of heat, and purifying by re-crystallizing from a solution in benzine.

Description. Colorless, prismatic needles or scales; mild camphoraceous odor and taste; neutral reaction; almost insol. in water; sol. in alcohol, ether, chloroform and fixed oils.

($C_{10}H_{13}OH$—150) THYMOL.—THYMIC ACID.

Obtained from oil of thyme by distillation; the portion distilling above 392° F. is agitated with NaOH and the thymol-sodium solution formed is treated with HCl to liberate the thymol, NaCl remaining in solution. Purified by crystallization from an alcoholic solution.

Description. Large, colorless crystals; aromatic, thyme-like odor; pungent, aromatic taste; neutral reaction; alm. insol. in water; sol. in alcohol (1), ether, chloroform and oils.

Impurities. *Carbolic acid:* Aq. solution + sol. Fe_2Cl_6 = blue color.

MENTHOL.

Found in all the plants of the mint family, and extracted from oil of peppermint, by rectifying by fractional distillation and subjecting the heavier distillate to a temperature of −10° C., or less, when the crystals of menthol separate. Occurs in snow-white acicular crystals.

Uses. As a local anæsthetic, and to relieve the pain of burns. Oil of peppermint is often met with in commerce, from which the menthol has been extracted.

Tests *to detect the removal of pip-menthol from oil of peppermint.* A test-tube partially filled with the oil under examination, is placed in a freezing mixture of snow and salt for 10 to 15 minutes. If the oil has not been tampered with, it will become cloudy, thick and of a jelly-like consistence, and if four or five small crystals of menthol are added and the tube replaced in the freezing mixture, the oil will soon form a solid mass of crystals.

If limpid or partially so, it indicates adulteration or removal of menthol.

FIXED OILS AND FATS.

The Fixed Oils or Fats, are solid or liquid bodies, derived from both animal and vegetable kingdoms, greasy to the touch, leaving a permanent fatty stain on paper, which is unaffected by heat.

Consistence. If liquid at ordinary temperatures they constitute the *true* or *fixed oils*, and if solid they are called *fats*.

Color, etc. Colorless, odorless and tasteless when pure, but as often seen, many are not darker than light yellow, and have a distinctive odor and taste, often due to impurities.

Specific Gravities. All lighter than water, ranging between 0.860 and 0.970.

Solvents. Insoluble in water, sp. soluble in cold alcohol, soluble in ether, chloroform, CS_2, benzol, benzine, turpentine and volatile oils.

Chemical Composition. Mixtures of two or more fats, having different fusing points, and which may be separated by fractional refrigeration. These fats are the compound ethers of the higher members of the fatty acids, the triatomic alcohol being *glycerin*, and the radical *propenyl*. In most cases they consist of two or three proximate principles, viz.: **Olein, Palmitin,** and **Stearin,** which may be called respectively, the *oleate, palmitate* and *stearate of propenyl.*

The acids belong to two series of the fatty acid group, of the general formula $C_n H_2 O_{2n}$, and the oleic acid group $C_n H_{2n-2} O_2$. Stearic acid, $C_{18}H_{36}O_2$; palmitic acid, $C_{16}H_{32}O_2$; oleic acid, $C_{18}H_{34}O_2$.

Olein (from ἔλαιον—oil) $C_3H_5''' (C_{18}H_{33}O_2)_3'$ is a liquid, while *palmitin,* $C_3H_5(C_{16}H_{31}O_2)_3$, and *stearin* (from στέαρ — suet) $C_3H_5(C_{18}H_{35}O_2)_3$ are both solids.

Purification. Purified by treatment with H_2SO_4, which carbonizes the impurities (or oxidized by permanganic or chromic acids, or the hypochlorites), agitating with water, decanting and filtering through charcoal to absorb coloring matter. Another method is by washing with a cold solution of an alkali carbonate.

Results of Heating. If solid they melt, or if liquid become thinner. When heated to about 572° F., they decompose, and evolve offensive and irritating vapors (causing a copious flow of tears) containing *acrolein*, C_3H_4O. They burn with a sooty flame, generating much heat.

Result of Exposure to Air. They acquire an acrid, disagreeable odor and taste and an acid reaction and are then said to be *rancid.* This change is due to the presence of impurities in the form of protein and mucilaginous componnds, or animal or vegetable tissue. This decomposition liberates the fatty acids, producing odorous and volatile acids (*butyric, valerianic,* etc.), *acrolein* and coloring matter.

Protection. Keep in a cool, dry place, away from light and air.

Restoration. By washing the rancid fat with warm water, or a weak alkali solution, and again washing with strong alcohol. Sometimes treated with powdered borax and dried sodium carbonate.

PREPARATION.—**From Animal Tissues.**

1. **Fusion,** by itself. *Example:* Cod Liver Oil.
2. **Fusion** in the presence of water. *Example:* Lard.

[In either case subsequent straining or skimming is resorted to, to remove the tissue.]

From Vegetable Tissues.

1. **Expression.** Either *cold* (oil of linseed), or between iron plates heated above the fusing point of the fat (olive and castor oils).
2. **Solution.** Accomplished by maceration or percolation, using CS_2 or benzin, and finally distilling off the solvent (oils of lobelia and pumpkin seed).
3. **Decoction.** The oil separates and rises to the surface of the water, during this process.

ADULTERATIONS. The high-priced fats are adulterated with cheaper grades, but on account of their similarity of composition, such admixtures are difficult to recognize.

A change in the fusing or congealing points is sometimes produced by such additions.

Sp. gr., color, odor and taste, often lead to their detection. Nitric acid and conc. sulphuric acid produce with different oils mixtures varying in color.

[Table of Officinal Oils and Fats, on page 193.]

EMULSIONS.

The suspension of oily or resinous bodies in a watery menstruum by the aid of a mucilaginous body.

Theory of emulsification. The oil globules are separated and each covered with a mucilage to prevent them from cohering. Milk and the yolk of egg (vitellum) are types of perfect emulsion.

Emulsifying agents. Gums, glyconin (Glyceritum Vitelli), Irish moss, Iceland moss, pancreatin, etc.

Method for preparing **Emulsio Morrhuæ** (containing 50% of oil). Put eight ounces of cod liver oil into a dry mortar and add 2 ozs. powd. acacia, rubbing with the pestle; when a uniform mixture results, add 6 ozs. of water *all at once*, and stir the mixture till a perfect emulsion results.

SOAPS.

Soaps are metallic salts of the fatty acids; the process by which they are formed is termed *saponification.*

PREPARATION. 1. **Soluble Soaps** (detergent, and soluble in water or alcohol). Made by boiling fats with a solution of soda or potash; the fatty acids unite with the alkali forming the soap, which remains dissolved in the water together with glycerin which has also been liberated from the fat. The *lye* is employed in a diluted state, and gradually added until in excess, thereby facilitating saponification. Boiling is continued until the mixture is transparent and tenacious. The excess of alkali is removed by adding NaCl, as soap is insoluble in solutions of most potassium or sodium salts. Potash soaps are *soft*, soda soaps *hard*.

OFFICINAL FIXED OILS AND FATS.

Name and Synonym.	Source.	Order.	Kingdom.	Method of Extraction.	Specific Gravity.
Oleum Adipis. (Lard oil)........	Lard (*Adeps.*)	*Pachydermata.*	Animal.	Cold expression.	0.900—0.920
Oleum Amygdalæ Expressum. (Sweet oil of Almond)......	Seeds (*Amygdalus communis var. amara or dulcis.*)	*Rosaceæ.*	Vegetable.	Hot expression.	0.914—0.920
Oleum Gossypii Seminis. (Cotton-seed oil)	Seed (*Gossypium herbaceum,* etc.)	*Malvaceæ.*	Vegetable.	Cold expression.	0.920—0.930
Oleum Lini. (Oil of Flaxseed. Linseed oil).	Seed (*Linum usitatissimum.*)	*Linaceæ,*	Vegetable.	Cold expression.	0.936
Oleum Morrhuæ. (Cod-liver oil)......	Fresh Cod Livers (*Gadus Morrhuæ,* etc.)	*Teleostia.*	Animal.	Fusion; expression; decoction.	0.920—0.925
Oleum Olivæ. (Olive oil)......	Ripe Fruit (*Olea Europea.*)	*Oleaceæ.*	Vegetable.	Expression; solution.	0.915—0.918
Oleum Ricini. (Castor oil)......	Seed (*Ricinus Communis,*)	*Euphorbiaceæ.*	Vegetable.	All four methods.	0.950—0.970
Oleum Sesami. (Benne oil)......	Seed (*Sesamum Indicum.*)	*Pedaliaceæ.*	Vegetable.	Expression.	0.914—0.923
Oleum Tiglii. (Croton oil)...	Seed (*Croton Tiglium.*)	*Euphorbiaceæ.*	Vegetable.	Expression.	0.940—0.955
FATS.					
Adeps. (Lard)............	Abdomen (*Sus. Scrofa*—Hog.)	*Pachydermata.*	Animal.	Fusion with wat'r and straining.	0.938 (about).
Cetaceum. (Spermaceti)......	Head (*Physeter Macrocephalus* — Sperm Whale.)	*Cetacea.*	Animal.	Fusion with water.	0.945
Oleum Theobromæ. (Butter of Cacao.)......	Seed (*Theobroma Cacao.*)	*Sterculiaceæ.*	Vegetable.	Hot expresssion.	(Suet should be kept in well closed vessels impervious to fat, and should not be used after it has become rancid
Sevum. (Prepared Suet)......	Abdomen (*Ovis Aries*—Sheep.)	*Ruminantia.*	Animal.	Fusion and straining.	

2. Insoluble Soaps. Made by combining a metallic oxide or an alkaline earth (as a base) with the fatty acids. Soaps of the alkaline earths are employed for waterproofing fabrics, by impregnating the fabric with alum or some calcium or barium salt, and digesting in a soap solution.

The soluble soaps decompose when used with hard waters, forming insoluble calcium soaps.

Description. Pure soaps (soluble) are mostly white, the color and marbled appearance being due to impurities or the presence of salts intentionally added to make them attractive.

Chemical Composition. One or more of the following salts of sodium or potassium. Examples of *soluble soaps:*

$$C_3H_5'''(C_{18}H_{35}O_2)'_3 \quad + \quad 3KOH \quad = \quad 3KC_{18}H_{35}O_2$$
$$\left(\begin{array}{c}\text{Stearin.}\\ \text{Propenyl tri-stearate.}\end{array}\right) \quad \left(\begin{array}{c}\text{Potassium}\\ \text{Hydroxide.}\end{array}\right) \quad \text{(Potassium Stearate.)}$$

$$+ \quad C_3H_5'''(OH)'_3.$$
$$\left(\begin{array}{c}\text{Glycerin.}\\ \text{Propenyl Hydrate.}\end{array}\right)$$

$$C_3H_5(C_{18}H_{33}O_2)'_3 \quad + \quad 3KOH \quad = \quad 3KC_{18}H_{33}O_2$$
$$\left(\begin{array}{c}\text{Olein.}\\ \text{Propenyl tri-oleate.}\end{array}\right) \quad \left(\begin{array}{c}\text{Potassium}\\ \text{Hydroxide.}\end{array}\right) \quad \text{(Potassium Oleate.)}$$

$$+ \quad C_3H_5(OH)_3.$$
$$\text{(Glycerin.)}$$

$$C_3H_5(C_{16}H_{31}O_2)_3 \quad + \quad 3KOH \quad = \quad 3KC_{16}H_{31}O_2$$
$$\left(\begin{array}{c}\text{Palmitin.}\\ \text{Propenyl tri-palmitate.}\end{array}\right) \quad \left(\begin{array}{c}\text{Potassium}\\ \text{Hydroxide.}\end{array}\right) \quad \text{(Potassium Palmitate.)}$$

$$+ \quad C_3H_5(OH)_3.$$
$$\text{(Glycerin.)}$$

SAPO.—SOAP. (Hard Soap. Castile Soap.)

Soap prepared from soda and olive oil.

Description. White or nearly white solid; alkaline taste and reaction; sol. in water, or alcohol. Should contain not more than 34% water, no metals, animal fats, or excess of alkali.

Officinal Preparations. 1. Linimentum Saponis (see Camphor).

2. EMPLASTRUM SAPONIS. (Soap Plaster). Contains powd. soap (10) incorporated with lead plaster (90).

SAPO VIRIDIS.—GREEN SOAP. (SOFT SOAP.)

Soap prepared from potassa and fixed oils. Linseed oil is often employed for this purpose. Although termed *green soap*, it is scarcely ever of that color unless artificially colored. Its usual color is brownish yellow.

Officinal Preparation. Tinctura Saponis Viridis (Tincture of Green Soap). Contains green soap (65) and oil of lavender (2), dissolved in alcohol (ft. 100) by maceration.

Officinal Insoluble Soaps. Linimentum Calcis (see *Calcium*). Emplastrum Plumbi (see *Lead*).

Reaction. $3PbO \quad + \quad 2C_3H_5(C_{18}H_{33}O_2)_3 \quad + \quad 3H_2O =$
$\quad\quad\quad \text{(Litharge.)} \quad\quad\quad \text{(Olein.)} \quad\quad\quad \text{(Water.)}$

$$3Pb(C_{18}H_{33}O_2)_2 \quad + \quad 2C_3H_5(OH)_3.$$
$$\text{(Lead Oleate.)} \quad\quad\quad \text{(Glycerin.)}$$

Water is required in the above reaction (as well as in the process of preparation) to furnish the elements to produce glycerin.

GLYCERINUM.—GLYCERIN ($\gamma\lambda\acute{v}\kappa v\varsigma$—sweet.)

A liquid obtained by the decomposition of fats or fixed oils, and containing not less than 95% absolute glycerin—($C_3H_5(OH)_3$—92).

Source and Preparation. Always a product of saponification. Discovered by Scheele in 1779, and called "the sweet principle of fats." First made during the process for making lead plaster (see reaction above), the soft plaster being well washed with water to dissolve out the glycerin.

The modern method for its production depends on the decomposition of fats or fixed oils by super-heated steam at high pressure, when the fatty acid rises to the surface of the glycerin solution.

$$\underset{\text{(Olein.)}}{C_3H_5(C_{18}H_{33}O_2)_3} + \underset{\text{(Water.)}}{3H_2O} = \underset{\text{(Glycerin.)}}{C_3H_5(OH)_3} + \underset{\text{(Oleic Acid.)}}{3HC_{18}H_{33}O_2;}$$

$$\text{or, } \underset{\text{(Stearin.)}}{C_3H_5(C_{18}H_{35}O_2)_3} + \underset{\text{(Water.)}}{3H_2O} = \underset{\text{(Glycerin.)}}{C_3H_5(OH)_3} + \underset{\text{(Stearic Acid.)}}{3HC_{18}H_{35}O_2.}$$

Purification. Purified by treatment with animal charcoal and fractional distillation.

Composition. A triatomic alcohol, often termed *glyceryl*, propenyl hydrate or propenyl alcohol.

[NITRO-GLYCERIN.—GLONOIN. ($C_3H_5(NO_2)_3O_3$). Obtained by the action of a mixture of concentrated HNO_3 and H_2SO_4 on glycerin, at a freezing temperature. A very explosive compound, soluble in alcohol, or ether, insol. in water; the basis of dynamite.]

Description. Glycerin is a clear, colorless liquid; syrupy consistence; hygroscopic; sweet taste, and neutral reaction; sol. in water or alcohol; insol. in ether, chloroform, benzol and the fixed oils; sp. gr. 1.250.

Properties. A great antiseptic and solvent.

Impurities and tests. *Butyric,* and *other volatile acids:* + dil. H_2SO_4 + Heat = odor. *Cane-sugar:* Warm with H_2SO_4 = dark color. *Sugars,* and *dextrin:* Heat and ignite = a porous coal remains. *Glucose:* + test-sol. potassio-cupric tartrate = yellowish-brown ppt. *Acrylic,* or *Hydrochloric acids:* + $AgNO_3$ = white ppt. *Sulphuric,* and *oxalic acids; calcium, iron,* and *metals:* Usual tests.

Officinal Preparations. 1. Glyceritum amyli (see Amylum). 2. Mucilago tragacanthæ (see Gums). 3. GLYCERITUM VITELLI (Glycerite of Yolk of Egg. Glyconin). Contains yolk of egg (45) thoroughly mixed with glycerin (55).

(HC$_{18}$H$_{33}$O$_2$—282) ACIDUM OLEICUM.—OLEIC ACID. (Elaic Acid.)·

May be made by forming lead soap (using almond or olive oil), decomposing with HCl and dissolving out the acid with ether or benzin, evaporating off the solvent and washing with water.

$$\underset{\text{(Lead Oleate.)}}{3Pb(C_{18}H_{33}O_2)_2} + \underset{\binom{\text{Hydrochloric}}{\text{Acid.}}}{6HCl} = \underset{\binom{\text{Lead}}{\text{Chloride.}}}{3PbCl_2} + \underset{\text{(Oleic Acid.)}}{6HC_{18}H_{33}O_2.}$$

Also made by chilling fats to 40° F. and expressing, the solid portion being rejected.

Description. A yellowish, oily liquid, becoming brown, rancid and acid on exposure to air; odorless; tasteless; neutral reaction; sp. gr. 0.900–0.910; insol. in water, sol. in alcohol, chloroform, benzine, etc. A solvent for fats and fatty acids. Unites with basylous radicals to form salts called *oleates*.

OLEATUM.—OLEATES.

OLEATUM HYDRARGYRI. (OLEATE OF MERCURY.) Contains 10% yellow oxide. See Hydrargyrum.

OLEATUM VERATRINA. (OLEATE OF VERATRINE.) A 2% solution of veratrine in oleic acid.

PRECIPITATED OLEATES.

Many unofficinal oleates are now being extensively employed. They are made by decomposing sodium or potassium oleate by a salt of the base required (both in solution), and subsequently melting, washing and drying the precipitate.

Aluminium Oleate—$Al_2(C_{18}H_{33}O_2)_6$. Made by the double decomposition between aluminium sulphate and sodium oleate.

$$Al_2(SO_4)_3 + 6NaC_{18}H_{33}O_2 = Al_2(C_{18}H_{33}O_2)_6 + 3Na_2SO_4.$$

Arsenic Oleate. $As(C_{18}H_{33}O_3)_3$.

Reaction. $AsCl_3 + 3NaC_{18}H_{33}O_2 = 3NaCl + As(C_{18}H_{33}O_2)_3.$

Bismuth Oleate. $Bi(C_{18}H_{33}O_2)_3$.

Reaction. $Bi(NO_3)_3 + 3NaC_{18}H_{33}O_2 = Bi(C_{18}H_{33}O_2)_3 + 3NaNO_3.$

Copper Oleate. $Cu(C_{18}H_{33}O_2)_2$.

Reaction. $CuSO_4 + 2NaC_{18}H_{33}O_2 = Cu(C_{18}H_{33}O_2)_2 + Na_2SO_4.$

Ferric Oleate. $Fe_2(C_{18}H_{33}O_2)_6$.

Ferrous sulphate and sodium oleate; boil the mixture to oxidize the ferrous to a ferric salt.

Manganese Oleate. $Mn(C_{18}H_{33}O_2)_2$.

Manganese sulphate and sodium oleate.

Nickel Oleate. $Ni(C_{18}H_{33}O_2)_2$. Nickel sulphate and sodium oleate.

Lead Oleate. $Pb(C_{18}H_{33}O_2)_2$. Lead nitrate and sodium oleate.

Silver Oleate. $AgC_{18}H_{33}O_2$. Silver nitrate and sodium oleate.

Sodium Oleate. $NaC_{18}H_{33}O_2$. Made by dissolving castile soap (1) in water (8); on standing, sodium palmitate deposits, and the solution containing the oleate may be decanted.

Tin Oleate. $Sn(C_{18}H_{33}O_2)_4$. Tin chloride and sodium oleate.

Zinc Oleate. $Zn(C_{18}H_{33}O_2)_2$.

Zinc sulphate and sodium oleate. Can be obtained as an impalpable white powder.

OLEATES OF THE ALKALOIDS.

To prepare these salts, the alkaloidal salt must be placed in solution, and an alkali added to combine with the acidulous radical, causing the alkaloid to be precipitated; after washing, draining and drying, it is then ready for solution in oleic acid.

ALKALOIDS.

Discovery really dates back to 1816, when Sertürner, a German apothecary, announced the existence of true morphine, and learned its characteristics.

Occurrence. In both animal and vegetable kingdoms. Existing in all parts of plants excepting perhaps the wood or stem.

Definition. Alkaloids are mostly crystallizable bodies of animal or vegetable origin, generally representing the active principles of the plants producing them. They have an alkaline reaction, combine with acids to form salts, but are distinguished from alkalies and alkaline earths by the fact that they do not saponify the fats, and are destructible by heat. When heated with an alkali, they evolve an ammoniacal odor.

Composition. They contain the elements C, H, O, and N, and are either compound *amines* or *amides* (the latter contain oxygen, while the former do not), or ammonia in which one or more hydrogen atoms have been replaced by a hydrocarbon radical.

Ex. Conine, $C_8H_{15}N = N \begin{cases} C_8H_{14} \\ H \end{cases}$ and may be looked upon as NH_3 with two H atoms replaced by the dyad radical C_8H_{14}.

Nicotine, $C_{10}H_{14}N_2 = \begin{matrix} N \{ C_5H_7 \\ N \{ C_5H_7 \end{matrix}$ is a *diamine*, or represents two molecules of NH_3, in each of which *all* the hydrogen atoms are replaced by C_5H_7.

Existence. They do not exist naturally in a free state, but as acid or neutral salts, in which the alkaloids are combined with such common acids as tannic, citric, tartaric, malic, acetic, etc., or some acid peculiar to the plant, as kinic, meconic, igasuric, aconitic, etc.

Solvents. Soluble in alcohol, chloroform, benzin, benzol, amylic alcohol, kerosene, etc.; and some are soluble in ether.

Insoluble in water.

Most of the alkaloids are *solid* bodies, but a few are *liquid* and volatile. *Ex.* Conine, sparteine, nicotine, lobeline. These are all *amines*, containing no oxygen.

Nomenclature. For the purpose of ready distinction from other principles, the terminations of all alkaloids are *ine* (aconiti*ne*, atrop*ine*), the Latin being *ina* (quin*ina*, strychn*ina*).

Glucosides and neutral principles all end in *in*. *Ex.* Glycyrrhizin, gelatin, glycerin, etc.

Formation of Alkaloid Salts. When forming salts, the alkaloids do not replace the hydrogen of acids, consequently the terms *sulphate, chloride*, etc., are incorrect when applied to an alkaloidal salt, but should be respectively, *hydrosulphate, hydrochloride*, etc. The type of these salts may be said to be ammonium chloride (or *ammonia hydrochloride*), forming their salts in the same manner that NH_3 and HCl produce the above salt.

Illustrations:

Type. NH_3 + HCl = NH_3, HCl, or NH_4Cl.
(Ammonia.) (Hydrochloric Acid.) (Ammonia Hydrochloride.) (Ammonium Chloride.)

$C_{17}H_{19}NO_3$ + HCl = $C_{17}H_{19}NO_3, HCl$.
(Morphine.) (Hydrochloric Acid.) (Morphine Hydrochloride.)

$2C_{20}H_{24}N_2O_2$ + H_2SO_4 = $(C_{20}H_{24}N_2O_2)_2, H_2SO_4$.
(Quinine.) (Sulphuric Acid.) (Quinine Hydrosulphate.)

$C_{21}H_{22}O_2$ + $HC_2H_3O_2$ = $C_{21}H_{22}O_2, HC_2H_3O_2$.
(Strychnine.) (Acetic Acid.) (Strychnine Hydro-acetate.)

$C_{17}H_{21}NO_4$ + HCl = $C_{17}H_{21}NO_4, HCl$.
(Cocaine.) (Hydrochloric Acid.) (Cocaine Hydrochloride.)

General Methods of Extraction.

I. *When the native alkaloidal salt* (the chemical combination of the alkaloid in the plant) *is soluble in water, and the alkaloid itself insoluble;* the addition of a strong alkali to an infusion or decoction of the vegetable substance, neutralizes the organic acid with which the alkaloid is associated, precipitating the alkaloid in a more or less pure form.

II. *When the native salt is insoluble,* or not freely soluble in water (as is more frequently the case). A dilute acid is then used for its extraction, so that its salt with an inorganic acid is obtained, and upon decomposition with an alkali, yields the quite pure precipitated alkaloid. In many cases, however, the extraction requires a more complex process, but all methods comprise the following six steps, viz.: 1. Solution. 2. Precipitation. 3. Re-solution. 4. Decolorization. 5. Purification. 6. Crystallization.

Decolorization: Effected by treatment with animal charcoal, or lime.

Theory of Isolation. The separation of the alkaloids may be thoroughly understood, by writing an equation to represent each step in which an important change occurs. The following method is suggested by the author.

First. To illustrate the extraction of morphine from opium, the native salt morphine hydro-meconate, soluble in a simple solvent. The + and − signs used, respectively indicating the basylous and acidulous radicals.

$\overset{+}{Mo}.\overset{-}{Mec}$. + NH_4OH = Mo + NH_4Mec. + H_2O.
(Morphine Hydro-meconate.) (Ammonium Hydroxide.) (Morphine.) (Ammonia Hydro-meconate.) (Water.)

Second. When the native salt is insoluble in a simple solvent.

Cinchona contains quinine hydro-kinate.

Reaction. $\overset{+}{Qu}.\overset{-}{Kin}$ + HCl = $Qu. HCl$ + Kin.
(Quinine Hydro-Kinate.) (Hydrochloric Acid.) (Quinine Hydrochloride.) (Kinic Acid.)

$2Qu.HCl$ + $Ca(OH)_2$ = $2Qu$. + $CaCl_2$ + $2H_2O$.
(Quinine Hydrochloride.) (Calcium Hydroxide.) (Quinine.) (Calcium Chloride.) (Water.)

Erythroxlon contains cocaine hydro-tannate.

$$\underset{\left(\substack{\text{Cocaine}\\ \text{Hydro-tannate.}}\right)}{2\overset{+}{\text{Coc}}.\overset{-}{\text{Tan.}}} + \underset{\left(\substack{\text{Sulphuric}\\ \text{Acid.}}\right)}{\text{H}_2\text{SO}_4} = \underset{\left(\substack{\text{Cocaine}\\ \text{Hydrosulphate.}}\right)}{\text{Coc}_2\text{H}_2\text{SO}_4} + \underset{\text{(Tannic Acid.)}}{\text{Tan.}}$$

$$\underset{\left(\substack{\text{Cocaine}\\ \text{Hydrosulphate.}}\right)}{\text{Coc}_2.\text{H}_2\text{SO}_4} + \underset{\left(\substack{\text{Sodium}\\ \text{Carbonate.}}\right)}{\text{Na}_2\text{CO}_3} = \underset{\text{(Cocaine.)}}{2\text{Coc.}} + \underset{\left(\substack{\text{Sodium}\\ \text{Sulphate.}}\right)}{\text{Na}_2\text{SO}_4} + \underset{\text{(Water.)}}{\text{H}_2\text{O}} + \underset{\left(\substack{\text{Carbon}\\ \text{Dioxide.}}\right)}{\text{CO}_2.}$$

Then to form cocaine hydrochloride:

$$\underset{\text{(Cocaine.)}}{\text{Coc.}} + \underset{\left(\substack{\text{Hydrochloric}\\ \text{Acid.}}\right)}{\text{HCl}} = \underset{\left(\substack{\text{Cocaine}\\ \text{Hydrochloride.}}\right)}{\text{Coc.HCl.}}$$

OPIUM.—GUM OPIUM.

The concrete milky exudation obtained in Asia Minor, by incising the unripe capsules of *Papaver somniferum.* (N.O. *Papaveraceæ.*) In its normal moist condition yielding *not less than 9% of morphine* by the officinal assay process.

OPII PULVIS.—POWDERED OPIUM. *Should contain* 12-16% *morphine.* Any powdered opium of a higher percentage may be brought within these limits, by admixture with powd. opium of a lower percentage in proper proportions, by the method given in Part I, page 31, for mixing solutions, etc., of different strengths.

Example. Having powdered opium, several lots, assaying 9, 11, 15 and 18%; how much of each shall I use to make 80 ozs. equivalent to 14%?

					Answer :		*Proof :*		
	9-	4	×	6.153	=	24.6 ozs.	4 × 9	=	36
14	11-	1	×	6.153	=	6.1 ozs.	1 × 11	=	11
	15-	3	×	6.153	=	18.4 ozs.	3 × 15	=	45
	18-	5	×	6.153	=	30.7 ozs.	5 × 18	=	90

13)80

6.153

79.8 ozs.

13)182 of 1%

14%

OPIUM DENARCOTISSATUM. (Denarcotized Opium.) Made by repeatedly macerating powd. opium (14% morphine) with stronger ether to remove narcotine (νάρκη—torpor), drying the residue, and adding to it powdered milk-sugar to restore the original weight.

Assay of Opium. U. S. P. (Mohr's modified process.) Opium (7 grams) is triturated with freshly slaked lime (3 grams) and water (20 cm³) to make a uniform mixture. Then water (50 cm³) is added and the mixture macerated with occasional stirring for one-half hour. Filter off 50 cm³ of liquid—representing 5 grams opium—add alcohol (5 cm³) and stronger ether (25 cm³); shake; add NH₄Cl (3 grams), shake one-half hour and let stand 12 hours. Counterbalance two small filters, place one within the other and decant the ethereal layer as completely as possible on a filter. Add stronger ether (10 cm³) and rotate, again decant the ethereal layer upon the filter, and afterwards wash the filter with stronger ether (5 cm³). Dry the filter and pour upon it the liquid in the flask; wash the flask and filter, with water (10 cm³); drain and dry the precipitate at 131°-140° F. Weigh crystals on inner filter; using the outer as a counterbalance. Multiply weight in grams by 20, and the product represents the percentage of morphine.

Explanation.   The above process is dependent upon the solubility of morphine in milk of lime, narcotine being only slightly soluble. NH₄Cl is added, forming CaCl₂ and NH₄OH, the latter precipitating pure morphine.

Reaction. $2NH_4Cl + Ca(OH)_2 = 2NH_4OH + CaCl_2.$

Ether is used to extract any narcotine that may be present, the alcohol dissolving coloring matter, resins, caoutchouc, etc.   It is reported, on good authority, that this process yields 10% less morphine than really exists in the opium, this amount being retained in the mother liquor.

Synopsis of a Method for the Extraction of Morphine.   An infusion of opium is prepared, then the meconate and lactate of morphine in solution are decomposed by the addition of NH₄OH, but which also precipitates coloring matter, and the other alkaloids, and in order to avoid this admixture with the precipitated morphine, alcohol is added to the solution to deprive it of its impurities and coloring matter. The crystals are purified by re-solution and filtration with animal charcoal.

CINCHONA.

The bark of any species of Cinchona containing at least 3% of its peculiar alkaloids and at least 2% of quinine.   (N.O. *Rubiaceæ.*) Contains about 20 alkaloids.

Cinchona Flava—Calisaya Bark.
Cinchona Rubrum—Red Bark.

Summary of Assay for Total Alkaloids.   Make a milk of lime and mix with 20 grams cinchona (80 powder, and dried at 212° F.); dry the mixture below 176° F.   (Kinate of calcium is formed, and the alkaloids are set free.)   Digest with alcohol near the boiling-point for an hour; cool and filter; add q.s. dil. H_2SO_4 ft. acid to test-paper (forming hydrosulphate of the alkaloids in solution).   Let the precipitate ($CaSO_4$) subside, filter the liquid, and wash the filter with alcohol.   Evaporate the alcohol from the filtrate, filter and wash filter with dil. H_2SO_4 until the washings give no turbidity with NaOH; concentrate by evaporation and add solution soda till strongly alkaline, forming Na_2SO_4 in solution, the alkaloids precipitating. Collect the precipitate on a filter, wash, drain and dry.   Multiplying the weight of the crystals in grams by 5 gives the percentage of total alkaloids.

Assay for Quinine.   Dissolve the total alkaloids from 2 grams cinchona in water with the aid of q.s. dil. H_2SO_4 to make the liquid acid to test-paper (thus making acid hydrosulphates of the alkaloids); add solution of soda to neutralize the solution, thus producing neutral hydrosulphates, a small amount of Na_2SO_4 being in solution.   Digest and cool to 59° F.   If crystals do not appear, the total alkaloids do not contain quinine in quantity over 8% of their weight, or quinine hydrosulphate 9%—(the other alkaloids remain in solution). If crystals appear, filter the solution, washing the crystals on the filter with sufficient water to make the entire liquid weigh 90 times the weight of total alkaloids taken. Dry the crystals at 140° F.

To the weight of the effloresced hydrosulphate of quinine so obtained, add 11.5% of its amount for water of crystallization, and 0.12% of the weight of the entire liquid for solubility of the crystals at 59° F. Multiplying the sum in grams by 5, equals the percentage of crystallized quinine hydrosulphate, equivalent to quinine in the cinchona.

PREPARATION OF QUININE.

Powdered cinchona is boiled with dil. HCl, forming soluble hydrochlorides of the alkaloids, which are decomposed by lime, precipitating the liberated alkaloids, leaving $CaCl_2$ and most of the impurities in solution. Dissolve out the alkaloids by digesting with alcohol, evaporate and dissolve the amorphous mass in dil. H_2SO_4, forming the hydrosulphate. Dissolve and filter with animal charcoal to purify, and crystallize.

Dissolve the crystals in water acidulated with H_2SO_4, and add water of ammonia till no further precipitation results, wash and dry.

Kerosene is now employed by many manufacturers in the place of alcohol.

General Tests for Alkaloids, yielding Characteristic Precipitates.

Marmés Solution, (CdI_2 (2); KI. (4); Water (12)) gives a gelatinous ppt.

Mayer's Solution of Iodohydrargyrate of Potassium ($HgCl_2$–13.5 grams; KI–49.8 grams; Water ft. 1 liter) produces a ppt.

Sonnenschein's Solution of sodium phospho-molybdate; yields a yellow ppt.

Schiebler's Solution of sodium phospho-tungstate; produces a ppt.

Precipitates are also obtained with, *Picric acid, mercuric chloride, platinic chloride, auric chloride, stannous chloride, tannic acid, Lugol's Solution, potassium iodide, lead acetate,* and *lead subacetate.*

ARRANGEMENT OF OFFICINAL ALKALOIDS.

Name, Synonym and Chemical Formula.	Source.	Natural Order.	Description.	Solubilities.	Properties and Doses.	Distinctive Tests.
Apomorphinæ Hydrochloras (Hydrochlorate of Apomorphine), $C_{17}H_{17}NO_2.HCl$	Morphine. (Decomposition Product).	Papaveraceæ.	Colorless, or grayish white crystals.	Water, 6.8; Alcohol, 50; alm. ins. Ether, Chloroform, al. ins.	Powerful einetic. Dose, ¼ grain.	ATROPINE. On heating the diluted green solution obtained by the action of sulphuric acid and bichromate potass. on atropine, the odor of roses and orange flowers is developed.
Atropina, (Atropine.) $C_{17}H_{23}NO_3$	Root and leaves of Atropa Belladonna.	Solanaceæ.	Colorless, or white acicular crystals.	Water, 600; Alcohol, v. s.; Ether, 60; Chloroform, 3.	Mydriatic and narcotic. Dose, $\frac{1}{130}-\frac{1}{30}$ gr.	
Atropinæ Sulphas (Sulphate of Atropine), $(C_{17}H_{23}NO_3)_2H_2SO_4$	do.	Solanaceæ.	White crystalline powder.	Water, 0.4; Alcohol, 6.5.	Mydriatic and narcotic. Dose, $\frac{1}{120}-\frac{1}{30}$ gr.	
Caffeina, (Caffeine.) $C_8H_{10}N_4O_2.H_2O$	Lvs. Camellia thea; Seeds Coffea arabica; Paullinia sorbilis.	Ternstræmaceæ. Rubiaceæ. Sapindaceæ.	Colorless crystals.	Water, 75; Alcohol, 35; sl. sol. Ether, Chloroform, 6.	Nervous stimulant. Dose, 1-3 grs.	ACONTINE. 1. Sulphuric acid colors it orange yellow, changing to brown. 2. Characteristic tingling sensation when a drop of very dilute solution is placed on the tongue.
Chinoidinum. (Chinoidine.) (Quinidin.)	Cinchona Bark Mixture of alkaloids (by-products)	Rubiaceæ.	Brown or black amorphous solid.	Water, alm. ins.; Alcohol, v. s.; Ether, sl. sol.; Chloroform, v. s.	Tonic and antiperiodic. Dose, 5-30 grs.	
Cinchonidinæ Sulphas. (Sulphate of Cinchonidine.) $(C_{20}H_{24}N_2O)_2H_2SO_4.3H_2O$	Cinchona Bark	Rubiaceæ.	White silky needles or prisms.	Water, 100; Alcohol, 71; Ether, sp. sol; Chloroform, 1000.	Antiperiodic, tonic and antipyretic. Dose, 5-20 grs.	
Cinchonina, (Cinchonine.) $C_{20}H_{24}N_2O$	Cinchona Bark	Rubiaceæ.	White prisms or needles.	Water, alm. ins.; Alcohol, 110; Ether, 371; Chloroform, 350.	Antiperiodic, tonic and antipyretic. Dose, 15-40 grs.	

Cinchoninæ Sulphas. (Sulphate of Cinchonine.) $(C_{20}H_{24}N_2O)_2H_2SO_4.2H_2O$	Cinchona Bark	*Rubiaceæ.*	Hard, white shining prisms	Water, 70 Alcohol, 6 Ether, 60 Chloroform, insol.	Antiperiodic, tonic and antipyretic. Dose, 15–40 grs.	
Codeina. (Codeine.) $C_{18}H_{21}NO_3.H_2O$	Opium.	*Papaveraceæ.*	White or yellowish prisms.	Water, 80 Alcohol, v. s. Ether, 10 Chloroform, v. s.	Sedative. Dose, ¼ gr.	
Hyoscyaminæ Sulphas. (Sulphate of Hyoscyamine.) $(C_{17}H_{23}NO_3)_2H_2SO_4$	Leaves, *Hyoscyamus niger.*	*Solanaceæ.*	Golden yellow or yellowish white crystalline powder.	Water, v. s. Alcohol, v. s.	Narcotic sedative. Dose, 1/60 gr.	
Morphina. (Morphine.) $C_{17}H_{19}NO_3.H_2O$	Opium.	*Papaveraceæ.*	White crystals or powder.	Alcohol, 10	Narcotic and sedative. Dose, 1/6 gr.	MORPHINE. 1. With solution of chloride of iron it gives a pale blue color, destroyed by acids or alcohol. 2. HNO_3 produces a red color changing to yellow. 3. Chlorine water & NH_4OH gives red color changing to brown.
Morphinæ Acetas. (Acetate of Morphine.) $C_{17}H_{19}NO_3HC_2H_3O_2.3H_2O$	Opium.	*Papaveraceæ.*	White or yellowish white crystalline powder.	Water, 12 Alcohol, 68 Ether, 60	Narcotic and sedative. Dose, 1/6 gr.	
Morphinæ Hydrochloras. (Hydrochlorate of Morphine.) $C_{17}H_{19}NO_3HCl.3H_2O$	Opium.	*Papaveraceæ.*	White, feath'ry acicular crystals.	Water, 24 Alcohol, 63 Ether, insol.	Narcotic and sedative. Dose, 1/6 gr.	
Morphinæ Sulphas. (Sulphate of Morphine.) $(C_{17}H_{19}NO_3)_2H_2SO_4.5H_2O$	Opium.	*Papaveraceæ.*	White, feath'ry acicular crystals.	Water, 24 Alcohol, 702	Narcotic and sedative. Dose, 1/6 gr. Magendie's Solutioncontains 2 grs. in each fluid-drachm.	
Physostigminæ Salicylas. (Salicylate of Physostigmine.) $C_{15}H_{21}N_3O_2C_7H_6O_3$	Seeds. *Physostigma venenosum* (Calabar Bean).	*Leguminosæ.*	Colorlessacicular or short columnar crystals.	Water, 130 Alcohol, 12	Mydriatic nerve sedative. Dose. 1/65 – 1/12 gr.	MECONIC ACID. Tincture of chloride of iron gives dark red color.
Pilocarpinæ Hydrochloras. (Hydrochlorate of Pilocarpine.) $C_{11}H_{16}N_2O_2HCl$	Leaflets. *Pilocarpus pennatifolius* (Jaborandi).	*Rutaceæ.*	Small white crystals.	Water, v. s. Alcohol, v. s. Ether, al. ins. Chloroform, al. ins.	Diaphoretic and sialagogue. Dose, ⅛ – ¼ gr.	

ARRANGEMENT OF OFFICINAL ALKALOIDS—*Continued.*

NAME, SYNONYM AND CHEMICAL FORMULA.	SOURCE.	NATURAL ORDER.	DESCRIPTION.	SOLUBILITIES.	PROPERTIES AND DOSES.	DISTINCTIVE TESTS.
Quinina. (Quinine.) $C_{20}H_{24}N_2O_2.3H_2O$	Cinchona Bark	*Rubiaceæ.*	White flaky powder.	Water, 1600; Alcohol, 6; Ether, 25; Chloroform, 5	Antiperiodic, tonic, antipyretic. Dose, 2-20 grs.	QUININE. 1. Solution in diluted H_2SO_4 has blue fluorescence. 2. Treated with chlorine water, followed by an excess of NH_4OH gives an emerald green color and coagulum, known as *Thalleiochin.* 3. HNO_3 does not redden it.
Quinine Hydrobromas (Hydrobromate of Quinine.) $C_{20}H_{24}N_2O_2HBr.2H_2O$	Cinchona Bark	*Rubiaceæ.*	Colorless lustrous needles.	Water, 16; Alcohol, 3; Ether, 6; Chloroform, 12	Antiperiodic, tonic, antipyretic. Dose, 2-20 grs.	
Quinine Bisulphas. (Bisulphate of Quinine). $C_{20}H_{24}N_2O_2H_2SO_4.H_2O$	Cinchona Bark	*Rubiaceæ.*	Colorless orthorhombic crystals.	Water, 10; Alcohol, 32	do.	
Quinine Hydrochloras (Hydrochlorate of Quinine.) $C_{20}H_{24}N_2O_2HCl.2H_2O$	Cinchona Bark	*Rubiaceæ.*	White lustrous needles.	Water, 34; Alcohol, 3	do.	
Quinine Sulphas (Sulphate of Quinine.) $(C_{20}H_{24}N_2O_2)_2H_2SO_4.7H_2O$	Cinchona Bark	*Rubiaceæ.*	White filiform crystals.	Water, 740; Alcohol, 65; Ether, slightly; Chloroform, 1000; Glycerin, 40	do.	
Quinine Valerianas. (Valerianate of Quinine.) $C_{20}H_{24}N_2O_2C_5H_{10}O_2.H_2O$	Cinchona Bark	*Rubiaceæ.*	White pearly lustrous crystals.	Water, 100; Alcohol, 5; Ether, slightly	do. (Also nervine) Dose, 2-10 grs.	
Strychnina. (Strychnine.) $C_{21}H_{22}N_2O_2$	Seeds; *Strychnos Nux Vomica* and *Strychnos Ignatia.*	*Loganiaceæ.*	Colorless octahedral crystals or powder.	Water, 6700; Alcohol, 110; Chloroform, 6; Ether, ins.	Tonic and spinal nervine. Dose, $\frac{1}{60}$ - $\frac{1}{20}$ gr.	STRYCHNINE. 1. To cold sulphuric acid add one drop of a solution of strychnine and a small crystal of potassium bichromate. A deep blue color results, becoming violet, cherry-red, and finally fading.
Strychninæ Sulphas. (Sulphate of Strychnine.) $(C_{21}H_{22}N_2O_2)_2H_2SO_4.7H_2O$	do.	*Loganiaceæ.*	Colorless white prismatic crystals.	Water, 10; Alcohol, 60; Ether, ins.	do.	
Veratrina. (Veratrine.)	Mixture of Alkaloids from *Asagræa officinalis.*	*Melanthaceæ.*	White amorphous powder.	Water, v. sl. sol.; Alcohol, 3; Ether, 6; Chloroform, 2	do. Dose, $\frac{1}{16}$ - $\frac{1}{4}$ gr.	

GLUCOSIDES.

Glucosides are proximate principles that yield when boiled with a dilute acid, *glucose* and a new body. They are usually active principles, yet unlike the alkaloids, they do not combine with acids, but unite with alkalies to produce salts, and are not precipitated by tannic or picric acids. A few are active poisons, others are harmless bitters, associated with resins, oils and alkaloids.

Solvents: Some are soluble in water, some in alcohol, and others in ether.

Officinal Glucosides, and Neutral Principles.

CHRYSAROBINUM.—CHRYSAROBIN.

A mixture of proximate principles (commonly mis-named *chrysophanic acid*), extracted from Goa powder, a substance found deposited in the wood of the trunk of *Andira araroba*.

Description. Pale, orange-yellow crystalline powder; odorless; tasteless; almost insol. in water, sl. sol. alcohol, sol. in ether and boiling benzol.

Officinal Preparation. Unguentum Chrysarobini. (Ointment of Chrysarobin.) Contains chrysarobin (10), and benzoinated lard (90).

($C_{20}H_{28}O_5$.) ELATERINUM.—ELATERIN.

A neutral principle extracted from Elaterium, a substance deposited by the juice of the fruit of *Ecbalium Elaterium*. (N. O. Cucurbitaceæ.) Extracted by dissolving out with chloroform, and precipitating with ether.

Description. Small, colorless scales or prisms; odorless; bitter, acrid taste; neutral reaction; insol. in water, sol. in alcohol.

Prop. Purgative. *Dose* $\frac{1}{16}$ grain.

Officinal Preparation. Trituratio Elaterini (Trituration of Elaterin). Contains elaterin (10), sugar of milk (90).

PICROTOXINUM.—PICROTOXIN.

A neutral principle prepared from the seeds of *Anamirta paniculata* (N. O. *Menispermaceæ*). Made by treating the kernel of the *Cocculus Indicus* seed (fish berries) with magnesia and hot alcohol; the evaporated solution is treated with animal charcoal and crystallized.

Description. Colorless, prismatic crystals; odorless; bitter taste; neutral reaction; sol. in water and alcohol.

Prop. Tonic and antispasmodic. *Dose* $\frac{1}{80}$ grain.

($C_{13}H_{18}O_7$.) SALICINUM.—SALICIN.

A neutral principle obtained from the bark of *Salix Helix*, and other species of *Salix*. (N. O. *Salicaceæ*.)

Preparation. A decoction of willow bark is deprived of tannin and coloring matter by precipitating with basic lead acetate, and the free acid neutralized with calcium carbonate.

The filtrate on concentration yields crystals, which are purified by recrystallization.

Description. Colorless, or white, silky crystals; odorless; bitter taste; neutral reaction; soluble in water and alcohol. On boiling with dilute acids the following decomposition takes place·

Reaction. $C_{13}H_{18}O_7$ + H_2O = $C_7H_6O_2$ + $C_6H_{12}O_6$.
(Salicin.)   (Water.)   (Saligenin)   (Glucose.)

Prop. Antifebrine. *Dose.* 20 – 30 grains.

      ($C_{16}H_{18}O_3$—246)   SANTONINUM.—SANTONIN.

A neutral principle prepared from *Santonica*. Made by exhausting a mixture of santonica and lime with diluted alcohol, thereby obtaining a solution of calcium santoninate, from which the alcohol is distilled, and acetic acid added to the residue; santonin precipitates, and calcium acetate is in solution.

Purified by treatment with animal charcoal, and recrystallization.

Distinctive reaction: Yields a scarlet red liquid gradually becoming colorless with alcoholic solution of potash.

Properties. Anthelmintic. *Dose.* Two grains.

($2NaC_{16}H_{19}O_4.7H_2O$—698)   SODII SANTONINAS.   (Santoninate of Sodium.)

Made by heating solution of soda with santonin till dissolved; filter and crystallize.

Description. Colorless, transparent crystals; becoming yellow on exposure to light; odorless; saline and bitter taste; slight alkaline reaction; sol. in water and alcohol.

Other glucosides (*unofficinal*) with sources: *Æsculin* (horse-chestnut); *amygdalin* (bitter almond); *arbutin* (uva ursi); *arnicin* (arnica); *colocynthin* (colocynth); *convallerin* (lily of valley); *convolvulin* (scammony); *crocin* (saffron); *daphnin* (mezereum); *digitalin* (foxglove); *gentiopicrin* (gentian); *glycyrrhizin* (licorice); *jalapin* (jalap); *populin* (willow); *quercitrin* (oak); *saponin* (soap bark); *thujin* (arbor vita).

ORGANIC ACIDS (*not mentioned before*).

      ($HC_7H_5O_5.H_2O$—188)   ACIDUM GALLICUM.—GALLIC ACID.

Found in nutgalls, sumach, uva ursi, etc.

Made by macerating powd. nutgalls with cold water for about a month, then expressing, and rejecting the liquid. Boil the residue with water and filter while hot through animal charcoal, and set aside to crystallize. Purified by re-crystallization. By this process, pure tannin, which is *digallic acid*, an anhydride of gallic acid, is converted into the latter.

Reaction. $C_{14}H_{10}O_9$ + H_2O = $2C_7H_6O_5$.
(Tannin.)   (Water.)   (Gallic Acid.)

Description. Nearly, or quite colorless silky needles, or triclinic prisms; odorless; astringent, acid taste; acid reaction; sol. in water (100), alcohol (4.5), ether and glycerin.

Impurities and tests: *Tannic acid:* + solution of alkaloids, gelatin, albumen, starch jelly, or tartar emetic with NH_4Cl = ppt.

Officinal Preparation. UNGUENTUM ACIDI GALLICI (Ointment of gallic acid). Contains gallic acid (10), incorporated with benzoinated lard (90). Avoid use of iron spatula.

PYROGALLIC ACID. ($C_6H_6O_3$)

Made by the sublimation of gallic acid, or powdered nutgalls.

Reaction. $C_7H_6O_5 = C_6H_6O_3 + CO_2$.
(Gallic Acid.) (Pyrogallic Acid.) (Carbon Dioxide.)

Properties. Readily reduces salts of mercury, silver, gold and platinum. Used with silver nitrate in photography, and for hair dyes and marking inks.

($C_{14}H_{10}O_9$—chiefly) ACIDUM TANNICUM.—TANNIC ACID. (TANNIN.)

Made by exposing powdered nutgalls to a damp atmosphere, macerating with ether, expressing, evaporating and drying below 212° F.

Description. Light yellow scales; faint, peculiar odor; astringent taste; acid reaction; sol. in water (6), alcohol (0.6) glycerin (6).

Test; see Gallic Acid.

Officinal Preparation. 1. Collodium stypticum (see Collodium). 2. Trochisci acidi tannici (contain 1 grain each); 3. Unguentum acidi tannici (contains tannic acid (10) incorporated with benzoinated lard (90).) Avoid use of iron spatula.

VALERIANIC ACID. ($HC_5H_9O_2$—102)

OCCURRENCE. Found in valerian-root, chamomile, wormwood, angelica-root, etc.

Preparation. Made from valerian-root by distillation; or artificially by the action of H_2SO_4 and potassium bichromate on fusel oil; the aqueous distillate is treated with NaOH, and the resulting salt of sodium valerianate decomposed by H_2SO_4, liberating valerianic acid.

Description. Colorless, thin oily liquid; disagreeable odor of valerian, and of old cheese; sour, acrid taste.

Substances Contributed by the Animal Kingdom. (Officinals.)

($HC_3H_4O_3$—90) ACIDUM LACTICUM.—LACTIC ACID.

Source. Produced during the spontaneous fermentation of milk-sugar, under the influence of casein; this transformation is termed *lactic fermentation.* A similar change occurs in dextrin, glucose, cane-sugar, etc., by the action of casein and other proteids, consequently lactic acid is met with in many vegetable products which have become sour.

Preparation. Now made from cane-sugar, which is changed into invert sugar by boiling with dil. H_2SO_4; solution of soda is added, and the mixture heated until it ceases to react with Fehling's Solution. H_2SO_4 is added to neutralize; the resulting Na_2SO_4 is partly removed by re-crystallization, and the remainder precipitated with alcohol. One half of the alcoholic liquid is heated, neutralized with zinc carbonate, mixed with the remainder and cooled. Zinc lactate crystallizes out, and yields the acid in solution when treated with H_2S, zinc sulphide precipitating.

Description. Nearly colorless, syrupy liquid; odorless; very acid taste and reaction; miscible with water, alcohol and ether; sp. gr. 1.212; contains 75% absolute lactic acid.

Impurities: IICl,H_2SO_4,sarcolactic acid, lead, iron, sugar or glycerin.

Officinal Preparation. Syrupus Calcii Lactophosphatis (see Calcium).

ACIDUM OLEICUM. (Oleic Acid.) See page 195.

ADEPS.—LARD.

The prepared internal fat of the abdomen of the hog, *Sus scrofa* (Class, *Mammalia.* Ord. *Pachydermata*), purified by washing with water, melting and straining.

Description. A soft, white, unctuous solid; melts at 95° F.; faint odor, free from rancidity; bland taste; neutral reaction; sol in ether, benzin and CS_2. Used as a base for ointments as *benzoinated lard*, in which form it is protected from rancidity.

Officinal Preparations. 1. Adeps benzoinatus (see page 175). 2. Ceratum (White wax (30), lard (70). 3. Ceratum resinæ. Basilicon ointment. (Resin (35), yellow wax (15), lard (50)). 4. Unguentum—Ointment. (Lard (80), yellow wax (20)).

OLEUM·ADIPIS. (Lard Oil.) See page 193.

CANTHARIS.—CANTHARIDES.

(Spanish Flies.) *Cantharis vesicatoria* (Class, *Insecta.* Order, *Coleoptera* (Beetles)). Collected chiefly in Hungary and Southern Russia.

Its blistering properties are due to the presence of *cantharidin* ($C_{10}H_{12}O_4$) which crystallizes in colorless prisms and scales; sol. in alcohol, ether, chloroform, acetic ether, glacial acetic acid, and oils.

Cantharis presents a shining coppery-green color; grayish-brown in powder, containing green, shining particles; odor strong and disagreeable. Should be kept in well-closed vessels containing a little camphor.

Officinal Preparations. 1. Ceratum Cantharidis (Blistering Cerate); contains powd. cantharides (35), incorporated with yellow wax (20), resin (25), and lard (25). 2. Ceratum Extracti Cantharidis (Cerate of extract of cantharides); made by percolating powd. cantharides (30) with alcohol, evaporating (to 15) and incorporating with resin (15), yellow wax (35), and lard (35), using heat. 3. Charta Cantharidis (Cantharides paper). 4. Collodium cum Cantharide. 5. Linimentum Cantharidis (Cantharides Liniment); contains cantharides (15), and oil of turpentine ft. 100 made by digestion. 6. Tinctura Cantharidis (Tincture of cantharides) contains 5% cantharides.

CARBO ANIMALIS. See page 160.
CERA FLAVA. See page 165.
CERA ALBA. See page 166.

CETACEUM.—SPERMACETI.

A peculiar concrete fatty substance obtained from the head of the sperm whale.

The upper jaw of the whale has a large cavity containing an oily liquid, which is removed and congeals into a yellow mass, it is drained, and expressed to remove oil; the pressed cake is purified by melting in water, skimming, boiling with KOH and washing with water.

Constituents. *Cetin* (cetyl palmitate, $C_{16}H_{33}(C_{16}H_{31}O_2)$), *myristic, lauric* and *stearic acids,* combined with alcohol radicals.

Description. White, somewhat translucent masses, of a scaly, crystalline fracture; pearly lustre; becoming yellow and rancid on exposure to air; odorless; mild, bland taste; neutral reaction; sp. gr. 0.945; sol. in ether, chloroform, CS_2, and boiling alcohol.

Officinal Preparations. 1. Ceratum Cetacei. (Spermaceti cerate.) Contains spermaceti (10), white wax (35), and olive oil (55). 2. Unguentum Aquæ Rosæ. (Ointment of Rose Water. Cold Cream.) Melt together expressed oil of almond (50), spermaceti (10), and white wax (10), and mix with rose water (30).

COCCUS.—COCHINEAL.

The dried female insect, *coccus cacti* (Class, *Insecta.* Ord. *Hemiptera.*) *Constituents.* Besides fat, mucilaginous and glutinous compounds, cochineal contains *carminic acid* ($C_{17}H_{18}O_{10}$) to which it owes its red color.

Carmine is obtained by treating a decoction of cochineal with a little alum, or cream of tartar, and setting aside to deposit.

Use. A coloring agent, and enters into the preparation of Tinct. Cardamom Comp.

FEL BOVIS.—OX GALL. OX BILE.

The fresh gall of *Bos Taurus* (Class, *Mammalia;* Order, *Ruminantia*). A green or brownish-green, viscid liquid, which is separated by the liver in the gall-bladder. It has a peculiar odor; disagreeably bitter taste; slight alkaline reaction; sp. gr. 1.018 – 1.028; contains *bilirubin* (a coloring matter); a fat, *cholestrin* ($C_{26}H_{44}O$), *glycocholic* and *taurocholic acids.*

Officinal Preparations. 1. Fel Bovis Inspissatum. 2. Fel Bovis Purificatum.

FEL BOVIS INSPISSATUM. (Inspissated Ox Gall.) Made by heating ox-gall to 176° F., straining, and evaporating to 15% of its weight.

FEL BOVIS PURIFICATUM. (Purified Ox Gall.) Evaporate ox gall to ⅓ its weight, treat with an equal vol. of alcohol, filter, distil off the alcohol, and evaporate to pilular consistence.

GLYCERINUM. See page 195.

ICHTHYOCOLLA.—ISINGLASS.

The swimming-bladder of *Acipenser Huso,* and other species of *Acipenser.* (Class, *Pisces.* Ord. *Sturiones.*) The officinal isinglass is that known in commerce as *Russian,* which is obtained from sturgeons in the Black Sea. The air-bag, or swimming-bladder, is cut open, washed, and dried by stretching on boards, the dried product being *leaf isinglass.* Sol. in boiling water, and boiling diluted alcohol.

Officinal Preparation. Emplastrum Ichthyocolla (Isinglass Plaster. Court Plaster). Made by coating taffeta on one side with a solution of isinglass in water, glycerin and alcohol, and on the other with tinct. benzoin comp.

MEL. See page 165.

MOSCHUS.—MUSK.

The dried secretion from the preputial follicles of *Moschus moschiferous* (the musk deer). (Class, *Mammalia*. Ord. *Ruminantia*.)

Constituents: Cholestrin, various fats and waxy substances, gelatinous and albuminous compounds, and salts. The odorous principle is probably formed by the slow decomposition of one of its constituents. When treated with KOH, ammonia is given off.

Officinal Preparation. Tinctura Moschi (Tincture of Musk. 10%).

OLEUM MORRHUÆ. (Cod Liver Oil.)

A fixed oil obtained from the fresh livers of *Gadus Morrhuæ*, or other species of *Gadus*. (Class, *Pisces*. Ord. *Teleostia*.)

The oil is separated and put into tanks in a cooling-room until it freezes, when it is placed in canvas bags and expressed, the product being an almost colorless liquid.

Constituents. Besides the common fats, *stearin, myristin, palmitin* and *olein*, small quantities of iodine, bromine, phosphorus and sulphur, also *gadium* ($C_{35}H_{46}O_9$).

Description. Colorless, or pale-yellow, thin, oily liquid; slightly fishy odor; bland, slightly fishy taste; faint acid reaction; sp. gr. 0.920–0.925; sol. in acetic ether, and ether, but scarcely in alcohol.

PEPSINUM SACCHARATUM. (Saccharated Pepsin.)

Pepsin, the digestive principle of the gastric juice, obtained from the mucous membrane of the stomach of the hog, and mixed with powdered milk sugar.

Preparation. The well-washed fresh stomach of the hog is finely chopped, and macerated in water containing HCl; the pepsin is separated from the solution, by the addition of sodium chloride, which causes it to float on the surface of the liquid, it is then drained and dried. To make *saccharated pepsin*, sufficient milk sugar is added to make a powder, 10 grains of which will dissolve 500 of coagulated albumen.

PEPTONES. When fibrin or coagulated albumen are digested with pepsin, peptones are formed which have the property of digesting an additional quantity of the same, to a limited degree.

Several *so-called* pepsins of commerce are simply dried peptones, and do not relieve the distress caused by certain digestive disorders in any considerable degree.

Description. A white powder; slight, but not disagreeable odor and taste; slightly acid reaction. Not completely sol. in water, leaving floccules of pepsin floating in the solution, which dissolve on the addition of a small quantity of HCl.

One part dissolved in water (500) containing HCl(7.5), should dissolve at least 50 of hard-boiled egg albumen in 5–6 hours at 100°–104° F.

Officinal Preparations. Liquor Pepsini (Solution of Pepsin. Liquid

Pepsin). A solution of sacch. pepsin (4%) in glycerin and water acidulated with HCl.

Tests to distinguish between Pepsin and Peptone.

Use a filtered 3% solution in water.

1. On boiling in a test tube; *Peptone* produces marked cloudiness and precipitation; *Pepsin*, a slight cloudiness without precipitation.

2. With strong HNO_3, the Pepsin solution gives slight opalescence, while the Peptone solution becomes yellow.

3. NaOH; precipitates Peptone, but not Pepsin.

4. NaCl; yields a white, gelatinous precipitate with Pepsin on standing; Peptone none.

5. $Ba(OH)_2$: with Peptone, a precipitate; with Pepsin, none.

6. Alcohol: with Pepsin a gelatinous ppt. insol. in water; with Peptone a granular ppt. sol. in water.

SACCHARUM LACTIS. See page 165.

SEVUM. (Prepared Suet. Mutton Suet.) See page 193.

VITELLUS. (Yolk of Egg.) The yolk of the egg of *Gallus Bankiva,* var. *domesticus* (Class, *Aves.* Order *Gallinæ*). *Composition:* 16% *Vitellin* (a proteid closely related to casein), 30% fat, 1.5% organic salts coloring matter and sugar, 0.42% *cholestrin* and 55% water.

[*Oleum ovi* (Oil of eggs). The fat expressed from the coagulated yolk, or obtained by exhaustion with ether.]

Vitellus is used as an emulsifier.

Officinal Preparation. Glyceritum Vitelli. (Glycerite of Yolk of Egg.) Contains fresh yolk of egg (45), and glycerin (55).

Unofficinal Products derived from the Animal Kingdom.

Ambergris; a morbid excretion from the intestines of the sperm whale, found floating on the sea. Used in making perfumes.

Sanguis (Ox Blood). *Castoreum* (Castor); the preputial follicles of both male and female animals *Castor fiber.*

Civet (from civet cat); used in perfumery.

Blatta orientalis (cockroach). *Egg Albumen.*

Extractum Carnis. (Extract of Beef.) *Formic Acid.*

GELATIN. (Artificial isinglass.) Obtained by boiling in water under pressure, bones, cartilage, skins, ligaments, etc.; on cooling, a jelly results which is dried in the form of thin sheets.

COLLA (Glue). Obtained by subjecting the offal of abattoirs and tanneries to a process identical with that for making gelatin.

Koumiss. Hirudo (Leech). *Lac* (Milk).

PANCREATIN. Obtained from the pancreas or sweetbread of sheep. An emulsifying agent, digesting the oils and fats.

TOXICOLOGY.

(Τόξικον—a poison; λόγος—a discourse.)

Poison. Any substance which, when introduced into the animal organism, swallowed, absorbed, or applied externally, will produce a morbid, noxious or deadly effect upon it.

The poisons are derived from all three kingdoms, viz.: *Animal:* (*Ex.* Cantharides, cochineal, etc.) *Vegetable:* (*Ex.* Euphorbium, ela-

terium, savin, etc.)　*Mineral:* (*Ex.* Mineral acids, copper salts, etc.)
ANTIDOTES.　Two classes.

First.　**Chemicals** that cause a decomposition with the poison,
giving rise to an insoluble or harmless body.

Second.　**Alkaloidal Principles** that have an antagonistic action
to that of the poison, thereby counteracting its effect.

General Remedies in Cases of Poisoning.

Evacuation of the stomach (except in poisoning by the mineral
acids) by means of the stomach pump, or the use of some of the following *emetics:* Warm water in copious draughts, water containing
a tablespoonful of mustard, salt water, zinc sulphate, copper sulphate, ipecac, tartar emetic accompanied with ipecac, and me-
chanically by tickling the throat with a feather, etc.

Demulcents: Mucilages of acacia, flax-seed, or slippery elm
bark; starch; egg albumen; olive oil; soapsuds; albumen, in the
form of milk, flour, blood, etc.

General Antidotes, in case the nature of the poison is un-
known.　A mixture of equal parts of magnesia, powd. charcoal and
hydrated oxide of iron, given in water.

CLASSIFICATION OF POISONS.

1. **Corrosive.** *Examples.* Mineral acids, oxalic acid, caustic alka-
lics, phosphorus, bromine, etc.
2. **Irritant.** *Examples.* Aloes, capsicum, colocynth, creasote,
croton-oil, elaterium, euphorbium, gamboge, jalap, savin,
scammony, etc.
3. **Narcotic.** *Examples.* Opium, HCN, hyoscyamus, cannabis
indica, etc.
4. **Narcotico-Irritant.** *Examples.* Digitalis, veratrum viride,
conium, colchicum, lobelia, aconite, belladonna, stramonium,
tobacco, nux vomica, etc.

CORROSIVES and IRRITANTS.　Their action is local, the Corrosives
causing vomiting, acting mostly on the mucous linings of the
œsophagus, etc., producing intense inflammation, while the Irritants
exert their irritating action lower down, and especially on the
bowels, producing *hyper-catharsis.*

NARCOTICS.　*Symptoms:* sleepiness, dimness of sight, stupor, delirium, etc.　Alimentary canal not affected, but lower bowels con-
stipated.

NARCOTICO-IRRITANTS.　Effects closely allied to the narcotics,
but having a more direct action on the spinal marrow and nerves,
producing more frequent occurrence of convulsions and paralysis.
They differ much from each in their action on the system, and
owe their properties to the presence of an alkaloidal principle.
Symptoms: Vertigo, coma, delirium, paralysis, or convulsions,
with pain and disturbance of the stomach and intestines.

The following table gives the most recently approved antidotes for many of the poisons :

Poison:	Antidotes:
Mineral Acids. (H_2SO_4, HNO_3, HCl, and nitro-hydrochloric acid.)	Give no emetic. Magnesia mixed with water, milk, chalk, whiting, potass. bicarb., fixed oils, demulcents. Laudanum (20 drops), if much pain.
Vegetable Acids. (Oxalic acid and salts. Tartaric acid and salts.)	Chalk, whiting, air-slacked lime with vinegar. (No soda or potash to neutralize acid.) Mustard water, olive oil, demulcents and stimulants.
Alkalies. (NaOH, KOH, NH_4OH, and their carbonates.)	Warm water till emetic; vinegar, lemon juice, or citric acid. Olive oil, demulcents, and laudanum (20 drops) if much pain.
Barium, lead, and their salts.	Epsom ($\frac{1}{4}$ oz.) or Glauber's salt (1 oz.) in water. Emetic (mustard water), milk and demulcents, and laudanum if needed.
Arsenic, and all its compounds.	Emetic (mustard water). Hydrated oxide of iron, or hydrated oxide of iron with magnesia, olive oil, albumen, demulcents, and laudanum.
Antimony salts, cantharides, colchicum, elaterium, iodine, copper, mercury, croton oil, savin, tansy, potass. bichromate, tin and zinc salts.	Albumen diffused in water. Emetics (warm water with $NaHCO_3$ or mustard), strong tea or coffee, or tannin, stimulants, laudanum (if needed), and demulcents.
Cannabis Indica, opium and morphine.	Emetics (mustard water) or stomach pump, cold affusions, strong tea or coffee; electro-magnetism. Keep patient awake and in motion. Artificial respiration.
HCN (see page 111) *and cyanides, alcohol, chloral, chloroform, ether, CS_2, etc.*	Emetics (mustard water), fresh air, keep body warm, rouse by ammonia, cold affusions, friction and mustard plaster to limbs, and artificial respiration.
Aconite, digitalis, ergot, lobelia, tobacco, veratrum, belladonna, conium, henbane, santonin, stramonium, calabar bean.	Emetics (mustard water); strong tea or coffee. Hypodermics of morphine; powdered charcoal; stimulants (whiskey, etc.). Warmth to extremities and artificial respiration.
Nux vomica and strychnine.	Emetics (mustard water), powdered charcoal, iodized starch, or tannin. To relieve spasms; inhalations of chloroform, or internally 25 grs. chloral hydrate, or $\frac{1}{4}$ oz. potassium bromide. *Lose no time.*
Silver nitrate.	Sodium chloride; emetics (mustard water)— demulcents.
Phosphorus.	Emetics ($CuSO_4$—3 grains every 5 mins.), f ʒ i old spts. turpentine, $MgSO_4$ ($\frac{1}{4}$ oz.). *No oils.*